The Truth About You

Susan Lewis is the bestselling author of thirty novels. She is also the author of *Just One More Day* and *One Day at a Time*, the moving memoirs of her childhood in Bristol. She lives in Gloucestershire. Her website address is www.susanlewis.com

Susan is a supporter of the breast cancer charity, Breast Cancer Care: www.breastcancercare.org.uk and of the childhood bereavement charity, Winton's Wish: www.winstonswish.org.uk

Praise for Susan Lewis

'Utterly compelling.' *Sun*

'Expertly written to brew an atmosphere of foreboding, this story is an irresistible blend of intrigue and passion, and the consequences of secrets and betrayal.' *Woman*

'A multi-faceted tear-jerker.' *heat*

'Spellbinding! You just keep turning the pages, with the atmosphere growing more and more intense as the story leads to its dramatic climax.' *Daily Mail*

'Sad, happy, sensual and intriguing.' *Woman's Own*

The Truth About You

Susan Lewis

arrow books

Published by Arrow Books 2014

2 4 6 8 10 9 7 5 3

First published in Great Britain in 2013 by
Century
Random House, 20 Vauxhall Bridge Road,
London SW1V 2SA

www.randomhouse.co.uk

Addresses for companies within The Random House Group Limited can be found at: www.randomhouse.co.uk/offices.htm

The Random House Group Limited Reg. No. 954009

ISBN 9780099550860

A CIP catalogue record for this book is available from the British Library

The Random House Group Limited supports the Forest Stewardship Council® (FSC®), the leading international forest-certification organisation. Our books carrying the FSC label are printed on FSC®-certified paper. FSC is the only forest-certification scheme supported by the leading environmental organisations, including Greenpeace. Our paper procurement policy can be found at www.randomhouse.co.uk/environment

Typeset in Palatino 11.5/13pt by Palimpsest Book Production Limited,
Falkirk, Stirlingshire
Printed and bound by CPI Group (UK) Ltd, Croydon, CR0 4YY

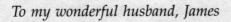

To my wonderful husband, James

Chapter One

'Exactly why are you looking so pleased with yourself?'

'Me?' Lainey responded innocently. 'I'm just enjoying listening to you.'

Stacy regarded her best friend dubiously.

'I am,' Lainey insisted. 'Keep going. I'm all ears.' Her own news could wait, since she really was keen to know more about the new man in Stacy's life. In fact it was making her heart sing to see how happy Stacy was now, after all she'd been through. Divorce could be a ferociously sadistic beast with a terrier-like grip that didn't let go until it had stripped its victims of every last vestige of morale, self-esteem, sometimes even looks, before it was done. Then there were the assets, money and kids, but better not get Stacy started on that, mainly because Derek, the offending spouse, had sliced off half her small inheritance (very sore subject), forced the sale of her gran's cherished country cottage (just as sore), and always claimed he didn't want kids (way beyond sore given that the new girlfriend was now pregnant). Best to keep her on the subject of Martin, who'd surfed in from the Net a few weeks ago and was doing far more to restore the shine to Stacy's pale blue eyes and freckly complexion than the endless chats over restorative vino and fresh Kleenex that Lainey had provided.

In spite of her loyalty to Stacy, Lainey's concentration wasn't as focused as she'd have liked it to be, since her own news was making her feel quite heady one minute and downright apprehensive the next. Actually, it wasn't such a big deal . . . Well, it could be, depending on how it turned out, but since she wasn't good with crystal balls or astral projection into next month for a quick look round, she'd better stop trying to second-guess the future and return to the present.

Stacy was still in full flow, and not in the least put off by Lainey busying herself about the kitchen making tea, folding washing, answering the phone and generally trying to keep on top of her hectic life. Having a large family – three children, a demented father and demanding husband – her energies were invariably channelled in several directions, most of which ended up going off at various tangents throughout the day, so that by bedtime she often looked back in wonder at what had happened to her original plans. Or she'd feel deflated by how much time had gone into achieving almost nothing, at least for herself, though she had to admit she'd never had much of a knack, or even desire, for putting herself first. She blamed her mother for that, since Alessandra – or Sandra as she'd preferred to be known, since it sounded more English – had rarely put her first either; had indeed seemed to go out of her way at times to make her eldest daughter feel as unwelcome in her own home as she had felt uncomfortable in her skin. And those Latin rages of Alessandra's, almost always directed at Lainey . . . It could make Lainey shrink to think of them even

2

now, and her mother had been dead for almost a year. Gone, but definitely not forgotten, if only because every time Lainey looked in the mirror the voluptuous Alessandra was looking back at her, with, perhaps, less of the fire, though her family weren't wholly convinced about that.

Lainey had little fondness for the resemblance to her mother, not because she hadn't loved Alessandra; actually, sadly, she had, which was why Alessandra's cruelty had hurt so much. It was simply that she'd always felt there was far too much of her mother, and now there was too much of her too. Her silky raven hair was too thick and unruly, her black eyes too large, her mouth far too full and kind of sloppy, and as for her overflowing bust, hips and thighs, as far as she was concerned they were just plain fat.

Scrumptious was how her husband, Tom, often described her. Or luscious, or succulent – there had even been occasions when he'd forgotten himself and called her juicy. Still, at least he found her sexy, albeit in a vaguely carnivorous sort of way, and provided she didn't allow herself to get too hung up about her overabundance in certain areas she could concede that on a good day she wasn't all that bad.

She just wasn't very good at putting herself first.

However, that was about to change, at least for a while. She'd actually, she realised, felt lighter since clicking on to pay for her new adventure, as though she'd shed a few pounds (if only). And a good long stare at herself in the mirror after making the commitment had shown her a thirty-six-year-old woman twinkling with a girlish kind of mischief that could lead her into all sorts of trouble.

3

Leave the past alone, she could hear her mother shouting, eyes flashing and nostrils flaring. *It is gone,* finito, *you are English not Italian.*

This was true, she was English, but only because she'd grown up in England. By birth she was Elenora Cristina, daughter of Alessandra Maria and *padre ignito.* Father unknown. Intriguing, kind of romantic if any of the stories she'd concocted for him over the years were true, but even if they were she couldn't imagine ever being as close to him as she was to her adoptive father, Peter. Everyone adored Peter, even his competitors, and there had been plenty of those during his long and turbulent career.

It was while Lainey, aged nineteen, was whirling her way through a period of work experience at the publishing house her father had founded that she'd first run into Tom Hollingsworth. Back then Tom had only published one book, and that hadn't done particularly well, so his agent had brought him to Winlock's hoping for greater things. They had certainly happened, to a degree that no one had even begun to imagine at the time: huge international sales, wide critical acclaim, and a highly rated TV series, *The Kingsley Way,* featuring secret agents Sebastian Kingsley and his exotic and troublesome wife, Alexis. (There had long been speculation that Alexis was based on Lainey, and while Tom would only smile enigmatically when this was put to him, Lainey would always hotly deny it.)

It was also said, by some, that Tom wouldn't be where he was today were it not for Lainey, but she knew that wasn't true. His talent was all his own, and she was as much in thrall to it as his legions of fans, whose need to know everything about him, his books, his life, his very raison d'être, often seemed

4

to push the boundaries of sanity. They should try living with him, she occasionally thought while whizzing out chirpy, informative responses to the volumes of adulation that poured in through every channel known to online connection. They'd love him even more. Not that she was biased, or couldn't see his faults, it was quite simply that, in spite of being fourteen years her senior, Tom was everything she could ever want in a man, and she liked to think she was everything he wanted too. He always said she was, and as far as she knew he never did anything to contradict it, but what he wasn't quite so good at were wonderfully romantic declarations of love. In fact, for a man whose very existence was all about words, he used depressingly few when it came to expressing his feelings. He did love her though, she was sure about that . . . Well, he was still with her after sixteen years, and not many of their friends could make such a heady claim to marital endurance.

It was amazing really that he had stayed, given how attractive he was to the opposite sex, and she knew he wasn't immune to their charms either, or their brazen offers, because she'd been in that position once. Not that she'd offered herself exactly, but nor had she made even a whimpered attempt to fight down the chemistry that had exploded between them virtually on sight.

She never liked to think of how much hurt she'd caused his first wife, Emma, except she did think about it, quite a lot, because her conscience seemed to enjoy chanting jolly little aphorisms like *what goes around comes around* or *you reap what you sow*. The fact that she hadn't actually known he was married until she was already head over heels and pregnant was no excuse, or not according to her conscience, anyway. She should have walked away the minute she'd found out, told him she wasn't prepared to break someone's heart in order to satisfy her own. Instead she'd let him leave Emma and his five-year-old son in order to start a new life with her.

'Don't be so sure you're the only one,' Emma had warned the day he'd moved out on her. 'And if he can do it to us, he can do it to you.'

During her most insecure moments – and largely thanks to her mother they occurred rather too often – those words would ring clearly in Lainey's mind, though she had to admit that her thoughts at the time had been along the lines of *he obviously loves me more, or he wouldn't be doing this*, and *I'm really, really sorry, I don't want to hurt you, but Tom has to make his own decisions.*

Such was the arrogance, the ignorance of youth. She'd never think that way now.

Sixteen years later she and Tom had two children, Tierney, fifteen, and Xavier, or Zav as they mostly called him, eleven. Max, Tom's eldest, was twenty-one and living in their annexe, though hopefully not for much longer. Lainey adored him, she really did, or at least she had when he was young. These days he was about as much fun to be with as an angry wasp. He still couldn't seem to work out who to be maddest at, his father for leaving when he was young, Lainey for taking Tom away, or his mother who'd abandoned him (as he liked to put it) by going off to pursue a new career in the States. The fact that he'd been nineteen and at uni when Emma had left didn't seem to earn her much in the way of forgiveness. If anything, it had provided him with the excuse he was looking for to drop out of his degree and take off travelling with just a backpack and a guitar for company, and a credit card already close to its limit. In the end, after more than a year of bailing him out of one scrape after another, Tom, out of fear that his son would return in a body bag, had flown to Bangkok and ordered him home.

'I don't have a bloody home,' Max had argued at the time. 'She's gone, hasn't she?'

'You've always had a home with us,' Tom had reminded him, which was true, because he had. 'You can even have the annexe to yourself now that Lainey's father has moved back into the main house.'

What a treat it was turning into, having Max, his music, his attitude and his parties as a full-time neighbour. If it weren't for the fact that he got on so well with Tierney and Zav, and was actually quite good with Peter, and indeed had moments when he could still make her laugh, Lainey knew she'd be buying him a ticket back to Bangkok.

'Lainey, Lainey, where are you? I can't find her.'

'It's all right, Dad,' Lainey soothed, going to assist her father in from the garden. 'She's only gone to the shops.'

Peter Winlock's watery blue eyes hunted the kitchen before coming to rest on Stacy first, then his daughter. 'Who?' he asked worriedly.

Lainey smiled gently. 'Stacy's here,' she told him. 'You remember Stacy, don't you? She's the one who drove into the back of your car the day she passed her driving test.'

Stacy's eyes closed in mock dismay. 'Hi, Peter,' she said, getting up to give him a hug. 'You're looking a bit dapper today in your old panama.'

Peter chuckled delightedly. 'The ladies always like this one,' he said, tapping his hat. He peered more closely into Stacy's eyes. 'I remember you,' he said, seeming thrilled. 'You drove into the back of my car.'

Stacy couldn't help but laugh. 'And I'm never going to live it down, am I?' she responded, without adding *even though it happened over fifteen years ago*.

'Cup of tea, Dad?' Lainey offered, going to reheat the kettle.

'Oh yes, I like tea,' he assured her, as though he rarely received such a generous offer. 'Do you like tea?' he asked Stacy.

Stacy would have answered, had Peter's attention not already begun drifting to whatever else he was seeing in his tragically muddled mind.

'Where is she, Lainey?' he asked anxiously. 'I can't find her.'

'It's OK, Dad, she's just gone to the shops,' Lainey assured him. 'She'll be back soon.' This was the best – the only – way, she'd discovered, to handle her father's never-ending search for her mother. Let him think she'd be home soon, and within a few minutes he'd have forgotten he was even looking for her. Of course it would come back to him at some point, but that was OK, they'd go through the charade again and would probably keep going through it day after day, week after week, until he was too addled even to think it any more.

Alzheimer's was so cruel, so random in its choice of victims, and showed no mercy for them either. It wasn't only memory it destroyed, it was dignity too, and her father had always been such a dignified man, and powerful in his field. By the time he'd sold his publishing house to one of the multi-nationals some twelve years ago, the company had been one of the mostly highly regarded in London.

Peter Winlock's name was still spoken of with respect and affection, and because Lainey adored him and always had, it was no hardship for her to take care of him. She even cleaned him up after incontinent moments, bathed him and soothed away his tears as he cried with shame.

It had been Tom's idea to buy this house – Bannerleigh Cross – from her parents. It was where she and her sisters had grown up, and there was barely a square inch of it that didn't feel special to Lainey. The stories her father had told her of its history had brought it to life in a way that had made her young heart long to know more about the colourful and romantic characters who'd once filled the rooms with laughter, tears, music and strife. Aristocrats and actors; politicians, doctors, adventurers – the tales had turned out to be as tall as the manor's elegant chimneys, but as a child she had never been able to get enough of them. Even now a part of her still believed in them, and on dark nights, if Tom was away and she was missing him, or her mother, she could almost feel the house and its ghostly occupants breathing its quiet energy back into her.

It was just over five years ago that they'd taken ownership of the place. By then her mother had been diagnosed with the cancer that had finally claimed her, and it had become clear that Peter couldn't cope on his own. The house was too big, and he was already absent-minded enough to be causing concern. By taking it over, Tom had reasoned, her parents would be able to stay in their beloved home for the rest of their lives, albeit in the smaller part of it that Tom and Lainey commissioned to be built on. If they did end up having to go into care at a later date, they'd have more than enough capital to make sure it was of the highest quality. Lainey and Tom would also have the rural idyll they'd both long dreamt of owning, and the children would be far better off growing up in the country, they'd felt, than they would in town.

It was this kind of generosity that told Lainey, without words, how much her husband loved her, and if the gesture could have been any greater she was at a loss to know how. He even helped with her father, taking over when she was numbed by tiredness, and should Peter happen to stumble into Tom's study while Tom was writing he was always given a far warmer welcome than any other un-thinking intruder. The rest of the family didn't dare to disturb Tom while he was at work, not even for minor emergencies such as broken arms or concussed heads. It was always Lainey who went hurtling off to school – or the hospital – to fetch the accident victim, and only later would Tom be told the story of what he'd missed.

It was amazing, she'd always thought, how easily he could turn the children's mishaps into giant adventures and end up putting a smile back on their faces. They adored him, as he did them.

He hadn't become particularly involved in the remodelling of Bannerleigh Cross; he'd simply left it to Lainey to make sure he had a place to work that was spacious and light with direct access to the garden, but not a part of the garden that was used by anyone who might disturb him. Even the gardener was encouraged to mow the lawn or strim the hedges on the days Tom wasn't around. So Tom's study was now where the old drawing room and library used to be, at the front of the dual-aspect manor with views across the sloping meadow that tipped into a bubbling stream at the edge of the three-acre estate. Since the lane leading from the village up to the house took a sweeping curve to the right when it became their beech-lined drive, the daily comings and goings took place out of his sight, mainly because Lainey had erected a sign directing everyone to the kitchen door, instead of the front.

The kitchen itself, which sprawled across most of the back of the house with several double French windows opening on to the patio, a hopeful-looking knot garden and the fields beyond, was still the true heart of the place, though it was twice its former size after absorbing the old back parlour, butler's pantry and garden room into its embrace. (All original features such as cornicing, ceiling roses and fireplaces had been lovingly restored and replaced; even the old flagstones were back where they belonged.) These days this bustling centre of activity was far more than a kitchen with a glossy black Aga at one end and vast inglenook fireplace at the other; it was a place to eat, watch TV, do homework, catch up on emails, stare at nothing if you were Peter, and occasionally relax on huge sofas around a roaring log fire with friends, glasses of wine and opinions that needed to be shared if you were Tom and Lainey.

Lainey never forgot how lucky she was to be here. In spite of the difficulties she had experienced with her mother, she harboured a sense of belonging here in the way that grass belonged to fields and stars belonged to night skies. Her father had always understood that and so did Tom, though what her sisters, her mother's favourites, thought, was never entirely clear, since they saw so little of them now.

'You're a good girl,' Peter said, as Stacy sat him into his comfy armchair at the window end of the battered old dining table. 'You drove your car into mine the other day, didn't you?'

Stacy feigned a collapse. 'And there was me hoping you wouldn't notice,' she groaned.

He patted her hand affectionately. 'Don't worry. We won't tell Sandra,' he assured her, using the very words he had at the time it had happened. Everyone had been nervous of Sandra's fiery temper, with the exception of Peter, who'd always seemed more enchanted than fazed by her operatic tantrums.

'Where's Sherman, Dad?' Lainey asked, referring to his faithful old golden Lab. As if she needed to ask. There he was, lying where he always lay when he brought Peter back from a walk, just outside the door waiting for permission to come in. It was Sandra who'd taught him to wait. Left to her he'd probably never have been allowed into the house at all. However, this was one of the few issues about which Peter had put his foot down. He loved his dog possibly as much as he loved his children, and as far as he was concerned Sherman had as much right to sit in front of the fire, or belly-flop on to the floor in the kitchen, as the rest of them. These days Sherman, who was getting on himself at thirteen, even slept on a rug at the foot of Peter's bed, and should Peter wake up in the night and seem not to know where he was, or if he got into some kind of difficulty anywhere, Sherman would bark to raise the alarm. This was partly why Lainey and Tom had recently moved Peter back into the

12

manor from the annexe, to make sure they always heard the dog. Now Peter's private living space, with its own shower room, cosy sitting area, fireplace, TV and beloved antique-book collection, was on the first floor, securely sandwiched between Tom and Lainey's master suite and the main family bathroom.

The children's rooms were on the second floor. Max, in the two-bedroom annexe, had turned it into a tip by day and party central by night. He invariably found his way into the manor at mealtimes, or for booze when his supplies ran out, or just to get under everyone's skin, with outstanding results.

'There you are, old boy,' Lainey was saying to Sherman as she ushered him in through the door. 'You come and lie down with Peter now. I expect you're both ready for a nap.'

Taking his biscuit to Peter's chair, Sherman slumped down next to his master and started to chew in a languidly satisfied sort of way. Peter wasn't watching him; his vague, rheumy eyes were gazing out of the window, though his hand automatically dropped towards the dog's head.

'You're a little miracle, Sherman,' Stacy declared, going to fill his drink bowl. And he was, because no one had ever trained him to bring Peter back from his walks, or to get him safely across a road, or to alert the family if Peter was distressed, he simply seemed to know what needed to be done and got on with it. 'I wish the male human species was a bit more like you,' she lamented, as Lainey answered the phone for the fourth time since Stacy had arrived. 'Trusting, loving and endlessly faithful.'

Smiling, as Peter turned to look at her, she gave him a wink and drew up a chair to keep him company while Lainey chatted to Hugo, Tom's publicist. Those calls usually went on for some time, since Tom was in high demand for various media or charitable events, even when he didn't have a book coming out. Apart from being a full-on house-wife and mother, it was Lainey's job, for which she was very well paid, to organise Tom's diary in a way that never took him away from the house when he wanted to write. Those dates were always care-fully worked out between them to take into account his annual deadline, the research trips that needed to be made, and the occasional visits to the set of the latest TV adaptation. Being a writer herself, Stacy was as admiring of Tom's success as she was, in some ways, indebted to it, since her regular column in one of the Sunday supplements was known to be loosely based on the hectic Hollingsworth family. Unfortunately the column had recently been axed due to a takeover at the paper, so, being freelance, she no longer had a regular source of income.

Though Stacy and Lainey had known each other since school, during their time at uni they'd drifted apart, until Lainey, in her capacity as junior publicist at Winlock's, had rung Stacy, who was just starting out on a local paper, to offer her an interview with the new le Carré, as Tom was being billed back then. The piece Stacy had concocted had not only turned into her very first double-page spread, it had gained her the interest of one of the nationals who had later offered her a job.

Since that time they'd barely gone a day without speaking. They'd been bridesmaids at each other's weddings; had often holidayed together with their husbands and later Lainey and Tom's children – Max too, when Emma had felt inclined to let him come.

Stacy had even been present at Zav's birth, though only because the baby had come early and Tom hadn't made it back from the States in time. Over the years they'd become closer to each other than they were to their respective sisters. In fact, Stacy often claimed that she'd never have survived the break-up of her marriage without Lainey's unflinching support. During that time she'd spent far more time at Bannerleigh Cross than she had at her own home, the other side of the village, mainly because Derek had refused to move out. He'd even thought it was OK to carry on his affair under the same roof, and Pauline, the little tart with no heart, had been happy to oblige.

When he'd heard what was happening Tom had informed Derek, a senior correspondent with CNN, that a man who behaved with no respect for his wife deserved no respect from others, so he needn't bother coming to Bannerleigh Cross again. Derek had moved out of the village soon after that, but then the house had to be sold so the proceeds could be divided, and thanks to a massive slump in the market he and Stacy had ended up with less than they'd paid for it. He'd also gone off with ten of the twenty thousand pounds Stacy had inherited from her gran, who had never been able to stand him, plus half the proceeds from the sale of her gran's cottage. That, more than anything else, was why she detested him with such a passion now. He needn't have taken his share of her inheritance, and he knew it.

These days she was renting the flat above her cousin's gift and accessory shop in Stroud, while Derek and Pauline, a Texan model with more teeth than hair, and more front covers than brain cells, were living it up on New York's Upper East Side.

15

At least her best friend was less than five miles from Stroud, and now Martin had appeared, the owner of a small but thriving nursery just off the A46, life was finally looking up again. She felt sure Lainey and Tom were going to love him when she got round to arranging a meeting. Certainly Lainey would, because Lainey generally loved everyone, and Tom probably would too, because as far as Stacy could make out there was nothing not to love.

'Sorry about that,' Lainey said, putting the phone down and typing a quick message to herself into the laptop she kept in the kitchen. 'Is Dad drinking his tea?'

'Yes, he's doing very well, aren't you?' Stacy replied, guiding the cup Peter was holding back to his mouth.

'Oh, who's that now?' Lainey grumbled as the phone rang again. 'Hello, Bannerleigh Cross.'

'Lainey, it's me, Sarah,' her middle sister announced sweetly. 'Is this a good time?'

'As good as any,' Lainey told her, turning to Stacy as she went on, 'What can I do for you, Sarah?'

Stacy's eyebrows rose.

'I thought I'd come and see Dad,' Sarah replied. 'Would tomorrow be convenient?'

Expressing no surprise, Lainey opened up her calendar, though she had no need to. 'Actually, he has swimming in the morning,' she said, 'but you could always take him, if you're free.'

Sarah was immediately hesitant. 'I'm not good with things like that,' she protested weakly. 'Perhaps we could do the afternoon?'

'Friday would be better, if you could manage that,' Lainey suggested. 'Why don't you come for lunch?'

16

'OK, if you're sure it's no trouble. I'll be there around twelve. Esther might come too,' she added, referring to their younger sister. 'I'll give her a ring and let you know.'

'That'll be lovely,' Lainey assured her. 'I haven't seen either of you for ages, so I'm already looking forward to it.'

Stacy was eyeing her sceptically as she put the phone down. 'So what pricked her conscience, one has to ask?' she commented. 'How long is it since she was last here?'

Lainey shrugged. 'A couple of months, maybe longer, and knowing her she'll cancel before Friday anyway.'

With a sigh, Stacy said, 'You know, what beats me is how they can opt out and let you take everything on yourself, when they're his *biological* daughters, for God's sake.'

Lainey's eyes clouded. She didn't much like to be reminded that Peter wasn't her natural father, when no father could ever have loved her more. 'He adopted me when I was four years old,' she said quietly, 'so I'm every bit as duty-bound to take care of him as my sisters are. Perhaps more so, considering how much he's given me over the years.' It was true, he'd never made her feel as though she mattered any less than the others; in many ways he'd seemed to go out of his way to make her feel the most special of all, which she guessed was a large part of why she and her sisters had never really been close. Of course, her mother hadn't helped, the way she'd so blatantly favoured the other two. This was very probably why Peter had always given her so much attention, to try and make up for it.

'I understand how you feel,' Stacy said softly, 'but they really ought to do more to help. It's not as though they live a million miles away, Cheltenham's only up the road, and they've both got cars and . . .'

'. . . busy lives,' Lainey came in quickly, 'and to be honest, I'm quite glad they don't come more than they do. We always end up in some sort of a row, and as soon as we start laying into each other I swear I can hear my mother cheering them on from the grave.'

'It would be completely typical of the old bat to do just that,' Stacy muttered, her dislike of Alessandra being no secret between them. 'Even though it was you who nursed her the entire time she was ill. You never let her down, not once, you even moved here, bought this house so you could take her for all her treatments, be there to deal with the aftermath, cope with her pain and temper . . .'

'Stace . . .'

'And where were your sisters all that time?' Stacy pressed on forcefully. 'Bloody nowhere, that's where they were. If they managed to visit more than twice a month then it's more than I ever heard about, and I know they didn't come, because I was here myself.'

Lainey sighed wearily and came to dab the drool from Peter's lips. How much of all this was he managing to take in? she wondered. Almost nothing, from the look of him, and though she was thankful for it, she could hardly bear how much she missed him.

Realising she'd probably gone too far, as usual, Stacy said, 'Sorry, I didn't mean to rant, and I know things got better between you and your mother towards the end, but honest to God your sisters don't even begin to understand how much hurt

18

they've caused you, and for your mother to have died without telling you . . .'

'Let's leave it now,' Lainey interrupted quietly. 'We can't assume Dad doesn't know what we're saying, and if he does it'll only upset him.'

Stacy immediately backed off, and wishing she was better at thinking before speaking, she took Peter's cup round the bar to the sink.

'Would you like to stay in the chair for your nap today?' Lainey asked Peter, holding on to both his hands.

His eyes came to hers and recognising her, he said, 'Lainey. How are you, my love?'

'I'm fine,' she assured him.

'Where's your mother?'

'She's gone for a little lie-down.'

'Oh, that's good. I expect she's tired after all that . . . business.'

'Yes, she is. And I expect you are too, so would you like a little zizz now?'

'Mm, yes I think so. I'm not in your way, am I?'

'Of course not. You're never in the way.'

'Are the children home yet?'

'No, I'll be picking them up in a minute. Stacy's going to stay with you while I'm gone.'

'Oh, that's nice. What time are we catching the train?'

'I'm not sure yet. I'll let you know when I come back.'

Seeming satisfied with that, he squeezed her hands and closed his eyes in a way that showed he'd had enough for now.

'I guess there's no train,' Stacy said, as Lainey came round the bar to join her.

Lainey shook her head. 'But I do have to pick the

kids up, so is it OK to stay with him? I mean, he should be all right on his own, but I'm worried he might try to cook or . . .'

'Of course I'll stay,' Stacy broke in. 'You don't even have to ask.'

Lainey smiled. 'What would I do without you? Oh, I remember, sink without trace!' Her eyes started to sparkle. 'Before I go I just have to tell you what I've done.'

Mirroring the sparkle, Stacy said, 'I knew there was something going on with you. So come on, spill.'

'I've actually booked it,' Lainey declared.

Stacy frowned.

'The villa,' Lainey cried laughingly. 'In Italy. We've got it for the entire month, from mid-July to mid-August while I go in search of my roots. The children are going to be so excited when I tell them. They're dying to go, and now . . .' She broke off as something smashed out in the hall. Throwing a curious, alarmed look at Stacy, she went to the door and quickly yanked it open.

It was no surprise to find Max standing over the shattered pieces of an antique vase, though she hadn't expected to find her bag in his hands.

'What are you doing?' she demanded, going to take the bag from him.

'It was an accident!' he cried. 'I was just picking it up. Like there's a crime in that?'

'I'll get a dustpan and brush,' she said, glancing meaningfully at the bone-china fragments.

'Don't tell me, it's worth a fortune,' he sneered, clearly trying to mask his concern. 'It has to be, because everything's valuable around here in the *capitalist's* paradise.'

Lainey stared directly into his moody dark eyes.

Handsome he might be, but when, she wondered, had he last shaved, or washed his shaggy fair hair? His clothes were hanging limply from his gangly limbs, and the smell of beer and tobacco was all over him. 'If you don't like the capitalist's house,' she responded smoothly, 'you don't have to stay,' and turning on her heel she started back to the kitchen.

'I wonder what *Tom* would have to say if I told him you were trying to throw me out,' he called after her.

I'm not trying to throw you out, I'm just trying to make you grow up, she wanted to shout back, but she knew better than to get into a tussle with him when he wasn't quite sober. Instead she rolled her eyes at Stacy as she picked up the dustpan and took it back to him.

'Dream on,' he snarled, and turning around he went back through the door he'd emerged from. Apparently his inner demons had laid full claim to his charm today.

After clearing up the mess herself, she emptied the pieces into a bag and stored it under the sink just in case she decided to show it to Tom. She knew she probably wouldn't, since she hated it when those two went at each other. However, she wasn't prepared simply to dismiss it right away. Something had to be done about Max's manner, particularly the way he seemed to have turned his anger on her lately. She'd just have to try and work it out at another time.

'I don't know how you put up with him,' Stacy muttered, as Lainey unhooked her keys from the board next to the back door.

'Nor do I,' Lainey responded, 'but, to be honest,

I've got other things to worry about right now, like my darling daughter and what sort of mood *she's* going to be in when I get her. Make yourself at home, or take another look at the villa. You'll find the link somewhere in my inbox. It's so gorgeous. We're going to love it there.'

'We?'

'You're coming too, I hope.'

Visibly brightening, Stacy said, 'Count me in, provided it's all right with Tom, of course.'

'He won't mind. Anyway, knowing him he'll write the whole time we're there, which is the reason I've gone for somewhere with a separate apartment that he can have all to himself. Besides, it's my treat. I've been saving up for this so I can spoil you all rotten while I go in search of who I might have been if my mother had stayed in Italy.'

Stacy cocked an eyebrow. 'So I take it you've gone for the villa in . . . what's the name of the place again?'

'Tuoro. Actually, it's just outside the village, up on a hill. Take a look. It's stunning. Bye, Dad, won't be long. Try to behave while I'm gone.'

Smiling at Peter's peacefully sleeping face, Stacy wandered over to the computer as Lainey ran out to the car. A few moments later she was clicking through to the villa that overlooked Lake Trasimeno and the village where Lainey's mother had apparently grown up. Perhaps her real father, too. Members of her family might even still live there. Clearly that was what Lainey was hoping to find out, and Stacy was happy to help, even though, in Stacy's humble opinion, to go looking for people who'd never expressed a desire to be found might not be a brilliant idea.

However, Tom might disagree with her on that, and she could only presume he did or he surely wouldn't be supporting the plan.

Chapter Two

Lainey was sitting in the car at the school gates, getting on with her emails while waiting for Tierney to come surging out with the crowds. Zav had just rung to remind her his football training had been swapped from tomorrow to today, so his friend Alfie's mother would be bringing him home. Great, this would give her some extra time to pop into the supermarket on the way back, and to pick up the dry cleaning that had been ready for at least a fortnight by now. Remembering she still had to call the caterer with numbers for Saturday night's dinner, she quickly dialled Tom's mobile to find out if he'd invited anyone else since they'd last spoken.

'Hi, darling, hope the shoot's going well,' she said into his voicemail. 'Call me back when you can. I need to talk about Saturday.'

Not long after she clicked off, he rang. 'Hey, it's me,' he said, sounding tired and slightly scratchy. 'Are you OK?'

'I'm fine, but I don't think you are. Problems your end?'

'A few. Where are you?'

'Waiting for Tierney. I had a long chat with Hugo earlier; we can discuss it when you're back. Did you get my message?'

'About Saturday? Yes, and apparently Guy can't make it. He's stuck in New York until early next week.'

'But Nadia's still coming?' Lainey was fond of Tom's agent, Nadia Roundtree, and would be sorry if she couldn't make it just because her husband wasn't around.

'She is,' he confirmed. 'I said it'd be fine for her to stay the night. Do we have room?'

'We'd have plenty if Max would find himself a job and move into a place of his own,' she couldn't help saying, 'but I can't see that happening any time soon.'

Sounding tired again, he said, 'Definitely not before Saturday, but I'll talk to him again. Please tell me he hasn't been giving you a hard time.'

'On and off, but nothing I can't cope with. Zav wants to know if you'll be back in time to watch him play football on Saturday.'

'Yeah, he texted and I should be.'

'Are you sure you're all right? You sound pretty fed up.'

He sighed wearily. 'I guess I am. It hasn't been an easy week so far, and there isn't much sign of it improving.'

'Are you on the set now?'

'No, but I ought to get back there. I'll call again later.'

After he'd rung off Lainey sat watching the girls beginning to trickle, then stream out of the old Victorian schoolhouse, claret-coloured skirts rolled up at their waists as high as they dared, white V-neck shirts popped open at the buttons to reveal lacy bras.

Not quite Essex comes to Gloucestershire, but almost.

Spotting Tierney ambling along with her new best friend, Skye Andrews, all glossy dark hair and electric-blue eyes, Lainey felt her usual pang of concern at how much older than fifteen she looked. True, she was going to be sixteen in a couple of weeks, but her height – she was already as tall as Lainey at five foot eight – her attitude, and the shapeliness of her figure made her seem closer to twenty. Though Lainey felt certain she was still a virgin, she most certainly didn't look like one, and she didn't always behave like one either.

There was some small comfort to be taken from the fact that half the girls in year eleven appeared equally sassy, even the weekly boarders, such as Skye, who'd spent a couple of weekends at Bannerleigh Cross over the past month or so. Lainey had to admit she hadn't particularly enjoyed the experience. Not that Skye was a difficult guest, on the contrary, she was always polite, helped out where she could, and as far as teenage attitude went, if she had one she clearly left it at the door before visiting friends' homes. It was the way Tierney had showed off in front of her that had grated on Lainey, carrying on as though having a famous dad was a total drag, and that living in a big house was more of an embarrassment than a privilege. Needless to say, she never acted that way around Tom, she wouldn't dare, and half the time Lainey was convinced she only did it in front of her to try and provoke a reaction. Lainey had learned not to rise to it, especially since discovering that Skye's family home, in the centre of London, was easily the size of theirs, and was actually only one of several lavish properties her stepfather had dotted around the world.

Watching Tierney and Skye now, taking their time over saying goodbye at the gates, one so exquisitely blonde, the other so stormily dark, Lainey could only feel glad that this was an all-girls' school. Heaven only knew what kind of havoc they'd wreak on boys of their age – actually any age – were they around them all the time. She couldn't remember her and Stacy being anywhere near as sophisticated when they were sixteen, but maybe that was because she didn't want to.

'Hey, Mum,' Tierney chirruped as she slipped into the car, her long bare legs seeming to take a while to come in after her. 'How's things?'

'Everything's fine,' Lainey told her, giving Skye a wave as she began reversing out of her space. 'How did the maths exam go today?'

'Yeah, it was cool,' Tierney replied, tossing her hair over one shoulder as she studied her mobile. 'GCSEs are so peak. I don't know why we're bothering when everyone knows they're a waste of time.'

'Not if you want to go on to do As. So you think you did well?'

Tierney shrugged. 'I guess so. I answered everything anyway. Oh, by the way, Skye's invited me to her place the week after exams are over. It'll be so cool, hanging out in London with her and her friends. They're completely amazing, and it's so dead around here.'

'I think we need to discuss that before you accept,' Lainey cautioned. 'We've never actually met her family . . .'

'Oh, Mum, lighten up, will you? Her rents are fantastic, just like you and Dad, but a bit stricter, which should make you happy. And there's no need to have a convo about everything I do. I'm going to be sixteen by then . . .'

'I'm aware of that and I'd like to know what you want to do for your birthday. Dad's agreed to a party . . .'

'Oh God, I so don't want one. There's no one around here to invite for a start.'

'Tierney, that's ridiculous. You've got dozens of friends in the area. What about Maudie?'

'Oh, don't start going on about her again. I'm still friends with her, all right? I'm just not hanging out with her quite so much. It's not a problem, it just happens, we move on, OK?'

'But I think she misses you . . .'

'*Mu-um!*'

'All right, all right. I'm just saying, you have lots of friends around here who you've known all your life, and whose sixteenths you've been to . . .'

'Which doesn't mean I have to have one too. I swear, I really don't want to spend my birthday with them. They're all so juvenile, like they really need to get out more, and I know you, you'll only try to join in with all your mum dancing and it is sooo embarrassing.'

Lainey had to laugh, mainly because she could see Tierney was trying hard not to. 'Which exams do you have tomorrow?' she asked.

Tierney was too busy texting to respond. 'Oh my God, that is so cool!' she suddenly cried.

Lainey waited for enlightenment, but unsurprisingly none came so she simply carried on driving, heading into town, while going over in her mind what further arrangements she needed to make for Saturday. If Nadia was coming without her husband they were down to eleven, unless she could persuade

28

Stacy to change her mind and bring the new man, but then they'd be thirteen and she wasn't sure she was comfortable with that.

'When's Dad back?' Tierney asked, as they drove into the supermarket car park.

'Saturday morning, or Friday evening if he can get away sooner. Why?'

Tierney shrugged. She was texting again. 'You're kind of unusual, you two,' she commented, seeming hardly to connect with her words, 'you know, still being together when everyone else's parents are split up.'

'Not *everyone's*,' Lainey countered.

'Well, just about. Oh God, it would be a total nightmare if you two broke up. I'd so hate it. I wouldn't know who to live with, because I love you both, and it would be the same for Zav . . .'

'Shall we change the subject?' Lainey cut in, knowing from experience how easily Tierney's teenage hormones could get her all wound up over nothing.

'I'm just saying, that's all. Loads of women have got the hots for Dad, which makes them totally sad, of course, but hey, someone has to be. Did I tell you, Mrs Kellaway, the English teacher, is mega struck on him? She's always asking about him, which kind of freaks me out. I mean, she's so *old* and like weird in the way she gets all steamed up over poems and stuff.'

'She's not that old,' Lainey objected, refraining from pointing out that Pamela Kellaway was probably still in her forties, while Tom was going to be fifty-one at the end of the year.

'Whatever,' Tierney murmured, going back to her phone.

'Are you coming?' Lainey asked, turning off the engine.

'No. I'll wait here and make sure no one offs the car.'

Rolling her eyes, Lainey took herself into the store, checking her own phone on the way and grabbing a hand basket to collect up the few items she needed.

Ten minutes later she was opening the back of the estate to drop in the groceries when she heard Tierney say, 'Shit, got to go.'

Waiting until she was in the driver's seat and starting the engine, Lainey said, 'Who was that?'

Tierney sighed. 'Do you really need to know?'

Lainey cast her a sideways look and turned in her seat to reverse out of the space.

'Talking about Dad,' Tierney drawled, as though the conversation hadn't been broken, 'do you reckon he was ever a spy himself? I mean, I know he says Ian Fleming based James Bond on him and all that rubbish – he's too young for one thing, and definitely not cool enough for another. But everyone says how realistic his books are, and when Mrs Kellaway asked if he ever used to work for MI5 . . . Well, he did once, didn't he?'

'You know he did, but it was a long time ago, just after he left uni.'

'He's still got loads of contacts though, you know, people he sees clandestinely, or who tip him off about stuff. I wonder if he had a codename when he was active, and if he did, what it was.'

Amused by the intrigue, Lainey said, 'What's brought this on? You've never seemed particularly interested before.'

'Nothing,' Tierney replied airily. 'I just thought, wouldn't it be cool if he was still a spy?'

Lainey had to laugh.

Tierney did too, and with a sudden gasp of what sounded like glee she went back to her phone, leaving Lainey to reflect on how following her logic these days was about as easy as deciphering her texts (not that Lainey ever snooped, well, maybe she might steal a glance or two if Tierney wasn't aware she was looking, much good it ever did her), or listening to her gabbing away to Skye on the phone.

Still, what really mattered, as Tom often reminded her, was that whatever might be going on in Tierney's overactive brain, she was at home most nights with them, and was apparently doing well at school. As for boys, true she was always talking about them, or drooling over some movie star or boy band, but apart from a couple of dates with her friends' brothers during the past year, she'd hadn't yet become involved in what might be termed a more serious relationship. Nor, to Lainey's relief, had she yet asked to go on the pill, unlike a few of the girls she'd grown up with whose mothers had given in rather than have to deal with the alternative.

Tierney would ask, wouldn't she, and not just go ahead and get a prescription without her mother knowing? Of course she would; Lainey had always made it perfectly clear that Tierney could come to her with anything, and it wasn't as if they didn't have frank conversations about sex, because they often did.

Lainey didn't even want to contemplate what Tom would say if he thought his precious daughter might be using contraceptives. He wasn't any too thrilled by the number of girls Max was bringing back to the annexe either, though mainly because of the example he was setting his younger sister and brother. Lainey had to leave that to Tom to handle, while she did her best with Tierney. As for Zav, since he was mercifully still too young to have developed an attitude, or spots, or sexually charged hormones, he was an absolute dream to live with when compared to the other two.

'So, like when you were my age,' Tierney said, clicking off the phone again, 'were you already into older men, or was it just when you met Dad?'

Both amused and vaguely curious as to why she was asking, Lainey said, 'Dad was my first boyfriend, so I didn't really know the difference.'

'That is so not true,' Tierney cried. 'You were nineteen when you two met, so there had to have been someone before that.'

'If there was, I can't remember his name now.'

Tierney scoffed. 'Yeah, right. Was it like amazing, when you and Dad first met? Did you think . . . I mean, did you know right away that he was the one?'

Remembering just how electrifying the occasion had been (though no way in the world was she going to tell Tierney that her parents had locked themselves in a conference room and gone for it, while the rest of the publishing team were waiting for them to join a meeting on the next floor), Lainey said, 'I'm not sure I knew he was the right one, exactly, but I definitely fell for him.'

Tierney was looking thoughtful. 'So do you think he'd have married you if you hadn't got pregnant?' she asked bluntly.

Lainey's heart caught on the words. They hadn't gone this far into her and Tom's past before, so there was a chance Tierney didn't know how sensitive this unexplored area was. 'I'm not sure,' she replied truthfully. 'He says he would have, but it's all a bit academic now, isn't it, because he did marry me and now here we are and you really ought to be asking him these questions, not me.'

'Yeah, and like he's going to answer them. Anyway, him being older and married and everything didn't really make a difference?'

Frowning, Lainey said, 'I wouldn't exactly put it like that. Why are you so interested all of a sudden?'

'No reason. Just making conversation. What were Granny and Grandpa like when you and Dad got together? Did they go ballistic about him being married and you being up the duff?'

Knowing she'd never forget how furious her mother had been, or the names she'd called her, Lainey said, 'You have to remember Granny was Catholic, so it was all pretty sinful as far as she was concerned. Not that I'm saying it wasn't wrong, because obviously it was, but it was harder for her to accept than it was for Grandpa.'

Tierney smiled. 'Grandpa's such a sweetheart, isn't he? I bet he was dead good-looking when he was young.'

'You've seen pictures, so you know he was.'

'How did he and Granny meet?' She swung round suddenly. 'Just a minute, she had you before she was married, so it was a bit much giving you a hard time when you did the same thing with me.'

Having thought so herself at the time, Lainey said, 'For all you know she was married to my real dad.'

Tierney frowned. 'Was she?'

'I don't know. She'd never tell me anything about him.'

'Did Grandpa know him?'

'No. He met her here, in England, after she'd left Italy. She was a waitress in a restaurant he used to go to – and kept going to, and kept going to until she agreed to go out with him.'

Tierney smiled. 'I can imagine him being a romantic, can't you? Oh my God, is that Max coming towards us in his Fiesta? Yes, it is. Flash him down, Mum, I need to speak to him and he's not answering his phone.'

Lainey had barely pulled to the side of the road before Tierney had leapt out and run over to an impatient-looking Max, who'd swerved to a halt the other side of the country lane.

Since she couldn't hear what they were saying, and wasn't particularly interested either, Lainey quickly checked her emails in case something important had come in.

Looking like I could be back on Friday evening Tom had written.

Pleased by the prospect of his early return, she sent him a quick reply, saying, *That's great. We all miss you, especially me. Love you. Xxx*

Though she rarely failed to sign off romantically, he almost never did, which she was well used to by now, though she wouldn't have minded if he made an exception once in a while.

'Do you love me?' she asked him from time to time.

'You know I do.'

'Then say it.'

'I love you. OK?'

Just like that, as if it were a duty, or a small ordeal that had to be endured. Yet when they made love, or simply spent time together, just the two of them, she never got a sense of him wanting to be elsewhere. Occasionally she'd feel his eyes on her while she was cooking, or working at her desk, and when she looked up he'd smile in a way that made her feel their connection as deeply as if it was something she could lose herself in. They were happy, she kept reminding herself, as close as it was possible for a couple to be, so why could she never quite shake the feeling that he was holding something back?

Because she was a mess of insecurities, that was why.

'OK, cool,' Tierney declared, getting back in the car.

'Did Max say where he was going?' Lainey asked, as she watched him drive on without glancing her way. Apparently he was still mad with her over something.

'No, but probably to Richmond's or Harry's. Oh my God, I forgot to take my phone. Did it ring while I was gone?'

'If it had I'd have answered it,' Lainey told her, pulling back on to the road.

'Well don't, OK? Don't *ever* answer my phone.'

Lainey's eyebrows rose.

Tierney kept her head down, checking her call log.

After a while, Lainey said, 'Are you revising tonight? Which exam do you have tomorrow?'

'RI, ugh! Like such a waste of time.'

'Good job Granny can't hear you, she'd be very upset to think you're not taking religious studies seriously.'

'Did you, when you were my age?'

'Of course.'

'Yeah, right.'

'I did.'

'Mum, you are such a bad liar. Anyway, even Granny never used to go to church until she got sick.'

This was true, and Lainey still wasn't sure that her mother had got any real comfort from her return to God. However, by then the two of them had become closer than they'd ever been, which had certainly provided some comfort for Lainey.

Tierney's attention had returned to her texts and remained there until after Lainey had taken a call from the caterers. 'So what's the big deal on Saturday?' Tierney asked, as they pulled up outside the house. 'Is it someone's birthday, or something?'

'No. Dad just wanted to invite a few people round. Do you feel like joining us? Guy's had to drop out so we're down to eleven.'

Tierney didn't answer. Lainey wasn't even sure she'd heard, she was so intent on whatever new message she'd just received, so leaving her to it she made her way to the kitchen, where Stacy was already opening a bottle of wine.

'Bit early, isn't it?' Lainey commented, dumping her bags on the counter.

'I'm in need,' Stacy told her. 'I've just been turned down for another job. The *Express* this time. They're not even going to bloody well interview me.'

Feeling for how awful the rejection must be,

Lainey went to give her a hug. 'It's their loss,' she murmured comfortingly. 'And think of it this way, Fate has obviously got something a whole lot better in store for you, it's just not quite ready to deliver yet.'

Stacy had to laugh. 'You have such a rosy way of looking at the shit in the world,' she told her. 'I guess it's why we all love you. Hey, T, how are you, sweetheart?' she said as Tierney came in the door. 'Exams OK today?'

'Yeah, cool,' Tierney muttered, keeping her eyes down as she pushed her way through. 'I'm going to my room,' she informed them.

'What about saying hello to Grandpa?' Lainey called after her.

'Hey, Grandpa,' Tierney shouted over her shoulder.

Lainey looked at her father, who apparently had no idea he'd just been spoken to. 'Is he OK?' she asked Stacy.

'He seems fine. He hasn't moved from the chair since you left.'

'In which case I'd better take him to the loo,' Lainey decided. 'Do you mind unpacking these bags and putting away whatever needs to go into the fridge?'

Half an hour later Stacy and Lainey were at the table with Lainey's laptop between them, ready to take a good long look at the villa in Italy, when the landline rang. Being the closest, Stacy reached for it.

'Hello, Bannerleigh Cross,' she announced, watching Lainey taking a sip of her tea. She couldn't have wine until Zav was home, just in case she needed to go and get him.

'No, this isn't Mrs Hollingsworth,' Stacy said, turning to Lainey. 'Who's calling, please?' Stacy's eyes widened. 'Can I tell her what it's about?' she asked. 'I see. Is he OK? Has something happened to him?'

Lainey's heart jarred.

'I'll pass you over,' Stacy said. 'It's a PC Darren Barry from Stroud Police,' she told Lainey. 'Apparently Max has been arrested for shoplifting.'

Lainey's insides sank.

'And he's drunk,' Stacy added.

Only just managing not to groan out loud, Lainey took the phone. 'Hello, Officer,' she said, 'I'm sorry if he's causing trouble. What can I do?'

'Someone needs to come and get him,' the policeman replied, 'and yours is the name he's given us.'

'How very sporting of him,' Lainey muttered, glancing up as Tierney came back into the room. 'I take it he's at the station in Stroud?'

'He is.'

'OK, I'll be there in about twenty minutes,' and feeling she'd rather brain him than collect him, she rang off and reached for her iPhone as it bleeped with a text.

'What's going on?' Tierney wanted to know.

'It's Max,' Lainey answered distractedly. *Ask your husband about Julia.* 'Oh, no, not another bloody nutter,' she groaned. Since both she and Tom were subjected to this sort of mischief-making on a regular basis, either through their phones or emails, she'd learned long ago that the only way to handle it was simply to ignore it. If it became a real nuisance, or in some way threatening, they usually handed it over to the police.

'OK, I'd better go and get him,' she said, dropping her phone back in her bag. 'He'd just better not vomit in my car is all I can say, or he's going to be seriously sorry.'

'Try not to be too hard on him,' Tierney called after her. 'Remember, it's not his fault he's all screwed up.'

Tierney's parting words were still smarting when Lainey led Max out of the police station over to the car. It seemed he'd driven himself into town (presumably already way over the limit) to help himself to a flagon of rough cider and a six-pack of Fosters from a bargain booze shop.

And got caught.

Not your day, Max, she was thinking sourly as she headed out of the station car park to start down the hill.

'I suppose you're going to tell Dad about this,' he snorted, using the back of his hand to wipe his mouth.

'You've been charged with shoplifting,' she reminded him. 'You're due in front of the magistrate tomorrow, so how on earth do you think you can keep it from him?'

He stifled a belch and lifted a greasy trainer on to the dashboard. 'He won't care, anyway,' he drawled. 'He's too fucking busy with all his fucking stuff going on to think about anyone except himself.'

Hating the swearing, but knowing he'd only increase it if she objected, she decided to ignore him and simply continued to drive.

'I guess you realise if you'd given me some cash it wouldn't have happened,' he declared, gazing out at the passing countryside.

'I don't recall you asking,' she snapped, wondering if he'd been trying to steal from her bag when he'd knocked over the vase. He'd never stolen from them before, but there was no knowing how far he might go to gain attention, or cause friction, or deliver some sort of payback for the damage he'd decided had been inflicted on him by the break-up of his parents' marriage.

He yawned, scratched his whiskery chin and slumped deeper into the seat. 'I forgot, nothing's ever your fault, is it?' he snorted.

Though she tensed, she refused to let herself go there.

'I guess you realise that if he'd been around for me when I was growing up, I wouldn't be in the fucking mess I'm in now,' he challenged.

She stayed silent.

'Would I?' he pressed.

'If that's what you want to believe.'

'It's a fact.'

'OK.'

'And we all know *why* he wasn't around when I was a kid.'

In spite of being as rattled as he intended, she kept her thoughts to herself, determined not to give him the satisfaction of a row.

'So no matter what you say, or what I do,' he rumbled on, 'it all comes down to one thing in the end: you took him away from me and my mum, so you've got to be to blame for the way everything's turned out.'

Before she could stop herself, she said tartly, 'I guess it would be a mistake to take on any responsibility for the way you are yourself, because you really wouldn't know how to handle something as adult as that.'

He didn't bite back right away, presumably because his booze-soaked brain was ticking too slowly to come up with something equally cutting. 'You think you're really clever, don't you?' he managed in the end.

'No, not really.'

More seconds ticked by as she fought to remind herself of how loving and easy he'd been as a child, and of how much she cared for him really, when he wasn't in one of these aggressively dark moods.

'You sit there in your posh house,' he suddenly blurted, 'driving your fuck-off car, with all your stuck-up friends, making out like you're the perfect wife to the famous author, when what you really are is a whore who steals other people's husbands.'

Reeling from the insult, she did her best to control the rage that flared up ready to explode.

'I bet you're going to tell Dad I said that,' he jeered.

Her voice was dripping with scorn as she retorted, 'It surprises me that you're still behaving like a boy when most twenty-one-year-olds I know are men.'

'What?' he snarled. 'What the fuck are you talking about?'

Since he knew exactly what she meant, she didn't bother to explain.

Clearly riled now, he said, 'You never gave a fuck about me, or my mum, the whole time I was growing up, did you? All you cared about was getting my dad and being the famous Mrs Hollingsworth. Well, fuck you, is what I say to you. And fuck him too.'

Turning off the main road to start heading towards the village, she replied. 'You'll be able to tell him yourself when he comes back on Friday. I'm sure he'll be interested to hear your observations on our marriage. As for me, I'd rather not hear any more from you, thanks.'

'Is that right? Can't take it, huh? Don't want to hear how he only married you because of who your father was. No way would you have got him otherwise.'

Suddenly wanting to hit him, she swerved dangerously over to the side of the road. 'You can walk the rest of the way,' she told him furiously.

'Oooh, the lady's really getting mad now. Throwing the stepson out on his ear . . .'

'Just go, Max. Get out of my car and next time you're in trouble *don't* call me.'

He looked at her with a triumphant grin on his face. 'I'm not going anywhere, man.'

'Get out,' she seethed.

'Are you going to make me?'

Knowing she couldn't, she put her head in her hands and made herself take a deep, steadying breath.

'Oh, for fuck's sake, she's crying,' he mocked.

'I'm sure you'd like it very much if I were, but all I'm actually doing is wondering why you have to be so goddamned unpleasant . . .'

'I'm just pointing out to you that my whole life is fucked because of you. I've had to grow up without a father . . .'

'Oh, for God's sake! You were with us every

weekend your mother allowed it. He's always been there for you . . .'

'No fucking way was he there for me, he was with you and *your* kids, the ones you tricked him into having to make sure you could hang on to him. So don't try giving me all that shit about him *being there for me* . . .'

'Stop it! Just stop,' she shouted. 'You win, OK? You've got what you wanted. You're hurting my feelings, making me feel like the most selfish person on earth. Is that enough for you? Do you want any more? Or have you finished now?'

Seeming only mildly pleased by her outburst, he simply shrugged and folded his arms. 'I don't know what you're getting so hysterical about, when it's me who's the injured party here . . .'

'Injured party?' she echoed incredulously. 'What the hell are you on? You're living in *my* house, doing your absolute damnedest to cause problems in *my* marriage, to upset Tierney and Zav . . .'

'That is so fucking not true,' he cried. 'When have you ever heard me have a go at them? Come on, tell me, because I'm interested to know the kind of shit you're telling yourself . . .'

'You can't seriously think they're not affected by the way you've been with me lately? I really don't know what's going on with you, Max, but I'm their mother, for Christ's sake; they feel as protective of me as you do of Emma. But answer me this, where's your mother now? Where was she when you rolled up from the gap year that got you seriously in debt? Did she care about you then? Was she waiting for you with open arms? Was she hell! She'd gone. Hello, States, new husband, new career, and did she invite you to join her? Did she even tell you she was getting married? If it weren't for your father you'd probably have been murdered in Thailand, or in prison for the rest of your life. Certainly you'd have been on the streets when you came back, because you had no job to go to, no plan to get one, and no intention, apparently, of feeling in the least bit grateful for what your father did for you. Instead you slouch around the annexe like a tramp, partying, smoking dope, doing God only knows what other kinds of drugs, getting pissed out of your head, and making me feel like hell every time you look at me. You're turning into a waste of space, Max Hollingsworth. A nobody, going nowhere, without a shred of decency in you and so much bitterness and self-pity it's eating you up like a disease. And you've got the cheek to try and tell me it's my fault when it was *your mother who brought you up, not me.*'

As she stopped the air seemed to reverberate around her. She felt so shaken, so stunned by her own explosion and the awful things she'd said, that she could hardly believe it had happened. He was barely twenty-one, for God's sake, not much more than a kid – though he liked to consider himself an adult – and she'd just laid into him as if he was to blame for every bad feeling she'd ever had about herself.

Seconds ticked by with neither of them speaking. She could hardly bring herself to look at him.

In the end, she said, 'I'm sorry. I didn't mean even half of what I just said, but honest to God, Max, you wind me up so badly at times that I wonder what the hell we're going to do with you. You never show any signs of wanting to help your-self, or to make something of your life, and I wish you would. Not for me, for *you*, because, believe it or not, I care about you, and I really do want the best for you.'

Still he said nothing, simply sat in his seat, staring straight ahead, the pale tightness of his mouth the only sign of how angry – and hurt – he was.

'I'm sorry,' she said again, and realising there was no point trying to repair this right now, she pulled back on to the road to continue the drive home.

Neither of them spoke again, nor did she answer her phone the several times it rang. She simply let the silence engulf them while wishing it were possible to open the windows and let her cruel words fly away in the wind.

When eventually she pulled up alongside Stacy's car at the house she was still trying to decide whether to tell Tom what had happened. She knew how unimpressed he'd be by the way Max had provoked her, and probably critical of her too for rising to it, but when she added in the drunkenness and shoplifting charge she dreaded to think of the unholy row it was likely to trigger between father and son.

After Max had got out of the car she walked round to the passenger side and looked up at his face. Though he kept his eyes fixed somewhere above her head, she could see he was still angry and no doubt trying to think of some way to punish her. However, he hadn't skulked off to the annexe yet, which she'd been expecting.

She wasn't sure what she wanted to say, apart from sorry, or shall we try to forget the last half-hour, but before she could utter a word he suddenly grabbed her to him and wrapped her in a rough embrace.

She was so shocked, so completely thrown, that it took a moment for her to realise that he wasn't intending to hurt her. By that time he was already pulling away, and without as much as a glance in her direction he walked to the annexe and closed the door behind him.

Chapter Three

It was Friday evening now and Lainey had been so busy all day that she could only feel relieved her sisters, as expected, had cancelled their visit. She'd really needed to catch up on the hours she'd lost yesterday taking Max to court.

Oddly, in a way amusingly, she and Max still weren't speaking, apart from by text, which was how she'd asked if he'd like her to drive him into town for his court appearance and he'd replied with an abrupt *Cool*. They'd travelled the whole way in silence, and when they'd got there they'd only spoken when necessary, mainly to the court officials. After the hearing, at which he'd earned himself a five-hundred-pound fine and four hours' community service, he'd asked to be dropped at his friend's house to pick up his car. Exactly how he was going to raise enough to pay the fine she had no idea. He'd have to work it out for himself, even if it meant swallowing his pride and asking for a loan.

With any luck he'd try to find a job so he could work off his debt in instalments. At least that way he'd be demonstrating a sense of responsibility that had so far escaped everyone's notice.

It was there though, Lainey was in no doubt of it, it was just a question of getting him to assert it, and the only way she could see of doing that was to start trusting him.

Good luck with that.

Hearing a car draw up outside she felt herself starting to smile. Though she knew some women might think it strange, or at least unusual, to experience heart flips as a husband of sixteen years arrived home, for Lainey it was gloriously normal. She adored the exhilaration of seeing Tom for the first time in almost a week; on occasions it almost felt as though she was falling in love with him all over again. And why wouldn't she when he was the most attractive man she'd ever met, albeit in a slightly quirky way, and life was never dull with him. Over time they'd become slightly less vigorous in their fervour, a little more tender in their togetherness, but their closeness had only deepened. He always said he needed her to keep him grounded, which might well be true, given how long he spent in his fictional world. And she needed him simply because she loved him so much. Though they rarely fought, when they did the rest of the family fled, since being in the same room wasn't safe when both had a tendency to throw whatever came to hand first. However, if Tom's latest book was singing along merrily almost nothing could rattle him, and when he was in a good mood it seemed everyone else was too – though Lainey knew from long experience that the creative flow could change from one day to the next, so it was best never to take anything for granted.

It was like living with a faulty time bomb, she would often tell him, meaning she never had any idea when he might erupt and when he did how great the explosion might be.

'And living with you, my darling,' he would counter, 'is like living with the tide – one minute I'm swept up in all the reasons why you're so vital to everything, and the next I feel as though I'm drowning in you.'

Though she understood what he meant, such words always stung her a little, since she knew she was guilty of being somewhat too needy at times.

Watching him now, as he got out of his car, laughing as he swung a joyous Zav up in his arms, she felt so much pride and love tangling with the other emotions in her heart that she barely noticed the other car pulling up behind his. Immediately Zav raced off to greet his uncle Grant, Tom's younger brother, and Cara, Grant's new wife. She'd had no idea they were coming tonight, but that was what it was like in their house, people were always turning up unexpectedly, which was why she generally cooked for more than the immediate family at mealtimes.

Tom was on his way into the kitchen now, and watching him she could feel their chemistry flickering into life. As he reached her and slipped his free hand into her hair, his smoky grey eyes told her more profoundly than words how glad he was to be home. She cherished those looks almost as closely as she cherished the lovemaking that would later follow, though tonight she felt he seemed slightly distracted.

Before she could ask, Grant and Cara came piling in the door behind him.

'I found them on my tail as I turned into the village,' he explained, picking up his mail as Cara swept Lainey into a bruising embrace.

'I swear you're looking too gorgeous,' Cara declared, her sunny blue eyes and cherry-red lips making her, in Lainey's opinion, the true beauty in the room. 'I hope you don't mind us turning up on you like this. I know you're entertaining tomorrow night, so I promise we'll be out of your hair long before anyone arrives. It was just that we couldn't be down this way and not drop in.'

'I'd have felt very offended if you hadn't,' Lainey informed her, meaning it. She was extremely fond of Grant and Cara, who'd recently married in the local church, after which a lavish reception had taken place here at the house. 'You can join the party if you like,' she went on, going to hug Grant. 'It'll be easy enough to set two more places.'

'Oh, we'd love to,' Cara assured her, 'but my gran's expecting us and we can't let her down.'

'What have you got cooking?' Grant wanted to know. 'Smells bloody delicious, whatever it is.'

'It's my favourite,' Zav piped up, his cheeky young face smeared with dirt and his mop of inky hair tumbling every which way. He was such a cocktail of Tom and Lainey that it was impossible to say where one of them began and the other ended. He was certainly more like his father in his insatiable passion for rugby, cricket and football, and had just been practising the latter solo in their paddock, waiting for Tom to come home. 'It's called cheesy burger bake,' he informed his aunt and uncle. 'Mum won't let us have it very often, because she says it's not healthy enough, but Dad really likes it too, don't you, Dad, so we're allowed to have it tonight and I helped to make it.'

'No!' Cara cried, impressed. 'Is there no end to your talents?'

'It's this big,' Zav ran on, stretching his arms as wide as they'd go, 'and we've got peach-flavoured ice cream for afters. Dad?'

'Zav?' Tom responded, abandoning his mail to twist the top off a bottle of wine.

'Are you definitely coming to my match tomorrow?'

'Absolutely,' Tom confirmed. 'I expect Uncle Grant would like to join us, if he doesn't have to rush off before lunch.'

'Count me in,' Grant replied, taking glasses out of a cabinet and passing them to Cara.

'Where's Tierney?' Tom asked Lainey as she emptied a bag of pistachio nuts into a bowl.

'Gone for a walk with Dad and Sherman,' she replied. 'They should be back any minute. Bliss.' She smiled, as he passed her a glass of wine. She wanted to ask him more about his week, whether things had improved by the time he'd left the set today – presumably not, given how pensive he seemed – however, as usual, their more personal conversations would have to wait until they were alone.

As they raised their glasses to friends and family the hall door opened and Max ambled in, looking, Lainey noticed with some surprise, as though he'd just washed his hair and very possibly taken a shower. What a turn-up!

Tom was eyeing his elder son with some interest. 'Everything OK?' he asked carefully.

'Yeah, cool,' Max responded, not quite meeting his father's gaze. 'Hey, Grant, Cara. Are you here for the weekend?'

'No, just tonight,' Cara told him. 'How's life with you?'

He shrugged. 'Kind of, you know.'

Tom's eyebrows arched.

'Actually, I'm on my way out,' Max informed them. 'Just thought I'd come and say hi before I go.'

'Where are you off to?' Lainey asked chattily as she started slicing a cucumber. 'Somewhere nice?'

'Bet he's got a hot date, good-looking guy like him,' Grant piped up.

'He's always got lots of dates,' Zav informed them. 'Are you seeing Christie tonight? I reckon she's really ream.'

Max looked amused by his half-brother's use of the slang term. 'And I don't suppose that would have anything to do with her cousin being signed up by West Brom?' he teased.

Zav laughed delightedly. 'We might get some free tickets if you go on seeing her, though it would be better if he was signed to Liverpool, wouldn't it, Dad? Just imagine, we could go to all the games, and we might even be allowed into the dressing rooms, because we know someone.'

'I should think Daddy could get you in anyway,' Cara suggested.

'He can, and he did,' Zav assured her. 'We went last season, didn't we, Dad? It was really cool. Max came too, didn't you, Max?'

'I did,' Max confirmed. 'Dad, is it OK to take the estate tonight? Crowded House are playing at Berkeley and we'll be able to get more of us in than if I take my Fiesta.'

Tom glanced at Lainey. 'I don't see any problem with that,' he responded, checking with her.

Shrugging, she said, 'Fine by me. Do you want some drinks to take with you? I expect I can find some food to pack up for a picnic as well.'

Max looked amazed. 'That would be totally awesome, if you can spare it.'

With a wry smile she went through to the utility room to fish out a cool bag, while Tom and Grant wandered outside with their drinks and Zav helped Cara to lay the table.

'Have you told him yet?' Max said quietly to Lainey.

Realising he was referring to his shoplifting charge, Lainey said, 'No, not yet, but I think I'll have to, because if it gets in the local paper and he finds out that way, there'll be all hell to pay.'

'There'll be that anyway,' he muttered.

Suspecting he was right, Lainey loaded him up with bottles and various snacks, before handing over the keys to the old estate that had been a part of the family since Tierney was born. As Max left through the back door Tom called out that he wanted to see him in his study between three and four the following day for a general catch-up.

'That might be a good opportunity for you to tell him yourself what happened?' Lainey suggested.

'Yeah, right,' Max retorted, and giving his father a surly salute he went off to the car.

'So how's Stacy getting on with the new bloke?' Cara wanted to know as Lainey returned to the kitchen. 'Have you met him yet?'

'No, I haven't. We invited them tomorrow night, but she's turned us down. She thinks our set, as she likes to call it, will be a bit much for Martin to handle before he gets to know us.'

Cara pulled a face. 'I guess I can see her point. What does he do, again?'

'He has a nursery – as in plants, not kids – just outside Stroud. I'm sure I've bought stuff there in the past, if it's the place I'm thinking of. Anyway, now Tom's back we'll probably meet up at a pub, just the four of us, one night next week. Apparently he's an avid fan of Tom's, so I don't think there's much danger of them not getting along.' As she finished speaking she was peering curiously through the window to where Tom and Grant seemed to be having some sort of disagreement over by the arbour. 'What do you think that's all about?' she asked as Cara came to join her.

'No idea, but they don't look happy, do they?'

'Shall I go and find out?' Zav offered, leaping up from the computer.

'No you don't,' Lainey retorted, grabbing him back. 'But you can whizz off and wash your mucky little face before we sit down to eat.'

'Oh, Mum.'

'Oh, Zav. Off you go.'

After he'd gone Cara said, 'Grant's looking really upset now. Actually, so's Tom. What on earth's happening out there?'

Both concerned and curious, Lainey said, 'Did Grant mention anything, before you came, about needing to discuss something with Tom?'

'Not a word. As far as I knew he was really looking forward to seeing him.'

Lainey watched as Grant put a hand on Tom's shoulder, while Tom regarded him in what looked to be a very steely silence. Tom turned away and Grant stood watching him, seeming helpless or maybe frustrated. It was difficult to tell from where they were.

Then suddenly everything changed as Tierney came streaking across the lawn, all long legs and flyaway hair, to throw herself into her father's, then her uncle's arms, while Peter, looking just as thrilled, followed in her wake with a limping Sherman.

'Oh no,' Lainey groaned, 'poor Sherman, his arthritis is obviously playing him up again,' and making a mental note to fit in a visit to the vet on Monday, probably after her father's appointment with the psychiatrist, she went to answer the phone.

Minutes later Tom was bringing a troubled-looking Peter in through the door.

'I didn't mean to do it,' Peter was saying. 'It was just there and I couldn't stop it.'

'Don't worry,' Tom soothed, 'we'll get it sorted.'

Guessing what was wrong, Lainey went to take over, but Tom said, 'It's OK. I'll do it.'

'Lainey, it was there and then gone,' Peter told her.

Gazing into her father's bemused blue eyes, Lainey cupped his face in her hands and kissed him. 'You'll be fine,' she assured him. 'Tom's going to get you all cleaned up, then we'll sit down for a lovely dinner.'

Peter nodded, and patted the hand Tom had laid on his arm. As they went out through the hall, the loyal Sherman padding on behind, Lainey turned to Grant, who'd followed them into the kitchen.

'Would you mind carrying the dog up the stairs?' she asked. 'He's obviously in a bit of pain, but he hates being apart from Dad.'

'Leave it to me,' Grant responded, and going after Tom and Peter he closed the hall door behind him.

'This must be so hard for you,' Cara sympathised, as Lainey drew in a shaky breath.

Lainey couldn't deny it.

'Does it happen often?'

'His incontinence? More and more these days,' she replied, glancing up as Tierney come in. 'It might be easier on him if he didn't realise it was happening; as it is, he feels so ashamed that he ends up getting into a terrible muddle. As if he's not in a big enough one already. Tierney, can you go and find out what's happened to Zav? I sent him to wash his face ten minutes ago and he hasn't come back yet.'

Tierney, who'd been giving Cara a hug, helped herself to a slice of cucumber as she left. 'Sorry, may I?' she asked, looking at her phone as she turned back again.

'May you what?' Lainey asked.

'Have a piece of cucumber?'

Lainey blinked in astonishment. 'Well, you've already eaten it now, but I hardly think you needed to ask.'

'I just don't want to seem impolite, or to take anything for granted,' Tierney explained, looking up from her texts.

Since she wasn't quite sure what to say to that, Lainey simply smiled.

'We're very lucky to have food whenever we want it,' Tierney reminded her, 'even if it is just a slice of cucumber. So many people in the world don't have anything, and I think it's wrong for people like us simply to stuff our faces and forget all about them.'

With a quick glance at a bewildered Cara, Lainey said, 'I don't think a slice of cucumber can qualify as stuffing your face, but your sentiments are admirable, my darling.'

Seeming pleased with that, Tierney spun round and went off in search of her brother.

'Don't ask,' Lainey muttered, as Cara seemed to

flounder for words. 'Let's just get the rest of dinner under way and do our best to pretend we're a normal family.'

Upstairs in her room, Tierney's whole attention was fixed on her laptop. He was there, online, taking time out to Instant Message her and ask if she was happy.

Just wait till she told Skye.

Her fingers almost shook as she typed in her answer.

I am now.

That's good.

Are you?

Of course. I'm in contact with you.

She desperately wanted to see him, but didn't have the courage to say so. He'd said the last time, though, that they would definitely get together again.

He was typing. You understand why I can't see you this weekend?

Her insides churned with longing. Yes, but I wish you could.

I know. I wish I could too. You have become very special to me.

She felt suddenly breathless, hot, desperate to see him if only on Skype, but there was no time now.

You're special to me too, she typed, and felt her insides flutter with the electric frissons of daring.

It's not long until your birthday.

Tomorrow week.

Will we be able to spend it together?

I'm working on it. I've told them I'm going to be at my friend's in London. She's OK with that, she'll definitely cover for me.

That's good. I'll make sure you have a really special time.

Thinking of the one kiss they'd shared she almost sobbed with dread and excitement.

Did you ask your parents for a Kindle? **he wanted to know.**

Yes.

Good. It'll give me a real kick to think of us reading the same books at the same time.

We could do that now.

Indeed we could, but I'd like to buy the books for you and send them to your reader. They'll be a gift from me to you.

Thank you.

Where are you at the moment?

In my bedroom. Where are you?

In a terrible dilemma over you. I can't stop thinking about
you.

Thrilled and tormented by the words, she knew
without any doubt that she was in love.

It's the same for me, she told him.

'Sweetheart, are you in there?' her father called
out, knocking on the door.

Tierney slammed down the lid of her laptop.
'Coming,' she called back, her heart practically
leaping from her chest. Running to the door she
threw it wide and all but bounced into her father's
arms. 'What are you doing up on our floor?' she
cried, teasingly. 'You never come up here.'

'I've been calling you, but you seem not to have
heard,' he replied as she linked his arm to walk him
along the landing to the stairs.

'Sorry, I got carried away with Skye. She's got all
this stuff going on, so I had to talk to her. Do you
know where Max is tonight?'

'Gone to some concert, apparently. Why?'

'Just wondered. Or Skye did. She's pretty hot for
him, but don't tell him I told you. Oh God, I was
supposed to find Zav. Has he gone down now?'

'Yes, he has. We're just waiting for you.'

Placing her hands on his shoulders as he descended
the narrow staircase ahead of her, she said, 'So how
are you? Did you have a good week in London? We
missed you, you know. I hope you missed us too.'

'Of course I did,' he assured her.

'Were you filming, or just casting and things?'

'A bit of both. But tell me about your week. How
are the exams going?'

'Yeah, cool. Think I'm doing pretty OK.'

Glancing at his mobile as it beeped with a text, he carried on down the main stairs into the hall before saying, 'Tell Mum I'll be right there, will you?' and disappearing into his study he closed the door behind him.

As he read the message his facial muscles tightened. *I sent your wife a text telling her to ask you about Julia. Just thought you should know.*

Quickly connecting to the number, he said, 'Why did you do that? What purpose do you think it's going to serve?'

'You know my purpose . . .'

'And you agreed to let me do it in my time.'

'That's the point, Tom, we don't have the luxury of time.'

His eyes darkened. 'The conditions you've imposed . . . You're making it damned near impossible . . .'

'Please don't be angry with me. I didn't want it to happen this way,' and before he could say any more the line went dead.

Chapter Four

Lainey was in front of the bathroom mirror, cleaning her teeth, when she heard Tom, in the bedroom, stretching luxuriously as he came awake.

Going to the door she stood watching him, early morning sunrays slanting a fence of light between them, lending the spacious room a soft, almost dreamlike feel. As his eyes came to hers she felt a pleasing warmth stirring to life. He'd been fast asleep by the time she'd come up to bed last night, one arm thrown behind his head, the sheet barely covering his hips.

It was how he was now, and as she went to him she could see he was as ready as she was to make his homecoming complete.

It was quite some time before she returned to the bathroom, still slightly dazed by the pleasure of their shared release, while he reached for his phone to check on any messages that had come in overnight.

'Are you OK?' he asked, when she stepped out of the shower.

'What do you think?' she asked, taking the towel he was offering. 'Don't I look it?'

He smiled teasingly and turned to the basins. 'You were frowning,' he told her reflection in the mirror.

'Really?' She was surprised. 'I guess I was just thinking.'

Since he didn't ask what about, she continued to dry herself as he started to shave.

Everything was so normal on the surface, so relaxed and as it usually was on a Saturday morning, yet somewhere behind this veil of benign preoccupation she couldn't help getting the sense of something being awry. Perhaps it wasn't him. In fact, it was probably her, since she was absorbed by the upcoming trip to Italy, which she'd yet to tell him she'd confirmed, and by what her mother might have been hiding all these years. She was even asking herself again, as she had through Alessandra's illness, if keeping secrets for so long had been responsible, at least in part, for bringing on the cancer.

How terrified her mother had been when she'd realised the seriousness of her condition. Lainey had been too, though she'd done her best not to show it. Perversely, it had also been a time of joy for her, since Alessandra had turned to *her* in her hour of need. It was the first time she'd ever felt truly special to her mother, and though they hadn't exactly grown close during the turbulent years that had followed – or not close enough for Alessandra to answer all the questions Lainey desperately wanted to ask – it had soon become clear that it was only Lainey who could fulfil her mother's needs. Not that Alessandra ever admitted to that, she had far too much pride to allow anyone to think she couldn't manage alone. However, as time had gone on and the deadly disease in her womb had spread to other parts of her, she'd become fretful, almost panicked if Lainey was too long away from her side. Whether she ever worried about how difficult it was for Lainey to watch her suffering Lainey had no idea, but what she did know was that there were times when she actually seemed to feel her mother's pain. It hadn't only been physical, though heaven knew that had been hard, she'd also felt the anguish and fear that had gripped Alessandra as her inner demons rose up to torment her.

'It's not your fault,' she'd told Lainey one day in a voice that had barely rasped from the clouded depths of her. 'It was never your fault.'

Lainey had soothed the crinkled skin of her cheeks. 'What wasn't?' she asked gently.

Alessandra's eyes were haunted, distant, dulled by pain. 'What happened . . . What they did . . .' she whispered. 'I'm sorry, Elenora. Can you forgive me? Please say you forgive me.'

Realising the words were opening small gateways into her past, Lainey held her mother's hand tightly as she said, 'Of course I forgive you, but I wish you'd tell me . . .'

'No, don't ask. The shame is not for you to bear. Forget them, Elenora. They are nothing to us now. Just take care of Daddy. Promise me, you'll take care of him.'

'You know I will.'

Alessandra's smile had been more of a grimace. 'I need to sleep now,' she whispered. '*Stai con me mentre dormo.*' Later Lainey had learned that this meant, stay with me while I sleep.

Her mother had spoken Italian often during her final days, but because she'd always refused to allow Lainey to learn the language Lainey had been unable to understand anything more than the cries of '*Nonnina, Nonnina.*' It was hearing her calling for her grandmother at the end that had wrenched the hardest at Lainey's heart. Who was Alessandra's grandmother? What had happened to tear them apart? Why had no one from Italy ever come to find their daughter, sister, niece, wife?

Tom's voice broke into her thoughts. 'You're still frowning,' he told her, tapping his razor on the side of the bowl.

Lainey's expression lightened. 'Just going through things for this evening,' she hastily improvised. It wasn't that he minded talking about her mother, it was simply that she really did need to start focusing on the day ahead. 'I'm trying to remember who's supposed to be arriving when, who's staying the night, which stall to get the flowers from when I go to the market. You can't imagine how stressful it is being me.'

With a droll raising of an eyebrow, he said, 'As long as that's all it is.' He scraped the blade across his jaw. 'If there was anything else, you'd tell me, wouldn't you?' he pressed.

Surprised, she said, 'Of course I would. And I hope the same goes for you. Actually, that reminds me, have you had some kind of falling-out with Grant? It looked pretty intense between you in the garden last night, and he didn't seem his usual chatty self over dinner. So has something happened I should know about?'

Swilling his razor, he said, 'He's trying to get me involved in one of his crazy investment schemes, and I'm not biting.'

Since this wasn't an unusual occurrence between the brothers, she let the subject drop and might have forgotten all about it had she not found Grant and Cara ready to leave when she went downstairs.

'What are you doing? What's happening?' she demanded, spotting their bags next to the kitchen door. 'You're surely not rushing off already? You haven't even had breakfast.'

'Cara's gran's had a fall,' Grant explained, coming to hug her. 'Nothing serious. We just thought we ought to get ourselves over there pronto.'

'Of course,' Lainey agreed. 'Gosh, I hope she's all right.'

'I'm sure she'll be fine,' Cara said, checking her phone. 'Lucky we're close by.'

Wondering if Cara was deliberately avoiding her eyes, Lainey tried to think what to say. Something wasn't feeling right about this, but how to put it into words without sounding offensive? 'Aren't you going to wait and say goodbye to Tom?' she asked, as Grant picked up the bags and started out to the car.

'I'll call him,' Grant replied, not looking back.

Cara held out her arms. 'I'm really sorry to miss the farmers' market,' she said, hugging her. 'I was looking forward to it.'

'There'll be other times,' Lainey assured her.

Cara smiled. 'Of course.' Now she was meeting Lainey's eyes in a way that felt oddly disturbing. 'Call me if you need anything, won't you?' she said kindly.

Puzzled, Lainey said, 'Likewise. And don't forget to let me know how your gran is.'

'Cara, are you coming?' Grant called out.

'Better go,' she said to Lainey, and with another quick squeeze she hurried off to the car.

Minutes after they'd driven away Tom came into the kitchen wearing a tracksuit and trainers, ready to go to football with Zav. 'Did I hear someone arriving?' he asked, taking a pitcher of orange juice from the fridge.

'Actually, it was Grant and Cara leaving,' Lainey told him. 'Apparently her grandmother's had a fall.'

Tom's hand paused in mid-air, but he said nothing, simply continued to pour.

'What's going on?' Lainey asked. 'Something's . . .'

'Just leave it,' he murmured. 'He'll get over it. Now where's Zav? Is he up yet?'

Since she didn't want to get into an argument when Zav and Tierney were likely to descend at any minute, she simply said, 'I haven't seen him, but . . .'

'I'll go and get him.'

He was only as far as the door before Zav came skidding along the hall straight into him. 'Hey, Dad. Great, you're up. Are we having pancakes for breakfast? You said last night we could.'

'Don't worry, I haven't forgotten,' Tom promised, ruffling his son's already ruffled hair. 'Going to give me a hand?'

'Sure am. Mum, have we got any eggs, or shall I ride my bike down to the farm shop and get some?'

'There are plenty in the basket,' Lainey told him, putting a pan next to the Aga. 'If you're going to toss them try not to let them land on your head, OK?'

Zav shouted with laughter. 'That's what I did last time,' he cried delightedly, as if his parents didn't already know. 'I'm rubbish at catching them, but Tierney's worse. How many shall we make, Dad?'

'About a dozen?' Tom suggested, starting to break the eggs. 'That should work out at about two each.'

Zav frowned as he counted on his fingers how many they were making for. 'I don't think that's enough,' he decided, holding up eight fingers.

'Uncle Grant and Auntie Cara had to leave early.' Lainey plonked an orange juice down in front of him. 'So we're only six if Max joins us, more for you if he doesn't.'

'I can eat six,' Zav informed her proudly.

'I know you can.' She laughed, catching his face in her hands and kissing him roundly.

'You're so sloppy,' he protested, wiping the kiss away. 'Dad never does that, do you, Dad?'

'He does to me,' Lainey told him with a twinkle.

'Wait till you have a girlfriend,' Tom advised his son.

'I don't like girls, they're stupid. Mum, can I have one of those chocolates? Please, please, please, please.'

'They're for after dinner tonight,' she said firmly, trying to make room for them in the fridge.

'That's so mean, I never get to have any of those and they're lush.'

'I'll save you one,' Lainey promised. 'Now, I guess as you two have breakfast under way I ought to go and rouse the rest of the house. Have you seen Grandpa this morning?'

'He was still asleep when I looked in,' Tom told her.

Glancing outside to check if the estate was back and seeing that it was, she said, 'I wonder if Max has company . . .'

'Are you kidding?' Tom laughed. 'You must have heard them all turning up in the early hours.'

Surprised that she hadn't, as she usually slept quite lightly, Lainey said, 'In that case I think I'll leave him. We can always rustle up more when they decide to surface.'

Upstairs in her room Tierney was huddled under the covers doing her best not to be hung-over. It wasn't easy when she'd downed a ton of vodka jelly over at Max's last night. It was seriously wicked, that stuff, nearly as good as the jägerbombs she and Skye had got wasted on the last time they were there. Skye had got totally off her face that night; she'd been in a bit of a state last night too by the time Tierney had staggered back to her room about four o'clock. Unlike Tierney Skye had gone to the concert with Max and his mates, so she'd been drinking all night, and smoking dope. Apparently she'd texted Max about eight o'clock and he'd offered to go and pick her up from school if she could sneak out. Obviously Skye had managed it, she always did, but Max, pig that he was, had refused to come back for Tierney. *You're still not sixteen*, he'd responded when she'd sent a text begging to be allowed to go too.

God, she hated him sometimes.

Still, at least he hadn't thrown her out when she'd sneaked over there after they'd all got home, nor had he stopped her tucking into the jelly, mainly because he'd been too into Skye to notice. The others had all been smooching about the place, snogging and doing other stuff it was too embarrassing to watch. Talk about some people needing to get a room. She was the only one who hadn't had a partner and not only because she was Max's sister so his mates had to keep their hands off, but because she wasn't interested in any of them anyway. As far as she was concerned they were just a bunch of mingers who thought they were seriously cool just because they smoked a few joints and got wasted while listening to loud music by bands she couldn't stand. Max was so weird the way he was into the same sounds as Dad. They even went to concerts together sometimes. No way would anyone ever catch her going to see sad old sacks like Eric Clapton or Jackson Browne or Billy Bragg. Most of her friends had never even heard of them. It was pretty embarrassing that she had.

She wondered if Skye was still over there, sprawled out unconscious on Max's bed the way Tierney had found her a couple of weeks ago. Skye had been going all the way with boys since she was fourteen. Actually, quite a few of their friends had, or so they said. Tierney was only sure about Skye – and about herself and Maudie in that neither of them had done it yet, but she was definitely going to.

Forcing her eyes open, she looked at the time and groaned. Ten past eight. Maybe she ought to make sure Skye had got back to school in time for her parents to collect her. If they turned up and found she wasn't there, Bannerleigh Cross was the first place they'd come looking, and since Skye wasn't officially supposed to be here . . .

Tierney flipped back the covers. No way could she risk being banned from going to Skye's when the exams were over, and if it came out that Skye was getting it on with Max there was no knowing how her dad might react.

Not bothering with a text she dialled Skye's number. 'Where are you?' she demanded in a whisper when Skye answered. 'Please tell me you're not still with Max.'

'No, one of his mates dropped me back at school about twenty minutes ago, so calm down.'

'Neither of my rents saw you leaving, did they?'

'There wasn't any sign of them so I don't think so. That was really cool last night, wasn't it? I just wish you could have come to the concert.'

'Me too. Bloody Max. I don't know what you see in him. He's such a jerk sometimes.'

'To you, maybe, but he's just looking out for you, which is kind of cute, if you ask me. Anyway, you didn't miss much. You were there for the party after, which was the best bit. That jelly is totally awesome, isn't it?'

'Totally.'

'So have you heard from you-know-who this morning?'

Tierney's insides fluttered and sank as she looked at her computer. 'Not yet,' she answered dismally. 'But it's still the middle of the night where he is.'

'Of course, and he'll definitely get in touch. He's completely mad about you.'

Tierney brightened a little. 'Do you think so?' She thought it was true, but she loved hearing Skye say it.

'Are you crazy? I've only ever seen him with you once, but I don't reckon he looked at anyone else the whole time.'

Thrilling at the mere thought of it, Tierney felt herself spinning with excitement as she remembered that night and how they'd snogged for the first – and only – time. He'd run his hands through her hair, down her back, and over her buttocks, pressing himself to her, letting her know how much he wanted her. She was so desperate for him to do it again, and to go further, that she felt almost faint with the thought of it. 'What about when Max nearly caught us?' she gasped breathlessly. 'Oh my God, I really thought he'd seen us.'

'He would have if I hadn't gone running up to him,' Skye reminded her.

'You were a brilliant lookout.'

'That's me, and I'm cool about being your alibi when you come up to London. Have you cleared it with your rents yet?'

'No, but I don't reckon there'll be a problem.'

'It's going to be like just the best sixteenth anyone ever had,' Skye assured her. 'You'll love it, I'm telling you, especially with him being so, you know, experienced and everything. That's what I love about Max, he really knows what he's doing . . .'

'Oh God, bordering on too much information,' Tierney broke in quickly.

Skye laughed. 'You wanted all the details before.'

'Yeah, when it wasn't my brother. Anyway, I'd better go . . .' She swung round as her computer beeped. 'Oh my God, it's him! He's only Skyping me,' she cried. 'I've got to go,' and abruptly ending the call she rushed to the computer and clicked on.

'Hey,' he said sleepily as his handsome face appeared on the screen. He looked like David Beckham with scruffy dark hair, or maybe more like Frankie in the Jonas Brothers. Whatever, he was totally, completely to die for *and he was Skyping her*. 'How's my favourite girl this morning?' he asked.

Her heart was thudding so hard she barely heard herself saying, 'I'm cool.' She wouldn't tell him about the hangover, she wasn't even sure she still had one. 'How about you?'

'Yeah, I'm good. I can't sleep, thinking about you. You look gorgeous when you've just woken up, by the way.'

Thrilled – and appalled – by the thought of waking up with him, she said, 'I wish you were coming this weekend.'

He sighed. 'Me too, but I have to stay here in New York. Something came up. Anyway, I'm not sure I can trust myself around you. You know what happened last time we were together.'

Feeling wonderful biting sensations in her most intimate parts, she said, 'I think about it all the time.'

His eyes burned into hers. 'Not long to wait now,' he reminded her, 'and you'll be sweet sixteen. Meantime, I want you to do something for me. Have you read the book everyone's talking about?'

Her insides lurched. He must mean *Fifty Shades of Grey*. Of course she'd heard of it, and knew exactly what it was about, but she hadn't actually read it yet, mainly because she knew if either of her parents caught her with it they'd go ballistic. 'It's like the first thing I'm going to download when I get my Kindle,' she told him, hoping it was the right answer.

He smiled. 'Really? I'll be interested to hear what you think of it.'

'Have you read it?'

His eyes seemed to narrow slightly as he said, 'I should go now, but first tell me what you're up to today so I can imagine you doing it.'

Wishing she had the courage to say she was about to get in the shower so he could think of her with no clothes on, or that she had plans to laze around the garden in a bikini so he could imagine her that way, she heard herself saying, 'I'm going over to my friend, Maudie's, to do some revising. She's a genius when it comes to physics.' As soon as the words were out she wanted to grab them back. Why did she have to go and remind him she was still at school? It was really going to put him off, and she couldn't bear it if it did.

'I'll try to catch up with you later,' he told her, and a moment later he'd gone.

She stared at the screen in despair. *Oh God, oh God, oh God.* What was she going to do? She always said the dumbest things and now he was going to think she was immature and stupid and a total waste of space, and if he thought that she'd just want to die.

'Tierney! What are you doing in there?' her mother called out.

'Go away!' Tierney seethed.

'Dad and Zav are making pancakes,' Lainey told her through the door. 'They thought you'd like some too.'

'I don't want any pancakes. I'm not hungry. Just *leave me alone.*'

There was a moment before Lainey said, 'Are you all right?'

'I'm fine. I just don't want to come down yet.'

There was no sound of her mother moving away. Tierney wanted to scream as she pictured her hovering outside. 'Can I come in?' Lainey eventually asked.

Tierney's fists were clenched. 'No!' she practically raged.

'You know, I think I will.'

'Don't you dare! This is *my* room and you're not invited.'

More seconds ticked by, and then Tierney's heart jarred at the sound of an email dropping into her inbox.

She quickly clicked on.

It was a gift from iTunes – *from him!*

Oh my God, he's sent me some music to download.

She found the message.

For you to listen to while revising. Xxx

The door opened and her mother came in.

'Well, at least you're up,' Lainey commented, casting a quick look around the room as though checking to make sure no one else was there.

'Of course I am,' Tierney replied sunnily, closing her laptop. 'I was just checking to make sure Maudie's still on for today. And actually, I'm dead in the mood for pancakes, especially Dad's. Zav's always have to be scraped off the floor.'

Lainey laughed. 'They're still pretty tasty though,' she commented, and grabbing a dressing gown she held it out for Tierney to slip into. 'Just as well it was me and not Dad who came up here,' she murmured over Tierney's shoulder, 'because wherever you were last night, and whatever you were doing, the smell in this room tells me that you were hitting the booze.'

Tierney froze. Her mother was a witch.

'I'm guessing you sneaked over to Max's,' Lainey continued, 'but we'll have a chat about it later.'

Keeping her back turned, Tierney started for the door. 'You're not going to tell Dad, are you?' she demanded, suddenly turning round and almost colliding with Lainey.

Before Lainey could answer Tierney was seized by a rush of elation, and grabbing her mother in a vigorous embrace she squeezed with all her might.

She didn't care if she was in trouble; he'd sent her some music, which made everything all right, and after breakfast she was going to race back up here to find out what it was.

After sending Tierney the mood-swinger on down for breakfast, Lainey went to knock gently on her father's door, pushing it open as she did so. Funny how once she'd never have dreamt of walking into her father's room without receiving his permission, while Tierney's door had always been open to her. Now the situation was completely reversed.

Finding Peter still fast asleep, she went to make sure he was breathing, much as she still did with the children, and after stooping to give Sherman a tousle she went quietly back to the landing. She'd leave him a while longer, then come back up to help him shower and dress.

By the time she got down to the kitchen a ragged pile of pancakes was gaining some height in the middle of the table, while jars of marmalade, maple syrup and honey were circling its base, and a pot of fresh coffee had been placed to one side, a bit like an old-timer checking out the new kids on the block.

'Auntie Daffs just called,' Tierney told her, grabbing their napkins from a drawer to start laying them out. 'She said she'll ring back later, but I was to tell you it's fine about . . . Oh my God, Mum, you're dancing. Please don't. Please, please. Oh God, Dad, stop!'

With 'The Hustle' playing on the radio, Lainey shimmied up to Tom who, with a frying pan aloft in one hand and a tea towel in the other, was already jigging his hips back and forth ready to bump them against hers. Zav was laughing and cheering them on, while spilling his latest pancake mix all over the Aga.

Tierney buried her face in her hands. 'You two are so sad,' she told them. 'No one dances like that any more.'

'We do,' Tom responded cheerily, still getting into the groove. 'Do you want us to show you how . . .'

'Don't even say it,' Tierney cried, appalled. 'No way am I ever going to want to dance like you.'

Loving her horror almost as much as her struggle not to laugh, Lainey went to cup her face and pressed a kiss to her forehead. 'Thanks for the message,' she said. 'Did Auntie Daffs say how she was?'

'Mum,' Zav piped up, 'is Auntie Daffs our auntie or yours?'

'Well, she's mine first, because she's Grandpa's sister, but she's . . .'

'She's our great-aunt,' Tierney told him, 'and she's definitely great, because for someone so old she's seriously cool. Can we start the pancakes now?'

'Go on, before they get cold,' Tom replied, readying Zav for his next throw.

'Watch this,' Zav cried as Max came yawning and stretching through the door, T-shirt riding up round his middle, jeans sagging below his boxers. 'I'm about to toss one. Can I do it now, Dad?'

'Slide it round the pan a bit more,' Tom instructed. 'That's it! Now tilt the pan forward . . . Good. Not too far. Remember the wrist action . . . OK, *go*!'

Zav flipped, the pancake flew and everyone cheered as it landed half in, half out of the pan.

'I nearly caught it, I nearly caught it!' Zav whooped excitedly, wiggling his hips and punching a hand in the air. 'You can have it if you like, Max.

Are you going to watch me play footie today? He can come, can't he, Dad?'

'If he wants to,' Tom replied. 'Don't you have guests?' he asked Max as Max slumped down at the table and helped himself to juice.

'They're still crashing.' Max yawned. 'Is there any coffee?'

'Tierney, can you get the phone, darling?' Lainey called as she went into the larder.

Bouncing round the table to go and do the honours, Tierney scooped up the receiver saying, 'Good morning, Bannerleigh Cross. How can I help you?'

Tom's eyes sparked with amusement.

'Someone's in a good mood,' Max grunted.

'Oh hey, Stacy,' Tierney was saying warmly. 'How are you? Yes, I'm cool thanks. Yes, Mum's here. OK. Mum, Stacy wants to know what time you're meeting this morning and where.'

'In the courtyard at Mills, around eleven?' Lainey replied.

Tierney relayed the message. 'I don't know,' she said, frowning, 'I'll ask. Stacy wants to know if she should book her flight yet, and if so to which airport?'

Taking the phone, Lainey said to Stacy, 'I'll look into it later today, so don't do anything yet. How did it go with Martin last night?'

'Yes, it was good,' Stacy replied, not sounding quite as upbeat as Lainey had expected. 'Just not sure . . . Well, he didn't stay over again and so now I'm wondering . . . Is he married, or a commitment-phobe . . . Nothing's ever straightforward, is it?'

'Tell me about it,' Lainey muttered. 'But did he say why he couldn't stay the night?'

'Should you be having this conversation with children in the room?' Max demanded.

'Feel free to leave,' Lainey told him.

Tom laughed.

Max glared at her, but couldn't quite hide the flicker of humour in his eyes.

'Let's talk about it later,' Stacy said. 'I've got some other news too, but it can wait till then.'

As Lainey rang off, Zav arrived at the table with his final messy pancake, while Tom brought a bunch of cutlery and mugs for the coffee. 'What was that about flights?' he asked, sitting down next to Max.

'To Italy,' Lainey announced delightedly. 'I've put a deposit on the villa near Tuoro that I sent you all a link to. Now all I have to do is sort out how we get there and who's actually going to come with us.'

'Me, me, I'm definitely coming,' Zav shouted. 'I've always wanted to go to Italy. Alfie says it's brilliant there.'

'Am I invited?' Max wanted to know.

Lainey was surprised. 'I didn't think you'd be interested. But you're welcome if you'd like to come,' she added hastily.

'It might be a good idea for you to spend the summer looking for a job,' Tom informed him.

'Yeah, right, that sounds like fun,' Max retorted.

'It's not supposed to be *fun*, it's supposed to be growing up and sorting out your life.'

Max groaned in dismay. 'I so don't need this . . .'

'Let's not spoil things,' Lainey insisted, trying to head off a row.

'I'm afraid I won't be able to come,' Tierney declared, her mouth half full of pancake.

Astonished, Lainey glanced at Tom as she said, 'What do you mean, you can't come?'

78

Tierney shrugged. 'What I said.'

'This isn't negotiable,' Tom informed her. 'It's a family holiday, so of course you'll come.'

'Sorry, I'm going to be sixteen by then, and I've got loads of things already planned for the summer.'

'What sort of things?' Lainey wanted to know.

Tierney flushed.

'Whatever they are, they can wait till we're back,' Tom said decisively.

Tierney's eyes glinted as she shook her head. 'No way,' she retorted. 'I'm staying here – and think of it this way, I'll be able to look after Grandpa, because he can't be on his own, can he? Or are you planning to take him too?'

'That was what Auntie Daffs was ringing about,' Lainey told her. 'She and Uncle Jack are coming to stay while we're away. And that means all of us, including you.'

Tierney's face was taut with defiance. 'As I just said,' she muttered through her teeth, 'I'll be sixteen by then, which means I'll be an adult, so . . .'

'It does not make you an adult,' Tom interrupted, 'and don't speak to your mother in that tone.'

'Why not? You always do.'

Stunned, Lainey could only watch as Tom put down his cutlery and glared at his daughter. 'You'll take that back right now,' he demanded, 'or you'll go to your room.'

'Why should I take it back if it's true?' Tierney protested.

'It isn't true,' Zav cried. 'Dad always speaks really nicely to Mum, doesn't he, Mum?'

'Actually, this isn't about me and Dad,' Lainey reminded them, wondering what was really going on with Tierney. 'It's about you, Tierney, and the

79

fact that we want you to come on holiday with us. It wouldn't be the same without you . . .'

'Oh, Mum, give me a break,' Tierney cried, her face colouring with frustration. She couldn't go away now. She had to stay here to be with *him*. 'This is all about you trying to find out about your family, if you've even got one . . .'

'Course she has, she's got us,' Zav pointed out.

'You know what I mean,' Tierney snapped at him. She fixed her mother with seriously determined eyes. 'I don't want to come to Italy,' she informed her, 'and if you make me I won't want to be a part of this family any more.' Rising to her feet she began stalking out of the room.

'Sit back down,' Tom ordered in a tone no one ever defied.

Tierney hesitated.

'Now!'

Pink-faced and steely-eyed, Tierney returned to her place.

'Eat your breakfast,' Tom commanded.

'I'm not hungry,' she replied sulkily.

Tom glanced at Lainey and carried on with his own pancake.

The others followed suit, eating in silence until Max said, 'Anyone fancy a game of Happy Families?'

Zav gave a shout of laughter as Lainey and Tom struggled to suppress their own.

'You all think you're so bloody funny,' Tierney cried savagely. 'Well, I don't. I hate you, all of you, and I can't wait to leave home.'

'Zav, pass the honey, son,' Tom said, reaching out a hand for it.

'So I'm invited to Italy?' Max asked Lainey.

'Of course,' she replied, sending a silent prayer

that he'd leave his black moods at home. 'As long as you pull your weight,' she added lamely.

He looked amazed, offended. 'Don't I always?'

She returned the look. 'Can't say I'd noticed.'

He appeared pained.

'Do you have any spending money?' Tom asked him.

'No, why, are you offering? Cool.'

Even Tierney had to choke back a laugh.

Tom narrowed him a look. 'Get a job anywhere, doing anything, until it's time to go, and you can come.'

'Does it have to be legal?'

Tom rolled his eyes as Tierney struggled with another laugh.

'I'll give you half my pocket money if you'll do my homework,' Zav offered.

'How much do you get?' Max wanted to know.

'A pound a week.'

Max's eyes rounded. 'Wow! And you'd give me a full fifty pence just for doing your sums? It's a deal.'

Knowing better than to rise to it, Lainey put a hand on Tierney's back and gave it a rub. 'Fancy coming to the market with me this morning?' she said softly. 'We could pop into Moonflower and see if they've received anything new since we were last there.'

Tierney was shaking her head. 'No thanks,' she said stiffly. 'I'm going to Maudie's for some revising. I hope that keeps you happy,' she shot at her father.

'Delirious,' he assured her. 'Are any of you three joining us for dinner tonight? Have they been invited?' he asked Lainey.

'No, we haven't,' Zav sighed. 'Or I haven't anyway, and I really want to come.'

'You're so weird,' Tierney told him.

'You say that about everyone,' he retorted, 'and really it's you who's weird, isn't she, Mum?'

'She's gorgeous,' Lainey replied, going to pick up the phone. 'Hello, Bannerleigh Cross.'

'These pancakes are seriously good, little man,' Max informed Zav as he reached for a third. 'You can cook for me any time.'

'Hello?' Lainey said into the phone.

'Hello,' Max and Zav echoed back.

Lainey turned away. 'Hello,' she said again. Someone was there, she could hear noises in the background, but whoever it was still didn't speak. 'I'm going to ring off now,' she told whoever it was. 'Goodbye.'

'Goodbye,' Max and Zav repeated.

Tom was regarding her curiously.

She merely shrugged. 'OK, I've got a lot to do before the party tonight, so you lot are in charge of clearing up here. If your friends wake up and want food,' she said to Max, 'eggs are down the road at the farm, bacon's two fields along to the right but can run fast, same goes for the milk, but in a separate field.' Enjoying her little joke, she dropped a kiss on Tom's head before running upstairs to start getting her father into the day.

An hour and a half later Lainey was hunting high and low for her mobile phone. If she didn't leave soon she was going to be late for Stacy, but she hated being out of contact in case there was some sort of emergency.

She'd rung her own number half a dozen times now, but before she could hear where in the house the phone might be the call was skipping straight through to voicemail.

'This is crazy,' she muttered angrily, turfing everything upside down in the kitchen again, certain this was where she'd last seen it.

She hoped Tierney hadn't taken it by mistake, but if she had she'd surely have answered it by now.

'Dad,' she said, barely even glancing across to where he was playing cards with his old sales director, Marty, who usually came to visit on Saturday mornings. Snap was all they managed these days, and Peter didn't even seem sure about that. How wonderful Marty was to spare his old friend this time. 'Dad, have you seen my phone?' she asked, yanking open the cutlery drawer and rummaging inside. He often hid things, probably unintentionally, but it had caused countless problems in the past.

'Have you seen Lainey's phone?' Marty repeated gently.

Peter frowned. 'Does she want to speak to me?' he asked, glancing up.

'Please don't tell me someone's put it in the dishwasher,' Lainey groaned, wondering if she could dare to tug it open mid-wash.

Deciding no one could really be that stupid (could they?), she started back along the hall intending to go and check the bedroom again, but got only as far as the bottom stair when she heard voices, or at least a voice, coming from Tom's study.

Looking up as the door opened, he seemed flustered as he said into the phone, 'OK, that's fine. I'll read it through. Sorry, I have to go now,' and he ended the call.

Regarding him curiously, Lainey said, 'What are you doing here? I thought you'd gone with Zav?'

'Max has taken him,' Tom replied, riffling round his desk apparently searching for something. 'I'm just about to leave, should be there in time for kick-off. Ah, keys,' he said, lifting them up to show her.

Sure something was going on with him, but having no time to press it now, she said, 'Have you seen my phone? I've looked high and low . . .' Suddenly spotting it on his desk she cried, 'What on earth's it doing in here?'

'I must have picked it up instead of my own,' he replied, still seeming distracted.

Since that could be the only explanation, she gave him a hasty kiss and after making sure her father and Marty were OK for drinks and sandwiches, she ran out to the car. Before starting the engine she quickly opened her mobile to let Stacy know she was going to be late. To her surprise the phone displayed an old text and when she realised what it was her heart gave a twist of confusion. *Ask your husband about Julia.*

She continued to stare at it. Why on earth would it be showing now, when it had been sent several days ago? She'd received dozens more since, so it should have been so far down the list as to be virtually lost, and yet there it was, filling the screen as though it had only just turned up.

To check that it hadn't – after all, whoever had sent it might have sent it again – she scrolled through the messages, and sure enough it had arrived on Wednesday. Today was Saturday. So the only logical explanation for why it was displaying now was because Tom had gone through her phone.

She couldn't imagine him doing that, but when

she considered what this message said, her head started to spin.

After watching Lainey's car disappear down the drive, Tom quickly reconnected to the call he'd interrupted when she'd come into his study. His expression was grim; frustration showed in every line of his face – and deepened when he found himself bumped through to voicemail. 'I'm sorry about just now,' he said, 'please ring me back when you get this message.'

Chapter Five

'I'm starting to think Zav and I are the only sane ones in our house,' Lainey was grumbling as she joined Stacy at a table in the shady courtyard of Mills Café. As usual on a Saturday morning the place was bustling with marketgoers, most of them hefting large bags of muddy veg and fresh crusty loaves. Lainey smiled and waved to a couple of neighbours as she sank into a chair that faced Mills's kitchen shop, where colourful tubs of handy gadgets were spilling like tombola prizes out of the door.

'So what's happened?' Stacy asked, pushing her empty coffee cup aside, and pulling in the fresh one Lainey had just bought. 'I must say you look a bit hassled.'

'Only because I'm late,' Lainey sighed, smiling at one of Zav's teachers, 'and Max has just rung to find out where his father is, like I'm supposed to know *everything*,' she added with a frustrated sort of laugh. Her eyes suddenly rounded. 'Oh God, Stace, you're not seriously planning to eat that enormous slice of carrot cake.'

Stacy blinked in surprise. 'Why, what else did you think I was going to do with it?' she countered with convincing confusion.

Lainey laughed. 'It's not fair. If I ate that I'd have

to stay on my treadmill for a week to work it off, and even then it wouldn't have budged. Anyway, tell me about Martin, have you heard from him today?'

Stacy's eyes twinkled. 'Wait for this . . . He rang a few minutes ago to say that his mother's invited us for dinner.'

Lainey almost choked on her coffee. 'You're kidding me,' she gulped. 'And you thought he was a commitment-phobe?'

Stacy shrugged. 'Let's not get too hasty. Maybe she invites all his new girlfriends to give them the once-over before he gets too involved.'

Lainey pulled a face. 'You're not painting a very dashing picture of this bloke,' she told her.

Though Stacy smiled, she said, 'Well, if he's that close to his mother, maybe it's why he's still single at thirty-eight.'

Lainey didn't disagree. 'Where does the mother live?' she asked, using Stacy's fork to carve off a tiny corner of cake.

'Painswick, apparently, so not far. I'm preparing myself for a gorgon, so anything less will be a bit of a kitten. Anyway, that's not my really big news, or it wasn't when I rang, and it still isn't actually, because you'll never guess . . . Is that mine or yours?' she asked, diving into her bag as a mobile started to ring.

'Mine,' Lainey replied, hauling out her own. 'Tierney,' she announced, and with a roll of her eyes she clicked on. 'Hi, darling, everything OK?'

'Yeah, I'm cool,' Tierney replied, sounding too bored for words, 'just wanted to let you know I'm going to stay at Maudie's tonight, OK?'

It took Lainey only a moment to decide that it

would probably be for the best, given the way Tierney had behaved during their last dinner party. Not that she'd been completely outrageous, in fact she'd been no more than a normal fifteen-year-old needing to flirt and opine and challenge, the way kids her age often did. The point was, no one really wanted to deal with a child trying to kick down the doors of puberty during what was supposed to be a relaxing evening for adults. 'Have you got everything with you?' she asked.

'No, but I can always borrow some of Maudie's stuff if I need to. I'll be back in the morning, I expect, but don't worry, I'll be quiet if you and Dad are still in bed with hangovers. I expect you will be. Hope the dinner goes well.'

'Thanks,' Lainey smiled wryly. 'Say hi to Maudie for me. Bring her back for breakfast if you like.'

'I'll ask her. Got to go now. Bye.'

A moment after Tierney rang off Lainey was answering her mobile again, this time to Max. 'Hi, isn't Dad there yet?' she asked with another apologetic glance at Stacy.

'No,' Max snapped stroppily, 'and Zav's just scored.'

'Yay!' Lainey cheered, holding up a hand to high-five with Stacy. 'Zav's scored a goal,' she told her.

'Yeah, great,' Max retorted sourly, 'but Dad's missed it, so where the hell is he and why isn't he answering his phone?'

'I don't know, Max,' Lainey answered with a pang of concern. What was going on with Tom? It wasn't like him to let one of the children down, at least not without giving a reason. 'He was about to leave the house the last time I saw him,' she said, 'so he should be there any minute. You tried the landline, I take it?'

'Yeah, Marty answered, and apparently Dad's car is still there, but he doesn't know where Dad is.'

Lainey frowned with confusion. *Tom's car was there, but he wasn't answering his phone.* 'Did Marty try the study?' she asked.

'I suppose so. Anyway, if you hear from him tell him from me that he's a lousy father,' and the line went dead.

'OK, well, I probably won't be passing on that cheery little message,' she muttered sweetly as she rang off.

Stacy was looking intrigued.

'It seems Tom's gone AWOL,' Lainey explained, 'which in his case probably means he decided to do some work before heading out and has got engrossed. You know what he's like. Anyway, where were we? I know, your really big news. So, come on, spill.'

Beaming, Stacy said, 'You remember my old boss at the paper, Diana Grimshaw? OK, she left a couple of years ago, but . . .'

'Yeah, yeah, I remember her,' Lainey confirmed. 'You always got on really well with her.'

Clearly pleased that Lainey remembered, Stacy said, 'Well, apparently she's part of this consortium that's setting up a new magazine and she wants to talk to me about coming on board.'

Lainey couldn't have felt more thrilled. 'That's fantastic news,' she cried, reaching across the table to embrace her best friend. If anyone was in need of – or deserved – a break, it was her. 'When did you hear?' she asked.

'Well, I knew yesterday that she was trying to get in touch,' Stacy replied, scooting her chair forward so a young mother could pass with an overloaded buggy, 'but we didn't actually manage to connect until this morning.' Her eyes came up, and for the first time in ages Lainey saw the confident, talented journalist she'd known so well starting to emerge from the protective cocoon that had almost smothered her. 'She wants me to go to a meeting on Wednesday, in town,' she continued, 'and if all goes well, I'll stay on to meet her partners on Thursday.'

'That's fantastic,' Lainey declared. 'They'll be very lucky to have you on board. So tell me, what's it about? When's it going to launch? Oh hell, who's this now?' she groaned, as her phone rang again. 'Actually, it's the caterer so I'd better take it.'

Waving her on, Stacy picked up her fork to start making a meal of her cake, only half listening as Lainey went through the menu for tonight's dinner and what time the caterers should arrive.

By the time Lainey rang off her mind was full of all she had to do while she was in town, so she remained distracted as she added new notes to the list she already had. Then she was ringing Tom to check he'd remembered to order the wine.

'I'm sure you did,' she said into his voicemail, 'but I haven't taken delivery of any yet, so I thought I'd better make sure. If there's a problem, we've definitely got enough in the cellar, but we'll need to bring it up. I expect Max can help with that. Have you spoken to him yet? He's been trying to get hold of you. Zav's scored a goal. Yay! OK, call me when you get this.' Ringing off, she returned her attention to Stacy. 'Sorry.' She grimaced. 'I'll turn it off now.'

'You don't have to do that. I'm used to it, with you.'

Lainey looked pained as a text bleeped into her inbox. It turned out to be Frankie and Dawn, two of the evening's guests, checking on what time they were expected. Since they had a country retreat locally they wouldn't be staying at Bannerleigh Cross, so Lainey texted back *7.30 for drinks*, and made another note to drop into the farm shop on the way home to pick up more eggs for breakfast.

The next text was from Max. *Still no sign of Dad. Zav really upset.*

Deciding to ignore it, since there was nothing she could do right now, Lainey tucked her phone away and returned her attention to Stacy. 'If it does work out with Diana,' she said, 'when do you think they'll want you to start?'

Stacy said, 'No idea, and we better not get too carried away, they might end up deciding against me.'

'No way.'

Stacy laughed.

'So come on, what's the magazine going to be about?'

'Apparently it's going to target women in their forties and fifties, though whether with fashion, cooking, travel, lifestyle . . . Actually, it's probably all of the above. I'll find out more on Wednesday.'

'Does she want you as some kind of editor, do you think? It sounds just your sort of thing. I wonder if it's going to be part of a weekend paper, you know, some kind of supplement, or a standalone?' Lainey was looking at her mobile. 'I'd ignore this call, I swear it,' she said, 'if it weren't the caterer again.'

Stacy waved her to answer and set about finishing her cake.

'I was thinking,' she said, after Lainey had dealt with the issue of who was providing coffee cups, 'if I am offered a job, I should make it clear right away that I've already booked a holiday.'

Lainey looked surprised, then doubtful. 'Just don't let it be a deal-breaker,' she cautioned. 'I mean obviously I want you to come to Italy, but if they're just starting out I should think they'd want all hands on deck.'

'Possibly, probably, but I should be able to come for a week at least. When are you going to book flights? I think we ought to do it soon, or we might not get the ones we want. Where do we fly into?'

'Pisa, if we go from Bristol. Perugia if we want to get ourselves all the way to Stansted, but I don't think we do. Ah, it seems my husband has surfaced from wherever he was hiding,' she declared as Tom's name flashed on her mobile. 'Hi, where are you?' she demanded, clicking on. 'Please tell me you're at the game.'

'Actually, I'm at home,' came the reply, 'but I'm about to go back to London.'

Lainey frowned, not sure she was liking the sound of this. 'Why? What's happened?' she asked, glancing at Stacy.

'I can't get into it now,' he told her. 'I just have to go.'

Lainey's eyes widened. 'But what about the dinner?' she protested.

'You'll have to go ahead without me.'

At that her temper sparked. 'Don't be ridiculous. They're your friends.'

'Yours too.'

'But they come to see you. Tom, what the hell's going on? Why do you have to go back to London?'

'I told you, I can't get into it now. We'll talk tomorrow.'

'No! I want you to tell me. How long are you going to be gone?'

'I'm not sure. Look, I have to go. I need to call Zav to apologise for missing his match . . .'

'Tom!'

'I'll speak to you later,' and the line went dead.

Stunned, Lainey looked at her mobile, then quickly rang him back. 'He's turned his bloody phone off,' she swore as she went straight through to voicemail.

'What's happening?' Stacy demanded.

Lainey shook her head in confusion. 'I've got no idea, except tonight's off apparently, and he's going back to London.'

Looking concerned, Stacy said, 'It must be something to do with the production. One of the actors has gone sick, or the script's not working.'

'If that's the case, why didn't he say so?' Her thoughts were tangling up in all sorts of suspicions, most of which were snaring on the text.

Ask your husband about Julia.

Quickly scrolling to the message, she passed it over for Stacy to read.

'Who's it from?' Stacy asked.

Lainey shook her head.

Frowning, Stacy read it again. 'So did you ask him?'

'I didn't take it seriously until . . . Well, until now, I guess . . .' She was dialling his number again. Once more she was bumped through to voicemail. 'He's not answering,' she said, clicking off the line. She wasn't sure what to think, or say, or do next.

'Have you tried calling whoever sent the text?' Stacy asked. 'Here, let me,' and taking the phone back she searched out the number. 'It's blocked,' she declared, after trying.

Lainey was racking her brains, trying to remember

a Julia. In the end her eyes returned to Stacy. 'Are you thinking what I'm thinking?' she asked quietly. There was only one explanation that was making any sense, and she really, really didn't want to go there.

'What I'm doing is trying not to jump to conclusions,' Stacy informed her.

Lainey got to her feet.

'Where are you going?' Stacy asked.

Lainey shrugged. 'Home, I suppose.'

'What about tonight's dinner? I thought you were getting bread . . .'

'I'll cancel it.'

Stacy's eyes widened. 'Isn't it a bit late? What about the caterers? They'll have everything . . .'

'They'll get paid,' Lainey interrupted. 'We've had to cancel at short notice before, so they'll donate the food to a local shelter.'

'Do you want me to come with you?' Stacy offered.

Lainey attempted a smile. 'It's OK, I'll be fine. Go and get the old gorgon some flowers, and if she turns out to be a kitten . . . Well, let's just hope she does.'

Lainey was experiencing so many strange feelings during the drive home that for long stretches of road she barely noticed where she was going. It seemed as though the world was trying to slip anchor, or to throw her into another dimension, but wasn't quite managing it.

Ask your husband about Julia.

Who had sent the message? Julia herself? Or somebody else?

She kept hearing Tom saying the name, *Julia,*

whispering it like a lover and feeling its sound like music. For her it was a stone, a beat falling out of time.

Why now? What had made the person who'd sent the text choose this week to contact her? What had happened to make it so urgent, so necessary for Tom to go to her today? Presuming that was where he'd gone. Maybe it wasn't.

Their village, Bannerleigh, looked from the air like a flamenco dancer, with arms circled overhead forming both sides of Acacia Avenue, with a green in the middle where local children often played cricket. The bottom end of the narrow high street, where a dozen or more almshouses, a handful of quaint cottages, the pub and its garden, and the church and graveyard clustered around a few cobbled lanes, was like the dancer's flying skirts. At the western end of the village the likeness came adrift, since the wider streets for the pricier houses, the playing fields and an ugly caged-in electricity grid had nothing of a dancer's legs. It was Max who'd first come up with the simile, when he was about nine years old and a friend had taken them up in a light aircraft. They'd only just come back from a holiday in Spain, where the caballeros at a flamenco show had sat him and Tierney on one of the white horses so they could ride around the stage and be a part of the magic.

It had been one of their more successful holidays.

Had Tom known Julia then? Surely to God it couldn't have been going on that long. If something *was* going on, and she didn't know for certain yet that it was.

What kind of a fool was she to doubt it?

Not wanting to run into anyone she knew, she

drove around the outside of the village, plunging through the light and shadow of leafy lanes searching her memory for some sort of sign, something that would tell her when the betrayal had begun.

If there was a betrayal.

Please God there wasn't.

Bumping over the cattle grid at the end of their drive she felt a sudden surge of anger, but quickly suppressed it. She had to deal with her father now, and Zav and Max. Thank God Tierney wasn't coming home tonight. Did she mean that? Probably not. Actually, yes she did.

What excuse was she going to give for the dinner being called off at such short notice? *Tom is having an affair and he's decided to spend tonight with his mistress instead of us. Her name's Julia, do you know her by any chance?*

Her head was spinning.

She needed to get a grip.

'Hi, Marty,' she said breezily as she sailed in through the kitchen door. 'Everything OK with Dad?'

'Right as rain,' Marty assured her. 'Went for a little walk down to the pub for our usual pint. You're back sooner than I expected. Can I give you a hand in with the shopping?'

'Oh, it's OK, no need,' Lainey assured him, tossing her keys on the worktop and glancing at the landline to see if there were any messages. No flashing light. Anxiety wrenched at her heart. 'I didn't get much today,' she said with a smile. Going to her father, she cupped a hand round his face and gazed into his liquid blue eyes. 'Hello you,' she whispered, feeling her emotions trying to break over the surface of her self-control.

'Hello, Lainey,' he said, covering her hand with his. 'Did you go to the market?'

She smiled and nodded, pleased that he'd remembered. 'And you went to the pub.'

'Marty's here,' he told her. 'I haven't seen the children this morning. Are they at school?'

'No, they're just out. Are you OK sitting there, or would you like to go for a lie-down?'

'I'm fine here. Did you go to the market?'

Dropping a kiss on his head, she turned back to Marty. 'Did you see Tom before he left?' she asked, busying herself with a search for nothing in particular. 'Did you speak to him at all?'

'Only to say cheerio,' Marty replied, reaching for his jacket.

She wanted to ask if Tom had taken an overnight bag, but she'd only embarrass herself and Marty. 'Thanks for coming,' she said warmly, giving him a hug. 'It always perks Dad up to see you.'

Marty smiled at his old friend fondly. 'Did you know,' he said to Peter, 'that the dot over the letter i is called a . . .' He scratched his head as though he'd forgotten.

Peter's eyes shone with mirth. 'A tittle,' he finished happily. 'And the most often used word in the English language is I.'

Marty held out a hand to shake.

They often ended their Saturdays with a factoid or two from a book they'd published over twenty years ago. It was amazing how easily Peter could recall the seemingly useless pieces of information, while trying to process what was happening now was a battle lost before it had begun.

After Marty had gone Lainey made an effort to straighten her mind. 'What am I going to tell them?'

she asked her father. 'What excuse shall I give for cancelling the dinner? Maybe I should go ahead with it?' She shook her head, knowing that she really didn't want to face their friends while she was feeling so . . . suspicious.

With a surge of anger, she cried, 'Am I supposed to make up a lie? Does he want me to say one of the children is sick? Or the house has caught fire, or I've been diagnosed with a terminal illness?'

Reaching for her bag she pulled out her phone. It was no surprise to find herself connected to his voicemail again. 'I know you've read the text,' she said tightly, 'so I'm asking, who is she?'

As she clicked off the line a rogue tear dropped on to her cheek.

'Lainey?' Peter said softly.

Quickly drying her eyes, she tossed back her hair as she turned around. 'Are you OK?' she asked gently.

'I think I might need the toilet,' he replied sheepishly.

'Of course, of course,' she cried, going to him, 'and how lovely you're able to warn me.' It didn't always happen that way, in fact it rarely did, but every now and again . . .

By the time she brought him back to his chair Max and Zav were raiding the fridge.

'What's for lunch, Mum?' Zav wanted to know. 'I'm starving. Are there any pizzas?'

'Have a look in the freezer,' Lainey replied, casting another glance at the landline even though she knew it hadn't rung.

'Where is it?' he asked.

Lainey frowned in confusion. 'What?'

'I said, where is it?'

'Where's what?'

'The freezer.'

'For heaven's sake, Zav, it's where it always is, in the second utility. What's the matter with you?'

'All right, all right, no need to shout. Want one, Max?'

Max wasn't listening; he was half out of the door talking to someone on his mobile.

While Zav went off for a rummage, Lainey took her father a fruit yoghurt and tried to think when his next medication was due.

'I scored two goals,' Zav announced as he came back into the kitchen. 'Max reckons I should have been man of the match, but Rufus Collins got it. He didn't do anything good. He nearly scored, though. It was a brilliant header that hit the post.'

'Well done, you. Two goals,' Lainey declared, hugging him. 'Did Dad ring you?'

'Yeah, he left a message to say sorry he couldn't make it. Where is he? Why didn't he come when he said he would?'

Lainey's heart flooded with love as she regarded him, all flushed cheeks and muddy kit. How was she supposed to answer his questions? 'Give those to me,' she said, taking the pizzas. 'I'll sort them out while you go and run a bath. Where are your boots?'

'I left them outside. Grandpa, I scored two goals today.'

Peter's face lit up. 'Were you playing football?' he asked.

Going to give him a hug, Zav treated Sherman to one too, then bounded off upstairs to clean himself up, shouting as he went, 'And it's a goal by Hollingsworth. And another goal by Hollingsworth.'

'So where is he?' Max demanded, pocketing his phone as he came back inside.

Busying herself unwrapping the pizzas, Lainey said, 'Something came up – he had to go back to London.'

'So what's so important that he just took off?'

'I'm not really sure. Something to do with the production, I think. He'll tell us later when he calls.' *If* he calls. What if he didn't? What was she going to tell them then?

She'd have to decide that when, if, the situation arose.

Max shrugged. 'Guess I'm off the hook for my paternal lecture this afternoon . . . Hang on, you've got that dinner tonight, haven't you?'

'It's been cancelled. Or it will be, when I get round to making the calls.'

Max looked puzzled. Then, clicking on his phone as it rang, 'Richmond, hey man, I was about to call you. Sure I'm up for it. I wasn't as wasted as some of you guys last night.'

As he chattered on, Lainey put the oven on to warm and started unloading the dishwasher. It was full of that morning's breakfast dishes, all sparklingly clean now, no longer running with honey, or syrup, or gritted with granules of sugar from the pancakes. She thought of how she and Tom had danced to 'The Hustle', deliberately teasing Tierney – and of how they'd made love earlier. It was hard to connect that part of the day with this part, and yet barely more than a few hours separated them.

Had he been thinking of Julia when he'd reached a climax that morning?

She had to stop doing this to herself, at least until she knew the truth.

'Lainey, what the fuck?'

Wincing at the language, Lainey turned to find Max glaring at her in an odd sort of way.

'What are you doing?' he demanded.

She didn't understand the question.

He looked at the floor.

It was littered with broken china. The last time she'd seen it like that was when her mother had flown into a rage with her father for putting things in the wrong cupboards. She hadn't known then that it was the beginnings of Peter's dementia.

'I'll get a dustpan,' Max said. 'Where is it?'

'In the utility room. Second cupboard on the right.'

It was only two plates, so not a disaster. She couldn't be sure whether she'd dropped or smashed them. She felt a sudden urge to smash more, but managed to control it.

She wanted him to come home. Or at least to call.

Who the hell was Julia?

Chapter Six

'Grant, it's Lainey,' she said when Tom's brother answered his mobile.

'Sure, how are you? Everything OK?' came the cheery reply.

'Yes, it's fine, well kind of . . . I was just wondering . . . It seemed you and Tom had a bit of a falling-out last night . . .' Where was she going with this? What did she really want to say?

'It wasn't serious,' Grant assured her. 'You know what we're like, at each other one minute, all forgotten the next.'

This was true, but then Grant had left in a hurry this morning . . . 'How's Violet?' she asked, referring to Cara's grandmother.

'OK. Just a bit shaken up, you know. She'll be fine.'

'That's good. Do send her my love.'

'Of course.'

There was an awkward moment before Lainey said, 'Can I ask what the row was about last night?'

Sounding oddly cagey, Grant replied, 'I'm afraid Tom's not very happy about the way some of his investments are performing. I kind of got him into them, and so he's holding me responsible.'

Much like the explanation Tom had given. 'Did

he – I don't suppose he . . . mentioned anything about someone called Julia?' she asked.

There was a brief hesitation before he said, 'No. Why, who is she?'

'I'm not sure. It's what I'm trying to find out.'

'I guess you've asked him. Stupid question, of course you have.'

'Actually, I haven't had a chance. He's gone off to London, and now I can't get hold of him.'

Grant still sounded baffled. 'So where does this Julia fit in?'

'That's what I'm trying to find out. She – or someone – sent me a text during the week telling me to ask him about *Julia*. Are you sure you've never heard of her?'

'Sure I'm sure.'

He sounded convincing. *Do you think he's involved with someone else?*

Realising she hadn't asked the question aloud, she was about to speak when he said, 'I'm going to try ringing him. I'll get back to you when I've spoken to him.'

After putting the phone down she turned around to find her father watching her quietly from his chair.

'What's wrong?' he asked, as she went to help him up.

'I'm not sure,' she replied, wishing with all her heart that she could turn to him the way she always used to, 'but it's not for you to worry about. Shall we go upstairs for a nap now?'

Compliant as ever, he shuffled along the hall with her holding his arm, Sherman following loyally behind. Thankfully the dog's arthritis didn't seem as bad today. He managed the stairs without having to rest, and he didn't lie down on his mattress until Peter was propped up against his pillows.

Sitting on the edge of the bed Lainey took her father's hand between hers, and was about to say she'd look in on him again in an hour when she noticed a tear rolling down his cheek. 'Oh, Dad, what's wrong?' she cried in alarm. 'Are you all right? Why are you crying?'

'Is your mother dead, Lainey?' he asked croakily. 'She is, isn't she?'

Lainey swallowed hard. 'Yes, she is.'

'When did it happen?'

'Just over a year ago.'

'Was I there?'

'Of course you were.'

He nodded, apparently relieved by that.

A moment or two later his eyes closed and she stroked a hand across his wrinkled forehead, smoothing away what little there was left of his hair.

'Talk to me,' he whispered. 'Tell me what's on your mind.'

His words, even his tone, were a warming echo from the past, when he'd always encouraged her to confide her problems so he could help her with them. It was funny how he'd managed to make things seem better, even when they weren't. 'Nothing's on my mind,' she assured him, 'apart from you and how tired you are.'

'Yes, I'm tired,' he agreed. A few moments elapsed. 'Is Marty coming today?'

'He's already been. You played cards together, and went to the pub.'

Peter smiled. 'That's nice. He's a good friend.'

As he drifted into a steady sleep Lainey continued to sit with him, watching his face, wondering what was really going on his mind. She didn't want to deal with what was going on in hers; it wasn't going to help her, and if anything it would only make things worse.

After a while she found herself gazing at the two photographs on the table next to his bed. The larger one was of her mother at her fiftieth birthday party, looking as exotic as a movie star with her smouldering eyes and wild raven hair. She was gazing out of the frame straight into Lainey's eyes, and Lainey could almost feel her fire burning inside her.

The other photo had been taken on Alessandra and Peter's wedding day, more than thirty years ago. They looked so young, even Peter, whose fortieth birthday had been just around the corner. There was very little grey in his hair then, few lines around his eyes, and his jaw had been finely chiselled and firm. Her mother, having recently turned twenty-one, was so fresh and radiant that Lainey could easily understand why Peter had fallen so hard. They were gazing into each other's eyes with a sense of surprise, it seemed, as though they'd somehow won first prize and weren't sure if it had really been meant for them. Peter was wearing a dark pinstripe suit with a mauve tie; Alessandra, toned and curvaceous, was in a knee-length cream dress with matching high-heeled shoes and a flower in her cascades of dark hair. Next to her, in a little cream dress of her own, and blue T-bar shoes, was four-year-old Lainey clutching a posy of sweet peas in both hands, her dark, tousled head tilted back as she gazed up at her mother and Peter. It was hard to see her expression, but Lainey liked to think she'd been as happy on that day as her mother clearly had.

Though she had no memories from before Peter had come into their lives, she knew that her mother had brought her to England when she was little more than a month old. They'd lived in Highgate then, with a distant relative of Alessandra's, a great-aunt once removed called Giovanna who'd treated her great-niece and the infant kindly, insofar as she was able to treat anyone in any way, given her many afflictions. In lieu of rent Alessandra had taken care of her old aunt and run the house, while Gayle, a young Australian nurse who'd come each day to give the old lady her vital insulin shots, returned on three evenings a week to babysit Lainey while Alessandra went to work as a waitress.

That was when she'd met Peter.

The question of why Alessandra had left Italy with such a young baby was one that had haunted Lainey for years, along with who her natural father might be. She'd searched the Internet, over and over, but it had yielded no answers so she'd created stories of her own. He'd been killed in a tragic accident and her mother had been so heartbroken that she could never bring herself to speak of it. Or maybe he'd been married to somebody else, so Alessandra had been banished from the country to save her Catholic family from the shame of having to bring up a *bastarda*.

Though the latter seemed a more likely scenario, if it were true surely her mother would have admitted to it eventually, at least to Peter, but as far as Lainey was aware her mother's past life had always been as closed to him as it had to her.

'It's not something she's comfortable discussing,' he'd tell her, 'so we shouldn't try to force her.'

Now, even if he had been protecting her from

some terrible truth, he probably couldn't remember what it was anyway.

Reaching into the cupboard beside the bed, Lainey pulled out her mother's handbag and sat with it on her lap, holding it in both hands. She knew if she opened it she'd smell the Chanel No 5 Alessandra had always used, probably with a faint tinge of mustiness now. She wasn't sure if she had the heart to do it. She missed her mother so much, in spite of – or maybe because of – the difficult relationship they'd shared. She felt sure Alessandra had loved her really, she'd just found it hard to show it – until the end, of course, when Alessandra had clung to her desperately, as though Lainey, and Lainey alone, could somehow make the demons go away. Maybe Lainey could have, if Alessandra had named them, but she never had, perhaps not even to the priest who'd come to hear her final confession.

Hearing the phone ringing elsewhere in the house, she kept hold of the bag as she ran along the landing to her and Tom's room. It was going to be him. He was ready now to explain what was happening and everything was going to be all right.

It turned out to be the mother of one of Zav's friends, asking if Lainey could do the school run on Monday instead of Tuesday.

After assuring her she could, Lainey rang off and quickly picked up again as another call came in.

'It's me,' Stacy told her. 'Are you OK?'

'Kind of.'

'No news, I take it.'

Feeling the words like small blows, Lainey said, 'Nothing.'

'And you've cancelled the dinner?'

'I rang everyone about an hour ago. I said there

was a problem on set that Tom had to attend to, and I seem to be coming down with something that I don't want to pass around. Anyway, tell me how you're feeling about meeting Martin's mother tonight.'

They talked on for a while, mostly about Martin and Stacy's prospective job, since Lainey didn't want to talk about Tom – if she did, she'd be in danger of giving life to the awful scenarios she was concocting in her head. Finally she said, 'Don't forget to call in the morning to let me know how it went.'

After ringing off she sank down on Tom's side of their bed, still clutching her mother's bag and trying not to imagine where he might be now. Was he thinking of her, worrying about how she was taking this sudden change to the day, perhaps to their lives? Had he stopped to consider what conclusions she might be jumping to? Was he at all concerned about what she might be going through? Did he intend to come back? If he did, would she end up wishing he hadn't?

Pressing a cheek to the soft leather of her mother's bag, she wondered what Alessandra would do if this were happening to her. Had Peter ever made her feel this anxious and vulnerable? He'd angered and frustrated her at times, that was for sure, but Lainey couldn't imagine her father ever giving Alessandra any concerns for his loyalty – or his love. They'd always seemed so close, so together in spite of Alessandra's fiery nature. Strangely, the only person who'd never fallen victim to her mother's often vicious tongue was Tom, probably because even she hadn't had the nerve for that. More than anything, Tom had made her laugh, or caused her to rethink an impulsive opinion or decision. She'd enjoyed battling wits with her son-in-law and husband, often running them round in circles in spite of having very little of their intellectual might.

Though Tom had his theories about Alessandra's past, he'd never attempted to draw her on the subject. As far as he was concerned it was none of his business, which didn't mean he wasn't interested, or unsupportive of Lainey's need to know more about her roots. If anything, he was as curious as Lainey was to find out what had caused Alessandra to abandon her native country. However, he saw no point in quizzing her when she'd made it so abundantly clear that she had no desire to be reminded of her life before coming to England, or of whatever family she might still have in Tuoro.

If there was anyone – a mother, father, grandmother, brothers, sisters, cousins – they certainly hadn't come looking for Alessandra, or not as far as Lainey was aware. In fact, all Lainey had to link herself and her mother to the small town on the edge of Lago di Trasimeno were their birth certificates. There was also the single page of a letter, which Lainey had found amongst her mother's papers following her death. It was in the handbag, along with Alessandra's crimson lipstick, her grey ostrich-skin purse containing fifteen pounds in cash, her silver and onyx rosary beads and a small phial of her favourite perfume.

Though Lainey probably knew the contents of the single page by heart, she slipped it out of the bag anyway and felt a wave of longing sweep through her as the scent of her mother came with it. It was when she was feeling at her lowest ebb that she missed her the most, which was odd really, given how rarely she had turned to Alessandra for comfort and advice.

The letter was written in Italian, but Lainey had paid to have it translated, and kept the neatly typed English version clipped to the handwritten original.

Tuoro, 8th September 1984

My dearest bambina,

Thank you for informing me of Giovanna's death. I was very sad to hear the news, but of course it was not a surprise as I know she has been ill for many years. May our dear Lord bless her eternal soul and take it into his keeping.

You write very lovingly of your new husband. He must be a good man to take your daughter as his own, as this is not always an easy thing for a man to do. Would you like me to tell your mother that you have named your child after her? I have not done so yet as I am unsure how she will receive the news.

I was disturbed to hear that you find it hard to look at the child without thinking of what happened, but please remember that she is not to blame. I know in your heart you are still angry, and I understand that, but I pray every day for . . .

This was where the page ended, and though Lainey had searched every pocket, drawer, handbag and cupboard in the house for the rest of the letter she'd never found it.

Those few short lines had left her with even more

questions than before, not least of which was why Alessandra had told the writer that she'd named her daughter after her mother when, according to the birth certificate, Alessandra's mother's name was Melvina. And why did the writer seem reluctant to tell Alessandra's mother that her grandchild bore her name?

From the handwriting and the tone of the letter Lainey thought the writer was probably a woman, but she had no way of knowing for certain, nor could she tell if she, or he, was in any way related to Alessandra. There seemed to be a degree of affection between them, however, and from the comments about Peter, and about finding it hard to look at her daughter without remembering, it seemed Alessandra had opened up to this person in a way she never had with anyone else.

Tom had wondered if the writer was a priest; Stacy felt it was more likely to be a close friend of the family, while Tierney had decided it was the grandmother Alessandra had called out for at the end. Lainey was inclined to agree with Tierney, but whoever the writer was, she had no idea if she would find this person when she went to Tuoro; having no name to help her get started, it was unlikely to be easy. It didn't matter, she was going anyway, armed with what little she did have, and if she ended up finding out nothing at all, then so be it. At least she'd have tried, and hopefully they'd have had a lovely holiday anyway.

Or they might have done, if Julia hadn't suddenly come into their lives.

It wasn't going to make a difference, she told herself forcefully. Everything would be sorted out just as soon as she spoke to Tom, and slipping the letter into the bag she went to return it to its rightful place.

'Oh God, Lainey, I'm sorry,' Nadia groaned, clearly embarrassed at turning up when she was no longer expected. 'I was driving and didn't check my messages. Don't worry, I'm out of here, just tell me, is everything all right? The kids are OK? Your dad's still with us?'

'We're fine,' Lainey assured her, reaching for her mobile as it rang. Did Nadia know Julia? Should she ask? Her heart skipped as she saw it was Tom on the line. 'Excuse me,' she said to Nadia, 'I have to take this, but don't go yet. Hello,' she said into the phone.

'Hi, it's me.'

'Yes, I know.'

There was a beat before he said, 'I just wanted to check you're OK, and to say sorry again for rushing off.'

Sounding colder, more hostile than she intended, she said, 'It might help if I knew why.'

'Yes, of course, but it's not a conversation to have on the phone.'

She could feel herself stiffening. Turning away from Nadia, she said, 'I know you saw the text, so who is Julia?'

He didn't reply.

Her eyes closed as an awful confirmation washed over her worst suspicions.

'Are you with her now?' she asked shakily.

'Yes, but it . . .'

She didn't want to hear any more. 'That's all I need to know,' she interrupted, and before he could speak again she cut the call dead. A voice inside was already telling her she should have let him speak, but another was shouting back, why? She didn't need the sordid details, especially not over the phone, or while his agent was there. They could talk later, face to face, when he came back. Presuming he was intending to come back. Of course he was; practically everything he owned was here . . .

'Sorry about that,' she said, forcing a smile as she turned to Nadia. 'Why don't you at least have a cup of tea now you're here? I was about to make one.'

Nadia regarded her uncertainly. She was a large woman with copious amounts of greying curls, electric-blue eyes behind fuchsia-pink framed glasses and a smile that could make a person blink, it was so sunny. It made her seem far younger than her forty-nine years, as did her almost flawless complexion.

'You're welcome, honestly,' Lainey assured her, glancing at her mobile as it rang again. Seeing it was Tom, she let it go through to messages and turned to put the kettle on. 'Actually, it's five o'clock, why don't we have some wine?' she suggested.

'Better not if I have to drive,' Nadia grimaced, 'but a cup of Earl Grey would really hit the spot.'

Tensing as the landline started to ring, Lainey might have ignored that too had Nadia not noticed it was Tom and scooped up the receiver to pass it over. 'Hi,' Lainey said evenly, more for Nadia's sake than Tom's.

'I know what you're thinking . . .'

'Nadia's here,' she told him. 'She didn't get the message about tonight being off, but it's lovely to see her anyway. Do you want to have a word?' and before he could object she returned the phone to his startled agent. 'I'm just going to check on Dad,' she

113

whispered. 'If he wants to speak to me again tell him I'll call him later,' and leaving them to it she ran upstairs to her father's room.

Ten minutes later she returned with Peter and Sherman, and though it was apparent as soon as Nadia greeted Peter that he didn't have any memory of who she was, his pleasure at seeing her made her smile.

'Sandra should be down in a minute,' he told her. 'I expect that's who you've come to see.'

Unfazed, Nadia said, 'That'll be lovely. Are you going to have some tea? I've just made a pot.'

'Oh, marvellous. I'll get Sherman some water . . .'

'It's OK, I'll do that, Dad. You go and sit down.'

As Peter made his way across the dining area, Nadia said, 'I hadn't realised the unit was shooting today. What a pain that they've run into a mess with the script. Actually, I never thought this latest adaptation was particularly well done, and I know Tom wasn't impressed with it either, so I guess it's not surprising they need him to go and sort things out.'

Lainey rolled her eyes as if to show how tiresome she found it on today of all days. What she was really thinking was how easily, how smoothly he'd apparently lied. Her husband the gifted storyteller.

Still, it presumably meant that Nadia didn't know about Julia, unless they'd concocted a cover between them while Lainey was out of the room. Since Nadia was fiercely loyal to Tom, it was certainly possible.

'How's Guy?' she asked chattily, referring to Nadia's extremely attractive and much younger husband. There were those, Lainey knew, who believed Guy had only married Nadia to get a share in her agency, and Max, who'd walked out of his work experience at the agency after some dispute with Guy, was amongst them. So, indeed, was Tom, though his affection for Nadia made him try harder than he otherwise might have to disguise his antipathy. As for Lainey, she put a lot of the male antagonism down to plain old-fashioned jealousy of Guy's more tender years, combined with his rock-star looks and undeniable charisma. It was true, she could wish he wasn't quite so flirtatious (she found it more irritating than flattering), and she hadn't been especially thrilled by the way he'd responded to Tierney the last time he and Nadia had come for the weekend. OK, he was probably only being polite, given how outrageously Tierney had flirted with him. Nevertheless, considering her age he could have toned down his response a little.

'Yes, he's fine,' Nadia was saying as she set about pouring the tea. 'Not about being stuck in New York till Tuesday, but hey, someone's got to do it.'

'What's keeping him?' Lainey enquired, carrying a bowl of water round to Sherman.

'Not what, who. Arnie Colefax is a year late delivering his latest book, so Guy is trying to keep him sober long enough to complete a first draft.'

'And he can do that by Tuesday?'

'He has to, or the publishers are demanding their money back. Frankly, it's all a bit of a mess, but he's Guy's client so I'm leaving him to sort it out.' She glanced at her watch. 'If tonight's dinner is off there's an old friend of mine not a million miles from here who I might drop in on, if he's around.'

'Is it anyone I know?'

Nadia's grin was impish. 'It is, but I'm not naming names. However, I will say that he was sitting to my left at the dinner you gave last Christmas.'

Lainey thought quickly, but they'd given so many

dinners since then, and been to so many other func-
tions that she simply couldn't remember who'd been
sitting where at any of them.

'OK, he was on your right,' Nadia told her. 'And
I think he was paying you rather a lot of attention
with a Christmas cracker.'

At that, it took only a moment for Lainey's eyes
to widen. 'You don't mean . . .'

'I do.' Nadia smiled, cutting her off.

She was referring to the head of Tom's publishing
house, whose ostentatious wealth and apparently
bottomless appetite for the good life had earned him
the nickname Trimalchio. Whether the epithet had
come from Scott Fitzgerald's working title for *The
Great Gatsby*, or directly from the *Satyricon*, Lainey
didn't know. What she did know, however, was
that Don Rhys-Lewis's rather dowdy wife of twenty-
seven years had sent him a postcard from Sydney
about a year ago telling him she'd run off with the
builder and wasn't coming back.

Hearing her father muttering lines from *The
Ancient Mariner*, she took him some tea and scooped
up her mobile on the way back as it bleeped with
a text.

*We need to talk. I'll be home tomorrow afternoon. Try
to arrange it so the children are out.*

Dropping the phone back on the counter top, she
was about to start drawing Nadia further on
Trimalchio when the door burst open and Zav came
in with tears streaking down his cheeks and something furry clutched in his hands.

'Mum, it got hit by a car,' he sobbed, 'and it isn't
dead. It's still breathing, so we have to take it to
the vet.'

Clocking Alfie hovering at the door looking

116

equally worried, Lainey said, 'Zav, we can't keep trying to rescue everything you find . . .'

'Mum! You've got to,' he shouted. 'It'll die otherwise and it'll be *all your fault.*'

Throwing an ironic glance at Nadia, Lainey went to inspect the wretched creature. A rabbit – and sure enough its eyes were open; it even blinked slowly as she put a hand on its side. 'Where's it injured?' she asked. 'Maybe it's just stunned.'

'No, there's blood on the other side,' Zav assured her, pulling free a hand to show her.

Sighing despondently, she said, 'Darling, I can't just leave Nadia here. She's our guest. Why don't you go and see if Max'll take you?'

'He's gone out. Mum, please. I don't want it to die. We have to try and save it. Please, please . . . Where's Dad? He'll take me, I know he will, because he cares about animals too, not like *you.*'

Stung by that, she said, 'Dad's not here.' She wouldn't bother to remind him that Tom had only ever taken him to the vet's once with one of his potential roadkill, whereas she took him on a pretty regular basis.

'Don't mind me,' Nadia told her, apparently amused by the scene. 'Far be it from me to stand in the way of a rescue.'

'Do you have to rush off?' Lainey asked, picking up the phone to find out where the emergency vet was located today. 'We should be back in under an hour, and now you've come all this way . . . Unless you're keen to get to Trimalchio, of course.'

Nadia twinkled. 'I'll give him a call while you're gone and let you know. Good luck with Basil,' she said to Zav. 'I hope you'll be in time.'

'Who's Basil?' he asked blankly.

Nadia nodded at the rabbit. 'Basil Brush,' she explained.

'He was a fox,' Lainey reminded her, 'but I'm sure this little fellow will have a name by the time we get back, if he manages to make it that far,' she added under her breath. 'Help yourself to anything. You can try having a chat with Dad, if you like. He might not say anything, but he enjoys having company. Oh, here's Tierney . . . What are you doing here? I thought you were staying at Maudie's. Hi, Maudie, how are you?'

'I'm good, thanks,' Maudie replied in an airy, cool-girl way that didn't quite suit her studious black-rimmed specs and limp, mousy hair.

'Tierney, can you keep Nadia company while I take Zav and his new friend to the vet?' Lainey said, reaching for her keys. 'We shouldn't be long.'

'I only came back for my laptop,' Tierney protested angrily. 'I can't stay . . .'

'You can until I'm back, surely?'

'No, I can't. For God's sake . . . Come on, Maudie,' and pushing her friend into the hall as though the shocked and surprised looks she'd left behind were nothing to do with her, she ran up the stairs.

'I'm really sorry about that,' Lainey said to Nadia. 'For the moment I'm afraid we'll probably have to put it down to her age, but I'll be having words with her . . .'

'Don't worry. I can remember what it was like to be sixteen, *just*. They're in their own worlds. You go on, I'm sure she'll be back down in a minute. I'll have a chat with her then.'

'What's the matter?' Maudie was demanding as Tierney shut the bedroom door behind them and swore repeatedly under her breath. 'What are you being like that for?'

Tierney's cheeks were burning, her eyes glittering wildly, but quickly jettisoning the last couple of minutes as though they hadn't happened she flopped on to the bed, arms and legs akimbo. 'Oh my God, Maudie, I am so in love,' she breathed ecstatically. 'You don't know what it's like. It's totally, completely amazeballs.' Suddenly she was back on her feet. 'I've got to listen to that music again,' and grabbing her laptop she opened up iTunes and started swooning as the first song began playing. She kind of preferred Adele's version of 'Make You Feel My Love', but he'd said to download Bob Dylan's and actually, with a bloke singing it she could more easily imagine it was *him* singing it to her.

Having heard all three songs enough times that afternoon, Maudie went back to the 'forbidden book', so caught up in it now that she couldn't bear to go anywhere without it.

After daydreaming through 'My Stunning Mystery Companion' by Jackson Browne and 'Don't Let Me Be Misunderstood' by The Animals (definitely Dad and Max type music, but she kind of liked it too, now she'd really listened to it), Tierney rolled on to her front to prop her chin in her hands. 'So come on, read out a bit more,' she encouraged Maudie. 'What are they up to now?'

Maudie's cheeks flooded with colour. 'No way am I saying any of this out loud,' she protested. 'It's like totally . . . I can't believe you're going to do all this stuff with him. Is that what he's expecting?'

Tierney shrugged. 'I don't know, but he definitely wants to know what I think of it.'

Maudie's eyes bulged as she continued to read. 'Oh my God, this is like totally . . . *weird.*'

'Let me see,' Tierney cried, grabbing the book.

Maudie pointed out the paragraph, and as Tierney read it she felt as though she was bursting inside.

She looked at Maudie.

Maudie looked back, and with squeals of hilarity they exploded into a gale of giggles.

'Hannah Armstrong, in year ten, reckons she's already done *everything* in this book with Aiden,' Maudie told her.

'No way!' Tierney exclaimed. 'She's not even fifteen yet – or no, she must be by now.' It was a bit galling to think that someone even younger than her was already so much more experienced. 'Do you reckon we're the only two virgins left at school?' she asked Maudie dismally.

'What are you looking so worried about?' Maudie objected. 'I'll be on my own soon.'

Remembering that was true, Tierney immediately perked up. 'Only seven days to go,' she declared, a ripple of nerves catching on a wave of excitement. 'Just think, this time next week I'll be with him.' Quickly rummaging for her iPhone as it rang, she saw it was Skye and clicked on. 'Hey, friend, how's things?' she cried cheerily.

'Yeah, they're cool,' Skye replied. 'Just getting ready to go for drinks at someone's house with the rents, then I'm meeting a couple of mates at a party. What's new with you? Have you heard any more since he sent the songs?'

'No, but I expect we'll IM or Skype later, or tomorrow or something.' How confident she sounded – and felt. 'When are you back?'

'That's why I'm calling. My mum wants to drive me down tomorrow, but I don't want to go back to school that early so will it be OK to come and stay with you?'

'Of course. No problem. My mum won't mind. Just let us know what time to expect you.'

'Sure. You get that I'll probably sneak over and stay with my shag buddy, though, don't you?'

'Duh, yeah.' Should she tell her Max was out with Christie tonight? 'Does he know you're coming?' she asked.

'I'll text him now. Are you still at Maudie's?'

'No, we just came back to mine so I could get my laptop.'

'OK, I have to go now. I'll text you tomorrow when we're on our way. Say hi to Maudie for me,' and Skye was gone.

After ringing off Tierney lay staring at the ceiling, going back over the conversation she'd had with him that morning and reliving how fantastic it felt just to watch him smile.

'Oh, Maudie, I think I'm going to erupt, or scream or do something insanely wild,' she cried, stretching out her arms. 'He is so cool and I love him so much.' Grabbing her laptop, she checked to see if there were any new emails. There weren't, so she called up his profile so she could gaze at his picture and pretend it was real. 'He is so completely to die for, isn't he?' she murmured dreamily.

Maudie was engrossed in the book.

Putting on the music again, Tierney lay back down and closed her eyes. She wondered what he was doing now. It was the middle of the day in New York, so he might be at a meeting somewhere, but even if he was he might still be thinking about her. She hoped he was imagining all the things she was.

'How do those books end, do you know?' she asked Maudie.

'I think they get married,' Maudie replied, without looking up. 'That's what Hannah Armstrong said, anyway, so I suppose she's hoping the same's going to happen for her and Aiden now. Like in her dreams.'

'It might,' Tierney said faintly. 'Actually, I reckon it will.'

Chapter Seven

It was Monday morning now and Lainey still had no idea who Julia was, or indeed where exactly Tom might be. Though she'd done as he'd asked yesterday and made sure the children were elsewhere for the afternoon, he hadn't come home. She'd waited and waited, paced the house, texted and rung him, but he simply hadn't turned up. She could still hardly believe it was happening as she veered from confusion to fury, to fear and all the way back again. He'd never done anything like this before. Why the hell wasn't he answering his phone? He surely had to know how worried she was. What if he'd had an accident? To her shame she realised an accident felt almost preferable to the thought of him being with another woman. At least that way their marriage might still be intact.

In the end, it was after five when he'd sent a brief message, saying *Sorry, lousy reception here. Will call tomorrow.*

Lousy reception here? What kind of lame excuse was that? Where the hell was he? Why didn't he get to a place where he could make a connection?

'He said he'll call tomorrow,' she told Stacy, when her friend came round to lend moral support. 'Not that he'll be home, so when exactly is he intending to come back?'

As much at a loss with that as Lainey, Stacy said, 'Have you tried him again since?'

Lainey shook her head. 'There doesn't seem any point. The calls just go straight through to messages. Anyway, don't let's start going round in circles with it all, tell me how you got on with Martin's mother last night.'

Stacy shuddered. 'Frankly, I'd rather forget the whole experience. She'll definitely be the reason he's still single at thirty-eight, and as far as I'm concerned he's going to stay that way.'

Lainey looked concerned. 'Are you saying you've broken up with him?'

'I have. I promise you, it had to be done.'

Since Stacy didn't look particularly upset, Lainey didn't challenge her. What she did though, stupidly, was encourage her to recall how she'd found out about Derek's affair with Pauline. It did neither of them any good, only served to depress Stacy and scare her.

Now, as Lainey went through the motions of preparing the children's breakfast, her mind was barely on what she was doing as she poured orange juice over Zav's cornflakes and had to start again.

'Turn it over, turn it over,' Tierney shouted, rushing into the kitchen with her school blouse barely buttoned, and her damp hair clinging to her face. 'Trey Songz's on and he is so cute. I am totally in love with him. *Turn it over*, Zav.'

'No way, I'm watching this,' he protested, grabbing the remote to protect his cartoon.

'That's just rubbish. Put on Massive R&B. Now!'

'Get lost!'

'Mum! Tell him. I have to watch Trey. Give me that remote,' she growled, trying to snatch it.

'No, you're not having it. Mum, get her off me. Stop! You're scaring Ronnie.'

Tierney did a double take. 'What?' she demanded in her right royal way. 'Who the hell's Ronnie?'

'He's my rabbit. He's there in the box and you're frightening him.'

Tierney stared at the box like it was a mistake Sherman had made. 'Shouldn't it be in a hutch, outside?' she protested.

'We'll let him go back in the wild when he's better,' Zav told her. 'Until then Mum said he can stay in here.'

Tierney shrugged. 'You're totally sad, do you know that? Now turn the telly over before I whack you.'

'No. It's not your telly, it belongs to everyone. If you want to watch Songz then go back to your room.'

'Mum, I swear, I'm going to do some serious damage if he doesn't give me that remote.'

'Where's Skye?' Lainey asked, starting to butter a pile of toast.

Tierney flicked back her hair. 'She's . . . still getting ready. Now will you please tell him . . .'

'Oh, *shut up*, Tierney,' Lainey snapped. 'If your father was here you wouldn't be watching the TV at breakfast anyway.'

'Only because he always has to have the news on. I just want to finish watching this *one* video, OK? Is that really too much to ask?'

'Zav was there first, now sit down and eat your breakfast or go back upstairs. I don't care which, just stop shouting and upsetting everyone's day before it's even begun.'

'It's not me, it's him,' Tierney seethed, elbowing Zav as she sat down at the table. 'If he'd do as he was told . . .' She broke off as a pan suddenly crashed on to the floor.

'If you'd damned well do as *you* were told and *shut up*,' Lainey raged, 'we could have a bit of peace around here.'

'Oh my God,' Tierney murmured, 'she's losing it.'

Clasping her hands to her head, Lainey cried, 'Yes, I'm losing it, and do you know why? It's *you*. You're so damned rude all the time, and you wait till I tell your father about the way you behaved with Nadia on Saturday, totally ignoring her and refusing to keep her company. Then you had the gall to tell me, thank God after she'd gone, that she's boring. How dare you say that about someone who's known you all your life and has only ever been kind to you? What's the matter with you, Tierney? You're turning into someone I don't know, and frankly I can't say I like you very much.'

'Well I don't fucking like you either,' Tierney shot back. 'You're always getting on my case about stuff and . . .'

'Hey, it's the happy Hollingsworths,' Max shouted over her as he came through the door. 'Can anyone join in?'

'I wouldn't bother if I were you,' Tierney snorted, 'she's in a vile mood.'

'Tierney, one more word out of you,' Lainey warned, 'and you're grounded for a week.'

Tierney looked about to protest before thinking better of it.

'Where's the alpha male?' Max asked, grabbing a slice of toast. 'Don't tell me, in the gym.'

'Why are you dressed like that?' Lainey demanded.

Max glanced down at his smart pale grey suit and clean white shirt. 'I'm going to work,' he told her.

She blinked.

'Christie's dad gave me a job,' he explained. 'It's only while his regular receptionist is off, but it'll get Dad off my back, and give me some spending money for Italy. When are we going, by the way?'

Since she'd reserved the flights in a fit of fury, or defiance, while she'd been waiting for Tom yesterday, Lainey was about to answer when Tierney said, 'I hope you haven't forgotten that I'm not coming.'

Lainey saw red again. 'I'll tell you what,' she raged, 'why don't I go on my own?' and slamming down a tea towel she stormed off into the hall, almost colliding with Skye as she came down the stairs.

'Wow, what's wrong with your mum?' Skye asked quietly as she entered a silent kitchen.

Tierney glanced at Max. 'Must be her time of the month,' she suggested. 'Or she's had a row with Dad.'

'Where is he?' Max asked again. 'I thought he was coming back yesterday.'

Tierney shrugged. 'Haven't seen him.'

'Hey, look at you in that suit,' Skye said teasingly as she shimmied up to Max. His eyebrows rose and a grin crooked one side of his mouth as she whispered in his ear.

'Do you have to do that here?' Tierney snapped. 'Some of us are trying to eat our breakfast.'

'I've finished mine,' Zav declared, pushing his bowl away. 'I'm going to find Mum.'

After he'd gone Skye peered playfully at Tierney. 'So, have you heard anything this morning?' she asked.

Colour instantly suffused Tierney's cheeks as her eyes shot to Max. 'What do you mean?' she demanded, trying to kick Skye under the table.

'You know what I mean.' Skye flicked back her hair.

Apparently catching on, Max broke into a grin as he said, 'So what's his name, T?'

'None of your business,' Tierney snapped, but in spite of herself she was starting to smile. She *loved* talking about him, even if she couldn't say much to Max, and since she'd woken up to a text saying *Good Morning Beautiful* all she really wanted to think about was him. Definitely not her mother, who was in a seriously foul mood and actually really needed to get over herself.

But still . . . Maybe she should follow Zav and go and make sure she was all right.

She was about to get up when Lainey came back into the kitchen. Though her face was still strained, her tone was much gentler as she said, 'I'm sorry I lost my temper. It's no way to send you off to an exam, so can we be friends again?'

Going to her, Tierney gave her a loving hug.

Lainey looked at Max. 'What time do you have to be at work?' she asked.

Glancing at his watch, Max said, 'I guess I ought to be going. Any chance of borrowing some cash for petrol? I'm pretty low and . . .'

'How much do you need?'

Startled by the quick response, he found himself eating air.

'Twenty? Fifty?'

His eyes widened. 'Fifty would be good. I'll pay you back,' he assured her.

Taking the notes from her purse, Lainey handed them over and turned to busy herself at the sink. 'We need to leave here in ten minutes,' she told Tierney and Skye.

They shot out of the kitchen, needing to finish their make-up before they left. Max tucked the cash into his inside pocket and was gone.

Taking a deep breath, Lainey allowed the quiet to settle around her, trying to use it as a calming force. She had to get a better grip, somehow separate what was happening between her and Tom – whatever that was – from what she needed to be and do for the children.

Thank God Vicky Morrison had texted just now to remind her she was doing the school run. She'd completely forgotten.

Where was Zav? She'd told him to go and clean his teeth.

Her eyes closed as a wave of dread swept out of nowhere. She might have no idea who Julia was, but what she did know was that she loved Tom more than anything and no way was she going to give him up.

Ring, she muttered desperately. *Get yourself to a place where there's decent reception and call me. What on earth can be so difficult about that?*

By the time Lainey drove back into the village, after dropping off the children and detouring to meet Stacy for a coffee, it was almost eleven o'clock and still no word from Tom. It was unsettling her badly now, but somehow she had to put it out of her mind or she was going to drive herself crazy.

Surely to God he wasn't really going to leave them.

Maybe he already had.

Stop doing this to yourself, just stop.

She couldn't imagine her life without Tom, didn't even want to, so she must clear her head and focus on getting her father and Sherman to the vet by one o'clock. Taking the dog for a check-up was always difficult, mainly because she knew the day was drawing close when the vet would say that his time had come. She didn't even want to think about how her dad was going to manage without his precious friend – or how empty the house would seem. As quiet and obedient as Sherman was, his wonderful presence amongst them was so filled with love and loyalty that it would be as though something vital had gone from their midst when he went.

As tears welled in her eyes, she tried to fight them back. Tom would come home today, and Sherman was going to be fine. She just had to stop being pathetic and get on with her life.

Ironically, she was due to spend the afternoon masquerading as Tom on Facebook and Twitter, responding to the dozens, perhaps hundreds of messages that had piled up over the weekend. What was she supposed to say when they hadn't had their usual Monday morning briefing over breakfast? This was when he generally gave her one or two tantalising details of plot for his readers to scoop up and discuss amongst themselves in their chat rooms. The feedback often proved highly entertaining for Lainey, and she'd share it with Tom over dinner.

It wouldn't be happening today – apart from anything else he hadn't written anything for over a week, or not that she knew of anyway.

Emerging from Bannerleigh's narrow cobbled high street to start skirting the village green, she frowned curiously to see a group of people straggling on to the road. Slowing the car, she was about to ask one of her neighbours what was happening when she glimpsed her father and Sherman at the heart of proceedings. Turning into the pub car park, she jumped out of the estate and felt her heart swelling with love and sadness as she heard her father reciting lines from what sounded like Shelley's 'Arethusa'. Why that poem on this day she doubted even he knew – he simply selected a work at random from the part of his memory that still stored his favourites and put his heart and soul into speaking them aloud.

As she joined the back of the group she sensed that he was only now beginning to register his audience, and the attention was daunting him. He began to stumble over the words, but seemed determined to press on as though afraid of letting them down. Moving forward, Lainey gently added her voice to his to help him to the end. *'Like spirits that lie / In the azure sky / When they love but live no more,'* they chorused together.

Taking his arm, she smiled and bowed as the onlookers applauded and he blinked in confusion.

'It's all right,' she whispered, 'we can go home now.'

He nodded and grasped her hand as she eased him past people he'd known for years, but didn't recognise now.

'I was keeping an eye out,' Anita Box, the pub's landlady, assured her as they got to the car park.

'Thanks.' Lainey smiled, knowing Anita would have put a stop to anyone mocking him. At least he had all his clothes on today; a couple of weeks ago Anita had brought him back in her car because he'd ventured out wearing only pants and an overcoat.

After settling him in the front passenger seat of the estate, and accepting the help of a young barman to lift Sherman into the back compartment, she drove on out of the village and a couple of minutes later they were stopping in front of the cattle grid to empty the mailbox. As usual there was a good handful of letters, and a couple of packages for Tom. The fact that she usually opened his mail gave her a moment's relief from the tension, since he'd surely never have allowed that if he had something to hide. A beat later the tightness of worry was back. Only a fool would take heart from such a hollow source of comfort, when there were so many other methods of communication these days.

'*At sunrise they leap / From their cradles steep / In the cave of the shelving hill,*' Peter murmured as they carried on along the drive.

Lainey smiled over at him. '*At noontide they flow / Through the woods below / And the meadows of asphodel,*' she recited.

Peter took a breath that turned into a wavering sigh.

'Would you like to come to the vet with us?' Lainey asked him.

He nodded absently and continued to gaze out of the window.

Deciding she'd better take him in case he wandered down to the village without Sherman to keep him safe, she drove around the back of the house, and seeing Tom's car her heart gave a painful lurch.

Not sure whether she was more relieved or anxious, she came to a stop and unbuckled her

132

father's seat belt. After making sure he was safely out and steady on his feet, she went to help Sherman.

'Here, let me,' Tom said, coming out of the house.

Unable to look at him, she replied, 'I can manage, thanks.'

He stood back, but as she struggled to heft Sherman's weight he stepped in again and took him.

'There you go,' he said softly, putting the dog on the ground.

Lainey took hold of her father's arm, and as she led him inside she could sense Tom's awkwardness. Was he feeling like an outsider in his own home, as though he didn't belong here any more?

Please God, don't let that be true.

She didn't know how to handle this. What was she supposed to say? More than anything she wanted to feel his arms around her, hear his words of reassurance, but considering what he'd put her through these past two days she knew that wasn't going to happen.

'He needs a shave,' Tom commented as he joined them inside. 'Would you like me to take him up?'

Somehow keeping her voice steady, she said, 'It's OK, I can do it.' If she was going to have to manage without him she might as well start now. The dread of it buckled her inside. How could he behave as though everything was normal when it was anything but?

'We need to talk,' he said quietly.

'Yes, we do,' she agreed, still unable to meet his eyes. 'But I'm afraid everything can't happen to your schedule. Dad needs a shower and then I'm due to take him and Sherman to the vet.'

Tom nodded slowly, and made the mistake of glancing at his watch.

133

'I'm sorry, do you have to be somewhere?' she snapped.

For a moment he seemed to be on the verge of replying, but in the end he simply went to answer the phone.

Without waiting to find out who it was, Lainey steered her father along the hall, and by the time she'd finished sprucing him and brought him back downstairs Tom had dealt with several more calls, something he rarely did on what was supposed to be a writing day. Their schedule stated that today – in fact, the whole of this week – was set aside for writing. He wasn't even in his study, he was still hovering about the kitchen seeming not to know what to do with himself.

'Lainey . . .' he began.

'Max has a job,' she declared, cutting him off.

He took a breath.

'He's standing in for the receptionist at Terry Flint's kitchen showroom.'

'Well, I guess it's better than nothing, and at least it'll earn him some money for Italy.'

'That's what he said. I've booked the flights, by the way.'

He made no comment, and when she turned to him her heart contracted to see how uncertain he looked. It wasn't like him. He was always so strong, so capable, the one who knew how to handle a crisis.

Was this a crisis?

She tried to think what to do. She needed to ask about Julia. The name was hanging between them, as transparent, as delicate as glass, but it seemed neither of them wanted to utter it. If they did it might shatter everything, and there would be no putting it together again.

'Do you have to take Sherman today?' he asked.

She glanced down at the dog, whose head was bowed, but at least his tail was up. His legs were no worse today than they'd been yesterday. She had painkillers, glucosamine, bandages to warm in the microwave. In truth, the only reason she was taking him today was to gain some reassurance that she was doing her best for him. They'd always give her another appointment and this with Tom needed to be sorted, no matter how hard it might be.

'I'll make Dad a snack and then come to your study,' she told him.

With a simple nod he turned and left, but his angst seemed to stay. It was charging the air, finding its way into her head and making it spin with so much dread that she barely knew where one fear ended and another began. It couldn't be that bad, surely. She was still imagining the worst, and it might not be that.

What else could it be? *Ask your husband about Julia.*

After calling the vet she made a coffee for her father, cut him a slice of frittata and settled Sherman next to him with a chew. She sat with them for a moment, loving the simple trust they shared, while wishing with all her heart that she could talk to her father. He'd never let her down, had always found a way to make her problems seem small, or at least less serious. What would he make of this?

Finally, dropping a kiss on his head, she left him to his snack and walked along the hall to Tom's study.

She found him standing at the window, staring across the lawn to the field that sloped down to the stream. She sensed a distance between them that had never been there before, and it panicked her to realise she didn't know how to close it.

Sounding sharper than she'd intended, she asked, 'So, what's going on?'

The way he continued to gaze out of the window made her wonder if he'd heard her, until he turned around to look at her. 'You need to sit down,' he said quietly.

Her heart jarred with a horrible beat. 'I don't want to sit down. I want to know what's going on.'

'I'm about to tell you. I just thought it might . . .' He shook his head. 'It doesn't matter.'

Not sure why, she suddenly crossed the room and sat on one of the calf-leather sofas. 'Is that better?' she asked, the anger in her dark eyes not quite masking the fear. 'Is this going to make it easier for you to tell me who *Julia* is?'

There, the name was out now.

'Lainey,' he said softly. 'I understand that you're angry . . .'

'Oh, you're right about that . . .' She put a hand to her mouth, as though to stop herself blurting out any more. Anger wasn't going to help her now, at least not until she knew what she was facing.

He came to sit with her, but didn't attempt to touch her. 'Julia . . .' His eyes dropped for a moment, as though the next words still weren't ready to come. 'Julia isn't my mistress,' he began. 'That's what you were thinking, isn't it?'

Though she neither admitted nor denied it, she could already feel the surging relief. 'So who is she?' she asked stonily.

'She's my daughter.'

At that her head reeled. *His daughter!* Of all the scenarios she'd created for herself, this one hadn't occurred to her at all. A mistress *and* a child! Oh dear God, how was she going to cope with this? What would it mean? 'You – you have a daughter?' she gulped, needing to be sure.

He nodded.

'Who with?' she managed. 'How old is she?'

He blanched.

'*How old is she*?' she repeated.

'Sixteen,' he answered quietly.

Her mind reeled again. Surely to God she hadn't heard that right. A daughter the same age as Tierney. She got to her feet, needing to escape him. 'Who's the mother?' she demanded.

'It doesn't matter . . .'

'Of course it bloody matters,' she raged, spinning round. 'When was Julia born? Before or after Tierney?'

He swallowed drily. 'A couple of months before.'

Her eyes widened with yet more shock. 'So all the time you were divorcing Emma, planning our wedding, preparing for the birth of *our* baby, there was another woman apparently already in the delivery room . . .'

'Yes, but . . .'

'So my mother was right, everyone was. You only married me because Peter Winlock was my father. If he'd found out you'd cheated on me, the way you'd already cheated on your wife, it could have meant the end of everything for you. So you kept your *other* affair a secret . . .'

'For God's sake, you're twisting everything . . .'

'How? Just tell me how I'm doing that when you've already admitted you have a daughter none of us have known anything about for *sixteen years*.'

His eyes were steely as he stared into hers.

137

He started to speak, but so did she. 'Who's the mother?' she repeated. 'And don't tell me again that it doesn't matter, or so help me . . .'

'It's Kirsten Bonner,' he broke in quickly.

At that she felt as though she'd been struck.

The ire seemed to go out of him. 'I'm sorry, I should have . . .'

'I take it we're talking about *the* Kirsten Bonner,' she cut in harshly. 'The one who used to front the Channel 4 arts programme?'

He nodded.

Finding it suddenly hard to breathe, she put her hands to her head. It was a long time, years, since the sassy, sophisticated, and exceptionally beautiful Kirsten Bonner had disappeared from the screen, but if Lainey was remembering this correctly (and how could she be in any doubt of it now), Kirsten Bonner had left to take maternity leave and had never returned. Though the decision in itself hadn't been especially sensational, the fact that she'd refused to reveal the identity of the child's father had set the press on fire back then. Speculation had been so rife, with so many famous and influential names being thrown around, that at least one commentator had remarked that it was a wonder Ms Bonner had managed to hold down a job at all if she was involved with so many men.

Lainey's eyes closed as the media frenzy of that time seemed to surge back around her. She remembered how sorry she'd felt for Kirsten Bonner, how she used to tell anyone who'd listen that the press ought to leave the poor woman alone and find some real news to report. 'Did it ever occur to them that she might be trying to save someone's marriage?' she'd even remarked. Never in her wildest imaginings had it occurred to her that Tom might be the father.

How stupendously naïve and delusional she'd been.

With a horribly sick feeling she remembered Emma's warning. *Don't be so sure you're the only one. If he can do it to me he can do it to you.* Did that mean Emma had known he was already involved with Kirsten Bonner? Lainey had to assume she hadn't, or being as bitter as she was back then, Emma would surely have gone to the papers.

Sixteen years on and still no one knew who the father was, though it was doubtful anyone cared any more. However, were it to come out that it was Tom Hollingsworth, it would be all over the news, which meant the press would be all over Bannerleigh, following her, Tierney, Zav, her father . . .

It was unthinkable. Too horrible for her to contemplate any further.

She turned back to Tom. He was still watching her, but she could feel the gulf widening between them. 'So what next?' she said hoarsely.

His answer was so shocking that she wished she hadn't asked. 'I'm going back to Hereford,' he told her.

'Hereford?'

'It's where they live, just outside.'

She was starting to shake. 'Are you saying you're leaving us?'

'No, what I'm saying . . .'

'So why are you going back? What about us? Tierney and Zav are your children too. What am I supposed to tell them?'

He dragged a hand over his ashen face. 'I was

hoping you'd say there are problems on set so I have to be there for another week.'

'Another *week*. You're going . . . Oh my God . . . You're asking me to lie to my children so you can go and be with . . .'

'To spare them being hurt. They don't need to know about Kirsten and Julia yet.'

'What do you mean, *yet*? Why should they ever have to know?'

'Julia's my daughter. I can't . . .'

'She's been your daughter for the past sixteen years, or so you're being led to believe. How do you know it's true? That woman could be lying . . .'

'It's true.'

Finding herself struggling to hold on, she turned back to the window.

'Lainey, I'm sorry,' he said wretchedly. 'I realise how hard this is for you. It is for me too . . .'

'Stop! Just stop,' she cried.

'. . . and it's come at a time when I . . . Well, when I was least expecting it . . .'

'*You* were least expecting it,' she echoed incredulously. 'What about the rest of us, who had no idea you had some kind of double life going on?'

'It's not like that.'

'Maybe not to you, but from where I'm sitting . . . She's *sixteen*, Tom. That's what you said, *sixteen*, which means you've kept her existence from me for all our married life.'

'Because I didn't . . .' He broke off as she clutched her head.

'I can't believe you've lied to me like that,' she seethed helplessly.

'Lainey, you need to listen . . .'

'Do I? Maybe I've heard enough. Maybe I just

140

don't want to hear any more about how you've made a mockery of our marriage . . .'

'For God's sake, will you let me get a word in?'

'Tell me you're not going back to them today,' she challenged.

His eyes closed. 'I can't do that. I have to go.'

'But *why*?'

He took a breath. 'It's complicated. I've made a promise . . .'

'You're making promises to another woman? What right does she have to make you keep things from your wife?'

He swallowed hard. 'She has no rights. She knows how much you mean to me, but for now I've given my word . . .'

'Let me talk to her. I need to find out what she wants, what she thinks she's going to prove by trying to destroy our lives.'

'All she wants is what's best for Julia . . .'

'And I don't want the same for my children? I take it you realise what this is going to do to them.'

He was speaking again, but she wasn't listening.

'Why now?' she cried. 'What's happened to make Kirsten Bonner suddenly decide . . . Oh God,' she groaned, as the truth dawned. 'Now my father doesn't know what's going on she thinks you're free . . .'

'Lainey, for God's sake, it's got nothing to do with that. What the hell do you take me for?'

She gazed at him harshly. 'I'm not sure I want to answer that,' she replied.

'Christ, you really are prepared to think the worst of me, aren't you?' he challenged, his face darkening.

141

'What am I supposed to think when you've already admitted you've been lying . . .'

'Not in the way you think . . .'

She pulled her hands free as he tried to take them and regarded him with wide, frightened eyes. 'Don't leave here today,' she said quietly.

'I have to. They need me . . .'

'And we don't?'

'Not in the same way.'

He reached for her again, but she took a step back. 'If you go,' she said, the words seeming to speak themselves, 'then I don't want you to come back.'

He appeared almost as stunned by that as she was. 'You don't mean that . . .'

'Yes, I do. That's the choice I'm giving you, Tom. You can stay, or you can go.'

There was an icy pause before he said, 'You know how I feel about ultimatums.'

'And this is how *I* feel about finding out that my husband had another child being born at the same time as my daughter, and that for the past sixteen years he's kept it from me. What else, Tom? How many more lies have there been? No, don't bother to answer. I don't want to hear any more. I'll be upstairs when you're ready to tell me your decision.' And somehow, considering how shattered she was inside, she made herself walk out of the room.

Ten minutes later he came into the bedroom to find her putting clothes into a suitcase.

'What are you doing?' he asked, appearing alarmed.

'Sorting out some things for the summer fete,' she replied, realising he'd thought she was packing for him.

He continued to watch her for a while, until finally he said, 'I'm leaving now, but I'll be back at the end of the week.'

Feeling his decision cut right through her, she spun round in a fury. 'You heard what I said,' she choked. 'I don't want you back if you're going to her.'

'Lainey, she's sick! That's why I have to go.' He sounded desperate.

She stared at him hard, not knowing whether to believe him. 'Who's sick, Kirsten or Julia?' she asked tersely.

'Kirsten.'

'What's the matter with her?'

He glanced away as he drew a hand over his face.

'You're lying!' she cried. 'You're making it up to give yourself an excuse to be with her.'

'I'm not lying!'

'Just go, Tom. Leave here now and don't bother coming back, because I don't want to live with someone who can't even . . .' She broke off as Sherman started to bark, and pushing past Tom she ran downstairs to check on her father.

He was sitting on the floor, struggling to get up.

'Dad, what happened?' she cried, going to him. 'Did you miss the chair again? Are you hurt?'

'Here, let me,' Tom said, easing her aside to raise Peter back to his feet.

'Silly old thing,' Peter was chuckling, though his ashen face showed he'd had a bit of a fright. 'I'm sorry, don't want to be a nuisance.'

'You're not a nuisance,' Lainey assured him. 'Were you trying to go somewhere, or were you intending to sit down?'

Peter only blinked.

'He needs changing,' Tom murmured. 'I'll take him upstairs.'

'No, you go,' she said, holding on to her father's arm. 'Obviously your sick girlfriend can't manage without you, but we can.'

As his face tightened she turned away, already wishing she hadn't said that, but it was too late to take it back.

A few minutes later, the sound of Tom's car starting down the drive made her want to run after him, but even if it didn't mean leaving her father in a vulnerable state, she'd never catch him now.

He was coming back, though, she reminded herself firmly. He'd said at the end of the week and it was Tierney's birthday on Saturday, so he surely wouldn't miss that.

The problem was he was going to be with another woman until then, a woman who'd had his child.

Dear God, how could he have led a double life all these years without her knowing?

Chapter Eight

'Where are the kids?' Stacy asked, putting a glass of wine in front of Lainey and pouring another for herself.

'Zav went to feed the ducks with Alfie,' Lainey replied, 'and Tierney's up in her room. She couldn't wait to get there, barely even said hello as she came through the door.'

Stacy's eyes rolled. 'And Max?'

'I'm not sure what time he's finishing. I guess we'll find out when he gets here.'

'Then you don't have to drive again today,' Stacy decided, 'so drink up.'

Though Lainey felt she needed it, when she took a sip she found the taste turning bitter on her tongue.

'So you haven't heard anything from Tom since he left?' Stacy said, going to close the hall door.

'We'd better keep it open,' Lainey told her. 'I want to be able to hear Tierney coming down the stairs.'

Returning to the table, Stacy glanced at Peter who appeared engrossed in an old movie, though whether he was taking anything in only he knew.

'To answer your question,' Lainey said, 'no, he hasn't rung, and I don't think he will.'

'He has to, eventually.'

Lainey only shrugged, and took another sip of

wine. 'I'm still trying to get over the shock of it all,' she confessed, wishing she could block out the image of a serenely gorgeous Kirsten Bonner with her dazzling smile and killer intellect. 'Never in my wildest imaginings . . .' She broke off, shaking her head as her heart caught on the dread of it. 'Except why not her? She's exactly his type. Tall, willowy, blonde, every man's dream, mother of his *sixteen-year-old* daughter who's no doubt a perfect copy of her perfect mother . . . It's all so bloody . . . *perfect*, isn't it?'

Stacy's smile was wry. 'You remind me of your mother when you're angry.'

Lainey didn't smile back. 'Do you think she really is sick?' she asked, not sure whether she wanted to believe it or not. Before Stacy could answer, she went on, 'If she is, why didn't he tell me straight away? No, he was lying, I know it. I think it's that he can't make up his mind who he wants to be with, me or her, so he's making out she's sick to buy himself some time with her.'

'Did he say what's wrong with her?'

Lainey shook her head. 'Just that she needs him. How sweet is that? And how bloody dare she need him? He's *my* husband, for God's sake, and he's got *three* other children besides the one he apparently has with her.' *How could he have a child with another woman?* She still couldn't make herself accept it.

'Speaking of children,' Stacy said, 'have you told yours anything yet?'

'No, but I guess I'll say he's stuck in London dealing with problems on the set.' Her eyes went to Stacy's. 'Do you think he has been leading a double life all this time?' she asked wretchedly.

'I've no idea,' Stacy replied gently, 'but . . .'

146

'. . . it's hard to think otherwise when the child is sixteen years old and her mother is as gorgeous as Kirsten Bonner,' Lainey finished for her.

'I was going to say, but he's always seemed so happy with you that it's hard for me to believe he's been cheating all this time. You'd know. Something would have been said, or your instincts would have picked up on it somewhere.'

'Well, they obviously had an affair sixteen years ago that I knew nothing about, which means he was cheating on Emma with *me and Kirsten*.' Her eyes closed as the guilt she still felt about taking him from his first wife closed in on her. 'This is my own fault,' she said softly. 'I deserve what's happening now for what I did to Emma.'

'That's ridiculous,' Stacy scoffed. 'It's all a very long time ago and Emma's been over it for years.'

'That doesn't mean it wasn't devastating for her at the time, because we know it was, and now I'm starting to find out how it feels.'

Stacy was about to respond when her mobile rang. 'Sorry, I have to take this,' she grimaced. 'I'll try and make it quick.'

As she got up to wander outside, Lainey found herself overwhelmed by images of Tom and Kirsten Bonner in a rural idyll with their beautiful child and sunshine all over them. How often did he go there? Had they found the place together, three, five, ten years ago, and moved in like newly-weds? How hard did Kirsten find it when he was with his other family? Presumably she'd had enough now, hence the text. She'd wanted to make sure Tom told his wife that he had other commitments that mattered as much as those he had with her.

'OK?' she asked as Stacy came back inside.

Stacy nodded. 'Just Diana wanting details of a few potential contributors. Anyway, what we need to do now is go back over what Tom said, because from what you told me on the phone . . .'

'There's really no point,' Lainey protested. 'I've told you everything anyway, and no matter what kind of spin we try to put on it, it's not going to change the fact that he's gone back there . . .'

'For the whole week?' Stacy interrupted. 'Maybe he's spending some of it in London, on the set.'

'That's not what he said, so I'm presuming he's intending to be with her. Actually, he's supposed to be writing. Maybe he's doing it there. For all I know he has his own study at her place. He's definitely taken his laptop, though not his shaving gear or toothbrush, which means he must already have them there . . .' Her voice faltered as images of his life with Kirsten rose up to torment her again.

'I have to say I'm not convinced by any of this,' Stacy informed her frankly. 'I mean, obviously Julia must exist, I can't think he'd lie about that, but as for him leading a double life with Kirsten . . . It would have come out by now if it were true. Someone would have discovered it, you know what the tabloids are like. Nothing escapes them for long.'

'Maybe this did, but even if you're right, I can't see how it makes it much better. He has a child with her, a child he's never told me anything about . . .'

'Maybe he didn't know himself . . .'

Lainey threw out her hands. 'How could he not know when it was all over the press at the time Kirsten was pregnant? The whole world knew.' Getting to her feet she went to fetch more wine from the fridge, hoping it might drown some of the

148

turmoil churning inside her. 'Even if he does come back at the end of the week,' she declared, 'I can't just roll over like some pathetic doormat saying oh do come in, Tom, please walk all over me, Tom. No, I won't do it. He made his decision when he was here today. I told him, if he left he needn't bother coming back, and he went anyway. I think that tells me everything I need to know.'

'But he's not someone who just walks out on his family . . .'

'He did it to Emma and Max.'

'That still doesn't mean he's doing it to you.'

'Maybe he already has. We only have his word for it that he'll be back on Friday, or Saturday, or whenever he's intending to come.'

'I know you don't believe he's gone for good . . .'

'How do I know what the hell to believe? These past sixteen years have clearly been a total sham . . .'

'Lainey . . .'

'No, think about all the time he spends at Dave Hill's place in Cornwall for "solitude when a book's not going well". He's obviously been with her, hasn't he, at her Herefordshire retreat, or whatever the hell it is. Convenient that, isn't it, a cosy little place at the back of beyond . . .'

'You're making this up,' Stacy reminded her. 'You've got no way of knowing if any of it's true.'

'I know she lives outside Hereford, because he told me.'

'I mean about him spending time there.'

'But surely you can see how easy it's been for him to lead a double life?'

'I repeat, you don't really believe any of this . . .'

'Actually, Stace, I do. You of all people will

remember how he neglected to tell me he was married when we were first together. If I hadn't got pregnant I'm sure he'd *never* have told me. I'd have had to find out for myself, and by then I'd probably have been history anyway, because he'd have been with Kirsten Bonner. Or maybe still with Emma, who knows? No, Stace, no matter how good a case you can make as devil's advocate, he's still not here, is he? He's with her. He even admitted it was where he was going, so please don't try defending him any more. You didn't see how torn apart he looks. This is big . . .' Her voice fractured on the undeniable truth of that, as tears stung her eyes.

Reaching for her hand, Stacy said, 'Don't you at least want to try to give him the benefit of the doubt? From what you've said, you didn't actually talk for long, so I'm sure there's more to come out.'

Drying her eyes, Lainey nodded, because actually it was true, they hadn't talked for long, and she hadn't really given him a chance to explain anything, so perhaps things weren't as bad as she feared.

And if she believed that she'd believe Tierney wasn't thundering down the stairs right now and making her way into the kitchen.

'You two on the wine already?' Tierney commented as she dumped her school bag on a worktop and yanked open the fridge. 'What's to eat? I'm starving.'

'There should be some frittata left,' Lainey replied, 'unless Zav's eaten it all.'

'I'll bet he has, greedy pig. Oh no, here it is,' and grabbing the last piece she stuffed it in her mouth, almost choking on a gasp as she knocked her bag to the floor.

'Oh, Tierney, why don't you take more care,'

Lainey grumbled, as her laptop and iPhone skidded across the flagstones.

'It's not my fault,' Tierney protested, making crumbs fly as she quickly stooped to gather everything up.

'Just a minute.' Lainey spotted a book she recognised. 'What's that doing here?'

'What?' Tierney countered, shoving the book under her laptop.

'Tierney, I saw what it was . . .'

'Yeah, all right, but it's not mine, OK?'

'Then why do you have it?'

'I'm looking after it for someone.'

Lainey's eyes turned flinty. 'If your father knew you'd as much as opened that book . . .'

'I told you, I'm looking after it for someone.'

'Presumably because her parents don't want her reading it either. Give it to me.'

'No way.'

'I said, give it to me.'

'And I said no way.'

Lainey's face turned white. She snatched the book away and tore out a handful of pages.

'Well, that was mature,' Tierney snapped.

'Go back to your room. You're grounded until we go to Italy.'

Tierney threw out her hands. 'That is such an overreaction.'

'Tierney, do as you're told or I swear to God we'll both end up sorry.'

Blanching at the outburst, Tierney started back down the hall. 'I'm going to talk to Dad about you,' she snarled, 'because I reckon you're losing it.'

'Good luck with that!' Lainey shouted after her. 'You're drunk, that's what's wrong with you . . .'

'Shut up, Tierney.'

'If you want to lose weight you should give up the booze.'

Lainey's eyes went to Stacy.

'You're not fat,' Stacy mouthed.

'And you're taking it out on me because you've had a row with Dad,' Tierney was ranting on. 'Well, I don't blame him for staying in London. I would too if I had to come home to you.'

'So would I if I had to come home to *you*,' Lainey shot back.

'I hate you.'

'The feeling's mutual.'

'I'm calling Dad now to tell him you're drunk and abusive and not fit to call yourself a mother.'

'Do it. And while you're at it, remind him it's your birthday on Saturday. Tell him you're going to be sixteen . . .'

'Duh, he knows that, and anyway, I told you, I'm going to Skye's this weekend . . .'

'We'll see about that.'

'Yes, we will and I'm going, so that's that.'

Allowing her the last word since it would go on all night if she didn't, Lainey went to close the hall door and took a large breath as she leaned against it.

'You're not fat,' Stacy repeated.

Lainey almost smiled.

'Lainey, are we going to swimming today?' her father asked.

'No, tomorrow,' she replied.

'Tomorrow,' he echoed in a whisper.

'Would you like some wine?' she offered, going to fetch a fresh glass.

As she reached the cupboard Tierney came

crashing back through the door. 'I've been in touch with Dad,' she announced. 'He's cool about me going to Skye's for my birthday, and he wants to know is he supposed to be in the studio for his radio interview tomorrow, or is it by phone?'

Lainey looked at Stacy, and could tell by her expression that she had registered the same as she had – first, that Tierney had managed to reach Tom, and second that having been talked into letting Tierney spend her sixteenth birthday with Skye in London, he now had no pressing reason to come back.

'Well?' Tierney prompted stroppily. 'Are you going to text him, or do I have to be the grown-up around here and do it for you? What have you had a row about, anyway?'

'Who says we've had a row?' Lainey countered.

Tierney shrugged. 'Seems pretty obvious. You're always in a vile mood when you two fall out. So, am I doing the texting?'

With a glance at Stacy, Lainey said, 'Tell him I don't know about the interview, he'll have to check with the programme's producer.'

'Isn't that your job?' Tierney needled her.

'Tierney, for heaven's sake, will you just do as you're told,' Lainey snapped.

Tierney's eyes flashed. 'All right, you don't have to shout! I just thought you were the one who organises everything . . .'

'I am, usually, but in this instance . . . Oh for God's sake.' Snatching up her phone, she pressed in a text: *Maybe Kirsten would like my job as well as my husband.*

'What did you say?' Tierney demanded.

'Mind your own business.'

'It is my business if my parents are behaving like idiots.'

'Don't you have some revising to do?'

'I've done it.'

'Then do it again, and give this to Grandpa before you go.'

Taking the glass of wine, Tierney carried it to Peter and sank on to the sofa beside him. 'Are you OK?' she asked, wrapping her arms around him.

Smiling, Peter patted her back. 'Yes, I'm fine. How are you?'

'Cool, I guess, or I would be if it weren't for Mum.'

Peter carried on smiling and patting Tierney's back. 'You've got a wonderful mother,' he told her, reminding Lainey of when he used to say the same to her.

'Yeah, right,' Tierney retorted, and planting a kiss on his cheek she treated Sherman to a hug and started to the door. 'I'm telling you,' she stated waspishly as Lainey topped up her and Stacy's wine, '*that's* what makes you fat, and if . . .'

'Tierney, why do you have to be such a horrible child?' Lainey cut in wearily.

'Maybe I take after you. Anyway, I'm not staying where I'm not wanted. Thank God I'm out of here on Thursday. I only wish it was sooner.'

A biting retort died on Lainey's lips as she lost the will to fight Tierney over something her father had apparently agreed to – that she could go to London as soon as term ended. Maybe it was a good thing for her to be away next weekend, particularly if things got any worse with Tom. 'I'll make sure your bag is packed ready for you to take to school,' she told her.

Tierney scowled. 'So kind,' she snipped. 'If you're making Dad feel that welcome no wonder he doesn't want to be here,' and flipping back her hair she stalked off along the hall.

'She really knows how to press my buttons,' Lainey sighed, returning to the table.

'And you owe me for that book. I'll have to replace it now and I don't see why I should pay when you're the one who destroyed it,' Tierney shouted from the stairs.

'You're not getting any money out of me for something that's going to pollute your mind and pervert your morals,' Lainey shouted back, quoting Tom.

'I'm *sixteen*, remember. It's not like I don't know about sex, and half the girls in my year have already done all that stuff.'

'If you believe that you're even stupider than you look. Anyway, if you haven't read it how do you know what's in it?'

'Duh, because everyone's talking about it. Maybe you ought to try reading it yourself, it might loosen you up a bit.'

Lainey caught Stacy's eye. 'I thought it was supposed to have the opposite effect,' she countered ironically.

'What?' Tierney retorted.

'Isn't it about bondage?'

Tierney groaned. 'Oh God, you're so not funny,' she told her, and before Lainey could attempt the last word she bolted up the stairs.

'It's almost as much fun being a mother,' Stacy commented, 'as beating yourself up on a Friday night.'

Lainey had to laugh, and glanced up as Max came

155

in from outside. 'Where's Dad?' he demanded angrily. 'He's not answering his fucking phone and I've been trying him all the way home.'

Cringing at the language, Lainey said, 'I take it your first day went well.'

Max grunted as he looked up. 'Yeah, great, if you don't count the tosser sales bloke who ought to stuff his fat fucking head in a microwave and turn it on. So where's Dad?'

'Have you tried texting? Tierney's been in touch with him . . .'

'When's he back? He's supposed to have got us tickets for Billy Bragg tonight and I bet he's forgotten.'

Suspecting he had, Lainey tried to think up an excuse.

'He has, hasn't he?' Max growled furiously. 'He's fucking forgotten, just like he always fucking forgets about me. I'm like a waste of space where he's concerned . . .'

'That is *not* true,' Lainey interrupted fiercely. 'He's got a lot on his mind at the moment . . .'

'Yeah, like I care,' and slamming on through the kitchen, he disappeared off to the annexe.

Lainey's eyes met Stacy's. 'And being a step-mother's even more fun,' she said drily.

'What's wrong?' he asked gently. 'You don't seem yourself today.'

'No, I'm cool,' Tierney assured him, tilting her head as she smiled. No way was she going to tell him she'd just had a bust-up with her mother, it would seem so juvenile. 'Are you still flying back tomorrow?' she asked shyly.

He nodded, and the way his smoky dark eyes

156

gazed from the screen made her heart flip right out. He was totally, mind-blowingly drop-dead; she could hardly speak she was so mad about him, and nervous, and excited. 'What have you been doing today?' he asked, sounding as though he really wanted to know.

She tried a nonchalant shrug. 'Nothing major,' she replied, not wanting to remind him that she'd been at school.

'Have you done any reading?'

Her breath caught as she nodded. Just him mentioning it was making her feel as though she was on fire down below. Was he really going to do to her what the characters were doing to one another in the book?

He smiled, and she felt she might faint.

'Have you thought about what you're going to wear on Saturday?' he asked.

Had she thought about anything else? It was keeping her awake at night, taking her attention from whatever exam she was sitting, dominating every conversation she had with Skye. 'I keep changing my mind,' she admitted, 'but I'm going shopping in London with Skye on Friday.'

He appeared interested in that. 'I'd like to buy you something,' he told her. 'Who's your favourite designer?'

Who was her favourite designer? Was he serious? 'Um, well, I like D&G, but they're kind of really expensive . . .'

'It doesn't matter. I'll get you something from D&G. How about shoes? Do you prefer Louboutin, or Jimmy Choo, or Hervé Léger?'

Her mouth almost fell open.

'Leave it with me,' he said with a smile. 'Just text

157

me your sizes and I'll have a nice surprise waiting for you.'

Wondering how she was going to get through the next few days, she asked, 'Where shall we meet?'

He gave it some thought. 'Send me Skye's address and I'll pick you up at the end of the road. I can hardly wait to see you.'

Boldly, she whispered, 'I can't wait to see you either.'

His eyes narrowed romantically as he said, 'You're so beautiful. I keep imagining us together and it's blowing my mind.'

It was blowing hers too.

'Do you want to get that?' he asked, as her mobile started to ring.

She glanced at it quickly. 'It's only my friend,' she told him. 'I'll call her back.'

'I should go now anyway,' he said. 'Don't forget to text me those details. I'll Skype again before the weekend,' and with a knowing lift of one eyebrow that just about flipped her mind he broke the connection.

'Oh my God,' she cried down the line to Skye moments later. 'He is so totally, unbelievably to die for. I can't wait till Saturday. Please tell me it doesn't hurt. No, don't go there, it'll only make me more nervous.'

'It'll be awesome,' Skye assured her. 'Anyway, I can't stay. I'm trying to get hold of Max, do you know where he is?'

'I think I heard him come in a while ago.' Tierney went to the window to check. 'Yeah, his car's there, but his music's on so I don't expect he can hear the phone. Shall I give him a message?'

'Yeah, tell him I can get out tonight if he can come and pick me up.'

'OK. I guess that means you'll be coming here?'

'I should think so. I'll have to be back by eleven, so it'll depend what time he comes for me.'

'Right, I'll go and tell him now.'

A few moments later she was rapping on the annexe door, but since the music was too deafening for anyone to hear she pushed it open and picked her way through the flotsam of Max's world to lower the volume. 'Max!' she yelled. 'Where are you?'

'What do you want?' he growled, coming through from the bedroom wearing only boxers and an open shirt. If he weren't her brother she might get what all the girls saw in him.

'Skye's been trying to ring you,' she told him. 'Apparently she can get out tonight . . .'

'Yeah, I got her messages, but Christie's managed to find some last-minute tickets for Billy Bragg so I'm not available.'

Tierney shrugged. 'So, you could at least call Skye back and tell her.'

'What's the point? If I don't ring she'll know I'm not free,' and changing the subject as though Skye's feelings didn't matter at all, he said, 'Lainey told me you've heard from Dad today. Where is he, do you know?'

Tierney shrugged. 'I think he's in London sorting out one of the scripts, and by the way Mum's been going off at me they've obviously had some sort of row . . .'

'Sorry, T, don't have time for this now,' he interrupted. 'I need to be out of here. Do you have any money?'

159

'Sure, but I'm not lending it to you, you never pay me back.'

He looked pained as he threw out his hands. 'You know I will, as soon as I get paid.'

'No I don't, and anyway, I thought Mum gave you fifty quid this morning.'

'She did, but I've got commitments, T, and believe me fifty quid doesn't go far.'

'You mean you spent it on weed.'

'Maybe. So, can you load me with twenty? I swear you'll get it back . . .'

'No way,' she snapped. 'I need it for when I go shopping on Friday.'

'I'll remember this next time you come to me for cash,' he called after her as she let herself out.

Ignoring him, since she'd never yet asked to borrow anything from him, she wandered on through to the kitchen to find out if her mother was in a better mood yet. She hoped so, because she was starving and she knew if she asked for food when her mother was in a bad temper, she was likely to be told to make it herself.

Finding Stacy at the Aga doing something with a tagine, Tierney glanced around the room, saying, 'Where's Mum?'

'She had a bit of a headache,' Stacy replied, 'so she's gone upstairs to lie down. Tea shouldn't be long now.'

In spite of knowing she ought to offer to help, Tierney said, 'I'll be back in a minute,' and leaving Stacy to get on with it she ran upstairs to her mother's room. 'Mum,' she called softly as she opened the door, 'can I come in?'

There was a gentle sigh before Lainey said, 'If you must.'

Since she was lying on her side with her back turned, Tierney went round to sit where she could see her, and instantly felt worried when she realised her mother had been crying. 'What is it?' she asked shakily. 'What's Dad done this time? Whatever it was, he wouldn't have meant it.'

Touched by how she'd leapt to her father's defence, Lainey reached for her hand and squeezed it. 'Everything's fine,' she told her. 'There's nothing for you to worry about.'

Tierney was eyeing her uncertainly.

Lainey smiled. 'I'm sorry I shouted at you earlier,' she said. 'Now tell me how your exam went today. What was it?'

'French oral. It was OK, I think I got through it.' Actually, she wasn't sure she'd done at all well, she'd been so busy thinking about *him*, but she was hardly going to tell her mother that. She was thinking about him now, and wishing she could go back to her room to Skype him again. 'Can I lie down with you?' she asked.

Lifting an arm so she could snuggle up to her, Lainey closed her eyes and inhaled the fresh, lemony scent of her daughter's hair.

'Tell me about when you and Dad first met,' Tierney said, hoping it would remind her mother of how much she loved him.

'Oh, Tierney, not now,' Lainey murmured.

Flattened, Tierney allowed a few moments to pass. What she was dying to ask was whether her parents had had sex on their first date, but she wasn't sure that would go down very well right now. Instead, she said, 'I know you and Dad slept together before you got married, otherwise I wouldn't be here – or I might, but you know what I mean . . .'

'Tierney . . .'

'I was just wondering, how long did you know him before you actually did it?'

There was a pause before Lainey said, 'As a matter of fact, it happened quite soon after we met, but if you're . . .'

'So he still respected you after? I mean, he wanted to see you again, obviously . . .'

'Tierney, are you trying to tell me something?'

'No! Like what?'

'Like you've met someone and you're . . .'

'No way have I met anyone, there's no one around here *to* meet. I'm just asking, that's all.'

'Who is it?' Lainey asked.

'I've just told you, there's no one.'

'If there is, you know you can bring him home. Dad and I would like to meet him.'

Shuddering to think how that scene would play out, Tierney replied, 'I think we should change the subject now, because you're totally getting the wrong end of the stick.'

'OK,' Lainey agreed.

After a while, Tierney said, 'You sound really tired.'

'I am.'

'You're not ill, are you? I mean, apart from the headache.'

'No, I'm not ill.'

A few more minutes ticked by.

'Are you sure you don't mind about me going to London for my birthday?'

'You know I mind, but if it's what you want . . .'

'It is, more than anything, and that's not being disrespectful to you and Dad. You've always given me great birthdays, but I'm not a kid any more. I need to do my own thing.'

'I understand that. I'll miss you.'

'I'll miss you too, but I'll be back on Monday or Tuesday. I know, how about we have a belated celebration at the pub we went to for Stacy's birthday last month? You and Dad really liked it there.'

'That sounds a good idea.'

Tierney waited to see if her mother would speak unprompted, but she didn't. So she began running through other topics they could discuss. Perhaps not the upcoming trip to Italy, it would only lead to a row, given that she had no intention of going, though she had to admit she was quite curious to know what Granny had been hiding all these years. Probably nothing more than the fact that she'd given birth out of wedlock, and hello, what was the big deal about that? OK, it probably meant more in a Catholic country, especially back when Granny was young, but even so, it was hardly a scandal now.

'Mum?'

'Yes?'

'Are you sure you're all right?'

'I just have a headache.'

'So you wish I'd go away?'

'No, it's nice lying here like this. We don't do it often enough these days.'

Tierney linked her fingers through her mother's and tried not to think about how hungry she was.

'Oh no.' Lainey smiled, as Zav came skidding along the landing and crashed into the door with a resounding thud. 'Mum! I'm outside. Can I come in?' he shouted.

Laughing, Tierney shouted, 'Where are you?'

'Outside!' he repeated indignantly. 'Where are you?'

'In here.'

With that the door flew open, and seeing his mother and sister lying on the bed he took a running leap to dive on to them. Catching him, Lainey pinned him down while Tierney tickled him until he managed to fight his way free and climb on to his mother.

'Surrender?' he demanded, punching his hands in the air.

'Never!' Lainey cried.

'Yes you do. I'm the champion, and tea's ready.'

'I'll race you down,' Tierney challenged.

Springing up from the bed, he was off like a shot with Tierney hard on his heels.

Given the choice, Lainey knew she'd probably stay in bed for the rest of the night, but it wouldn't be fair on Stacy, and would probably end up worrying the children. So, getting to her feet, she went into the bathroom to splash some water on to her face.

Since sending the message suggesting Kirsten might like her job, there had been a resounding silence. She wasn't sure what she'd expected, though it had never been like him to engage in a row by text.

She wondered what he was doing now, how he was feeling, if he was even thinking about her and the kids.

Reaching for a towel, she started to dab her face, but stopped as her heart turned over. They were due to fly to Italy in less than two weeks, and she felt suddenly afraid that he might decide not to come with them. He knew how much this trip meant to her, and he'd always supported it, but maybe it was no longer a priority for him.

Regarding her flushed cheeks in the mirror, she felt herself stiffening with anger and resolve. Whatever he decided, she'd booked everything now, and no way was she going to cancel.

Chapter Nine

It was Thursday morning now, and the only messages Lainey had received from Tom were either work related or to ask if she was all right. Her replies had been brief, giving him whatever information he was seeking, while saying nothing about herself; nor did she mention his radio interview on Tuesday.

When she'd tuned in she'd half expected to find he'd withdrawn from it, but he was there – or at least at the end of the phone – and listening to his light-hearted banter had left her boiling with rage and frustration. It wasn't that she'd wanted him to sound broken, or tormented, or even distracted (actually, maybe she had), she just hadn't been prepared for him to sound his usual witty, erudite self. No one listening would ever have dreamt that he might have been in the process of walking out on his wife and children to be with the nation's forgotten sweetheart and their teenage daughter. He'd made the presenter and other guests laugh, repeatedly, and had gamely joined in other discussions that weren't focused on him. She'd wondered if Kirsten and Julia were in the room with him, providing a live audience of two while he spoke down the line. It was what she, Zav and Tierney had often done, Max too if he was around and in the right mood. After the broadcast was over she'd usually sit with him to discuss what had been said and how well it might have gone down.

Being an expert in the field of interviews, Kirsten had undoubtedly done that for him on Tuesday; very probably she'd done it many times in the past.

It had been a horrible couple of days since, two of the worst Lainey could remember.

'Are you all right?' Tierney had asked when she'd come down for breakfast this morning. 'You look terrible.'

Knowing she did, Lainey had managed an ironic sort of smile as she lopped the top off a boiled egg. As she'd put it in front of Tierney, a row of soldiers lined up around it, she'd wondered what Kirsten Bonner gave Julia for breakfast. No doubt something proper and healthy like fresh fruit and muesli. They had those things too, it was just that neither of her children liked them. Nor did Tom, come to that, only her, but she hadn't had any this morning; she'd had no appetite.

'Mum, you're not getting in a state about me being in London for my birthday, are you?' Tierney had asked as Lainey had helped carry her bags out to the car. She was taking them to school ready to leave with Skye as soon as the final exam was over.

'No, no, I'm fine,' Lainey assured her. 'I just didn't sleep too well last night.'

Dumping her stuff in the back of the estate, Tierney turned to gaze frankly into her eyes. 'You've got to make up with Dad,' she stated. 'Life is too short to go on like this and whatever he's done, it can't be that bad.'

Thank God it didn't seem to have occurred to

Tierney that he might already have left them. She really wouldn't want her thinking that, especially when it might not be true.

Please God it wasn't.

She kept wondering how she could doubt it, how she was even managing to contain her anger, though there wasn't much point to it when he wasn't here to receive it.

'Have you packed all your presents?' she asked Tierney as she went round to the driver's side.

'I think so. Zav, you're in the back, not the front,' Tierney snapped.

'I know, I was just getting my iPod,' he retorted, his small frame weighed down by the enormous bag on his shoulders.

'You can't take it to school,' Lainey told him.

'Yeah, but I can listen to it in the car, can't I?' he cried. 'It'll save me listening to you two going on about all your stupid stuff.'

With a sudden sunny smile, Tierney wrapped him in an embrace and planted a smackeroo on his forehead.

'Yuk!' he protested, wiping it off.

'You know you love me really,' Tierney teased, getting in beside her mother.

'I do not,' he assured her, climbing in the back. 'Mum, are you taking me to football after school or is Alfie's mum?'

Unable to remember, Lainey said, 'I'll text you later to let you know.'

'I'll be fine,' Tierney insisted when Lainey finally dropped her off. 'Everything will, I promise.'

Lainey took the small comfort as if it were a prediction and tucked it deeply into her heart. From Tierney's lips to God's ears. She disliked that phrase, but it was what had come to her mind and she wanted so much for everything to be all right that a little assistance from above, or anywhere, wouldn't go amiss.

At the school gates Tierney turned to wave, and Lainey felt tears stinging her eyes. It wasn't that she minded about Tierney wanting to spend her sixteenth with friends (well she did, but realised she had to learn to let go), it was more that it felt as though everything was slipping away.

Checking the time now and calculating that Tierney would be midway through her biology paper, she sent a message for her to pick up when she came out. *Hope exam gone well. Have a good journey to London. Don't forget to call tonight. Love you, Mum xxx*

She jumped as the phone rang, and seeing it was Stacy she clicked on. 'Hi, how's it going?' she asked. 'Have you met Diana's backers yet?'

'I have,' Stacy confirmed, 'and everything's looking good so far, but that's not the reason I'm calling. Have you seen today's *Guardian*?'

A bolt of unease jarred in Lainey's chest. 'No,' she replied. 'Do I want to?'

'I'm not sure. Tom's got a piece on page nine about why the Coalition might not survive the next parliamentary session.'

Lainey was still bracing herself in case Stacy went on to tell her something that might hint at, or even reveal, the personal events in his life, but it seemed that was it. 'Do you think he wrote it this week?' she asked, certain that no request for such a piece had gone through her, which was what normally happened.

'Given the detail, he must have.'

169

Lainey's head started to throb. So while she was here tearing herself apart, not knowing from one hour to the next what the future might hold, he was at Kirsten's dashing off articles about what it might bring for a bunch of irrelevant politicians.

Didn't he care about her feelings at all? He must have known she'd see the piece, or at least hear about it, so was that what he wanted, for her to realise that life was going on as normal for him – though with Kirsten at his side now, instead of her?

'Are you still there?' Stacy asked.

'Yeah, I'm here,' Lainey replied, biting down on her fury and pain. 'Tell me more about your meeting with Diana's backers.'

'I will when I see you. I just wanted to know if you'd seen . . .'

'When are you back from London?' Lainey interrupted. 'Why don't you come over on Saturday night? We can open a bottle or two . . .'

'Oh no, please tell me that doesn't mean Tom's not coming back,' Stacy protested.

Lainey's heart skipped a beat. 'I don't think we should count on it,' she replied tersely. 'He seems very comfortable where he is, and now he's given Tierney permission to go to Skye's . . .' She didn't want to go on with that. 'Did you tell your new bosses you're going to Italy?' she asked. *Please don't let her back out, please, please.*

'I did, and Diana's sure we can work something out. Worst-case scenario, I won't be able to stay for the entire month.'

It would do, just as long as she was there for some of the time, especially if Tom backed out. He wouldn't though, would he? 'That's great,' she told Stacy. 'With the way things are I might not go for that long

170

myself. Or, who knows, if I find I have family there I might end up staying for good.'

There was a wryness to Stacy's tone as she said, 'I know you're not writing your marriage off that easily.'

It was true, she wasn't. The trouble was, until Tom came back there was precious little she could do to save it, if it was even in trouble, and she still wasn't entirely sure about that. *Of course it's in trouble, you fool. He's shacked up somewhere with another woman. How much more trouble do you want than that?*

In her worst moments, when the anger about where he was and the way he was hardly in touch became so intense she could hardly bear it, she came close to packing up his belongings, loading them into a lorry and sending them to Kirsten. If she had an address or phone number she might well have done it, but she had neither, and an Internet search hadn't revealed anything particularly useful about the woman either. At least, not as far as her residence was concerned. What Lainey had discovered was that Kirsten Bonner had written several children's books and three chick-lit novels in the past ten years, all under the pseudonym of Beverly Crane.

Had Tom helped her to get published?

Only an idiot would imagine he hadn't.

It was unnerving Lainey badly to find herself wondering when lawyers might start becoming involved. Would he try to force her to sell the house? The mere thought of it incensed and terrified her. She couldn't give up her beloved home, but she couldn't imagine giving him up either. He was the centre of her world. Everything revolved around him in a way she hadn't quite seen until now. She'd always thought she was the one who held everything together, whom they couldn't manage without, but it was Tom, with his humour and strength, discipline, encouragement, support and love, who made sense of it all.

He wasn't going to leave. He'd be back at the weekend, as promised, and somehow they'd manage to sort everything out.

It was around four on Saturday afternoon when Lainey took a break from her duties at the village fete to pop home to see if Tom was there. She was so afraid he might not be that she almost tripped over in the rush of her relief when she saw his car in its usual spot. Since Max, Zav and her father were all down at the village hall, she sent a text to Max telling him to take over her stall, as she was going to be longer than she'd expected.

Finding no sign of Tom in the kitchen she went through to his study, trying desperately to ignore the terrible nerves inside her. Everything was going to be fine, she kept telling herself. The sense of rejection she was feeling wasn't real, it was all in her head. He was back to stay, she wasn't going to walk in and find him packing his books.

'Hi,' he said, looking up from his desk as she appeared in the doorway. 'I'm sorry, I forgot about the village fete today.'

'It's OK,' she replied stiffly, 'as long as you didn't forget it's Tierney's birthday.'

His eyebrows arched. 'I'd never hear the end of it if I did,' he responded. 'I spoke to her first thing. I didn't get the impression she was missing us much.'

Lainey knew she was supposed to smile, but she couldn't quite manage it. 'She's very happy with her Kindle, apparently,' she said. She wouldn't tell him about the book she'd confiscated the other day – actually, torn up – it would serve no purpose now. 'I downloaded a copy of *The Lost Generation* for her,' she informed him.

His interest was immediately piqued, and she knew he'd be remembering the last time they were in Paris, as a family, when they'd introduced the children to Shakespeare and Company, Sylvia Beach's wonderful bookshop next to the river. *The Lost Generation* was the story behind the shop, which had fascinated Tierney at the time, and apparently delighted her when she'd found it on her Kindle this morning.

She couldn't help wondering if he'd been in touch with Kirsten during that weekend.

Were all their memories going to be sullied now by his affair?

'How long are you staying?' she asked, feeling her hands clenching at her sides.

His eyes narrowed slightly at the tightness of her tone, but his own was calm as he said, 'Look, I understand this past week can't have been easy for you . . .'

'Don't patronise me,' she snapped.

He took a breath. 'It wasn't my intention. I just want you to know that . . . Well, obviously I need to explain what's happening. It's why I'm here, so we can talk.'

She felt dizzied by a horrible beat in her heart. That didn't sound as though he was staying. 'Well, it's very kind of you to spare the time,' she told him, 'but maybe I don't have it right now . . .'

He made the mistake of sighing.

'Don't you dare be like that with me!' she raged.

'While you've been tucked away in the back end of nowhere with your bloody mistress and daughter, writing articles for a newspaper, debating the merits of a useless government, not sparing a thought for anyone else . . .'

'There was never a moment when you weren't on my mind,' he broke in angrily. 'I wrote the piece as an escape, to try to make myself think of something else for a while, and as for . . .'

'Oh, lucky you, being able to find an escape. It wasn't quite the same for me, I'm afraid, because I was here taking calls for you, dealing with your publishers, your agent, your publicist, your public, your *children*, undoing your commitments, making up excuses for why you weren't ringing people back. In other words I was *lying* to try and spare people's feelings, the way you've been lying to me for years . . .'

'Jesus Christ, Lainey . . .'

'I know what you're doing,' she shouted over him, 'you're trying to find a way of cutting yourself loose from us that's not going to end up all over the press. You wouldn't like that, would you, because you're a very private man really, and we all know how private she is, hiding behind her pseudonym, *Beverly Crane*. So how are you going to make this work without causing too much fuss?' Her eyes were bright with fury; tears were streaming down her cheeks.

'Lainey, stop,' he implored, trying to take her hands. 'This is the very reason I didn't call, because I didn't want this happening on the phone. I wanted to be here so I could explain properly . . . Don't,' he urged, as she tried to back away. 'It's OK, I swear. It's going to be all right.'

'How can it be if you're leaving?' she heard herself choke.

'I'm not leaving,' he insisted. 'At least, not in the sense you're seeing it.'

'What other sense is there?' she cried. 'If you think you're going to split your time between her and me you can damned well think again, because even if she's willing . . .'

'That's not what I'm suggesting,' he told her forcefully. 'Now will you please stop jumping to conclusions and listen. I have to be with Kirsten for a while. She needs me . . .'

Lainey's hands went up. 'Stop right there,' she said furiously. 'I couldn't give a damn what she needs, what matters to me is my marriage and my children. I thought they mattered to you too, but apparently . . .'

'Of course they do, nothing matters more, but I told you on Monday, Kirsten's sick . . .'

'And I'm supposed to care about that? Let someone else look after her.'

'Lainey, she has cancer. She needs treatment and someone has to take her.'

'So why does it have to be you?'

'Because that's what she wants.'

His eyes were burning into hers as he watched her processing his words: his mistress was seriously ill, she needed him beside her, her daughter needed her father . . . His loyalty was to them now, not to his family here. Where did they fit in? Would they ever fit in again?

As she gazed back at him she felt a sudden urge to get away from him, to escape to a place where she wouldn't have to listen to any more, or to deal with whatever came next.

175

'I'm sorry that she's sick,' she said hollowly, 'I wouldn't wish that on anyone, but as for where it leaves us . . .'

'It doesn't *leave* us anywhere.'

'Don't be a fool,' she snapped.

Throwing out his arms, he said, 'You think you've got this all worked out, don't you? You've told yourself . . .'

'We need to decide what we're going to tell the children,' she cut in.

'Lainey, you're rushing ahead before we've even had a chance to discuss this.'

'Actually, *you* need to decide,' she informed him, 'because it's *you* who's doing this to them.'

'I'm not doing anything to them. I'm simply trying to support someone who's sick, and in my shoes you'd do exactly the same.'

She almost laughed at that. 'And if I were in your shoes, how would you feel about me going off to take care of a family I'd never even mentioned until a week ago? A man I'd had another child with . . .'

'This is absurd. I don't have another family . . .'

'But you do. By your own admission you have a sixteen-year-old daughter with a woman whose needs now outrank ours. I can see why they would, I can even see that they're your responsibility, but if you're asking me to condone your relationship with Kirsten Bonner by letting you live between here and there, the answer is *never.*'

His eyes were steely as he said, 'You know, I was hoping we might have a more reasonable conversation than this, but clearly . . .'

'Then perhaps you can tell me what's reasonable about having a child with another woman and

176

keeping them a secret all these years?' she shot back.

'Dad! Dad! You're back,' Zav cried, suddenly bursting into the room. 'You have to come down to the village hall,' he insisted, grabbing Tom's hand. 'They're waiting for you to do the auction.'

'Zav, this isn't a good time, son,' Tom protested.

'But you promised . . .'

'Just go,' Lainey told him.

Tom's eyes came back to her, and remained there as Zav continue to tug his arm. 'OK,' he said to Zav, still staring at Lainey, 'run back and tell them I'm right behind you.'

'Yay!' Zav cheered, and blowing his mother a kiss he zoomed off.

Waiting until the kitchen door slammed behind him, Lainey said, 'So, are you going back to Kirsten's tonight?' As the question tore through her heart she could already see the answer in his eyes.

'I promised Julia I would.'

And how could he deny a child whose mother had cancer? Especially when the child was his.

She stared at him hard, hating him and everything that was happening, while longing for him to take her in his arms. If he told her now that he loved her, that he was sorry and Kirsten meant nothing to him, she might find a way to deal with this. As it was, he simply looked at her, his eyes masking whatever he might be feeling for her. 'You know, you really don't make things easy,' he told her.

'Well, I'm sorry about that . . .'

'I meant for yourself, not for me. If you were prepared to listen, to try to understand . . .'

'I have listened, and I understand perfectly. Now you need to go to the village. Don't worry about

177

coming home after the auction. We won't keep you, you can head straight on back to Kirsten's.'

'Lainey, please . . .'

'Do I need to ask if you're coming to Italy with us next Saturday?'

His eyes closed in despair.

Not sure whether she wanted to scream or beg, she said, 'I always thought you wanted to be there for me when I made this trip.'

'Of course I do, it's just the timing . . .'

'I'm not changing it. We'll go without you.'

He took a breath, and dashed a hand through his hair. 'If you feel you have to . . .'

'I do.'

'OK, but I wish you'd wait, because it's obvious, at least to me, that your mother was trying to protect you from something.'

'And whatever it was happened a long time ago. It can hardly hurt me now, and I could have relatives there, people who remember her . . . I might even have . . . a father.'

'You have Peter.'

'Of course, and I'm never going to think of anyone but him as my real father, but I want to know about my roots. I can see that you might not understand that, because you've always known who you are, where you're from, but I haven't.'

'Then at least talk to Father Michael before you go. He was with your mother at the end, he heard her final confession . . .'

'Whatever she might have told him he'd be honour bound to keep it to himself, and you know it.'

'But she's dead now, and if he does know something . . .'

'He doesn't.'

'Why don't you ask?'

'I don't need to. You know how the Catholic Church works. The confidentiality of the confessional is sacrosanct, both before and after death,' and feeling more devastated than she could ever remember, she turned on her heel and walked out of the room.

'Do you know how they describe that dress on the D&G website?' he was asking as he reclined on the bed, watching Tierney admiring herself in the mirror. 'They say it's virginal and seductive at the same time.'

Giggling as she went funny inside, she struck a model pose with her weight on one leg, and her lips moodily pouted. She could see exactly why they'd describe it that way, because it was like a little girl's dress in a way, with a round neck and lace collar, puff sleeves and flouncy skirt that reminded her of a party dress she'd had when she was six. It was dead short, and really showed off her legs, especially now she'd put on the Jimmy Choo ankle boots he'd also bought for her. She didn't want to think about how much it had all cost, but she knew it was mega, like probably in the thousands, which just went to show how much he liked her.

'Do you feel virginal and seductive?' he asked, topping up her champagne.

She smiled shyly and gazed at him from under her lashes. 'I might,' she answered teasingly.

They were in a totally awesome apartment, overlooking the river, somewhere around Wandsworth, she thought, but wasn't entirely sure. She'd been too nervous during the drive here to take much notice of where they were going. Anyway, it belonged to a friend of his apparently, who was happy to let them have it for the weekend while he was in Frankfurt.

'You certainly look it,' he murmured, patting the bed for her to come and join him.

Feeling anxious and excited again, she perched beside him, crossing one leg over the other as she took a sip of her drink. She'd already had two Breezers at Skye's to give herself courage. Skye had warned her she'd need them. It was definitely good to be at least half wasted for her first time, she'd said.

'You won't feel so shy, and it won't hurt so much either,' Skye had declared.

'Why, does it hurt a lot?' Tierney had asked worriedly.

'Depends how relaxed you are, and if he bothers to make sure you're, you know, in the right mood, but I don't think you'll have any problems with him. He's dead experienced, so he'll know what he's doing.'

He hadn't touched her yet, apart from on the back when he'd steered her in through the door. It didn't seem to matter, because she was definitely already in the mood. Everything down there was burning and throbbing like it had a life of its own, and her boobs felt enormous in their new lacy push-up bra. She was sure if he as much as brushed his fingers over them she'd sob or cry out or do something equally embarrassing.

'Do you know what you are?' he said lazily.

She wasn't sure how to answer that.

'*You* are my guilty pleasure.'

She giggled, and lowered her eyes as she sipped. She'd never tell him this, but she really didn't like that expression, maybe because her stupid parents had spoiled it for her by saying it made them want to throw up.

'You're beautiful,' he said softly, folding her hair back over her shoulder. 'You do things to me it's not fair to do to a man, do you know that?'

Her heart was pounding so hard it almost hurt.

'Do you want to get that?' he murmured, as her phone started to ring.

She shook her head, and without checking who it was she turned it off.

He smiled, and she felt overwhelmed all over again by how totally drop-dead he was.

She gave a sob of nerves as he began lowering the zip at the back of her dress, and again as he sat up and touched his lips to her neck. Gazing into her eyes, he eased her arms free of the sleeves. Her nipples were showing large and hard through her bra, and what he said about them made them harder than ever. She felt dazed, disoriented, almost as though she was floating.

She was going to be his submissive, he would be her master, he was telling her, just like in the book. She had to do as she was told, while he undertook to ensure she was satisfied in every way. 'Do you know what it'll take to satisfy you?' he asked, lying her down on the bed.

Actually, she didn't, not really.

'Would you like me to show you?' he offered, drawing the dress down over her thighs.

She nodded, uncertainly.

He looked at her new lacy thong and his eyes narrowed with approval.

She started to kick off her ankle boots, but he stopped her.

'Not yet,' he instructed, 'I want you to keep them on.'

She watched as he lifted her leg to replace the boot, and almost cried out when, without warning, he dropped a hand to her inner thigh.

'Are you wet?' he asked. 'Touch yourself and tell me if you're wet.'

She stared into his eyes, not sure what to do.

'Do it now,' he urged.

As she slid her fingers into the thong he began removing his tie.

'Well?' he prompted.

She swallowed noisily. 'Yes, I'm wet,' she whispered, knowing she'd never been so wet in her life.

'Take off the bra,' he commanded.

Feeling dizzy again, she did as he said and found herself barely able to breathe.

'Exquisite,' he murmured, as her boobs fell free. The tie was in his hands now, and she realised it was just like the one that featured on the cover of the book.

'Happy birthday,' he whispered, reaching over her.

Oh crap, she was thinking to herself. But it was OK, even if he gagged her she'd still be able to let him know if she needed him to stop and he definitely would, she felt sure of it.

Anyway, she wasn't going to want him to stop because she was totally, completely dying for this to happen.

Chapter Ten

'Oh no, Dad, what are you doing?' Lainey cried above Sherman's barks as she rushed to the Aga to grab a burning pan from the heat.

Peter stood aside helplessly, seeming not to understand there was a problem.

'Another minute and we'd have been on fire,' Lainey told him, using a chuckle to try and keep her tone light. She didn't want to scare him, but even if she did she knew he'd have forgotten it by the next time he took it into his head to do some cooking.

Plunging the pan under a rush of cold water, and standing back as a cloud of steam hissed out from it, she said, 'Are you hungry? Shall I make you something to eat?'

'I have to take Mummy her breakfast,' he told her.

Lainey looked at him sadly. It was three o'clock in the afternoon, they'd not long finished lunch and she couldn't be sure whether he was meaning his own mother, or hers. Yesterday she'd found him searching for his mother's tap shoes – she'd been a championship dancer in her time, as had his father. 'Why don't you come and sit down?' she said, taking his arm. 'I'll bring you a nice cup of tea . . .'

'I have to take Mummy's breakfast,' he repeated. 'She'll be upset if I don't.'

'Then let me see to it, OK? I know what she likes and you've done enough for today.'

Offering no more resistance, he allowed her to lead him to his chair, where Sherman settled next to him and earned himself an extra chew for raising the alarm. 'You're such a good boy,' Lainey murmured, stooping to fuss him. 'I don't know what we'd do without you, I really don't.'

By way of answer Sherman thumped his tail on the floor and carried on gnawing his chew.

'We have to take Mummy's breakfast,' Peter said, as Lainey went to put the kettle on.

'Yes, I'm going to make it now,' she assured him, glancing out of the window to see Nadia, Tom's agent, pulling into Tom's empty space. She was only passing, she'd said on the phone, but she wanted to drop a present off for Tierney's sixteenth.

'Can't let such an important date pass without marking it, can we?' she declared as she came in the door. 'So where is she? No, don't tell me, still sleeping off the effects of last night's party. Did she have it here? You're looking very up together if she did.'

'She's with her friend in London,' Lainey replied with an ironic smile.

'I see, spreading her wings. Well, it happens, I guess, and you're looking a little like you wish it wouldn't.'

Lainey shook her head. 'I'm fine,' she assured her. 'Probably had one too many myself last night.'

Nadia rolled her eyes. 'You and me both. Anyway, I think she'll like what I've got her. I did a bit of research to find out what girls her age are into these days, so hopefully I've scored a hit.' Putting the beautifully wrapped gift on the counter top, she looked around the room. 'Tom not here?'

Feeling the words like a pain, Lainey said, 'No, he's away this weekend.'

Though Nadia's eyebrows rose in surprise she didn't ask where he was, which made Lainey wonder if she knew about Kirsten. As friends as well as agent and client she and Tom had come through a lot together over the years, including the break-up of both their marriages, Tom's in the earlier days, then Nadia's about ten years ago. There wasn't much they didn't tell each other, so it was likely Nadia did know about Kirsten.

'Oh, it's Guy,' Nadia announced as her mobile rang. 'Another husband who's away for the weekend. Time we girls gave ourselves a bit of a treat, if you ask me,' and clicking on she wandered outside to answer the call.

Taking her father some tea, Lainey perched on the arm of his chair and rested her cheek on the top of his head as she gazed at nothing. Where was Tom now? With Kirsten, of course. Was he thinking about his wife? Would she see him again before she went to Italy?

Where the heck was all this going to end?

'Is that Lainey?' Peter asked, patting her hand.

'Yes, it's me.' Lainey smiled, straightening up.

Peter nodded and leaned forward to pick up his tea. 'You're a good girl,' he told her.

Pressing a kiss to his forehead, she went to fetch her own tea and sat down at the table to try Tierney's mobile again. Still no answer. Nor had Tierney so much as texted or emailed today. *Please don't let her have drunk so much that she's still in bed at this late hour.*

'Max? It's Lainey,' she said into her mobile.

'Yeah, I got that. What can I do for you?'

'Have you heard from Tierney today?'

'Not so far. I expect she tied one on with Skye and her mates last night.'

'I'm sure you're right. Where are you?'

'In Bristol, about to go and see a movie.'

'OK. Well, if you hear from her first, please tell her to ring me.'

'Will do,' and he was gone.

'Does Mummy have some tea?' Peter asked.

'Yes, I took it up just now,' Lainey replied.

Glancing down as her phone beeped with a text, she saw it was from Zav and opened it. *Going to watch cricket with Alfie and his dad. Back about teatime. Is that OK?*

Texting a quick yes back, she dialled Stacy's number and left a message for her to call when she got home. Though they'd spent hours talking about the situation with Tom and Kirsten last night, drinking far too much in the process, she was still in sore need of her friend's support.

Glancing up as Nadia came back in, she started to get up. 'Tea?' she offered. 'I've just made some.'

'Don't worry, I'll pour,' Nadia insisted. 'What about you?'

Lainey held up her mug. 'So, what are you doing in this neck of the woods?' she asked. 'Don't tell me you've been to see Trimalchio again.'

Nadia twinkled. 'As a matter of fact I was at a school reunion last night, over at Westonbirt.' She shuddered. 'I knew there was a reason I hadn't stayed in touch with most of them.'

Lainey laughed, and looked down as her mobile rang. Her heart jolted to see it was Tom, and she quickly clicked on.

'Hi, have you spoken to Tierney today?' he asked.

Frowning as their concerns fused, she said, 'No, but I've left a couple of messages. I wondered if she'd forgotten to take her charger, except she could always use Skye's.'

'Maybe you should try calling Skye to make sure everything's all right.'

'I would if I had a number.'

'You mean you don't?'

Stung, Lainey snapped, 'OK, I'm the world's worst mother for not having a number for my daughter's best friend . . .'

'What about Skye's parents? Can you contact them?'

'No, and before you start having a go at me . . .'

'How the hell could you let her go off without knowing exactly where she was going?' he demanded.

'She was going to Skye's, and if you hadn't given me so much else to think about maybe I'd have remembered to get a number. As it was . . .'

'We need to get hold of the school,' he interrupted. 'They'll know how to contact Skye's parents.'

'It's Sunday, and the end of term,' she reminded him. 'There won't be anyone there.'

'So we don't try? We just give up? Is that what you're saying?'

'No! I'm saying I'll call Maudie. She's sure to have a number for Skye, and if she doesn't she'll know someone who does.'

'Thanks,' Tierney said, taking her phone from him as she sat into the Audi, barely closing the passenger door behind her. 'I hope you didn't mind having to bring it.'

'Why would I mind when it's given me the chance to see you again?' he replied with a smile.

Did he think she'd left it at the apartment on purpose? She hadn't, she'd thought it was in her bag until she'd got back to Skye's around eleven this morning. It was gone five now, and had taken all this time for her to make contact with him, then for him to go back to the flat to collect it.

'Are you OK?' he asked, seeming genuinely concerned.

She gave a nonchalant flick of her hair. 'Yeah, yeah, I'm cool,' she assured him with the ghost of a smile.

Touching his fingers to her chin, he turned her to face him. 'You were sensational last night, do you know that?' he murmured.

His eyes were amazing, gazing into hers like he could see everything she was thinking. She hoped he couldn't, because she hadn't felt sensational, or not all of the time. It made her feel a bit better to think he hadn't gone off her, though.

He put a hand on her leg and she found it kind of weird the way her body could do one thing, while her mind did another. It was like she wanted it, but didn't.

'So how's it feeling to be a woman?' he said softly.

He'd asked her that last night, and this morning, and she still didn't know how to answer. The truth was, no different really, apart from the bruising feeling where she'd never had bruises before, and the memories of everything he'd done to her. Some were amazing, while others . . . Well, she didn't really want to think about them, because she definitely hadn't liked it as much as she was probably supposed to.

'The apartment's still free if you don't have to rush back,' he whispered.

Her eyes were fixed to the gates outside Skye's house. She wanted to go with him, but didn't. It was all so confusing. 'They're waiting for me,' she said hoarsely. 'Skye's mum and stepdad are taking us out for dinner tonight.'

'I see. Then you mustn't let them down.'

She lowered her head so her hair was masking her face.

'I'll call you, OK?' he said gently.

She nodded awkwardly.

'Off you go now,' and leaning across her he opened the door for her to get out.

Certain he could see her bottom as she stepped up on to the pavement, she clasped the hem of her dress and half walked, half ran back to Skye's. When she reached the gates she turned to see if he was still there. He was, and when he waved she smiled. She really loved him, and definitely wanted to see him again, but she couldn't help thinking it was easier on Skype.

'How did it go?' Skye pressed urgently, as Tierney rushed into the bedroom they were sharing.

'OK,' Tierney replied, quickly closing the door.

'So when are you seeing him again?'

Tierney's heart twisted strangely. 'I'm not sure. He's going to call me. I suppose it'll depend on when he can get away.' Feeling suddenly miserable, she slumped down on a chair

'What's wrong?' Skye asked. 'I thought you'd feel better once you'd seen him again.'

Tierney shrugged. 'I do. I mean, I kind of do, but at the same time . . .' She took a breath as she tried to sort out her mind. 'It's like I said earlier,' she attempted to explain, 'part of it's fantastic, and I don't regret what happened, or anything, but . . .' She shrugged awkwardly, not quite knowing how to put her feelings into words.

Sitting up to give this her full attention, Skye said, 'Listen, the first time's always a bit weird, you feel like kind of empty after, but it's not as though he doesn't want to know you. He said he'd call, and I bet anything he does.'

Though Tierney liked the sound of that, it still wasn't cheering her up much.

'I reckon we should read more of the book,' Skye suggested. 'It's a total turn-on, and with all the stuff you said he was into last night . . .'

'You know what's weird,' Tierney said, watching Skye rummaging for the book, 'when you read about it it's dead hot and all that, but when it happens to you for real . . .' She broke off as the sense of help-lessness and fear she'd experienced last night staged a shaky return. 'He kept saying I'd get to like it,' she said, 'I just had to give it time.'

'I expect he's right,' Skye responded wisely. 'Remember, you'd never done *anything* until last night, so maybe it was a bit full on for your first time. I know it would blow my mind if Max were to get into all that. I wonder if I can talk him into reading the book?'

Feeling very doubtful about that, Tierney suddenly remembered her phone, and grabbing it from the dressing table where she'd dropped it she turned it on. 'Oh my God,' she murmured, as it began bleeping like mad. 'I have to ring the rents, looks like they're doing their nuts trying to get hold of me,' and going to her mother's number she pressed to connect.

'Tierney, thank goodness,' Lainey cried, answering

on the first ring. 'We've been really worried. Why didn't you call sooner?'

Glancing at Skye, Tierney said, 'Sorry, I left my phone at one of Skye's friend's last night, and I've only just got it back.'

'Well, at least you're all right. Where are you now?'

'At Skye's. So what's all the fuss about? Why are you trying to get hold of me?'

Sounding exasperated, Lainey said, 'It isn't like you not to call when you're away, and when you weren't answering your phone . . .'

'Yeah, well, I'm OK, and you don't have to keep checking up on me.'

Her mother fell silent, and Tierney immediately felt horrible for snapping at her. 'So how is everyone?' she asked, trying to sound a bit friendlier.

'We're fine, thank you,' Lainey responded. 'Nadia's just called in. She brought you a present.'

'Oh God,' Tierney muttered.

In a tone that told Tierney Nadia was close by, Lainey said, 'Yes, isn't that lovely? Would you like to speak to her?'

No! She definitely wouldn't. 'I'd really love to,' she replied hastily, 'but Skye's parents are taking us out for dinner and they're already in the car.'

With a sigh, Lainey said, 'OK. Actually, I was wondering if you'd like to invite Skye to Italy with us? Or perhaps you'd rather ask Maudie?'

Tierney hesitated. She didn't want to go to Italy at all, or she hadn't before, but now, actually, she was thinking maybe she did, especially if Skye could come too.

But what about Maudie? It was going to seem a bit mean choosing Skye over her.

'Zav's taking Alfie,' her mother told her.

Great, two idiot boys splashing about the pool getting on everyone's nerves. 'I'll let you know,' she said, deciding she had to think about it.

'OK. So when are you coming home?'

Tierney shrugged as she glanced at Skye. 'I'm not sure. Tomorrow, I expect. Is Dad back yet?'

'He was, but he's had to go away again. He's been trying to get hold of you.'

'Where's he gone?'

'To Hereford.'

'Why? What's there? Is he researching or something? Please tell me you've made up by now.'

'Yes, we're speaking,' Lainey confirmed. 'Now, what time should we expect you tomorrow?'

'I don't know. I'll text when I'm on the train.'

They both fell silent then, until Lainey said, 'Are you all right?'

'Yeah, I'm cool,' Tierney replied weakly. 'I'd better go.'

'OK. I'll give your love to Nadia.'

Tierney's eyes closed as images of what she'd allowed Nadia's husband to do to her last night came flooding back, and she felt seriously sick. 'I'll see you tomorrow,' she said, and before her mother could ask again if she was all right, she quickly rang off.

'I've heard from Tierney,' Lainey said into Tom's voicemail. 'Apparently she left her phone at a friend's, so she's OK. She's not thrilled about you being away again though, so I think you should speak to her.'

As she rang off she wandered outside to wave Nadia off, and as the car disappeared around the corner of the house she stood staring at the garden, wondering if they would ever enjoy it as a happy family again.

Hearing the phone ringing, she turned back inside.

'It's me,' Tom announced when she answered. 'What exactly have you told Tierney?'

Bristling, Lainey said, 'I haven't told her anything, why?'

'She's just accused me of having an affair,' he said tightly, 'and that could only have come from you.'

'Don't be ridiculous. She's got her own imagination, and it doesn't take much to leap to that kind of conclusion when you're away so much. She's scared, and this was her way of testing you. So what did you tell her?'

'That it was nonsense, of course. What did you think I was going to say?'

'Well, I'd hope you wouldn't break it to her on the phone, but obviously you do need to tell her.'

'Of course. I'd hoped we could do it together.'

She could already feel herself reeling away from it. 'If I agree to it, it'll be for Tierney, not for you,' she told him.

His silence was as cold as the dread in her heart. 'I'll let you know when I'm coming,' he retorted, and with that the line went dead.

Sitting down at the table she pressed her hands to her head, hardly knowing what to do with herself, where to turn or who to talk to. She knew Stacy would come soon, but right at this moment she was feeling such an urgent longing for her mother that she thought she might go mad.

'The woman's got cancer, Lainey,' she could

almost hear her saying, 'so what do you expect him to do, just abandon her?'

Surely Kirsten had other family who could take care of her, but even if she did, it wouldn't be the same for Julia as having her father around, knowing he was there to make things as right for her mother as he could.

It wasn't as if she wanted to take him away from Julia, though actually she probably did, but even if she could, how would she feel then, knowing the child was trying to cope on her own? If anything, Julia needed her help too, but it wasn't likely that Kirsten would want that. Nor did she, really.

She just wanted Tom.

'Are you sure you want a man who's apparently been cheating on you all your married life?' she could hear her mother saying. A man, she added to herself, who never tells you he loves you? She guessed she now knew why he didn't, and the truth of it hurt so much that she couldn't prevent herself from breaking down.

It had all been a sham. She'd never mattered as much to him as he had to her, and now she was losing him to the woman he'd really loved. How was she going to bear it? She couldn't even begin to think of her life without him, while he was probably desperate to find a way to be with Kirsten for good. How scared he must be of what she was going through. He'd be asking himself all the time if she was going to make it, and no doubt punishing himself for not marrying her when he should have, sixteen years ago.

Suddenly realising that Sherman was barking, Lainey pulled herself together to go and see to her father.

Finding him standing at his bedroom window, staring out at the twilight, she put an arm around him and rested her head on his shoulder. 'Are you OK?' she whispered. 'Did something disturb you?'

It was a while before he answered, but it wasn't easy to make out what he was saying. It didn't matter, he was calm, and simply being with him was calming her too.

'Do you know where Mummy is?' he murmured softly. 'Can you see her, Lainey?'

Wishing she could, even if it was only to prove that the impossible could happen, Lainey said, 'I wish I could, Daddy. Can you?'

He didn't answer, only rested his head on hers and patted her hand.

Chapter Eleven

'What the hell's up with him?' Tierney muttered the following morning, watching Max leap into his car and roar off across the gravel, before veering up on to the grassy bank and all but losing control of the steering as he left the house.

Keeping her tone even, Lainey said, 'Dad's been having a chat with him . . .'

'Oh God, they are so immature,' Tierney broke in irritably. 'What does Max have to do to please Dad? He's got a job now. Oh no, don't tell me he's been fired already.'

'No, he's not due in until twelve today.' Lainey glanced down the hall to where Tom was emerging from the annexe. He'd rung while she was collecting Tierney from the station to let her know he was at the house and about to speak to Max. The call had left her feeling so wretched that she'd had a terrible struggle hiding it from Tierney. She just didn't know how she was going to face her family being torn apart by the person they all loved so much.

Now she was feeling bad for not having been there to offer Max some support, since his relationship with his father was already troubled enough. It might have helped him to feel a little less alone in the betrayal if she'd provided a silent reminder that she was as affected by this as he was. Except how could that possibly help anyone?

'Aren't you going to open your present from Nadia?' she said to Tierney, whose holdall was spilling over the floor as she tugged out her washing.

Presuming Tierney hadn't heard as she went to dump her clothes in the machine, Lainey repeated the question.

'OK, don't keep on,' Tierney snapped. 'I'll open it in a minute, all right? I'm trying to do this now. If I don't you'll just go on and on, nag, nag, nag. It's all you ever do. I wish I hadn't bothered to come back now.'

Finding herself wishing the same, Lainey swung the holdall up on to a counter top and was about to zip it back up again when a dress she hadn't seen before caught her eye.

'Wow!' she said, taking it out. 'This is pretty. Did you get it . . .'

'What are you doing, snooping in my bag?' Tierney seethed, snatching the dress away.

'For heaven's sake, I was just saying how nice it is. What's put you in such a bad mood?' A stroppy Tierney really wasn't what she needed this morning, in fact it was so far from what she could take after a near sleepless night that she feared for her rapidly vanishing self-control.

'I'm not in a bad mood, I'm just saying, that's all. God, what is it about everyone in this house? I can't do anything without someone having a go . . .'

'Oh shut up,' Lainey snapped.

Tierney's eyes narrowed dangerously, but for once she didn't answer back, simply slung the bag over her shoulder, picked up her phone and turned to leave.

'What about the present?' Lainey urged. 'You can't usually wait to open gifts from Nadia . . .'

Letting her bag drop to the floor, Tierney sighed irritably as she seized the prettily wrapped package as if it were some kind of punishment.

As Lainey watched her loosening the ribbon and peeling back the paper, she was experiencing an uneasy sense of disconnect from the people she loved. Tom and Tierney were both behaving like strangers; her father was in another world, her mother had gone and was never coming back . . . What was happening to her life? How was she supposed to go forward from here when she no longer knew where here was?

Shaking herself as Tierney opened a designer box to reveal the most beautiful gold-tone bangle, she said, 'Wow. Can I see it?'

Saying nothing, Tierney shoved the box and bangle across the bar.

Frowning, Lainey asked, 'Tierney, what's the matter with you? This is a *Chloe* bangle. Apart from being lovely, it probably cost a small fortune and it's a really thoughtful gift.'

Tierney's face was pinched, her irritation clearly mounting as she replied, 'Yeah, all right, it's lovely. What else do you want me to say?'

'Aren't you going to try it on?'

'Not right now.'

'Then how about texting Nadia to say thank you?'

'I'll do it when I get upstairs, OK? Why are you having a go at me? Just because I don't want to put it on now doesn't mean I'm not grateful. Honest to God, you're so in my face all the time . . .'

'Tierney.' Tom had entered. 'Don't speak to your mother like that.'

'Oh, so everyone's going to have a go at me now!' Tierney cried, throwing out her hands. 'Great! Go for it. It's so lovely to be home – *not*.'

Drawing her into an embrace, Tom said, 'Shall we try to calm things down a little?'

As Tierney's arms went round him Lainey's heart turned inside out. What kind of relationship did he have with Julia? Were they as close as he was with Tierney?

'No one's having a go at you,' he was saying, 'but I've no doubt Nadia put a lot of thought into that present . . .'

'And that's my fault? I didn't ask her to.'

'That's hardly the point, and you know it. So come on, what's eating you? Why are you so grumpy today?'

'I'm not, or I wasn't until *she* got on my case.'

'All right, that's enough,' Tom said, keeping an arm round her as she started to sob. 'Why don't you take your things upstairs and come back down when you're ready? There's something I need to discuss with you, and I'd rather you'd calmed down a bit before I get started.'

Apprehension instantly shone in Tierney's eyes. She turned in panic to her mother.

'It's OK,' Lainey told her, knowing it was anything but. 'Go on up now, or would you like me to come with you?'

Tierney seemed unsure.

Picking up the present and her phone, Lainey started to lead the way, but came to a stop as Tierney shouted, 'No, it's OK, I can go on my own,' and brushing past her mother she charged along the hall and up the stairs.

For several moments Lainey and Tom stood

listening to her footsteps, the slam of her door and the abrupt start of her music. Lainey was no more sure of what was going on in her mind now than she was of what might be in Tom's. She only knew that once again it felt as though everything was spiralling out of control and she had no idea what to do to bring it back.

In the end she was the first to move, going to pour herself a coffee. After the hours she'd spent awake in the night going over and over what she wanted to say to Tom, the reasoning, the pleading, the utter despair, she seemed unable now to summon anything more than, 'Would you like one?'

Looking round to find out what she was offering, he said, 'Thanks,' and pulling out a stool to sit the other side of the bar, he buried his face in his hands.

'Just in case you're in any doubt,' she began, 'I want you to know that I treasure our marriage, our children, our life together more than anything. It means the world to me, because I love you, or I did before I found out . . .'

As her voice faltered he said, 'You surely can't think you mean any less to me . . .'

'Actually, that is what I think, because I know I'd never be able to do to you what you've done to me.'

His eyes were fixed harshly on hers. 'You just don't get it, do you?' he said. 'You just can't see . . .' He broke off as the landline rang, but neither of them made a move to get it.

His eyes were still on hers and she began to feel as though she was drowning.

As though sensing it, he reached for her and pulled her into his arms. She shook as she sobbed, drily. She needed him to go on holding her like this, to tell her that everything was going to be all right, that he would stay if it was what she wanted. It was, more than anything, but only if he wanted it too.

'I'm sorry,' he murmured, 'I'm so sorry, I just need to get her through this chemo . . .'

'But how long's that going to be?'

'A few more weeks, then we can . . .'

'About time you made up,' Tierney commented, coming into the kitchen. 'It was going on just a bit too long, if you ask me.'

Tom's tone was ironic as he said, 'I don't recall that anyone did, but thanks for your opinion.'

Tierney slanted him one of her more surly looks.

At least she seems in a better mood now, Lainey was thinking. She's probably made up with Skye after some teenage row, or the time of the month blues were passing.

'So where are we going for my birthday dinner?' Tierney demanded, going to the fridge. 'Is it tonight, or tomorrow? I need to know so I can tell Maudie when she can come over.'

Lainey tensed as she looked at Tom. He surely wasn't going to let Tierney down over this.

'Well, now you're back we'll go tonight if you like,' he answered in as cheery a voice as he could muster.

Realising he'd probably intended to return to Kirsten this afternoon, Lainey moved away, furious that he could even consider leaving the house so soon after telling Tierney about his other life.

'So, what's the lecture about?' Tierney asked, going to plonk herself in her father's chair at the table.

Tom frowned.

'You said just now that you wanted to talk to me,' Tierney reminded him. 'So here I am.'

He glanced at Lainey, who gave a brief shake of her head. If they were taking Tierney out to dinner tonight she didn't want the occasion spoiled by his news. It would just have to wait.

'OK, if you've changed your minds that's cool by me,' Tierney was saying. 'So where shall we go tonight? I was thinking about the pub we went to for Stacy's birthday.'

Leaving them to discuss it, Lainey ran upstairs to get her father ready for his visit to Age Concern, already wondering if Tom would stay the night or drive back to Kirsten in the early hours. She had to find a way to make him stay, but if even if he did, how was she going to feel knowing that he'd rather be somewhere else? She couldn't even be sure he'd sleep in their bed, or that she actually wanted him to. Of course she did, she simply couldn't bear the thought that they might never make love again, but on the other hand, if they did, how was she going to feel when he left in the morning?

Finding her father dozing in his chair, a photograph of her mother lying in his lap, she picked it up and felt more tears tightening her throat as she gazed into Alessandra's beautiful eyes. She tried to imagine what she might say to her now, but there were no answers in the silence, no advice she could call on. There was only the fact that she was going to Italy, and that her mother would have strongly disapproved.

What were you hiding? Lainey whispered in her heart. *What happened that you could never talk about? Did you do wrong to someone, or did they do wrong to you? You look so happy with Daddy, so whatever sadness,*

*regrets, demons you brought with you from Italy must
surely have been overcome . . .*

In spite of everything that was happening, or
maybe because of it, the pull of Tuoro, the small
town, village, of her birth, seemed to be growing
stronger by the day. Perhaps it was the need to get
away for a while that was driving her desire to go.
She was going to hate being there without Tom, but
while he was supporting Kirsten through chemo
she had to do something to distract herself from
the fear that he was using this as a way to break
away from her.

Tierney was upstairs in her bedroom. Maudie had
gone home a few minutes ago, and though Tierney
knew she should call after being so short with her,
she wasn't ready to apologise yet. Anyway, it wasn't
her fault they'd fallen out. Maudie shouldn't have
kept going on about her, Tierney, always trying to
be like Skye and doing things she didn't really want
to do. Like she didn't have a mind of her own. If
she hadn't wanted to go with Guy on Saturday she
wouldn't have, and just because she wasn't in a big
hurry to see him again didn't mean she'd gone off
him. It only meant she didn't want to rush things.
Plus she kept feeling really bad about Nadia, but
she hadn't told anyone that, not even Skye.

It would definitely be better if she went to Italy
with her parents, and since she'd texted Skye as
soon as Maudie had stormed off to ask if she could
come too, it was too late now to invite Maudie,
especially when Skye had texted straight back to
say *deffo, yes*.

That was great, they'd have a totally fab time,
unless Max did end up coming and decided to bring

Christie. Should she warn Skye about that? Actually, why bother when Skye and Max were only shag buddies, and it wasn't like Skye didn't have other partners too.

Looking up as the familiar warble of Skype broke into the room, a shudder of nerves coasted so rapidly through her that it made her feel slightly sick. He'd said he'd call at five, and here he was. He'd also told her how he wanted her to be dressed when she connected. It was feeling totally wicked and weird and she really wasn't sure she wanted to answer.

As the ringing stopped she started to panic. He was going to think she wasn't interested now, and she was.

To her relief he called again.

'Well, well,' he murmured as soon as her image got through to his screen, 'look at my guilty pleasure tonight.'

Dizzied by her own daring, sitting there with no top on, she said, 'Hi, how are you?'

'How about totally hot for you?'

Kind of liking the answer, she stole a glance from under her lashes. He was so amazingly to die for that she couldn't understand why he made her nervous.

'When am I going to see you again?' he asked. 'I think it'll have to be soon, don't you?'

Not sure what to say to that, she only shrugged and wondered when would be the best time to tell him she was going to Italy. Before she could make a decision her mother's voice cut across everything.

'Tierney?' she called, knocking on the door.

'Oh my God!' Tierney gulped, and rapidly disconnecting she grabbed her T-shirt and tugged it over her head. 'Yeah, what do you want?' she shouted, shaking so badly she could hardly get her arms in the sleeves.

'I was hoping we could have a chat,' Lainey answered.

'What about?' she asked, kicking her bra under the bed.

'Well, going to Italy for one. I wondered if you'd decided who you'd like to take.'

'Oh, Skye's coming,' she answered, going to open the door. Seeing Lainey's face, her eyes widened with alarm. 'Have you been crying?' she demanded accusingly.

Lainey smiled. 'Of course not, I just got something in my eye.'

'Where's Dad?'

Lainey took a breath. 'He's . . . He had a call . . .'

Tierney's face paled. 'He's gone away again, hasn't he? When's he coming back? I thought we were going out tonight . . .'

'We are, but he won't be able to join us.'

'Why not? Where's he gone? What's so important that he has to go now?'

Putting an arm around her, Lainey said, 'I want you to come downstairs. Zav's there and we need to have a little chat.'

'Oh my God, Mum, Dad's not leaving us, is he? Please say he's not . . .' Her voice shook with panic.

'Sssh,' Lainey soothed.

'He can't, I won't let him.'

Lainey smiled past the lump in her throat.

'Why didn't he come and see me before he left?' Tierney demanded, as they started down the stairs.

'He wanted to,' Lainey assured her, 'but there was a bit of an emergency with someone he knows . . .'

'Who?'

'That's what I'm about to tell you. Now, please try to calm down, for your own sake as well as Zav's.'

As they walked into the kitchen Lainey's heart contracted to find Max at the table with Zav. His eyes came to hers and she could see straight away how angry he was with his father.

'Are you OK?' the two boys asked, almost in unison.

Lainey smiled. 'I'm fine,' she assured them, even though she wasn't. Thank goodness none of them had been around when Tom had got the call telling him Kirsten had been rushed to hospital: she wouldn't have wanted them to hear what she'd said. She didn't even want to remember it, while fearing Tom would probably never forget it.

'With any luck she might die,' she'd blurted.

His shock had been no greater than her own. 'You don't mean that,' he'd said darkly.

'No, of course not,' she'd cried, burying her face in her hands. 'I'm sorry. I don't know what came over me. I understand that she needs you now, that Julia does too, but we're supposed to be taking Tierney out this evening. What are you going to tell her?'

'The truth,' he'd replied. 'Why on earth would I tell her anything else?'

'But you can't just come out with it and then rush off as though it's no big deal. She's going to be traumatised by this . . .'

'Don't you think I realise that? But what do you want me to do? I can't pretend I didn't receive the call . . .'

'Go!' she'd cut in sharply. 'Just go and leave the children to me. I'll tell them myself . . .'

'I don't want you to do that.'

'It's not about what you want. It's about what they need, and frankly if I'm going to be the only parent they have around for the foreseeable future perhaps I am the one who should be dealing with this.'

He hadn't argued any further; he hadn't even attempted to embrace her before leaving. He'd simply said, 'I'll call you later,' and then he was gone.

Now, she was asking herself if she should do this while Max was there. Asking him to leave was only going to make him feel even more shut out than he probably already did, and she didn't want to do that to him. And what about her father, sitting there in his chair smiling absently out of the window? Should she break the news in front of him? He almost certainly wouldn't register what was being said, unless Tierney started shouting, of course, which was highly possible.

Deciding it was probably a good idea for Max to stay, since he might be of some help with Tierney, should it be needed, she sat down at the table with Tierney, feeling Zav's eyes watching her curiously.

Apparently sensing what was about to happen, Max said, 'Would you rather I left? I mean . . .'

'No, no, you're a part of this family,' Lainey reminded him, adding, 'whether you like it or not.' She was the only one who smiled at her attempt at humour.

She looked at Zav, who was still seeming more baffled than anxious, though he clearly sensed something was up. 'OK,' she said, finding herself taking heart from Max's presence, even though she still didn't know the details of what had transpired between him and Tom. 'I'd hoped Dad would be the one to tell you this,' she began, 'but he's not here, and so . . .'

'Oh my God, you really are splitting up,' Tierney panicked.

'Just listen, T,' Max said gruffly.

Tierney shot him a look. 'You know what this is about?' she challenged.

He nodded. 'Dad told me this morning.'

She turned back to her mother. 'Is Dad ill?' she cried. 'Is that why he keeps going away, because he has to get treatment?'

'No, he isn't ill,' Lainey answered. 'Now please stop trying to second-guess what I'm about to tell you and let me get on with it.'

Perching on the edge of her seat, Tierney clasped her hands tightly together and waited.

'It seems,' Lainey said, realising she had no idea how any of this was going to come out, 'that Dad has another . . .' She'd been about to say family, but couldn't bring herself to, not yet. 'Well, he has a daughter who I didn't know anything about until the beginning of last week.'

Tierney's jaw dropped as her face turned white. 'You're kidding,' she murmured.

Lainey was looking at Zav, wanting to be sure he'd understood so far.

'How old is she?' Tierney asked.

Max gave a snort of contempt. 'You're going to love this,' he told her.

Regretting he was there now, Lainey said, 'She's sixteen, apparently, and her name's Julia.'

Stunned, Tierney looked from her to Max and back again. 'Like the same age as me?' she said, as though needing to be sure she'd heard right.

Lainey nodded.

'I don't believe it,' Tierney declared. 'I mean, how can he have a daughter the same age as me?'

'He can't,' Zav told her knowledgeably.

Not sure how Zav had deduced that, Lainey said, 'That's where he's had to go today, to be with Julia and her . . . and her mother.'

Tierney's shock was hard to watch. 'You mean . . . Oh my God, Mum, are you saying that he's gone to live with them?'

Lainey glanced at Max. 'To be honest, I'm not sure what he's doing,' she replied. 'I don't know what he said to you, Max . . .'

Max only shrugged. 'I didn't give him a chance to say much,' he confessed. 'I was just like, no way do I want to hear about how he cheated on my mother *twice*. Sorry,' he muttered to Lainey, 'but you know what I mean.'

Of course she did, and she felt ashamed that it had taken her so long to realise how Max would see this. To him it must seem like he and his mother had hardly mattered at all back then, and for all Lainey knew he was right.

'So he was cheating on you *and* Emma?' Tierney's statement was also a question.

Glancing uneasily at Max, Lainey said, 'I think it would be more accurate to put it Max's way and say that he was doubly cheating on Emma.'

'So what happened when *Julia* was born?' Tierney cried angrily. 'Is she older or younger than me?'

'A couple of months older, apparently. I don't know, Dad hasn't told me the details . . .'

'If he does,' Max cut in scathingly, 'he'll have to own up to lying to us for years, and he definitely won't want to do that.'

Lainey put a hand to her head, needing to stop it throbbing.

'Dad doesn't lie,' Zav said loyally.

Lainey's eyes went tenderly to his. She wouldn't contradict him, because she had no desire to push his dad off his pedestal. Luckily neither Max nor Tierney seemed inclined to crush him either.

'Have you met this *Julia*?' Tierney asked.

Lainey shook her head. 'I don't really know anything about her, apart from her age – and who her mother is.'

'You mean you know her mother?'

'No. She was . . . She presented an arts programme that Dad appeared on. It'll be how they met, I'm sure.'

'At the same time as he was seeing you,' Tierney snorted in disgust.

'It must have been before,' Lainey replied, feeling the betrayal so deeply that she wanted desperately to stop this now and go upstairs to be alone.

'Do they know about us?' Zav asked.

'Yes, I'm sure they do,' Lainey told him.

'Do we have to meet them?' Tierney wanted to know.

'You can count me out if we do,' Max growled.

Dragging her eyes from him, Lainey said, 'None of us has to if we don't want to.'

'I definitely don't,' Tierney declared. 'Frankly I just want them to fuck off and die.'

Lainey winced as she said, 'Actually, Julia's mother – her name's Kirsten – has cancer, which is why Dad's having to spend so much time there.'

'He never told me that,' Max protested.

Lainey looked at him, not sure what to say, but she knew what he was thinking, because she found herself thinking it too. What if it wasn't true? What if it was just an excuse to try and make the break easier?

Realising that was nonsense, that Tom would surely never tell such a terrible lie, she pushed it out of her mind.

'When's he coming back?' Zav asked.

'Who cares?' Tierney retorted. 'He's been cheating on Mum, on all of us, for years, so why would you even want to see him?'

Zav's eyes filled with tears as he looked at Lainey.

Opening her arms for him to come and sit on her lap, she held him tightly and fought down her own emotions.

'He won't just leave us, will he, Mum?' Zav begged.

Wishing there was a way to offer comfort without lying, Lainey said, 'I'm not really sure.'

An awful silence fell as the uncertainty of what they were facing seemed to drift around them like ghosts.

'So what happens now?' Tierney asked in the end.

Lainey shrugged. She only wished she knew. 'We go to Italy, as planned,' she answered, 'and maybe by the time we come home . . . Well, maybe things will be different with Kirsten, and Dad will have made up his mind what he wants to do.'

Max said, 'Why should he get the choice of whether he stays or goes? He's hardly earned it.'

Lainey couldn't argue with that.

'I really hate him for this,' Tierney seethed. 'As far as I'm concerned I never want to see him again,' and leaping up from her chair she ran out of the room.

Had Zav not burst into tears, Lainey might have

gone after her. 'I don't want him to leave,' Zav wailed. 'I want him to stay here with us. Can't you make him, Mum? Please.'

Only wishing she knew how, Lainey said, 'I'm sure he'll be back soon, so you can have a chat with him yourself, OK?'

Zav nodded, but didn't stop crying. 'I wish this Julia and her mother didn't exist,' he sobbed. 'Everything was all right until they came along.'

'I know,' Lainey soothed. She looked at Max, and could see how hard he was struggling too.

'I think what's really important for you two,' Lainey said, hugging Zav closer and wishing she could take Max's hand, 'Tierney as well,' she added, 'is to know that whatever happens with Julia and her mother, it's never going to change how much Dad loves you.' She was sure of that, she had to be, or there wouldn't be any point to anything any more.

'Tierney and Zav maybe,' Max said gruffly, 'but definitely not me.'

'That's not true . . .'

'Yes it is. No, it's OK, Lainey, I get what you're trying to do, but you don't have to. I'm cool with it. I've been here before, but you haven't, so it's you who matters now, and what he's doing to you.'

Feeling her throat tightening at his sensitivity, she told him, 'I'll be fine, don't worry about me.'

Looking up at her with teary eyes, Zav said, 'Dad loves you too, doesn't he?'

Hugging him to her, Lainey tried to think what to say, but there was nothing that he'd want to hear, so she simply kissed his head and tightened her embrace.

After a while he asked, 'Can I ring Dad?'

'Of course. I'm not sure if you'll get through

212

straight away, but you can always leave him a message,' and connecting to Tom's mobile, she handed her own to Zav.

'Dad, it's me,' he said shakily into the voicemail, 'please don't leave us. We really love you and we want you to stay.' As he rang off his eyes went to Max, as though, being the eldest and so like their father, he was the next best thing. 'Will you come and watch me play cricket later?' he asked.

'Course I will, mate,' Max responded, 'be glad to. We can go and have a knock-around now if you like.'

Sniffing as he straightened himself up, Zav nodded and went into the utility room to get the bats.

'Thanks,' Lainey said quietly to Max.

He only shrugged, and following his brother outside he left Lainey preparing herself to go upstairs and deal with Tierney.

Tierney was lying on her bed, trying not to hear the Skype ringtone that kept burbling out of the computer every couple of minutes. She knew it was him, but she couldn't speak to him now.

She didn't want to speak to anyone, especially not her dad. If he thought she was ever going to have anything to do with *Julia* and her stupid mother, whatever her name was, he could bloody well think again. So what if she had cancer, it still didn't change the fact that he'd been cheating on Mum for years, and her mother just didn't deserve it. God, she hated him. He was such a hypocrite, always going on about morals and standards and stuff, and all the time he was having an affair with someone he'd been seeing since *before she was born*.

She couldn't bear to think how that must be making her mother feel. She didn't want anyone to hurt her mum, ever, because annoying and random as she could be, she was totally brilliant too, and there wasn't anyone Tierney loved more in the world. She used to love her dad the same, but not any more. No way did she ever want to see him again, even if Zav did. He was history to her now, totally over.

Feeling another rush of tears welling up, she rolled off the bed and crawled across the room to pick up her phone. It was going off almost as regularly as the computer, telling her she had texts. If there was one from her dad she'd delete it.

The first was from Skye. *Parents flying to Morocco on Friday, so getting train to yours. Sx*

For no reason she could think of, the message made her cry again. Her heart skipped a beat when she saw the next text was from him. *Trying to Skype. Where are you? Missing you, my beautiful girl.*

She read it again, and considered sending a reply asking him if they could run away together. Would he want to do that? She'd promise him anything if he did, just to get out of here.

Feeling all fussed and horrible at the thought of leaving her mother, she quickly scrolled on to her next message. It was from Maudie, saying sorry for the things she'd said earlier.

Wishing desperately that she'd asked Maudie to come to Italy now, she started to call her, then stopped when she realised she couldn't speak to anyone yet.

The last text was from Skye again, giving page numbers she should go straight to in the dreaded book.

She didn't want to read any more of it.

Everything was going wrong.

Where was her dad? Why hadn't *he* sent her a message?

'Tierney, can I come in?' her mother asked from the other side of the door.

'No!' Tierney shouted, without really knowing why. 'Go away.'

'Please let me in.'

'I said go away.'

'We need to talk.'

'You might, I don't.'

There were a few moments of quiet before her mother said, 'Well, if you change your mind . . .'

'I won't.' Tears were streaming down her face again. She had no idea why she was being mean to her mother, when really all she wanted was to go out there and try to make her feel better.

Getting to her feet, she used her fingers to wipe her eyes, and the back of a hand for her nose as she went to turn off the computer. She stood still for a moment, trying to collect herself. 'All right,' she said shakily, 'you can come in now.'

When nothing happened she went to open the door. The landing was empty; her mother had already gone, and now she hated herself so much she just wanted to curl up in a tiny ball and die.

Chapter Twelve

Lainey's smile was hesitant as she joined Father Michael on a bench not far from her mother's grave. It was the first time she'd seen him since the funeral, and she felt guilty for never going to church on Sunday, even though she wasn't Catholic and he probably didn't expect to see her there.

She'd just left a bunch of lilies on Alessandra's marble tombstone, and spoken to her softly in her heart as she'd arranged them. *Love from me and Daddy, the children too, of course. If you can see us, if you know what's happening, please tell me what to do.*

Her only response had come from a faint stirring of a breeze.

Are you angry about me being here, at the church? Do you know what I'm about to do?

Though Lainey didn't believe in the afterlife, or didn't think she did, she felt it best to keep an open mind.

'Thank you for seeing me,' she said to Father Michael.

'It's always a pleasure,' he replied, smiling with the reassuring mix of kindness and wisdom that had helped her so much during her mother's final days. 'How have you been keeping?'

'Yes, fine, thanks,' she said, feeling the strain of

the lie stretching through her like a pain. 'And you?'

He sighed softly. 'Oh, I'm not going to grumble,' he replied. 'What news of your dear father? Is he still with you, at Bannerleigh Cross?'

'Oh yes. It's his home, and I hope it always will be.' She didn't want to believe Tom would end up forcing a sale, but with the way things were she couldn't be sure of anything. 'His dementia is worsening,' she admitted. 'He's very detached, hardly ever speaks, apart from to recite poetry at times.'

Father Michael's eyes softened with regret. 'It is a tragedy indeed when such a brilliant mind falls victim to this horrible disease,' he murmured. 'And what about those sisters of yours, are they helping to take care of him?'

Lainey merely raised her eyebrows.

'Ah, I see things haven't changed on that front. It's lucky he has you and Tom, so it is.' He leaned in mischievously. 'Can you tell me when the next book's coming out? I'd like to impress a couple of colleagues with my inside info.'

Wondering what he'd make of the other inside info she could give him, she said, 'It's due at the beginning of December.'

Where would they be by then? How was she going to stop herself breaking apart?

Father Michael was twinkling. 'I'll look forward to it,' he promised, 'but I'm sure you didn't come here to talk about that. So what can I do for you?'

Lainey's mouth felt dry, her insides liquid and shaky as she said, 'It probably won't surprise you to hear it's about my mother.'

'No, I can't say it does, may God rest her soul.'

She smiled gratefully. 'I think you know,' she began, 'well, obviously you know that she came here from Italy, just after I was born.'

He nodded that he did.

'You probably also know that she never talked about the family she left behind, at least not to me.'

He neither confirmed nor denied it.

'Well, the thing is,' she went on, 'I've decided to go to Tuoro – that's where she was born – to see what I can find out about her and . . . well, maybe about my father too. I mean my birth father, obviously, not Peter.'

He nodded understandingly.

She glanced down at her hands, summoning the courage to come to the point. She was sure he already knew what it was, but in his typical priestly way, he was allowing her to get there in her own time.

'I know I'm not really supposed to ask this,' she continued, 'but before she died did my mother ever say anything about what had happened to make her leave Italy the way she did?'

Taking her hand, he held it gently between both of his as he said, 'Even if I were allowed to break the seal of the confessional, which of course I am not, I'm afraid I still wouldn't be able to give you the answers you're seeking.'

Lainey's eyes gazed deeply into his, absorbing his words and realising that he'd answered her question; at the last her mother still hadn't spoken of what she'd kept hidden for almost forty years.

'Do you think I'm wrong to try to find out about my roots?' she asked.

He gave it some thought, tilting his silvery head to one side, while still cradling her hand. 'I think it would be highly unusual if you weren't curious,' he replied in the end.

She waited for more, but it seemed that was all he had to say for now. 'Tom thinks . . . He was all for me going to Italy a while ago, he was planning to come with me, but now he seems to have . . . reservations.'

'Did he say what they were?'

'He thinks my mother could have been trying to protect me from something.'

'And you don't agree with that?'

'I don't disagree, because of course it seems likely he's right, but if she was . . . Whatever happened was over thirty-six years ago. I can't see how it could hurt me now, and wouldn't you want to find out who you really were, if you were me?'

He allowed some moments to pass as he considered the question. 'Yes, I probably would,' he replied. 'I'd go even further and say that as they're your roots, you have a right to know more about them.'

Lainey's breath caught on a dry sob as she smiled. She'd had no idea until now just how much his approval would mean to her. 'Thank you,' she whispered.

He patted her hand and squeezed it gently. 'Is that all that's troubling you, Elenora?'

Lainey found her throat tightening. Only her mother called her by her full name; it was the first time she'd heard it in over a year.

'It isn't, is it?' he prompted.

Her head went down as she fought back the tears. She so desperately wanted to tell him about Tom and Kirsten and Julia that it almost came tumbling out.

'Perhaps I can help,' he suggested.

She shook her head. 'Thank you, but I'll be fine. I just . . . Well, I hope some time in Italy will help to straighten things out for me in more ways than one.'

'Then I shall pray that it does, and if you change your mind and would like to talk, you know where I am.'

As she walked back to the car she felt the phone vibrating in her hand, and opened her messages to find one from Tierney saying she was going to Maudie's for the night, and another from Stacy confirming that she could fly to Italy on Saturday, but could probably only stay for a week.

'The good news, though,' Stacy continued, 'is that I'll be back in Gloucestershire tonight, so I'll come straight to you from the train. My car's at the station, so don't worry about picking me up.'

Though she'd spoken at length to Stacy over the past couple of days, telling her everything that was happening, the thought of actually seeing her was as uplifting as anything could be at this time. Things never felt quite so bad when her best friend was around.

By the time she got home she'd received several calls from Tom; she hadn't taken them since she hadn't wanted to speak to him while driving. She knew already, because he'd texted her this morning, that Kirsten had been discharged from hospital, but he hadn't said when, or even if he was coming home again.

Surely he'd be back before they went to Italy? He knew how upset the children were now she'd broken the news, so she couldn't imagine he'd want a whole month to pass before seeing them again. If they actually stayed for a month, and she wasn't entirely sure at this stage that they would.

'*Mum!* I'm not feeling the love,' Zav cried indignantly as she walked through the door.

Looking up from her phone, she quickly put it down and went to give him a hug and a kiss. 'Better?' she asked, smoothing his hair. What had he been saying? Her mind was all over the place – she didn't seem able to concentrate on anything any more.

'Really soppy,' he told her, but his dear, handsome face was gazing up at her lovingly, showing he wasn't cross, only teasing – and worried, and confused and not quite as sure of himself as he'd been a couple of days ago. 'So, are you coming?' he asked.

'Where?'

'To feed the ducks with me and Grandpa and Max. They've already gone down to the pond, so we'll have to run to catch them up.'

Kissing him again, she said, 'Why don't you go on ahead? I have a few calls to make.'

He stayed where he was. 'To Dad?' he asked uncertainly.

She nodded. 'One of them, yes. Have you heard from him today?'

He shrugged. 'Kind of. He rang to ask how I was, so I told him I thought he should come home, but then we got cut off.'

'Didn't he call you back?'

'No, he texted to say he'd be home as soon as he could. Do you want to see it?' And sliding his phone out of his pocket he handed it over.

Please don't worry, son, I'll be back as soon as I can. If I don't make it before you go to Italy have a lovely time, take care of Mum and Tierney, and remember how much I love you. PS call any time you want to while you're away, don't worry about how much it's costing.

Lainey's insides were so tight with anger and despair it was hard to speak. So he wasn't coming back before they left, or not by the sound of it, and he'd told Zav by *text*.

As soon as Zav had gone, she snatched up her phone. 'What the hell do you think you're doing?' she cried when she finally got hold of him. 'I've seen your text to Zav. He's a child. He needs you . . .'

'Lainey, I'm doing my best here,' he shouted over her. 'It's not easy this end either, and frankly, you're in a better position to cope right now than Kirsten is.'

'Is that so? Well, frankly, I shouldn't have to be coping without you and nor should the children. Have you spoken to Tierney yet?'

'I've tried, but she doesn't want to listen. Just exactly what did you tell them?'

'What the hell do you think I told them? Isn't the fact that you have a daughter by another woman enough to shatter their world? They trusted you, Tom, as did I. We believed in you in a way you clearly never deserved. Actually, do you know what, I don't want to have this conversation any more,' and before he could object she ended the call and turned off her phone.

A moment later the landline rang, but the machine was on and she left it on as she poured herself a large glass of wine and carried it outside. There was nothing to be gained from speaking to him now; they clearly couldn't communicate civilly and hearing his frustration, knowing Kirsten might be listening, was too much for her to take.

'I'm going to focus on Italy now,' she told Stacy

when she arrived. 'We leave on Saturday . . .' Her voice faltered, and Stacy putting an arm around her shoulders made it even harder to hold on. 'I wish Tierney would come home,' she said. 'She's not handling this very well, and we really need to talk.'

'Where is she now?'

'At Maudie's. I spoke to Cass earlier, Maudie's mother, to ask her to call if Tierney didn't seem herself. To be honest, I wanted to be sure Tierney was actually there. The last thing we need is her running off to London or somewhere to try and punish her father. And me. For some reason she seems to be angry with me too.'

'Mm, she probably can't deal with seeing you hurt,' Stacy commented, refilling their glasses. 'It's making her feel helpless, and probably guilty too, in the way kids do when their parents are having problems.'

Lainey nodded agreement. 'Do you think,' she began, dangerously close to the edge again, 'that this really is the end for me and Tom?' *Please say no, please, please, please say no even if you don't mean it.*

'What's difficult,' Stacy replied, 'is not knowing what he actually *wants* to happen when Kirsten gets through this – *if* she gets through, and we still don't know how serious it is. I take it you haven't asked him that question.'

Lainey shook her head. 'There hasn't been much of a chance, and to be honest, I really don't want to hear the details of what's been going on all these years. Much less do I want to see him break down over another woman. I know it's cowardly, and I'll have to go through it at some point, but for the moment I just can't bring myself to.'

Understanding that, Stacy said, 'This trip to Italy

223

couldn't have come at a better time. The last thing you need is to be sitting around here, waiting to find out what's happening over there.'

Not denying it, Lainey said, 'You know, it keeps reminding me of when you and Derek first broke up. He'd never come right out and admit it was over between you. He just kept stringing you along, letting you think you could work things out . . .' She was so tense all of a sudden that her whole body seemed to ache with it, and as a terrible sense of dread came over her she could barely move, or think past it. What had been so particularly bad for Stacy was how cruel Derek had been in the end. Was Tom going to reach that point too? Would there come a time when he really didn't care about her feelings at all?

'Tom isn't Derek,' Stacy said softly. 'He has way more qualities and though this is going to be hard to hear, one of them is that he's trying to be there for Kirsten and Julia at the same time as trying to keep things together with you.'

Lainey smiled weakly. 'It's not going to work, though, is it, because whatever happens now, we can never go back. Kirsten and Julia will always be there and I guess we'll just have to wait and see who he really wants to be with.'

'Don't listen to Maudie,' Skye was saying into the phone, 'she's just a sad little virgin who doesn't know the first thing about blokes.' Tierney turned away from Maudie, afraid she could hear. 'You're mad about him really,' Skye ranted on, 'it's just all this stuff with your rents that's messing with your head. I'm telling you, it screwed me up big time when mine broke up, but then I realised, well someone told me, actually, that I had to stop going on like they were my responsibility. And you have to do the same. They're grown-ups, they can figure stuff out for themselves, and if they can't, it's not your fault. You've got your own life to lead, just like I have mine, and look at me now. I've got all the freedom I could wish for, and it's really helped me to grow up.'

Tierney couldn't deny that, since Skye was the most mature person for her age that she knew. She wanted to be like that too, totally cool about stuff, never letting anything get to her, but she wasn't making a very good job of it right now.

'I'll be there tomorrow,' Skye reminded her. 'We can have a chat then, but meantime, definitely go to see Mr Grey.' This was what she'd started calling Guy. 'It's what he wants, and you know it's what you want really.'

If it was, then how come the whole thing had started creeping her out?

After ringing off, she turned back to Maudie.

'You're going to go, aren't you?' Maudie challenged, her blue eyes glittering harshly behind their black-rimmed frames.

'I don't know,' Tierney mumbled. 'I've said I would . . .'

'So what? You're mad getting into this if it's not what you want. He's just a perv, really. OK, a dead-fit perv, but he's getting off on some seriously weird stuff.'

Though Tierney couldn't deny it, she wasn't really thinking about him any more. Her mind was on Julia and what she might be like. Whoever she was, Tierney already hated her for taking their dad away. She had no right to, even if her mother was sick.

He belonged at home with her, Zav and Max – and with Mum, who was totally destroyed . . .

Tears welled up in her eyes. She couldn't bear to think of her mother hurting, it was the worst thing in the world, but she didn't want to talk to her either, and she especially didn't want to talk to her dad, who kept texting and calling.

'Please call me back, Tierney,' he'd urged her earlier. 'I promise I'd come there if I could, but things are difficult here. Julia's not as strong as you, she needs . . .' She'd deleted the message at that point, because what the hell did she care about Julia?

All she cared about, in fact, was what she was going to do tonight. 'I promised him I'd be outside the Hope and Anchor by eight,' she told Maudie.

'So text to say you can't be there now,' Maudie retorted. 'Make up an excuse like you have to go somewhere with your mum, or you're not very well.'

Tierney's eyes fell to her phone. The truth was, the only person she really wanted to see was her dad, though she'd never tell him that, and anyway it couldn't happen while he was with Julia, so she might as well go and see Guy. Except she didn't really want to see him, even though she'd told him on the phone that she did, and now he'd driven all this way. He'd even booked them into a hotel for the night, and Maudie was going to be her alibi.

Opening up her messages, she pressed in a text. *Really, really sorry, but crisis at home so can't make it.* Bracing herself, she hit send.

A minute or so later she received a reply. *I don't believe it. Am already here and mad to see you. Can't you work something out?*

Tierney's eyes went anxiously to Maudie's. 'What shall I say?'

Maudie thought. 'Just ignore it,' she decided. 'It's not like he's going to go charging up to the house to get you, is it?'

True, he wouldn't do that, but all the same . . . 'He'll be so pissed off.'

'And? He'll get over it.'

Tierney started as her phone rang. Seeing it was her dad she immediately clicked on. 'I don't want to speak to you,' she growled. 'I hate you for what you've done . . .'

'Tierney, we need to talk . . .'

'About *Julia*, great, like I'm dying to hear all about her. You're a hypocrite and a liar and if you think . . .'

'Will you please listen . . .'

'No! I don't want to hear anything you have to say, especially not about her.'

'You've never even met her . . .'

'And I'm not going to either. She's nothing to do with me, and nor are you now, so go away and leave me alone.' As she ended the call she broke into tearing sobs. 'I hate him,' she seethed. 'What he's done, the lies he's told, it just makes a mockery of everything.'

Looking on dolefully, Maudie said, 'I don't think it means he doesn't care about you, though.'

Reaching for her phone as it bleeped with another text, she saw it was from Guy and passed it to Maudie.

Can you meet me in the morning?

'If it weren't for my mum,' Tierney said, 'I'd run away with him now, but I can't leave her to cope with this on her own. It wouldn't be fair, she hasn't done anything wrong, and I've been really mean to her . . .' She started to cry again as she thought of

227

how short she'd been with her mother earlier, when she must be going through hell.

Still holding Tierney's mobile, Maudie checked it as it rang. 'It's her,' she announced. 'Do you want to answer it?'

Sniffing as she nodded, Tierney sat up and held out her hand. 'Hey,' she said as she clicked on.

'Are you all right?' her mother asked.

'No. Dad just rang. He wants to talk, but I told him I'm not interested in anything he has to say.'

Her mother sighed. 'Maybe it's a good thing we're going away,' she said. 'A bit of distance, a change of environment, might do us all some good.'

A spark of hope leapt in Tierney's chest. 'So is he coming?'

There was a pause before Lainey replied, 'No, he's not coming.'

Tierney's heart sank. 'Mum, you're crying,' she wailed. 'Please don't cry. We don't need him there. It'll be all right.'

'I'm not crying,' Lainey assured her.

Knowing she was, Tierney said, 'Do you want me to come home?'

'It's OK, you stay and have a chat with Maudie. I'll be fine.'

'Are you sure?'

'Of course I am.'

'Love you.'

'Love you too. Goodnight.'

'Goodnight,' Tierney whispered back, knowing that all she wanted in the world right now was her mother's arms around her.

After ringing off she swung her legs over the side of the bed and pushed her hands through her hair.

'What are you going to do about you know who?' Maudie asked worriedly. 'He's still waiting for an answer.'

Picking up her phone, Tierney began pressing in a text.

Everything going mental here. Sorry. Will get in touch again when back from Italy. 'There,' she said, passing it over for Maudie to read, 'satisfied?' and telling herself everything was going to feel ten times better once Skye arrived around lunchtime tomorrow, she went into the bathroom to turn on the shower.

The following morning Lainey was upstairs packing Zav's suitcase. Though he was supposed to be helping, she'd agreed to let him go with Max to collect Tierney and on to the station for Skye. He seemed to be seeing Max as a Tom substitute, and the way Max seemed happy to be there for him was very much to Max's credit. She knew how much it would please Tom, if he could see it, though his feelings would surely come heavily loaded with guilt for causing so much insecurity and heartache in his younger son that he needed Max's support.

As far as she knew, there had been no more contact between Tom and Max since Max had stormed off the other day. She was sure, though, that Tom would have tried to talk to him, much as he had with Tierney and Zav, but it was pointless attempting this by phone. They needed to see him, to have him show them he still cared and that no matter what, he would always be their dad.

More than anything right now she wanted to hear his car pull up outside, to know he was back, even if it was only to see them before they left in the morning. Better still would be to hear him say he'd changed his mind and was coming after all, except, given what was hanging over them now, would that really be a good idea?

Reaching for her mobile as it rang, she saw it was him and clicked on.

'You rang earlier?' he said, without a hello.

She had, but hadn't got through, and since she hadn't really known what she wanted to say she'd rung off without leaving a message. 'It was nothing,' she told him. 'Or actually, I suppose I was wondering how things were over there.'

'Really?' He sounded incredulous. 'And you care?'

Stung, she said, 'Please don't take that attitude with me. I'm trying . . .'

'All right, all right, I'm sorry,' he cut in sharply. 'It's been a long night and actually, if you must know, things aren't all that great.'

Not entirely sure how she felt about that, given Kirsten's condition, she said, 'So is she . . .? Is this a primary?'

'No, it's a secondary, but I don't want to get into discussing it now. I need to get back there, and anyway this reception's not good enough. Can you hear me OK?'

'Yes, I can hear you perfectly. So I'm guessing we're not going to see you before we go.'

Sighing, he said, 'I promise you, if I could make it happen, I would, but I'm afraid I can't. I'll try ringing the children again . . . Actually, I finally managed to speak to Max last night, but he ended up telling me to go fuck myself, so I can't say it went well.'

'I'm sorry about that,' she responded, without really meaning it.

'I've got to wonder, Lainey,' he continued, 'exactly what you've been telling them.'

Outraged, she cried, 'What *I'm* telling them? Can I remind you, you're the one who spoke to Max in the first place, not me, and it seems you somehow forgot to tell him that Kirsten has cancer. Just how did that manage to slip your mind, Tom?'

'I don't know what you're trying to imply with that,' he raged back, 'but for your information, I didn't get as far as that before he stormed out. And now we know what difference it makes, absolutely none, because he still won't speak to me, and nor will Tierney.'

'And I suppose you're about to blame me for Tierney being hurt and angry too. Well, before you do . . .'

'I'm not going to do anything of the sort,' he broke in furiously, 'and this is getting us nowhere. The reason I rang is to tell you that I've left money in the top right-hand drawer of my desk for the children to spend in Italy.'

Taking a moment to bring herself down, she said, 'I'm sure they'll be very grateful, though I don't imagine for a minute that it'll make up for you not being there.'

To her surprise he didn't rise to it, and her words suddenly seemed petty.

His silence continued, but she knew he was still there, and as she pictured him in her mind's eye a fierce longing engulfed her.

'How are you feeling about going?' he asked quietly.

Don't be nice to me, she wanted to cry, *it just makes*

it worse. 'I'm fine,' she replied, more stiffly than she'd intended.

'Have you managed to make contact with anyone in Tuoro yet?'

'I don't have any names,' she reminded him, 'apart from my grandparents, and for all I know they're not even alive.'

'So you never received a reply to the letter you sent?'

'The one addressed to Signor and Signora Clementi, Tuoro sul Trasimeno? You know I didn't. Maybe you've forgotten with so much else on your mind.'

'No, I hadn't forgotten, I just wondered if something might have turned up in the last couple of weeks.'

'No, it hasn't. I'll be starting from scratch, more or less.' *Which is why I need you. We were always going to do it together.*

As though he might have been reading her mind, he let the silence run until they finally spoke at the same time.

'You first,' he said.

'No, you,' she insisted. 'What were you going to say?'

'I was going to wish you luck,' he said. 'I hope you find what you're looking for.'

Her eyes closed as emotion threatened to overwhelm her.

'And you?' he prompted. 'What were you going to say?'

She'd been about to ask when she might see him again, but instead, she said, 'It doesn't matter. It wasn't important. I should go now, I've still got a lot of packing to do.'

'OK. I'll try calling the children again, but if I can't get through, please don't let them think I don't love them.'

'Of course not.' She waited for him to say the same to her, but they either lost the connection at that point, or he simply rang off.

Chapter Thirteen

'Oh my God, what if it turns out you're Bruno Tonioli's long-lost sister?' Tierney cried as they wheeled their luggage out of arrivals into the blistering heat and bedlam of Pisa airport. Every café and coffee bar was overflowing, the traffic was in chaos and there seemed to be queues to join queues whose ends were nowhere in sight.

'Who?' Zav said, wrinkling his nose as he checked to make sure he had mobile reception.

'You know, the bloke off *Strictly*,' Skye replied. 'The crazy one.'

'That would be so hilaire,' Tierney declared, ducking to avoid Max's guitar as he swung round to watch a couple of passing girls.

'You think you're so funny,' Lainey commented, relieved that everyone seemed in good spirits and that their driver had taken charge of her and Zav's overloaded trolley.

'Oh, Mum, what if you're related to Fabio Cannavaro?' Zav gasped eagerly. 'That would be so cool. We could get to see all the matches,' he told Alfie, who was looking faintly bemused.

'Trust you to come up with a footballer,' Tierney sighed irritably. 'No, I reckon she's going to be related to Nancy Dell'Olio . . .'

Skye and Stacy burst into laughter.

'. . . or Donatella, or Giorgio Armani. Just imagine if you were, Mum. That would be like so amazing.'

'Personally, I'd say there's a good chance Pavarotti's your dad,' Stacy put in reflectively.

Lainey sliced her a look.

'More like Berlusconi,' Max put in. 'The rate he knobs around he's probably everyone's dad. What are those parties he has? Bunga bunga. We're definitely going in for some of those while we're here.'

'What, just the five of us?' Tierney grimaced.

'We're seven,' Lainey reminded her.

'No way are you two coming,' Tierney shot back.

'Charming,' Lainey muttered, struggling to keep an eye on the driver as he weaved through the crowds to where he'd left the car. That would be just perfect, if he turned out to be a fraud and she lost all her luggage before they'd even got on the road.

It was hard to believe that no more than two hours had passed since they'd left a wet and windy England, every one of them in a tense or querulous mood after getting up so early. Now, along with their coats and boots, the edginess seemed to have been shed and everyone, including Lainey, was feeling the pleasing anticipation that came with the start of a holiday. It was all going to be fine, she kept telling herself, just as long as she didn't think about Tom.

'Mum, have you got any suncream?' Tierney called out from behind her.

Digging into her bag, Lainey found and passed back a tube of factor thirty, and received a groan of protest in response.

'I'll never get a tan with that,' Tierney complained.

'You're already a gorgeous colour,' Skye told her,

sounding both envious and annoyed. 'It's me who needs to bronze up a bit. Max! What are you doing?' she cried as his trolley crashed into hers.

'Sorry, this thing is out of control,' he growled, grabbing his guitar before it fell off the top. 'Shit, man, it's hot. Lainey, has this place we're going got a pool? It better have, or we're going to fry.'

'It has a pool,' she confirmed, helping Stacy to steer her trolley round a rowdy group of Brits. 'Oh my God, look at the queue for the car rental. Max, are you sure you want to pick one up here? Why don't you wait till we get there?'

Instantly persuaded, since it seemed half of humanity was waiting for the car-hire buses, Max swung his trolley along after them to where their driver was waiting next to his vehicle and Zav and Alfie were flirting with a couple of Italian girls in the next car.

'That's my brov,' Max declared, giving Zav a playful cuff. 'Getting his priorities right as soon as we arrive.'

'Will you listen to him?' Tierney groaned, handing her vanity case to the driver, who looked as though he ought to be modelling for Calvin Klein.

Flipping back her silky hair, Skye treated him to an outrageously suggestive smile as he took her bag next. 'Thanks,' she said, breathily.

Lainey's and Stacy's eyes met with no small irony.

'Interesting times ahead,' Stacy murmured as they began piling into the air-conditioned interior, Zav and Alfie in the far back, Max, Skye and Tierney in the middle and Lainey and Stacy behind the driver.

'You wait,' Max was saying to Zav and Alfie over his shoulder, 'once these Italian chicks clock yours truly they're going to come flocking, so we'll have plenty of bunga bunga, guys.'

As Tierney attempted a withering put-down, and Skye thumped him, Lainey looked at Stacy again and rolled her eyes. Heaven only knew what they'd let themselves in for, coming away with two hormonal teenage girls and a budding musician who was so full of himself. She shuddered to think of how grown-up Zav and Alfie might be by the time they got back.

Best not to dwell on it now, and deal with whatever disasters arose when, if, they ever did. On the other hand, worrying about them and how she was going to keep them all entertained might just be better than tormenting herself over Tom. He wasn't here, nor was he going to come, so she had to put him out of her mind and focus on how wonderful it was to be in the country of her birth.

And it was wonderful, she decided, even calming, in its way, or it might be if she could force herself to detach from all she'd left behind and start to unwind. Actually, she felt sure it was already having a beneficial effect, because she really was loving the sound of Italian being spoken, even though she didn't understand it, and the thought of exploring a history and culture that she was a part of was quite enthralling. Not that she was experiencing a natural affinity or anything, it was far too soon for that, but as they left the airport complex to start heading south, the sun-baked Tuscan countryside was definitely rousing something inside her.

She could hardly take her eyes from the swathes of dry brown fields and feathery grasses rolling away from the road to the languid stretch of mountains sitting watchfully on a close horizon. Their tops were hazed by heat, their slopes blotched by the odd cloud shadow. They passed windmills rotating imperiously against a backdrop of pristine blue; pylons linking like messengers across the landscape, orderly saplings, tangled woods and acres of sunflowers, their faces turned away from the road. It made her think of Tom and how he was turning his back on her, and the ache in her heart grew heavier and harder to bear.

Signs to Firenze began appearing, and for some reason a flood of memories rose up from the past. It wasn't as though they'd ever been there, but she found herself remembering the places they had visited, the holidays they'd loved, the romantic weekends without kids, the excitement of new adventures with them. She began searching for signs from those days she might have missed or decided to ignore over the years: unusual silences, long phone calls she'd thought were to Nadia, or his publisher; an eagerness to get home when they'd seemed to be having such a good time. It was all there, and as the pain of it clenched around her heart she closed her eyes. Where was he now? What was he doing? Was he thinking of them, wondering how their journey had gone, feeling sorry he wasn't with them, or glad? More likely he wasn't thinking of them at all. He'd always been good at that, switching off, or compartmentalising as he called it. If only she could do the same.

By the time they reached the border with Umbria they'd been driving for over two hours and the others were all fast asleep. Stacy's head was on Lainey's shoulder, her phone still clamped in her hand. Since her job on the magazine had been confirmed, she'd been working all hours, rushing around the country interviewing potential contributors, and reporting back to her bosses at the end of each day. Her plan was to spend most of her time in Italy on the computer researching and writing articles for the first edition, submitting ideas for future issues and perhaps concocting a travel blog for the magazine's website.

How much was Stacy actually going to see of the country? How ill she could afford this time away. Lainey felt terrible for not trying harder to persuade her to put her job first, but she hadn't been able to face the thought of coming without her. *It's only a week*, she reminded herself, *and if she needs to go back earlier I'll drive her to the airport myself.*

'Lago Trasimeno,' the driver suddenly announced, glancing at her in the rear-view mirror.

Experiencing an almost childlike surge of excitement as she caught her first glimpse of the lake's easterly shores, Lainey broke into a smile. The sparkle of water was soon gone, masked by dense woods and warehouses, but she was here at last, very close to where her mother had grown up and their roots were buried. She turned to gaze out of the other window, across the rolling plains to where a medieval-looking town, maybe a city, was perched in a sprawl and tumble over a distant hillside.

'Is Cortona,' the driver told her. 'There is Tuscany. Here, where is lake, this is Umbria.'

Knowing Cortona was the closest large town to Tuoro, Lainey said, 'How much further do we have to go?'

'Is only few kilometres,' he assured her. He glanced at the dashboard. 'Is very hot today, thirty-seven degrees.'

'Very hot,' she agreed, already longing to step back into its scorching embrace.

'Mum, have you got anything to eat?' Zav called sleepily from the back.

'Yeah, I'm starving,' Tierney piped up. 'Are we there yet?'

'Almost,' Lainey replied, pulling a handful of energy bars out of her bag. 'We'll have to go to the supermarket later,' she informed them, and grinned past the hurt she'd caused herself as they gave a collective groan. That was usually Tom's line when they arrived on holiday, *We'll have to go to the super-market later*, and he always gave her a mischievous wink as he was treated to the same unimpressed response.

Yawning and stretching, Stacy dragged a bottle of warmish water from her bag and passed it around. 'I need a swim,' she declared, fanning herself with a sodden tissue.

'You and me both,' Skye responded. 'I can hardly wait to get my clothes off.'

Max responded with something Lainey didn't quite catch, but whatever it was it made Skye squeal with laughter, and Lainey felt sorry all over again that Tom wasn't around to keep an eye on things.

'We're there!' Tierney suddenly cried. 'Look, it's a sign for Tuoro.' She bounced forward to wrap her arms round her mother's neck. 'How do you feel?' she asked. 'Getting all déjà vu-ed, or anything?'

Smiling, Lainey said, 'Not yet. I'll let you know if it happens,' and taking in every last detail of the passing terrain, from signs to a lakeside restaurant and campsite, to a removal-lorry park and an avenue of limes, she waited, almost breathlessly, for a burst of something, anything, whether awe, belonging, or simple pleasure, to ignite inside her. So far nothing much seemed to be happening; however, as they progressed along a leafy boulevard and began climbing towards the walls of what appeared to be a very old village she realised she was starting to feel faintly nervous, as though the ghosts of her past were watching her approach.

'It looks really boring,' Zav declared, as they rounded the outskirts of the village and continued to climb.

'What do you mean?' Lainey cried. 'It's beautiful.' It wasn't, at least not from the main road, but she felt sure the briefly glimpsed narrow streets, running between a mishmash of old and new houses, led to a cornucopia of hidden character and promise. Indeed, as they rounded a steep bend past a news-paper kiosk on one side and an antique shop on the other, a small park full of plane trees appeared in front of them, making her think of all the boules they'd played during holidays in France. There were no boules here, but the space seemed a similar sort of mecca for the community's older folk to while away the time. The thought that one or two amongst them might know her grandparents, perhaps even her mother, caused a quick surge of adrenalin to catch on her hopes. There was even a chance that one of *them* was her grandmother or grandfather, an aunt or uncle, a cousin – even a sister or brother, though they all looked a bit too old for that.

Was her father there?

Her mind turned instantly to Peter, who'd seemed upset when she'd left that morning, though he'd been unable to articulate what was bothering him.

'It was there, and then gone,' he kept saying.

'Was it a pain?' she'd asked, smoothing his hair.

'There and then gone.'

'Did you lose something?'

'There and then gone.'

She'd call Aunt Daffs in a while to make sure he'd settled down.

After turning left at the plane-tree park where a cobbled road seemed to run down to the heart of the village, they drove on past the Carabinieri and some apartment buildings, around another bend in front of a rather grand-looking building called Teatro Communale dell'Academia (a theatre school?) and a small car park with recycling bins next to the road. From there the climb up the hill grew steeper and twistier, and though Lainey was dying to turn round to catch a first real view of the lake, she was determined to wait till they were at the villa, where it wasn't going to disappear on her again.

Two kilometres later (not one, as it had claimed on the website, nor was it a reasonable walk to the village), they reached the end of a winding dirt track and passed through a set of tall iron gates. They were high enough now for a sweepingly panoramic view of the lake, and though the website had prepared her for the vista, the reality simply took her breath away. Its seemingly endless stretch of sparkling waters completely dominated the heart of the valley, rolling for miles in each direction and out to the gentle swells of a mountainous horizon. Around the shores were other towns with their foundations in the waters, and appearing to float on the otherwise empty surface were three small islands.

'Wow,' Stacy murmured.

'Is very beautiful, no?' the driver said, sounding as proud as if the enchanting scenery was all his.

'Can you swim in it?' Skye wanted to know.

Realising the driver hadn't understood, Lainey said, 'According to my guidebook you can. Apparently there's a beach down there somewhere, and you can take boats, or ferries, over to the islands.'

'I definitely have to get a car,' Max announced, 'cos no way can we get down there without one.'

'My brother bring car,' the driver told them. 'Is already here. Fiat Bravo, *si*?'

'*Si*,' Lainey agreed. 'That's for me. We need another for Max, is that possible?'

'Another car, *si*. My brother bring. We tell him,' and inching carefully around a curve in the drive, he beamed happily as they all gasped at their first sight of the villa. It was everything Lainey had hoped for and more. The thick stone walls and vine-covered terraces were glimmering sleepily in the afternoon sun, while gnarled old olive trees and colourful tumbles of flowers surrounded it. The shutters were all open, as was the front door, but to her surprise they drove on round to the side of the villa and up a steep slope. At the top was an exquisite grassy lawn with a footpath leading to a rose- and jasmine-covered pergola, where a raven-haired woman around Lainey's age was waiting to greet them.

'Hello, hello,' she cried warmly, coming across the lawn as Lainey began the exodus from the car. 'I am Adriana,' she declared, shaking Lainey's hand, 'and I am very happy to welcome you to Villa Constantia. You are Signora 'ollingsworth, *si*?'

Responding to her friendliness, Lainey said, 'Yes, I am, but you must call me Lainey. And this is Stacy.'

'I am much pleased to meet you, Stacy,' Adriana informed her with a smile that seemed to grow more dazzling by the minute. 'And these are the children, but oh no, they are so grown up. Hello everyone, I am Adriana and I hope you are going to have a very nice holiday at this villa.'

'Where's the pool?' Zav wanted to know, looking around.

'Zav, where are your manners?' Lainey exclaimed. 'Adriana's just said hello to you.'

'Oh, sorry. Ciao,' he said, coming forward to shake her hand.

'Ah, *si parla italiano*,' she cried happily.

Zav's face was a picture as he turned to his mother. 'I only know ciao,' he confessed.

As everyone laughed, Adriana said, 'The pool – *la piscina* – she is down in the bottom terrace. You can reach by the steps you see inside the, how you say, *cespugli*?'

Hazarding a guess, since there was only one set of steps that she could see, Lainey said, 'Bushes?'

'*Si, si*, inside the bushes,' Adriana confirmed.

'Can we go and look, Mum?' Zav pleaded.

'In a minute,' she promised, 'you need to help unload the car first.'

'Hi, good to meet you,' Max declared, holding out a hand to shake Adriana's. 'I'm afraid I don't speak Italian either, but I'm definitely willing to learn.' He wasn't a sophisticated flirt, although he probably thought he was.

'This is very good,' Adriana told him enthusiastically. 'Perhaps I give you the address of the school of my friend. He is very good teacher.'

Stifling a laugh at the subtle put-down, Lainey watched the girls introduce themselves while Max went to collect his guitar, then turned to take in the view again. It was spectacular, utterly mesmerising, with not a single cloud in the sky to disturb the vast swathe of blue, nor a vessel on the lake to ripple the glassy waters.

'It is very special, no?' Adriana asked, coming to stand with her.

'Very,' Lainey agreed, feeling both entranced and intrigued by what memories this view might have evoked for her mother. Had she ever climbed this high, played in that lake, explored the closest island where, according to the guidebook, lace was made and fishermen lived? Certainly she would have felt this sun scorching her limbs, and heard the orchestra of cicadas drowning the birdsong. Had her family home been up here on the undulating hillside, or tucked away in the heart of the village whose red rooftops were glinting in the sunshine? Where was the school she'd attended, the friends she'd known, the church where she'd made her confessions? Perhaps talking to the priest would be a good place to start her search.

'Are you from this area?' Stacy was asking Adriana.

'No, I am from Perugia,' Adriana replied, with a wistful sigh. 'Tuoro is the home of my husband's family, and this villa belong to my brother-in-law, Marco. He cannot be here today to greet you, so I do this for him.'

'Does he live nearby?' Stacy asked, ignoring the matchmaking light that shot to Lainey's eye.

'Yes, he live close to Tuoro, in same place as me and my husband where we each have a home and our business. Sometimes we stay here, at this villa, when it is not let, and we have a holiday. You will see inside, it is like two apartments. You passed the door to the one downstairs just now, and here, under the pergola, is door to the one upstairs. This work well when I come with my husband and children and Marco has with him his wife and son. We can be separate, but together. I will show you.'

Clocking the wife and son, Lainey threw Stacy a regretful look as they wandered across the lawn towards the villa.

'What's the name of the town over there?' Stacy said, pointing to the western shore.

'This is called Castiglioni del Lago. Is very beautiful town. You visit one day while you are here to see the market and the wonderful shops of food. Of course also the Castello del Lione, which is very old fortress.'

'Actually, Mum's here to try and find her family,' Tierney piped up from behind them.

Adriana's eyes rounded with interest. 'You have family in this region?' she asked Lainey.

Thrown by being thrust so abruptly into the deep end, Lainey said, 'I'm not sure. I mean, it's possible. I was born in Tuoro, but my mother left when I was a baby . . .'

'Ah, so you are Italian?' Adriana cried happily. 'This makes sense to me, because you, if you don't mind me saying, look Italian.'

Lainey smiled. 'I'll take that as a compliment, but I'm afraid I don't feel very Italian. Like my children, I don't even speak the language.'

'Your mother did not teach you?'

'No, sadly, but like my stepson, I'm keen to learn, so perhaps I could go to your friend's school.'

The way Adriana's eyes twinkled told her there was no such school. 'But what is the name of your family?' she prompted. 'Perhaps I have heard of them, or even know them.'

With a glance at Stacy, who was clearly encouraging her to seize the moment, Lainey said, 'My grandparents on my mother's side are called Clementi. Melvina and Aldo Clementi.'

Adriana was frowning. 'Maybe we ask my husband or brother-in-law when they come. They know everyone because they spend much time here when growing up, and now with our business.'

'What do you do?' Stacy asked.

Adriana threw out her hands. 'We do everything, but first, close to here we have a vineyard and olive grove, and we also have shops in Roma and London where we sell our produce and many other things Italian. Marco, this is my brother-in-law, he is meeting with very important supplier in Montepulciano today. This is why he cannot be here. You know Montepulciano? Is very famous for the wine.'

Lainey smiled as she nodded. The wine was one of Tom's favourites.

'And now I show you inside the villa,' Adriana declared. 'You see we are on the terrace that has very splendid views of Lago Trasimeno. You understand that this is very special lake, because is one of only fifty-two in the world recognise by UN for, how you say, *ambiente* – envir – onment?'

Lainey and Stacy both nodded.

'*Si*, environment quality. You can swim, and if you want to sail or windsurf there is very good school in San Feliciano which I can give you address for. There is much horse-riding, and hiking and visits to wineries and oil presses. Many things to do, you will find inside lots of information that I bring for you.'

Following her through the open double doors,

leaving Tierney and Skye going into a huddle over one of their phones, and Max tuning up his guitar, Lainey tucked an arm through Stacy's as they looked around the spacious and mercifully cool kitchen-cum-sitting room. Definitely not at the top end of luxury, but it had a distinctive charm about it, with a shabby-chic half-kitchen to the left (next to no worktop space, a slimline dishwasher, mini fridge, two cupboards and a sink – not really big enough for them, but it would have to do). To the right was a large round table covered by a flowery plastic cloth, and ahead was a seating area boasting three tan leather sofas, an impressive marble fireplace flanked by towering bookshelves and a large dark wood cupboard which turned out to house all the cutlery and crockery.

'And in here,' Adriana was saying, turning through a door next to the kitchen, 'we are having two bedrooms and one very large bathroom. You can do as you please, of course, but this is usually where the children sleep. Twin beds in this room, and again in this one.'

'Perfect,' Lainey responded, deciding on one for Tierney and Skye and the other for Zav and Alfie.

'And now we see the other wing,' Adriana declared, turning back into the sitting room and going to open a door to one side of the fireplace. 'This is where we have small hall and two double bedrooms, each with their own bathroom. One has very lovely terrace, but no view from inside room, the other has view, but no terrace.'

'You choose,' Lainey said to Stacy. 'I'm happy with either.'

'You paid, you get to choose,' Stacy insisted.

Lainey smiled at Adriana. 'We'll sort it out, but

both look gorgeous, thank you. I'm just a bit worried about Max. Are there any other rooms up here?'

'No, but there is the apartment downstairs, where is one bedroom and bathroom, a kitchen with very large fridge, and big sitting room where is Sky television and the Wi-Fi if you need.'

'I definitely do,' Stacy assured her. 'Maybe I should have the apartment, if I'm going to be working most of the time.'

'No, please don't leave me sharing a wing with Max,' Lainey shuddered. 'I can stand his music, I can even put up with his humour, but I'd rather know nothing about his bunga bunga parties, thank you very much.'

'Is that me you're talking about?' Max demanded, coming in after them. 'This place is seriously cool. Where's my room?'

'We've decided to let you have the downstairs apartment all to yourself,' Lainey announced generously.

His eyes narrowed suspiciously. 'You're kidding me. A whole apartment? My own front door?'

'All yours. Just try to remember, when you're partying it up down there, that there are other people in the house and two are of very tender years.'

'Oh, you and Stacy can handle it,' he assured her. 'I might even invite you if you're especially nice to me.'

Slanting him a look as Stacy laughed, Lainey turned back to Adriana. 'It's wonderful,' she told her. 'I know we're going to love it here.' She wasn't allowing herself to think of how much Tom would have approved, because it just wasn't relevant.

'I really hope so,' Adriana was responding as they walked back to the sitting room. 'I will just go through the alarm and gate codes with you now, and how some of the things work.'

The basic training didn't take long, and Lainey was on the point of asking about supermarkets and restaurants when Zav and Alfie came charging in from the terrace.

'Hey, Mum.' Zav was waving his phone. 'I just had a text from Dad. He wants to know if we arrived safely and if we had a good flight.'

Before Lainey could answer, Tierney snapped, 'Tell him to mind his own business.'

Catching Adriana's surprise, Lainey stared hard at Tierney.

'Well, he didn't want to come,' Tierney cried, throwing out her hands, 'so why should we tell him anything about what we're doing?'

'No way am I going to be in touch with him,' Max declared, pushing past to go back outside.

'Me neither,' Tierney snorted.

Zav looked worriedly at Lainey.

'Send a text back if you want to,' she said gently.

'Yeah, but what shall I say?'

'Whatever you want to say.'

Zav looked down at his phone and shrugged. 'I want him to come,' he said quietly.

Afraid for how much it would upset him if he asked and Tom said he couldn't, Lainey went to put an arm around him. 'Just tell him it's lovely here and you're about to have a swim,' she said, 'and then I think you and Alfie should go and explore the pool.'

As they ran off cheering, she turned to Adriana, who was discreetly studying a brochure. 'Families!'

she commented, trying to make light of the last few minutes.

With a sympathetic smile, Adriana put the brochure down as she said, 'I shall leave you to settle in now, but if you need anything you will find my number, and Marco's, in your welcome pack. There are some basic supplies in the fridge, but if you want the supermarket it is back down the hill through the village, turn left in the direction of Perugia and you will see on left-hand side. Oh, and if you are thinking of eating out tonight I can recommend La Pergola in the village, or you can drive up to the top of the hill where you will find Lo Scoiattolo. The Squirrel. Here they do very good pizzas and pasta for the young ones.'

After she'd gone and all five children were cavorting about in the pool, Lainey sank down in a chair on the terrace and could have kissed Stacy as she brought out two glasses of chilled white wine.

'Orvieto,' Stacy informed her, 'so nice and local.'

'Perfect,' Lainey responded, inhaling the bouquet.

'Here's to a wonderful holiday,' Stacy toasted. 'Let's hope it's successful in every way.'

Smiling faintly, Lainey touched her glass to Stacy's and took a sip. 'He texted me too, asking me to let him know that we've arrived safely.'

Apparently unsurprised, Stacy said, 'So are you going to?'

'I suppose I shouldn't just leave it to Zav. I'd like to speak to him really.'

'Then call.'

Raising her eyebrows as a piercing Tierney scream erupted from the pool area, followed by some gigantic splashes, Lainey picked up her mobile and pressed to connect. 'Hi,' she said into his voicemail, 'just to let you know that we've arrived in one piece and it's beautiful here. I'd say we were missing you, because we are, but it's probably not what you want to hear.' She glanced at Stacy and continued. 'Please don't forget to stay in touch with the children, even if Max and Tierney don't call or text back. It'll mean something to them anyway.' She took a breath. 'OK, that's about it for now. You know where we are if you need to speak to us, and you might not want to hear this either, but I love you,' and already regretting saying it for how needy it might have made her sound, she rang off.

'Mum? Are you awake?' Tierney whispered into the darkness.

Rolling on to her back, Lainey reached out to turn on the lamp, but couldn't find the switch. 'What are you doing here?' she asked softly.

'Can I get in with you?'

Flipping back the sheet and moving over to make room, Lainey settled Tierney's head into the crook of her arm and said, 'You haven't fallen out with Skye already, have you?'

'No, no, she's just . . .' Tierney stopped, unsure about admitting that Skye had gone down to the lake with Max, where there was supposed to be a disco. 'I just couldn't sleep,' she said lamely.

'Why's that?'

'I don't know. I guess Dad and everything. Why aren't you asleep?'

'I was until you came in.'

'No you weren't.'

'How do you know?'

'I can tell. A bit like you can always tell with me.' Lainey smiled, and for a while they lay quietly

252

gazing through the mosquito nets to where a host of stars were lighting the night sky. The only sounds to be heard were the cicadas mingling with the faint thrumming of music somewhere in the valley.

'Does this place feel like somewhere you belong?' Tierney asked after a while. 'You know, like on an instinctive level?'

'We haven't even been into the village yet,' Lainey reminded her.

'No, but you know, it can still happen. I'll be glad for you if you do find your family . . .'

'. . . they'd be your family too . . .'

'. . . provided they're nice, but we live in England and all my friends are there, so if you were . . .'

'Sweetheart, no matter what happens on this holiday, Bannerleigh Cross will always be our home.'

Tierney fell silent.

Knowing what she was thinking now, Lainey was about to try and reassure her when she said, 'What if Dad moves them in?'

In spite of feeling certain it would never happen, Lainey's heart gave a horrible jolt.

'We can't live there with them, and you remember what Stacy's husband did, how he moved his girlfriend in . . .'

'Dad would never do that to us.'

'He might, while we're here. We could get back and find they've taken over . . .'

'Tierney, he wouldn't do that.'

'How do you know?'

'I just do, but if you're really worried, you should call him and tell him what's on your mind.'

'I don't want to speak to him.'

'Yes you do.'

'No, I don't.'

'You're just angry and confused, we all are, but you love him really . . .'

'Do you still love him?'

Lainey's breath caught on the question. 'Yes,' she said, because why would she lie? 'Yes, I do, but we have to sort things out . . .'

'Are you going to get divorced?'

'Oh, Tierney . . .'

'You are, aren't you?'

'Things haven't gone that far yet . . . I don't want to, obviously, but if it's what Dad wants . . .'

'If it is I'll never, ever, speak to him again.'

Giving her a hug, Lainey said, 'I won't hold you to that, because it's not what I'd want for you. Remember, he's been a wonderful dad up to now, and I'm sure that won't change . . .'

'He's not here. That's a change. He's never not come on holiday with us before.'

'No, but it doesn't mean he doesn't love you.'

'If it means he doesn't love you, then I'm with Max, I'll never want to see him again.'

'Darling, Max has his own issues with Dad that you mustn't let yourself get dragged into.'

Accepting that was true, and that she didn't want to be a part of it, Tierney spread her arms and legs to cool them as she said, 'If you end up finding out you've got a father, who's still alive, what will you do?'

'Well, I guess that depends on who he is, how he is, where he is . . . It's impossible to say.'

'But Grandpa will always be our grandpa?'

'Of course he will. He adopted me, so we're every bit as much his family as Auntie Sarah and Auntie Esther and all of their children.'

'I kind of miss him, don't you? I mean, I know he's still there, but I'm talking about the way he used to be, always loads of fun and full of stories. I wonder what he'd say if he knew about Julia?' She turned to look at Lainey. 'You know, it'll be really weird if you end up finding your real dad just as I'm losing mine.'

'Tierney, you'll never lose Dad, that you can be sure of.'

Tierney fell silent again. It was hard for her to articulate how she felt about sharing her father with someone she'd never even known about until a few days ago. He didn't belong to Julia, even if he was her dad too. He belonged with them, her, Mum and Zav – Max too, obviously, who was only texting and inviting Christie over for a week. How was that going to be for his shag buddy Skye?

What did she care? It was their business, not hers.

She needed to focus on her parents breaking up and Guy getting in a state about her not showing the other night, and then weirding out about her going to Italy. It was like he was desperate to see her, and he just needed to chill. Already today he'd sent like about forty texts and even though it proved that he was totally mad about her, she wished he'd stop, because it wasn't really what she wanted any more.

'Come on, spill,' Lainey prompted.

'Spill what?'

'All that nonsense you've got going on in your head.'

Tierney stopped breathing; like her mother was able to read her mind? No way. She just couldn't know about Guy. No, she was still thinking this was all about Dad. And it was, because Tierney was really worried about what might happen, how broken up her mum was going to be if they did get a divorce. She had to do something to try and keep them together, but the only idea she'd come up with so far had been more Skye's than hers, and she wasn't sure it would work for her parents. In fact she knew it wouldn't, but maybe she should give it a try all the same. So, bracing herself, she said, 'Don't bite my head off, OK? Just hear me out before you say anything, but you know, everyone's saying that this book, *Fifty Shades of Grey* . . .'

Sighing, Lainey said, 'So you've read it.'

'Only bits, but you haven't read any of it, and everyone's saying it does wonders for their sex life, so maybe, if you . . .'

'Tierney, this isn't about sex. And it's definitely not about bondage, unless you're suggesting I use some kinky way of tying him to me.'

As they laughed, they rolled into each other's arms and felt the complexity of their relationship turning very simple for a while.

'So are you going to tell me who keeps texting you?' Lainey asked in the end.

Tensing, Tierney said, 'What do you mean?'

'I'm guessing he's someone you met in London when you were with Skye?'

'No. Yes, I mean, he's like no one really. Don't let's talk about him. Let's work out how we're going to make things right between you and Dad.'

'That's for us to do, not you.'

'Have you spoken to him since we got here?'

'No.'

'Do you want to?'

'Tierney . . .'

'I'm not sure if it's right to play hard to get. Sometimes it works, and sometimes it doesn't.'

'You have to stop worrying about us,' Lainey scolded.

'He rang Zav just as we were going to bed.'

'Really? Do you know what he said?'

'No, Zav didn't say.'

Lainey turned her gaze back to the stars. It wasn't so much what Tom might have said to Zav that was upsetting her, it was the fact that he hadn't called her.

'Are you OK?' Tierney asked, turning to her.

Lainey's eyes were closed; her whole body was tense. 'Of course,' she said, the words seeming to unwind her a little.

They listened to the sound of a car coming slowly along the gravel drive.

'It must be Max,' Tierney said.

As a second door banged shut, Lainey remarked, 'Seems he's found himself some company. That didn't take long.'

'Like father like son,' Tierney muttered.

Lainey reached for her hand.

'They ought to learn how to be faithful,' Tierney commented tartly.

'If Dad had learned that a long time ago you wouldn't be here,' Lainey reminded her.

Tierney turned away. She was thinking of how she was part of Guy being unfaithful to Nadia and hating herself for it, but that was mainly because she was starting to hate him now. 'You know when you had sex for the first time,' she ventured. 'Was it like, dead romantic, or did you hate it?'

'To be honest,' Lainey said, 'I was pretty drunk

and the boy I was with, Stuart, was in the same state, so I don't remember all that much about it.'

'But you do about the first time with Dad?'

'Yes, I definitely remember that.'

'If you'd known he was married, would you still have, you know, gone with him?'

Lainey's throat was drying, and her head was aching. 'I'd like to say no, I wouldn't have,' she replied, 'but I'm not sure that's the truth. I was very attracted to him; the chemistry was pretty overpowering.' For her it still was, but she was very much afraid that it was no longer the same for him.

'Mm, I can understand how you felt, because sometimes it's like you have to do something even though you know it's wrong, or it might hurt someone else. You just get this feeling that you *have* to do it, like your body's got a mind of its own.'

Lainey's eyes narrowed as she turned to her. 'What are you trying to tell me?' she asked cautiously.

'Nothing! I'm just saying, that's all.'

'Tierney, for God's sake, you haven't got yourself involved with a married man?' Panic was already taking hold, because if she had, then Lainey's own troubles were going to seem small by comparison, especially if Tom were ever to find out.

'Of course I haven't,' Tierney cried. 'That's not what I said. Why do you have to go and say that when I was just trying to be helpful?'

'I'm sorry, I'm sorry. It's just . . . I guess I'm tired, and not thinking very straight. Why don't you go on back to your own bed now? We've got some exploring to do in the morning and I'd like to be nice and fresh for it.'

Sitting up, Tierney said, 'Are you nervous about what you might find out about Granny's past?'

'Yes, actually, I am a bit.'

'What, like in case your father turns out to be a mass murderer?'

Lainey sighed. It wasn't as though the thought hadn't occurred to her, but at this stage she wasn't going to allow herself to run with it. 'Let's just hope he doesn't,' she responded.

'He won't be,' Tierney said confidently. 'He'll either be dead, or married to someone else . . . Oh my God, what if it turns out you're as big a surprise to his wife as *Julia* was to you? That would be seriously weird, wouldn't it?'

'Tierney, go to bed, please.'

'I'm gone. Love you.'

'Love you too.'

As the door closed behind her, Lainey turned to stare at the night sky again. Her thoughts were so tangled, her hopes and fears so inextricably enmeshed that she couldn't imagine sleep coming any time soon. She wondered if Tom might be awake too and thinking of her.

More likely he was fast asleep with Kirsten lying beside him, perhaps with her hand in his, or his arm around her, and Julia in a nearby room.

How on earth was she going to bear this?

Chapter Fourteen

'Who do you reckon it is?' Stacy murmured, as she and Lainey looked down from the hot, but shady terrace to where a large black Audi was passing in front of the villa on its way, presumably, to the slope where their hire car was parked. No entryphone buzzer had sounded, and as far as they knew the gates had closed automatically behind Max when he'd left an hour ago with the girls. (To hook up with some British dudes he'd met at the disco last night, he'd informed Lainey in his cool-guy, don't-bother-me-with-stuff way, before leaving.)

For one head-spinning moment Lainey wondered if it was a taxi and Tom had decided to turn up and surprise them. Perhaps that was why Zav had seemed more relaxed after he'd spoken to his dad last night, because he'd known he was coming today.

Though it didn't seem likely, anything was possible, and she longed with all her heart for it to be true. What would happen after that she had no idea, she just wanted it to be him.

As the Audi came to a stop, a blaze of sunlight on the windscreen was making it impossible to see who was driving, and with tinted windows at the back there was no way to tell if anyone else was in the car.

Throwing Stacy a look, Lainey watched the driver's door open, and as a man in his mid- to late thirties got out she felt her jaw starting to drop.

'Whoever he is, he's mine,' Stacy muttered, as quite possibly the most gorgeous-looking male they'd ever seen removed his sunglasses and started towards them. He was tall, slender but muscular, with carelessly tousled black hair and a shadow of stubble around his chin that made him look like a rock star, or a movie legend, or someone any woman would want to wake up next to.

Moving past the disappointment of it not being Tom, Lainey went forward to greet him. 'Hello,' she said smiling, holding out a hand to shake. 'I'm guessing you're Marco, Adriana's brother-in-law?'

'That is right,' he confirmed, his large hand closing loosely, yet somehow firmly around hers. His expression was tinged with curiosity as he regarded her, and yet was so openly warm that, in an odd sort of way, it seemed to make his looks less daunting. In fact, perhaps he wasn't quite so drop-dead after all, she decided, since his nose was a bit crooked and his eyes a little close together. However, they had such a mesmerising intensity about them that she was finding it almost as hard to meet them as she was to look away. 'And you are Mrs Hollingsworth?' he asked politely.

'Lainey,' she corrected. 'Please, call me Lainey. Or Elenora, if you prefer.' She almost laughed as she imagined Stacy's face behind her. 'It's very nice to meet you,' she told him. 'We love the villa. It's perfect, and the view is . . . *bellissima*.' She instantly felt foolish, because it was probably the wrong word and she shouldn't even have attempted it, knowing nothing of the language. How many years had it been since she'd found herself tongue-tied in front of a man? In truth, she wasn't sure she ever had.

'Excuse me, can anyone join in?' Stacy asked, peeping over her shoulder.

Lainey spun round and almost bumped into her. 'Sorry,' she said. 'Marco, this is Stacy Greenfield, my closest friend. Stacy, this is Marco, Adriana's brother-in-law. Our landlord.'

'It's lovely to meet you,' Stacy said, shaking his hand while treating Lainey to an elbow out of the way. 'You have a stunning place here. I can only wonder why you don't live in it yourself. I know I would if it were mine. Unfortunately, my darling *ex*-husband left me with so little that I can't even buy anywhere in England, never mind abroad, and I think I should really stop talking now, because I'm starting to make a fool of myself.'

Spluttering with laughter, as Marco's eyes twinkled, Lainey said, 'Would you care for a coffee? I was about to make some.'

'Oh, no, no, I'm fine, thank you,' he replied, in accented but perfect-sounding English. 'I have come simply to introduce myself, and to check that you have managed to decipher the code for the Wi-Fi.'

'Actually, now you come to mention it,' Stacy said, 'I *am* having a bit of trouble. I was going to ask Max to sort it, but if you can help . . .'

'I will be happy to. It is very long and hard to read. A lot of people have difficulty.' He turned to Lainey.

She smiled quickly as though she'd been caught staring, which actually she had.

'My sister-in-law tells me that you are hoping to find your family while you are here,' he said.

Surprised, though feeling suddenly, absurdly,

proud of her Italian roots, she said, 'That's right. I was born in Tuoro, so I'm here to find out if anyone might remember my mother, or even my father.'

He was nodding with interest.

Behind him Stacy's eyes were widening, but Lainey wasn't sure what message she was trying to send.

'I'm afraid my Italian is non-existent,' she ran on, filling an awkward silence, 'but I'm hoping to find someone who speaks English.'

He frowned. 'I'm afraid that won't be easy in Tuoro,' he lamented, 'or certainly not amongst the older generation. We are not a major tourist destination, you see, so the locals have not found the need to speak your language.'

Lainey grimaced her disappointment. 'Perhaps you can recommend a translator?' she suggested.

His frown disappeared. 'But I will be very happy to help you,' he declared, as though the matter had already been decided. 'My sister-in-law would like to help too, and my brother. We are all very intrigued.'

'Oh my goodness,' Lainey responded, not knowing what else to say. 'I'd be extremely grateful if you could, but I don't want to take up your time. I understand how busy you are . . .'

Behind him Stacy was drawing a frantic zip across her mouth.

'It is August,' he reminded her. 'There is less for us to do during this month, so we are pleased to be of assistance. In fact, Adriana has already contacted our grandmother because she spends many years growing up in the village. She lives in Firenze now, but she tells Adriana that she knows the name of Melvina Clementi.'

Lainey's eyes widened. 'Do you think it might be the same Melvina Clementi?' she asked.

He grimaced an apology. 'I am not sure,' he confessed. 'I will need to give our grandmother more information, but she has already told Adriana who we can to speak to in the village who possibly knows – or knew – Melvina and Aldo Clementi.'

Lainey's eyes were bright as she turned to Stacy. She'd never even dreamt she might get off to such a promising start.

'Tuoro is not a big community,' Marco explained. 'Of course it is bigger now than when my grandmother was young, but she still has a few friends here of her generation.' He pulled a mischievous face. 'She calls them *dei vecchi* – the oldies – but she will be ninety-one next month. She is like a woman half her age.'

Loving the sound of her, Lainey turned as Zav and Alfie came trudging up from the pool. 'My son and his friend,' she explained to Marco, and realised that he probably considered them a pair of heathens, since Adriana had rung earlier offering to take them to church along with her own little brood. Lainey had felt obliged to forgo the kindness, since neither Zav nor Alfie were very familiar with the house of God or what was expected of them inside.

After high-fiving with the boys and telling them they must meet his son, Benito, who was ten apparently, and spoke very good English, Marco excused himself to take a phone call. As he wandered back to the car Lainey stifled a laugh as Stacy murmured, 'Please hand me a Kleenex if I'm drooling.'

Tugging her into the villa behind Zav and Alfie, Lainey said, 'All that and he seems a really nice bloke too.'

'Some women have all the luck,' Stacy complained, reminding them both of the wife. 'I wonder what she's like.'

'Probably just as stunning.'

Stacy sighed dejectedly. 'I'm sure you're right. Makes me wish I was a Catholic.'

'What?' Lainey cried with a laugh.

'Well, God definitely didn't hold back when it came to giving out looks to you Italians, did he, and most of you are Catholic, so I'm figuring it's divine reward for your unquestioning faith, apart from in your case, of course, but you've still got the genes.'

With a wry roll of her eyes Lainey went to make sure Zav and Alfie were all right, and by the time she came back Stacy was on her way down to Max's apartment with Marco to sort out the Wi-Fi.

Half an hour later, appearing flushed with triumph and oddly bleary-eyed, Stacy returned to declare that Marco had gone off to get his son and would meet them down at the main piazza in an hour.

Lainey blinked her astonishment.

Stacy shrugged. 'I was going to ask about his wife,' she said, 'but as he didn't mention her I thought I wouldn't bother either.'

Though Lainey broke into a laugh, her eyes were regarding Stacy carefully. 'Promise me you won't go falling for him,' she said seriously. 'The last thing you need is a complication with a married man . . .'

Stacy's hands flew up defensively. 'I was just being friendly,' she protested. 'Anyway, meeting up was his suggestion, not mine, and I thought, as it's Sunday, and our first full day here, I ought to forget about work and start in earnest tomorrow. Is that OK with you?'

Lainey smiled. 'Of course. I just don't want you ending up getting hurt again, that's all.'

Coming to cup her hands round Lainey's face, Stacy said, 'Will you please stop worrying? Sure he's to die for, but even if he were my type, which actually he isn't, my priority right now is very definitely my job. While yours, my gorgeous Italian *amica*, is finding your family, and since he's offering to help I think we should pack ourselves into our little Fiat Bravo and be on our way down the hill, don't you?'

Having no argument with that, Lainey called for the boys, scooped up her keys and led the way outside. By the end of the day, she was thinking to herself as she locked the villa door, she might actually have spoken to someone who knew, or used to know, her grandparents, or even to her grandparents themselves! The thought of that caused a ripple of excitement mixed with trepidation to run through her. She'd better start deciding how she was going to handle it if they refused to see her, because if they did, given the fragile state of mind she was in, the rejection would be doubly hard to bear.

On the other hand, they might welcome her with open arms and even rejoice in being able to introduce her to her father.

And if you believe that, she told herself grimly as she got into the car, *you'll believe Tom's on his way here and Kirsten Bonner was only ever a figment of a cruel imagination.*

Leaving the car in a shady spot at the edge of the village, Lainey and Stacy wandered up a wide flight of steps into a cobbled street lined with quaint old stone houses and flower-filled pots. The boys, seeming not to feel the heat, charged on ahead, eager to find food, drinks and any kind of entertainment there was to be had.

'It's so pretty,' Stacy said, gazing up at the tightly shuttered windows and old-fashioned lamplights. 'I wonder if your mother ever walked along this street. I guess she must have if she grew up here.'

Finding it surprisingly easy to imagine, Lainey continued to look around as they strolled into a tiny piazza with a fishmonger's tucked into one corner and washing-covered balconies angled across another. There was no one around, nor any sounds coming from inside the dwellings, just a lazy ginger cat watching from a shadowy doorway and the occasional flutter of birds in the eaves. Sauntering on, they arrived at what turned out to be the main street, though it was barely wide enough for one car to pass along its cobbles. There were more people around here, bustling in and out of the food shops where fruit, veg, pasta and all manner of homewares were spilling out of boxes and barrows. It was far from crowded, however, and everyone was speaking Italian, making Lainey realise how many English voices they'd always heard during their travels through France and Spain.

They paused in front of a butcher's shop where every conceivable type of sausage was arranged in slices over trays in the window, or hanging in oily, garlic-stuffed glory from hooks in the ceiling. The smell of roasting chicken wafting out of the door set Lainey's taste buds stinging.

'The piazza's down here,' Zav informed them, as he and Alfie came running back towards them.

'Is Marco there yet?' Stacy asked, catching Zav's arms as he aeroplaned into her.

'Didn't see him. Mum, are we going to have some lunch now? I'm starving.'

'Look!' Alfie cried, pointing. 'That shop's called Speede-bene,' and howling with laughter they zoomed off back to the piazza.

Spotting an old lady lumbering slowly towards them, weighed down by heavy bags and probably a lifetime of woes, Lainey gave her a smile. '*Buon giorno, signora,*' she said warmly.

Whatever the old lady said in response was lengthy and mellifluous and seemed very friendly. She even put a bag down to pat Lainey's cheek before moving on.

'She could have been your granny,' Stacy teased as they continued on to the piazza.

'You can mock,' Lainey responded airily, 'but how lovely if you were right. She was adorable.'

'She certainly seemed to think you were. I wonder if you reminded her of your mother.'

Lainey's eyebrows rose as she slanted her a look.

'Well, you might have,' Stacy shrugged. 'You definitely remind me of her sometimes.'

'I'm going to take that as a compliment,' Lainey decided, and spotting a *panetteria* on the edge of the piazza she took off for a browse – and came away with a greasy slab of herb-crusted focaccia, two still warm *filones*, a *panbrioche*, and half a dozen sticky sweet pastries. 'Well, we do have five children to feed,' she pointed out as Stacy gaped at the size of the bag. 'Anyway, we're on holiday, so no time to be thinking about diets.'

'Unless you're about to have lunch with an Adonis,' Stacy reminded her.

Lainey paused, turned around and pushed the bag into Stacy's hands.

Laughing, Stacy followed her on to the small piazza where a central fountain was sparkling in the midday sun, and a rather grand limestone-fronted *municipio* was flying a collection of stately flags over a temporary bandstand. The café tables, spaced out like small islands below a cluster of white parasols and strings of bunting, were starting to fill up. Marco was already there with his son, Benito, who was busily showing some sort of electronic device to Zav and Alfie.

'Adriana and my brother, Lorenzo, will join us soon with their children,' he informed them as he got up to greet them, 'so we shall be quite a large party. I hope this is all right with you.'

'Of course,' Lainey assured him, sinking into the chair he was holding out.

'Thank you,' Stacy smiled, as he quickly moved to offer her a seat too.

'Elenora? What will you have to drink?' he offered, as a waiter arrived.

Liking his use of her real name, Lainey eyed his beer and said, 'I think I'll have one of those.'

'Mm, me too,' Stacy responded to his glance her way.

'*Due birra,*' he told the waiter, '*e due coca.* This is OK with you,' he said quickly to Lainey, 'for the boys to have coca, the same as Benito?'

'They'll be in seventh heaven,' she assured him, smiling at Benito, who had very definitely inherited his father's looks, though his eyes, she noticed, were a startlingly violet shade of blue. What an impact he was going to have on the girls when he got older.

Moments after the waiter vanished Adriana and her family turned up, greeting Lainey and Stacy almost as old friends, in spite of the fact that this was the first time they'd ever set eyes on Lorenzo. Though he appeared much older than both Adriana and Marco, and was nowhere near as striking as his brother, he oozed as much charm as good humour and was clearly a favourite with the kids.

'Adriana tells me you are Italian by birth,' he declared, cutting straight to the heart of matters as he pulled up a chair, 'but you do not yet speak the language?'

'I'm going to learn,' Lainey promised. 'I meant to take lessons before coming, and I would have if I'd managed to find the time.'

'Is no problem for us,' he assured her, 'we in this family must speak English for our business, but I think for you, if you are Italian, it would be very good to learn.'

'Stop bullying her,' Adriana chided, 'and please order us some drinks. Giana, Nico, Coca-Cola for you?'

'*Si, si,*' they cried in unison, their eagerness showing how rare a treat this was. Since neither could be any older than seven, Lainey wasn't surprised by that; certainly she hadn't allowed her own children to drink Coke before they were ten, and even now she tried to limit Zav to one, at the most two, a day.

It was amusingly comforting to find they shared the same values.

'. . . *e lui a pagere il conto,*' Lorenzo was telling the waiter, after adding his order to Marco's.

The waiter laughed, while Marco rolled his eyes. 'My brother has said that I will pay the bill,' he explained to Lainey and Stacy. 'He is a very good comedian. We think he will perform as a clown at the Ferragosto Toreggiano.'

'This is festival we have every year in the village,' Adriana explained, 'to celebrate Hannibal's defeat of the Romans, which happen here at Tuoro . . . I think two hundred years BC?' She looked at Marco.

He pulled a face. 'A long time ago,' he said, making everyone laugh. 'Some of the villagers will dress like soldiers of that time and walk through the streets,' he continued, 'and there is a party at La Ronde, which is another piazza at the end of Via Garibaldi.'

'That's over there,' Benito cried, pointing in the direction of a narrow side street that started out between an optician's and a *lavanderia*. 'Papa, can we take Zav and Alfie to show them?' he asked eagerly.

'Of course,' Marco replied, putting a hand on his son's springy dark hair. 'There is no traffic in this direction,' he assured Lainey. 'They will be perfectly safe. Ah, here are our drinks,' and clearing his phone from the table he whispered something in Benito's ear as the waiter set down his tray.

Smiling at the way Benito flushed with pleasure as he looked up at his father, Lainey took her beer and called to Zav and Alfie to come and get their Cokes.

'I praise Benito for speaking English,' Marco confided to Lainey as the children carried their drinks to the next table. 'He can be self-conscious about it sometimes, but today he is doing very well.'

'He seems almost as bilingual as you,' Lainey commented, taking a much-needed sip of her beer.

'He has an English mother,' Marco explained, a light of irony in his eyes.

Surprised, though not sure why, Lainey replied, 'Ah, well, that would certainly help.' She wondered if it would be rude to ask where his wife was today. Deciding it probably would, she simply said, 'Not that having an Italian mother helped my bilingual skills. She wouldn't allow a single word of the language to be spoken in her hearing, and if anyone as much as suggested coming here on holiday they usually ended up sorry.'

'She was a very passionate woman,' Stacy put in drolly. 'A bit like Elenora, really.'

As everyone enjoyed the moment, Lainey allowed her eyes to flutter closed and felt the heat of the day mingling with the very real pleasure of being here. What would her mother say if she could see her? Probably best not to think about that when she was on a mission to exhume whatever skeletons Alessandra had buried. Feeling a knot tightening in her heart as she wondered what Tom might be doing now, she looked around again and the tension slowly passed.

'So tell us what you know about your family?' Lorenzo prompted, after they'd made their menu choices and the children had disappeared off to La Ronde. 'You were born here, I think, and your parents too?'

'My mother was,' she confirmed, 'but I don't know about my father. His name isn't on my birth certificate and my mother would never tell me anything about him.'

Lorenzo's eyebrows rose with intrigue. 'Aha, I think we have a case for Inspector Poirot,' he declared, rubbing his hands together as though casting himself in the role.

'He was not an inspector,' Adriana reminded him.

Lorenzo batted it away. 'Detective, inspector, what I am saying is we have a big mystery that we must solve, and I think Isabella, our grandmother, is going to be important in this. She has a very good memory for a woman her age, and she knows everyone in Tuoro.'

'She used to,' Marco reminded him. 'It's been a long time since she lived in the village, and many new people have come since then.'

'But we only want the old ones,' Lorenzo pointed out, 'and there is nothing to be afraid of, because most of them have lost their teeth so they cannot bite.'

Adriana groaned. 'Not funny,' she told him, though the others were laughing.

'I think it's quite likely,' Lainey said, 'that my father, if he's still alive, won't want to know me, but that's all right. It'll just be good to know who he is, or was, and to find out why my mother never came back to Tuoro again after she left. She didn't even stay in touch with her own mother, or not that I know of, and I haven't been able to find out anything about my grandfather either. Apart from his name.'

'Aldo Clementi,' Stacy supplied, in case anyone had forgotten. 'And Melvina, his wife.'

'Grandmama reminded us to look at the records in the town hall,' Adriana informed them. 'If your parents were married in Tuoro there will be a record of it here, in the *municipio*. Do you think they were married?'

Lainey shook her head. 'I'm not sure, but somehow I doubt it.'

'It is definitely worth a look,' Marco put in. 'I can do this tomorrow when I am here for a meeting with the *segretario comunale*.'

Grateful for how quickly he was getting on to

this, Lainey was about to thank him when Stacy asked Adriana, 'Did your grandmother say whether she knew Alessandra, Lainey's mother?'

Adriana shook her head. 'But I ask only if she knows Melvina and Aldo, and she says she know them a little, but not well. She says Melvina was a very strong – *carattere*?'

'Character,' Marco provided.

'*Si*, character, and she feels sure that a lot of people will remember her because she was *molto molto bella*.'

Understanding that to be extremely beautiful, Lainey said, 'Did your grandmother know if she still lives in Tuoro, if she's even still alive?'

'What she said was that there were rumours about Melvina and Aldo before they leave Tuoro, so it is not likely that they are still here. She did not want to discuss what were the rumours, because she has no idea if they are true. She will speak to you about them, she says, if you do not find anyone who can tell you what they know. You understand, she is not confident that her information is good, so she would prefer you to speak to older people in the village first. But,' she continued, 'she advise us to go gently, because it could be we wake up ghosts that many of the older people will wish to stay dead.'

Lainey turned to Stacy, feeling almost as alarmed by that as intrigued.

'Do you have the letter with you?' Stacy prompted.

Lainey shook her head. 'It's at the villa, but I can remember most of it. There's only one page,' she explained to the others, 'and I've no idea who wrote it, but whoever it was addressed my mother as *mia cara bambina*, so it must have been someone who was fond of her.'

'We've wondered,' Stacy added, 'if it might have been Alessandra's grandmother who wrote it, or a relative anyway.'

'What does it say?' Marco prompted.

'Well, one of the oddest things about it,' Lainey began, 'is that my mother seems to have told the writer that she named me after her mother, Melvina, but obviously it isn't true. Melvina isn't even my middle name, because that's Cristina. The writer then asks if she should tell Melvina that Alessandra has named her child after her, but she seems worried about how my grandmother might take it.'

Marco and Adriana were frowning in confusion.

'Go on,' Lorenzo encouraged.

'I can remember the last paragraph word for word,' Lainey told them. 'It says: "I was disturbed to hear that you find it hard to look at the child," meaning me, "without thinking of what happened, but please remember that she is not to blame. I know in your heart you are still angry, and I understand that, but I pray every day for . . ." and then it stops. Obviously there were more pages, but I've never been able to find them.'

Adriana and Marco exchanged glances. 'Well it certainly raises a lot of questions,' Adriana commented, glancing at Lainey's phone as it rang.

'Tierney, my daughter,' she informed them and clicked on. 'Hi, darling, where are you?'

'You mean where are *you*?' came Tierney's testy reply. 'We're at the villa, but no one's here so we can't get in.'

Rolling her eyes, Lainey said, 'Didn't you take any keys?'

'Duh, no, or I wouldn't be calling.'

'OK, well, you'll have to come and get them

because we're about to have lunch. We're on the main piazza in the village. You won't be able to miss us. Have you eaten? You can join us if you like.'

Going off the line to consult the others, Tierney came back, saying, 'Count us in, but there are five of us. Is that OK?'

'Sure, if you don't mind,' she calculated quickly, 'ten of us.'

'*Ten!* Who's with you? Oh my God, don't tell me you've found your family already.'

Lainey smiled as she looked at Marco, Adriana and Lorenzo. 'I wish I could say I had,' she responded, thinking what a blessing it would be if her search could lead to them. 'I'm sure we've still got a way to go on that,' she continued. 'Don't be long, we've already ordered,' and ringing off, she was about to finish her beer when the church bells started to ring.

Curious, she turned in search of a dome or a bell tower above the rooftops, but the piazza was too closed in to see beyond its walls. 'Is that signalling the end of Mass?' she asked.

Checking his watch, Marco said, 'No, it's too late for that. It must be a baptism, or maybe a special communion.'

As she continued to listen Lainey could feel herself being oddly drawn to the melodic chiming, as though it was calling to her, or at least trying to remind her a church was there. To Marco she said, 'I think I should talk to the priest.'

'By all means,' he agreed. 'He is a very amenable person, but he has not been here for more than ten years, so I am not sure what he can tell us.'

'Ah, something I almost forget,' Adriana suddenly

cried, as Lorenzo went off to round up the children. 'Grandmama tell me you should also go to Isola Maggiore – this is the biggest and closest of the three islands in the lake – because she is sure it is where your grandmother used to work with the lace.'

'Lace?' Stacy echoed.

'*Si.* For many years the women of the island make most beautiful lace,' Adriana explained. 'Perhaps it is where your grandparents lived, I don't know, but it is a very short boat ride to get there and you will see that some women, even today, are still making the beautiful linens.'

Lainey glanced at Stacy, as Marco said, 'I can go with you in the afternoon tomorrow, if you would like me to help with the translation.'

Ignoring Stacy's kick under the table, Lainey broke into a smile. 'That would be lovely, thank you,' she replied. 'Just tell me what time to meet you and where, and I'll make sure I'm there.'

Much later in the day Lainey and Stacy were stretched out on sunbeds beside the pool, soaking up the sun through a leafy bower, and half dozing as they listened to Max playing his guitar. He was nowhere in view, but the sound of his Bob Dylan and Billy Bragg renditions were carrying melodically over the hillside, as were the accompanying voices of his small audience comprising Tierney, Skye and the two new friends Max had hooked up with at last night's *discoteca*, as they were now calling it. They seemed pleasant enough boys – or young men, since they were around Max's age – and being English, from Cheshire, there was no problem with the language. Apparently there were

277

plans to hit the *discoteca* again tonight, and Lainey had found herself agreeing to Tierney and Skye going with them.

'If you don't we'll just sneak out anyway,' Tierney had warned, before she'd even had a chance to object.

'You're not old enough to get in,' Lainey had pointed out.

'Yes we are, and anyway no one checks IDs here and we both look eighteen, so there won't be a problem.'

Since it was too hot to argue, Lainey had let it go; after all, she had to start allowing these freedoms at some point, and now seemed as good a time as any. Actually, her only real concern was Skye and how hyper she'd been at lunchtime, to a degree that Lainey had wondered if she'd been drinking before coming to join them at the café.

Keeping her eyes closed and trying not to think of Tom as Max broke into 'Take It Easy', one of Tom's favourites, she half turned to Stacy as she said, 'Tell me, what did you make of Skye earlier?'

Raising a lazy hand to shield her eyes, Stacy replied, 'I guess embarrassing is the first word to come to mind. She didn't seem to know who to flirt with first, Max, the new boys, Lorenzo or Marco.'

Lainey shuddered as she recalled it.

'I guess we mustn't forget her age,' Stacy continued. 'All those hormones, being in a new place, away from home . . .'

Prepared to accept that, since the music was drawing her deeper into memories of Tom and how easily aroused they'd always become in the sun, Lainey reached out for her mobile as it rang. Seeing who it was made her heart turn over. 'It's him,' she said to Stacy, and clicked on before considering whether or not she wanted to speak to him.

'Hi,' he said, 'is this a good time?'

Matching the evenness of his tone, she said, 'As good as any. What can I do for you?'

'Actually, I was just wondering how it was going over there. If you're all settled in and finding your way around OK.'

'We're doing fine, thank you.' And if they weren't, what exactly did he propose to do about it? 'Zav's missing you.'

'I've spoken to him a couple of times,' he assured her, 'I think he understands why I can't be there. So what's the place like?'

The words flew out before she could stop them. 'I don't understand why you're interested. I mean, you could have been here to see it for yourself . . .'

'Would you rather I rang off?'

Swinging her legs off the bed, she went to sit on the edge of the pool.

'Are you still there?' he asked.

'Yes, I'm here,' she replied.

He took a moment before saying, 'So how are Tierney and Max? I still can't get either of them to take my calls or answer my texts.'

'Does that mean you still think I'm turning them against you?'

'No, of course not. I'm sorry I said that, you didn't deserve it.'

'Actually, I don't deserve any of this, but it's still happening.'

She could almost see his face, the tautness of his mouth, the vein that stood out on his temple when he was trying to stay calm.

'Are you going to tell me anything about what's happening over there,' he asked, 'or am I wasting my time?'

Since she really didn't want him to ring off, she said, 'Everything's fine. The villa's perfect, the view of the lake is stunning and the village isn't the most charming I've ever seen, but it's quaint.'

'So, have you decided how to go about finding your family?'

Gazing out across the glittering miles of the lake to where the horizon was as smudged by heat as the whole vista was by time, she said, 'Actually, I've already got someone willing to help out on that.' The thought of Marco and embarking on her search with him, instead of Tom, was making her feel almost resentful. Except she'd have needed his help anyway, since Tom was no more familiar with Italian than she was. 'He's the owner of the villa we're renting,' she continued, 'and his grandmother sort of remembers Melvina and Aldo.' She felt an urge to tell him how good-looking Marco was, but knowing he'd see straight through the puerile effort to make him jealous she managed to stop herself.

'And Alessandra? Does anyone remember her?' he asked.

'Not that I've come across so far. Marco's grand-mother says we should speak to people in the village – and on an island in the lake – because she's sure we'll find someone who knew my grandparents better than she did.'

'So it doesn't seem likely that they're still there?'

'No. Apparently there were rumours before they left, but I don't know yet what they were.'

'That sounds interesting.'

'Or ominous.'

'Indeed. Has there been mention of any other family members?'

'None so far, but it's still early days.'

He fell silent, and she felt herself on the brink of tears as she wondered what he was thinking, where he was while making this call. Somewhere out of Kirsten's earshot, presumably. She watched a dragon-fly, graceful and iridescent, skimming across the sparkling surface of the pool. He should be here, she was thinking, *he should be here.*

'Am I allowed to ask about Max and Tierney now?' he asked carefully.

'Of course,' she replied. 'They're OK. You might be able to hear Max playing his guitar . . .' She held up her phone and wondered if he could make out the familiar sound of 'Fall at Your Feet' by Crowded House. It was another favourite of Tom's; in fact almost everything Max played, whether on his guitar or his iPod, had been influenced by his father.

'Did you get that?' she asked, bringing the phone back to her ear.

'I did. He's improving.'

'He has an audience, so that's probably helping.'

'Oh?'

'Only Tierney and Skye, and a couple of friends he made last night. Zav and Alfie got bored and went inside to watch a DVD.'

There was a smile in Tom's voice as he said, 'Seems I've still got some work to do on my younger son's musical tastes. I'm surprised Tierney's there. It's not usually her sort of thing.'

'No, but I think she's quite keen on one of the new friends, Brett, so she's prepared to suffer it. I've said she and Skye can go to the local disco tonight.'

'Are they old enough?'

'Apparently they're not as strict here as they are at home, and it's not as if we're in Rome, or Florence. It's all very local and not even particularly touristy, apart from down by the lake where there's a camp-site and said disco. Please don't send her a text telling her what time to be back and to make sure she has her phone and doesn't let her drink out of her sight. I'll go through all that before she leaves, and Max will be there. You know how protective he is of her.'

'I also know how irresponsible he can be, so no later than midnight, and no more than two alcoholic drinks.'

Unable to stop herself, she said, 'If you want to lay down the rules you should be here. As you're not, I'll make the decisions.'

He didn't argue, he simply said, 'If you need any backup, just call.'

'And what, leave a message? You never answer your phone.'

'I do when I'm in range. If I'm not, texts usually manage to get through.'

'So I'd best not count on you in an emergency?'

Sighing, he said, 'I should probably go now.'

'Yes, you probably should.'

'I'll call again tomorrow.'

'Actually, I wish you wouldn't. It's hard enough being here without you; having you calling out of guilt or pity or whatever's driving you . . .'

'Is concern for my family not enough?'

'It might be if it was genuine.'

'You seriously think it isn't?'

She knew it was, for the children. She stared hard at the water, fighting back tears.

'If I could be there, I would,' he told her.

'Really?' she responded, and unable to hold it together any longer she disconnected the call, put her phone down and slipped soundlessly into the pool.

Chapter Fifteen

Tierney had never been to a shop like this before in her life. She kind of knew they existed – there was one in Bristol, and she thought there was probably one in Cheltenham too, but no way had she even looked in the window, much less walked through the door. Here, in Italy, they seemed to be everywhere; they were even advertised on hoardings on the side of the road with graphic pictures, and, typical of Skye, she'd insisted they come in to find out exactly what kind of stuff they sold.

As if the window display with all its rubber toys and frilly knicks could have left them in any doubt.

The worst part of being in here was knowing that Max, Brett and Ricky were waiting outside in the car, finding it hilarious that they'd had the nerve to venture in. They had to know Skye was only doing it for a tease; once she had a drink in her she just couldn't help herself, it seemed, but all this kinky paraphernalia and the explicit pictures on the walls were reminding Tierney too much of Guy.

He'd only sent her one of the photos he'd taken of her the night she was with him. Seeing herself like that had made her feel so sick with shame that she'd erased it straight away, without even mentioning it to Skye. She hadn't answered it; in fact she'd hardly replied to any of his texts since being here, so why wasn't he getting the message?

Now she was wondering if the photo had been some kind of threat – do as I say or these shots will go public.

Please, please, please God don't let that be true.

He hadn't said that, so she had to put it out of her mind or she'd go mental with terror. She was just going to think about normal stuff now, such as Brett, who seemed really sweet and funny and into lots of the same things she was. He'd danced with her loads of times at the *discoteca* last night, and when Max – bloody Max – had made her go on to Coke, Brett had only done the same. How lovely was that?

'What do you think?' Skye asked, sauntering out of a fitting room to stand in front of a mirror.

Tierney's jaw dropped. A beat later she was giggling. Luckily no one else was in the shop, apart from the girl who was on the till, and she hadn't stopped jabbering on the phone the whole time they'd been there.

'Shall I get it?' Skye wondered, turning to get a glimpse of herself from behind.

'Are you serious? When are you going to wear it?'

Skye regarded her incredulously. 'Duh, it's a swimsuit, so when do you think I'm going to wear it?'

Tierney shrugged. It didn't look much like a swimsuit to her, or at least not one she would wear, the way it plunged right down to below Skye's navel and barely covered her boobs. Starting to feel a bit claustrophobic, she said, 'Come on, we should go.'

Skye looked annoyed. 'We can't without buying

something,' she protested. 'I'm going to get this. So what are you going to get?'

'Nothing. I don't want anything.'

'You have to buy something. Brett's expecting you to.'

'No, he isn't, and anyway, what's it got to do with him?'

'You must have seen his face when we said we wanted to come in here. I'm telling you, he's out there like practically gagging for it.'

'Then he'll just have to gag, because I'm not buying anything.'

Returning to the cubicle and leaving the curtain open as she changed back into her sundress, Skye said, 'I don't get what's wrong with you lately. You're always in a mood, and it's not like you've got anything to be in a mood about. There's Mr Grey practically . . .'

'Don't talk about him.'

'Oh, excuse me for breathing. I thought he was your . . .'

'He's not normal,' Tierney broke in waspishly. 'In fact, he's pervy. Maudie thinks so too.'

'Oh, well, let's all agree with Maudie the virgin, why don't we?' Skye scoffed. 'That girl hasn't got a clue what it's like to be kissed, never mind shagged by a bloke. She's just jealous, that's her trouble. Jealous and a minger.'

Rushing to Maudie's defence, Tierney said, 'She's *not* a minger, and the trouble with you, Skye, is everything's always about sex, and actually there's more to life.'

Skye's eyebrows arched in amazement, but she said no more as Tierney turned away and walked outside into a wall of heat.

What she really wanted, more than anything, she realised, was to talk to her dad – not about any of this, she wouldn't even want to talk to her mum about that. She just wanted her dad to be here, the way he always was on holidays, bossing them about, driving them mad, but making everything kind of special and fun.

She wondered if he was doing that with Julia and her mother now. Probably not, given that Julia's mother was ill. He could have in the past, though, lots of times, and they, his real family, had known nothing about it. It was so horrible to think of that she couldn't allow herself to or she'd start crying or something, and Skye would think it was because they'd rowed and it had nothing to do with her.

She should have asked Maudie to come.

Or *Julia* – as if!

What was Julia like? Probably blonde and gorgeous and really popular with everyone. Tierney wondered if she'd had sex yet, or been into a sex shop, or even had a boyfriend.

Actually, she couldn't care less about Julia, or anyone else come to that. She just wished everyone would go away and leave her alone, and never, ever mention the word sex again.

Lainey couldn't help laughing at the way Marco was trying to extricate himself from the fifth or sixth friendly greeting he'd run into during their short walk from his car to the pier. Though she wasn't at all surprised to find he was so well known, she was bewildered, as well as amused, by how extensive the greetings were. Surely a lot more was being said than a mere 'Hi, how are you?' or 'Nice to see you.' In fact, for how long each encounter took, with everyone seemingly oblivious to the blazing sun, she felt certain they must be exchanging a day-by-day account of the past month's events.

'As we say in England,' she commented, when he finally parted from a jaunty middle-aged man who ran the campsite they'd just passed, 'never use three words when fifty will do.'

Enjoying the humour, he said, 'Italian people are very effusive by nature. We cannot help it, so if I talk too much today, you must tell me to stop.'

Knowing she'd never do such a thing, especially when he was being so kind, she cocked an eyebrow at the saucy billboard outside the *discoteca* (was it really a bare bottom? Perhaps it was a cleavage – it was difficult to tell) and strode on towards the jetty. It wasn't a strip club, surely. She'd have words with Max tonight, because if he was taking Tierney to such a place and Tom were to find out . . . Actually, she'd deal with it herself, she didn't need Tom's backup.

Since speaking to him yesterday, she'd felt so down and stressed by what was happening that she'd almost rung Marco earlier to call off their trip to the island. Now she was nothing but glad that she hadn't, since her spirits had lifted considerably during the past twenty minutes, so she was going to stay focused on her search, and on how fortunate she was to have Marco's company, as well as his help. On the drive down the hill he'd filled her in on his visit to the town hall, where he'd found a record of Melvina's marriage to Aldo, but none bearing the name of Alessandra Clementi. This had come as no surprise, since it had hardly been likely he would turn anything up when her father was *ignoto*.

As she listened to Marco now, explaining about the sculptures they were passing beside a children's playground, she couldn't help reflecting on what she'd learned about him over breakfast that morning. It had come out when Stacy had wondered aloud why no one ever spoke about his wife.

'I expect it's because she left him and went back to England with another man,' Zav casually informed them.

Lainey wasn't sure who'd been more shocked, her or Stacy. Since Zav must have got his information from Benito they didn't doubt that it was true, but it was hard to imagine someone leaving a man like Marco. Of course, they barely knew him yet, and judging him merely on his looks and charm was a bit like judging a house by a glossy front door. It could be hiding all manner of evils inside. Or a broken heart, she couldn't help thinking, and if Marco's wife really had left him for another man, there was a good chance he wasn't feeling much better than she was right now. If he wasn't, he was very good at hiding it, but hopefully so was she.

'Excuse me, but you are looking very – *pensieroso*?' Marco was searching for the word. 'Pensive!' he cried laughingly. 'I am sorry, did I interrupt?'

Laughing too, she said, 'No, no, not at all. Or at least I'm glad you did. I want to thank you again, not only for coming with me today, but for taking Zav and Alfie to spend the afternoon with Ben while Stacy works.'

He seemed surprised. 'It is very good for Ben to have the company of English boys his own age. He is, of course, close with his cousins, but the children, they change so quickly as they grow up – and Ben, having parents of different nationalities, is caught between two cultures, which is good in one way, but hard for him in another.'

Since she didn't feel it would be right for her to mention what she knew about his wife unless he did, Lainey said, 'He's a very sociable – and handsome – little boy.'

With no small irony, Marco said, 'I would take all the credit, if he did not have a very beautiful mother who makes sure to look after his manners.'

Smiling, and liking him for speaking kindly of his wife in spite of what their differences might be, Lainey turned to watch the ferryboat shunting its way into dock. She needed to focus her mind on Isola Maggiore now, which she could see across the way, covered in trees, seeming almost close enough to swim to, though she wouldn't be willing to give it a try.

How many journeys, she wondered, had her mother, or grandmother, made over this short stretch of water? What had been in their minds, who had they been going to see, what had troubled them or made them happy? Having no idea what she would learn at the other end, what might have happened in storms or sunshine, crisis or calm, she could only allow herself to board the ferry and hope, if either of them was looking down on her now, that they weren't as hostile to her search as she feared.

'Do you know the story of how the lake receive its name?' Marco asked, as they went to stand at the ferry's bow ready to start the short crossing.

'No, but I hope you're going to tell me.' Lainey smiled, enjoying the rocking motion of the boat and the swish of the waves lapping its sides.

'It is from,' he began, turning to sit on a bench

seat, 'an Etruscan prince who came to these shores and fell in love with a beautiful nymph, Agilla. She fell very deeply in love with him too, but then the prince died – I do not know how – and so the lake bears his name, Trasimeno. It is said that when the wind blows over the water it is the sound of Agilla still mourning the death of her lover.'

Lainey pulled a face. 'That's so sad.'

He smiled wryly. 'I'm sorry, but don't worry, I think they were very happy while the prince was alive.'

'How long were they together?'

'Oh, fifty years I think. Possibly one hundred. A very long time.'

Her eyes sparkled. 'I know that's not true.'

He seemed curious. 'How do you know?'

'Because she was a nymph and nymphs don't exist.'

He threw out his hands. 'How can you say this?' he cried. 'You spoil the story for me now.'

Laughing, she turned back to gaze out over the sun-dappled waters, feeling nature's beauty and romance wafting over her as gently as the breeze. She couldn't stop herself wishing Tom was here to share it, but a brutal reminder of where he actually was quickly moved her thoughts on.

The island was coming into clearer view now, with all kinds of boats bobbing about the shoreline, and through the dense forestation on the hillside she could see the double bell gable of a church glinting like opals in a bed of emerald green.

Minutes later they were following the island's jetty into a small clutch of market stalls whose wares were mostly for tourists: guidebooks, beach balls, name bracelets, and an assortment of handcrafted lace. Though there were plenty of people around, the only language she could make out was Italian; however, the music blaring from a nearby café was unmistakably Madonna.

'This is Via Guglielmi,' Marco explained, as they reached a meandering brick-laid street with pictur-esque stone houses each side of it, and troughs of tired-looking flowers adding their colour to so much grey. 'This is named after the Marquis Guglielmi, a very rich man, who lived here for many years in the nineteenth century and made the Franciscan monastery and church into his villa. It was his daughter, Elena, who brought a lady from Turin to teach the local women to make the lace, which became famous around the world.'

Liking the sound of Elena, Lainey looked around for some signs of women sitting outside their doors pursuing their craft, but there were none. She tried to imagine what it might have been like when her grandmother, Melvina, had worked here, presum-ably as a much younger woman, and decided that it had probably been a hotbed of rivalry and gossip, given the meagre size of the community.

'This is the Museum of Lace,' Marco explained, crossing the street towards what looked like a small mission house with its flat facade, oblong windows and arched front door. 'If you would like to go in and look around, we can do this, but first I will ask if they know who is the best person to talk to about our search for Melvina.'

Twenty minutes later, after browsing the few display cabinets of antiquated lace collars, tablecloths and tassels, they stepped back out into the blazing sun armed with the name and address of an old fisherman who, they'd been told, knew everything about the island and everyone who had lived on it during his lifetime of almost eighty years.

Since Via Guglielmi was the only street on the island, they were soon knocking at Signor Donata's scratched front door and gazing up at the tightly shuttered windows for some signs of life. After several more attempts to rouse him they had to accept that he was either deaf, or not at home.

'I will see if we can get round the back,' Marco decided, 'he could be in the garden,' but as he started towards an alley that ran down the side of the house a bent and very frail-looking man appeared, blocking the way.

After establishing that he was Signor Donata, Marco quickly set about introducing himself and Lainey, and explained why they were there. The whole time he spoke the old man's rheumy eyes kept flickering to Lainey, as though he was assessing the truth of what he was hearing. In the end he nodded, and turned back into the alleyway, beckoning for them to follow.

The garden at the back of the house was mostly overgrown, with an old fishing boat slumped in the grass close to the lake, as though exhausted by its lifetime's work. On a bumpy patio there was a round marble-topped table with four plastic chairs and a collapsed parasol barely clinging to its spokes.

'*Vuoi qualcosa da bere?*' the old man asked, looking at Lainey.

'Would you like a drink?' Marco translated. 'It would be polite, but I'm not sure what he's going to offer.'

Amused, Lainey said, 'I would love one, thank you. *Grazie.*'

Several tranquil moments passed while Signor Donata went inside to do the honours, leaving Lainey and Marco to watch a mangy cat emerge from beneath the boat and pad towards a gaggle of fat geese pecking about the edge of the lake. By the time Signor Donata returned, Marco had managed to struggle the parasol up over its rusty pole to provide them with some much-needed shade.

The drink turned out to be a syrupy sort of orange squash with lots of foam around the top and ice cubes at the bottom. Given how thirsty she was, Lainey had no problem swallowing it almost in one, then promptly wished she'd waited when Signor Donata watched her put her glass down again before lifting his own and saying, '*Salut.*'

Catching Marco hiding a smile, she whispered an apology and sat quietly listening as Marco returned to his explanation of why they were there. This time she heard her grandmother's name mentioned several times, and her mother's, and saw the way the old man's eyes seemed to sharpen. He started to nod, slowly, but the rugged texture of his skin was making his expression hard to read.

Finally Marco turned back to her. 'I have told him that you are Melvina and Aldo Clementi's granddaughter,' he said, 'and that you are hoping to find out something about your family while you are on holiday here, in Tuoro.'

Lainey smiled at the old man, hoping to encourage him to speak freely.

His eyes remained on hers as he began speaking in a voice so gravelly and low that she wondered if Marco was able to follow. Since he didn't interrupt, she had to assume that he was, and so she waited and listened, trying to gauge from their

294

expressions what was being said, but it simply wasn't possible.

In the end, after asking several questions, all of which seemed to receive the answer '*No,*' or '*Non posso dirvi,*' Marco began his translation.

'Signor Donata says he remembers your grandmother, Melvina, but he knew better your great-grandmother, Maria. She came from Passignano, but she lived here, on the island, with your great-grandfather, Alberto, for all of her married life. Alberto was a fisherman born on the island and she, like many of the ladies, worked at making the lace. When her daughter Melvina is old enough she is making the lace too.' He glanced at the old man, who was gazing at nothing as he listened to his story being told in a language he didn't understand.

'He says that Melvina was very beautiful,' Marco continued, 'and that she had very high spirits. All her young life she was in mischief, but everyone loved her so everyone forgave her. It was when she became older that the real trouble began. Each time she goes to the mainland she says she will never come back. She hates the island, she tells her parents. She wants to have a better life, the same as the noble ladies who come to buy the lace. Maria and Alberto were afraid of the way she began behaving with the men who sometimes came with the ladies. People used to say that she was trying to find herself a husband, and anyone's husband would do as long as he was rich.'

Lainey pulled a face. Were she not certain that both men were staunch Catholics, she might have made some sort of quip about her grandmother's morals. In the circumstances, she felt it better to keep quiet.

Marco's eyebrows arched ironically as he seemed to read her mind. 'Signor Donata says that Melvina did find herself the husband of someone else,' he continued. 'His name was Luigi Valente. Everyone knew him, because he lived in a grand villa close to Cortona and he was the host when many of the wealthy people who want to buy the lace come to the region. He was a man who always had an eye for the pretty girls, Signor Donata says, and Melvina was prettier than most.'

The old man suddenly spoke again, at some length, using his hands to emphasise whatever point he was making.

When he'd finished, Marco said, 'He wants you to understand that he is only repeating what he has heard from his wife over the years. He himself never saw Melvina with Valente, but her relationship with him was common knowledge, and his wife saw them together often, sometimes here on the island, or in Tuoro. It was said that when she became pregnant Valente paid your grandfather, Aldo Clementi, to marry her, and Aldo agreed because he was very much in love with Melvina. Apparently Valente bought them an apartment in Tuoro where he visited Melvina many times over the years, and Aldo he always turned a blind eye.

'Your great-grandmother, Maria, was so ashamed of her daughter's behaviour that she would no longer see her. She banned her from the house, even from the island, but Melvina did not care. She was besotted with Valente. When her son was born she did not even try to pretend he was the son of Aldo. She told everyone he was the son of Valente, and Valente did not deny it. It is terrible for Aldo, for Maria and Alberto too, but Melvina she had no

296

shame. It is said,' he continued, his voice turning grave, 'that Valente's wife caused the accident that killed Melvina's little boy when he was two years old, by putting a curse on him.'

Thrown by this unexpected revelation, Lainey looked hard at the old man, wishing she could ask him herself if he actually believed in the curse. Surely not?

Marco was speaking again. 'After the death of her son Melvina came to grieve on the island, where Maria took care of her and tried to make her well again. Aldo came too, and it is said that Valente sometimes visited, but Signor Donata does not know if this is true. Though he saw him often on the island over the years, he cannot recall whether he came during those months. He thinks if he did it is not likely that Maria and Alberto would allow him to enter their house. All he knows is that by the time Melvina and Aldo returned to Tuoro she was pregnant again, and no one could say for sure if the little girl, when she came, was the child of Aldo or Valente.'

'Was the little girl . . .' Lainey cleared her throat. 'Are we talking about Alessandra now, my mother?'

Marco nodded. '*Si*, this is Alessandra. Because of what happened to her son Melvina insisted to everybody that Alessandra was the daughter of Aldo. As Alessandra grows up she spends much time here on the island with her grandparents, who adore her. It is easier for them to keep her safe from Valente's wife and her curses when she is here, and this they must do because Melvina continued to be the mistress of Valente.

'Signor Donata says that all the years of Alessandra's childhood Melvina was often travelling with Valente, or staying with him at his villa when his wife was away, *maledendo la sua anima immortale con i suoi peccati*. Damning her immortal soul with her sins, was what he said.'

Knowing how offensive this conduct would be to a man of Signor Donata's generation, Lainey couldn't help feeling ashamed of her grandmother's behaviour.

'I think, from what else Signor Donata has told me,' Marco was saying, 'that Alessandra was like her mother in many ways, in that she was very beautiful and spirited. She was a favourite here on the island, but when she was fifteen, maybe sixteen, she returned to Tuoro to live with her mother. It is said by the people of the island that her grandmother, Maria, died from a broken heart after what happened to her beloved Alessandra.'

Feeling herself tensing, Lainey said, 'So what did happen to her?'

Marco shook his head helplessly. 'I have tried to persuade Signor Donata to tell me, but he either doesn't know, or doesn't want to say.'

Turning to the old man, Lainey begged, 'Please will you tell me what happened to my mother? It's very important for me to know.'

His eyes stayed on her as Marco translated.

A moment or two passed before Signor Donata explained to Marco his reasons for not going any further.

'He says,' Marco told her when the old man had finished, 'that he doesn't want to believe what he was told. He thinks some people were wrong in what they understood and that he hopes for your mother's sake, and for yours, that they were.'

Feeling her insides starting to liquefy as a terrible

suspicion formed, Lainey said, 'Can you ask him,' hoping she wasn't about to offend Marco – or Signor Donata, 'is he saying that Valente could be both my father and grandfather?' In other words, it was possible that her mother had slept with her own father.

Looking as worried by this as she was, Marco said, 'Are you sure you're ready to know the answer to that?'

Actually, she didn't think she was, but how could she possibly leave here without asking?

'What he says,' Marco began after Signor Donata had spoken at some length, 'is that we should talk to Carlotta Calduzzi?' He glanced at the old man for confirmation of the name and received a nod.

'She was your mother's friend from a very young age,' Marco continued, 'and Signor Donata is sure that she is still in Tuoro. He says if anyone can tell us the real truth of why Alessandra left and never returned, it will almost certainly be Carlotta.'

As they took the ferry back to Tuoro Lainey stood gazing at the village on the hillside, a sleepy, benign-looking clutter of old houses at the centre of a careless modern sprawl. It was as though the younger generations were tumbling away from their roots, pulling themselves free of the past, making new stories for the future of this valley. Yet they were still connected to the heart of the community, as though not wanting to flee too far, which wasn't so very different to how it had been for Melvina and Alessandra.

Until Alessandra had left, never to return.

'Are you OK?' Marco asked as she let go of a sigh.

'I think so,' she replied, 'though learning that I could be the daughter of incest . . .' Even saying it was stirring its horror inside her; that it might be true was making her feel sick to her soul. 'It would explain why my mother would never tell me who my father was.' She was gazing at the village again, and wondering if her mother's ghost was watching her from a hidden window. Melvina's too, and Aldo's. Perhaps even Valente's.

'We do not know this for certain yet,' Marco reminded her. 'It could be that Aldo was your grandfather.'

Appreciating the reassurance, she turned to him, saying, 'According to your grandmother Aldo and Melvina left Tuoro many years ago. Do you think she might know where they went?'

'We can always ask,' he replied, taking out his phone.

A few moments later he shook his head regretfully as he said, 'She is not able to tell us. They had already gone by the time she came to the village, and she never heard that they came back.'

'But she knew about the rumours. She told Adriana about them, though she wouldn't say what they were.'

He was frowning as he thought. 'Incest is a very grave sin,' he declared, 'it would be hard for anyone to speak of it, particularly those of my grand-mother's and Signor Donata's generation. But if Carlotta Calduzzi was your mother's friend, she will be younger, and perhaps she will not find it so difficult to tell us what we need to know.'

Touched by the 'we', Lainey nevertheless felt compelled to say, 'It's hard to imagine anything worse than what we're suspecting, but just in case it does go that way, perhaps now would be a good time to say I'll understand if you'd rather not continue. Heaven only knows what we're going to uncover . . .'

His hand was up. 'Without a translator,' he came in gently, 'you will not uncover anything, and I am not such a faint heart that I cannot stand a little scandal.'

She almost smiled. 'It's not so little,' she reminded him. 'As you said, it's a very grave sin, and with you being Catholic . . .'

'Do not let that trouble you,' he insisted. 'I am . . . What?' he said as she suddenly regarded him curiously. 'Did I say something?'

'No, I did. I'm thinking about the way my mother turned her back on the church. For years, right up until the months before she died, she'd never set foot in one . . . If she'd been party to incest, either knowingly, or unknowingly, the shame would be terrible, but I thought God forgave everything if you confessed.'

His eyes were teasing as he said, 'A few Hail Marys and you're all pure again? But you are right, He does forgive our sins if we confess them. Perhaps your mother was so ashamed that she could not bring herself to tell anyone, even the priest?'

'I don't suppose it'll help us if we try to find the priest who was in Tuoro at the time,' she reflected. 'Even if he's still alive, he won't break the seal of the confessional. Perhaps he refused to grant her absolution and that's why she'd have nothing to do with the church again.'

Marco was looking doubtful. 'A priest will only refuse absolution if he believes the person is intending to sin again,' he told her.

'Which would mean that she was a willing party to the incest, presuming she knew that Valente could be her father, and she might not have known. Perhaps it's why Melvina rejected her. She was jealous because Valente preferred Alessandra and Alessandra refused to give him up.'

'But she did give him up, because she went to England.'

'After Melvina told her the truth, that he was her father?'

'If it was the truth. And then we must ask ourselves, why did Melvina and Aldo also leave Tuoro?'

Realising they still had a long way to go in their search for answers, Lainey sighed heavily and took his hand as he helped her off the boat.

'I will try to find out if Carlotta Calduzzi is still in the village,' he said, as they walked back to his car. 'I think, as your mother's friend, she is going to be our best bet from here.'

'Wow, there seems to be a bit of a recurring theme going on here,' Tierney commented, pausing in the critical task of painting her toenails blue. 'I mean first your granny gets herself knocked up before marriage, then your mother, then you.'

Lainey eyed her meaningfully. 'Please don't feel free to carry on the tradition,' she retorted archly, making Skye laugh. She hadn't mentioned the possibility of incest yet, and wasn't sure she would even if it turned out to be true. She'd have to discuss it with Tom first. Apart from Stacy, who was currently on the phone, he was the only one she'd feel remotely comfortable confiding in. However, he hadn't called yet this evening and though she wanted desperately to speak to him, she didn't feel right about ringing him.

Thank God her mother had never told Peter her secret, if it really was as bad as Lainey feared.

It could hardly be any worse.

Could it?

Unable to imagine it, she picked up her wine and watched Stacy pacing up and down the lawn in the twilight, making plans with Adriana for how they were going to structure their day together tomorrow concocting a column on Umbrian cuisine. This would be for the new magazine's first edition, and regular foodie features from various parts of the globe might follow. Thinking selfishly, Lainey just hoped Adriana's contribution would enable Stacy to stay on after the weekend, because she wasn't much relishing the thought of being here without her.

She had Marco and Adriana now though, and at least she was making some headway with her search.

'So how come you two are here this evening?' she asked Tierney and Skye. 'Where's Max?'

Skye shrugged as she said, 'He's gone to watch some Led Zep tribute band, but don't ask me where.'

'Castiglione del Lago,' Tierney sang out with a dramatically Italian flourish. 'Sad, if you ask me, but then Dad and Max's taste in music always has been.'

'Talking about music,' Lainey said, 'I saw the disco down at the lake earlier, and it looked like a strip club to me. Please tell me I'm not right.'

'You're not right,' Skye responded, not even looking up from the butterfly tattoo she was carefully pasting on to her ankle.

'Like as if we'd go to a strip club,' Tierney snorted in disgust. 'What are you on?'

Lainey watched as she snatched up her phone to read a text.

'Oh, for God's sake,' she muttered, and slammed the phone down again. Her face was so pinched and pale that Lainey asked, 'Who was that?'

'No one,' Tierney snapped.

Skye looked up at her.

Lainey glanced at Skye, and back to Tierney. 'If it was Dad,' she said, 'maybe you ought to have a chat with him.'

'It wasn't Dad, OK? And even if it was, I don't want to speak to him. He's got another daughter he can have a chat with if that's what he wants.'

Hearing the hurt behind the anger, Lainey said softly, 'She's not taking your place.'

'Oh, right? So that's why he's there now, and not here?'

'He won't be seeing it that way.'

'Well, too bad, because I am, and anyway, I don't know why you're sticking up for him, when it's *you* he's really cheating on, like you're nobody now.'

Feeling the hurt, Lainey lowered her eyes.

'Oh God, Mum, I'm sorry,' Tierney cried, coming to hug her. 'I shouldn't have said that, it just came out, but I didn't mean it, honest. You're not nobody, you're the best mum in the world, even Max says so, and you're not even his. I'm sorry, I'm sorry, please say you forgive me?'

'Of course I do,' Lainey replied, leaning back so Tierney could sit on her lap.

Skye said, 'When my dad walked out on us, my mum got her revenge by going out and finding someone else. I reckon that's what you ought to do, especially if he's loads richer than Tom. It really hacked my dad off when he found out my mum had got herself a multimillionaire.'

Before Lainey could respond, Stacy, having joined them and overheard the last part of the conversation, asked, 'Ah, but did it make him come back?'

Watching her sit down, Skye said, 'He definitely wanted to, but my mum wasn't interested any more. She's happier now than she's ever been.'

Why, Lainey wondered, was she getting the impression that Skye didn't believe her own words? Or perhaps she resented the fact that her mother was happy.

'Well, that's good,' Stacy remarked, 'but I expect it took her a while to get there.'

Skye rolled her eyes. 'Tell me about it. She was really broken up at first, couldn't stop crying, or anything. She was like so depressed. What seriously used to get to her was the way he kept avoiding seeing or speaking to her. He was kind of worried, obviously, because he knew she was in a state, but rather than come round or ring her to find out how she was, he'd ring me instead. She used to hate that. She'd say it made him a coward and a hypocrite, but I didn't mind. At least it meant I got to talk to him, not that he was ever very interested in me.'

'I'm sure that's not true,' Lainey protested.

Skye merely shrugged, and turned to watch Zav and Alfie coming out on to the terrace.

'Are you OK?' Lainey asked. Zav nodded, and looked askance at Tierney on her lap.

'You're such a baby,' he told his sister.

'Yeah, and you're such a grown-up,' she shot back.

'Glad you noticed,' he replied, with a little

swagger of his hips that made everyone laugh, including Tierney. 'Mum, is it OK if we go for a swim?'

'I don't see why not. Just make sure the lights are on down there, and don't forget to bring the wet towels back up with you.'

'OK, will do. Come on Alfs, race you!'

As they shot off across the lawn, Lainey was about to top up her and Stacy's wine when Zav shouted back, 'By the way, Mum. Dad just rang and said to tell everyone goodnight.'

As Lainey's heart sank, Skye said, 'God, that's exactly what my dad used to do. Tell Mum this, tell her that so he didn't have to speak to her himself.'

'Actually Tom does ring me,' Lainey told her, trying not to sound defensive.

Skye merely shrugged. 'I'm just saying, that's all, but if I were you I know what I'd be doing now and that's getting it on with Marco. He's totally drop-dead and rich, I reckon, and it definitely looks like he's got the hots for you . . .'

'Skye, for God's sake,' Tierney cried, 'this is my mother you're talking to and no way is she interested in Marco, even if he is interested in her . . .'

'Which he's not,' Lainey quickly added.

Skye wasn't fazed. 'That's because you don't want her to be interested,' she told Tierney, as though Lainey hadn't even spoken, 'but I'm telling you . . .'

'That's enough,' Lainey cut in sharply. 'I really don't need your advice, thank you, Skye, and I'd appreciate it if you didn't air your opinions quite so freely in the future.'

Chapter Sixteen

'I don't think your mum likes me very much,' Skye commented, as Tierney came in from the bathroom.

Tightening the towel around her, Tierney said, 'She'll like you even less if she finds out what you were doing after everyone went to bed last night.'

Sighing wearily, Skye rolled over on the bed to stare thoughtfully up at the ceiling. 'You know what your trouble is,' she said after a while, 'you're jealous.'

Tierney almost gasped. 'Jealous of *you*, with my own brother? What are you on?'

'No, I don't mean that, I mean you're jealous because your dad's got another daughter, because your mum's getting it on with Marco . . .'

'She so is *not* getting it on with Marco! She went out with him once, yesterday, because he speaks Italian and she doesn't, so why are you trying to make something of it?'

Skye merely shrugged, then raising a long slender leg she began inspecting its golden perfection. 'You should have come down to the pool last night,' she said, as Tierney freed her hair from a towel and shook it out. 'Brett was really disappointed when you didn't.'

Though Tierney felt sorry if she'd let Brett down, no way was she going for a moonlight swim while Skye was wearing the bathing suit she'd bought in the sex shop. She'd known what would happen, all the attention would be on Skye, and though she, Tierney, was only interested in Brett as a friend, she'd have felt dead stupid hanging about in her bikini with no one taking any notice of her.

'I heard you screaming,' she said, going to brush out her hair, 'and I expect Mum did too, so chances are she'll want to know what was going on.'

Rolling on to her front and resting her chin in her hands, Skye said, 'Would you like to know?'

'Not really,' Tierney lied.

'Yes you would, so I'll tell you. They grabbed the swimsuit off me and I ended up going with all three of them.'

Tierney's hand stopped in mid-air as her eyes went to Skye's in the mirror.

Bursting into laughter, Skye sat back on her knees and reached for her make-up bag. 'They got the swimsuit,' she confessed, 'but I only went with Max.'

Tierney was watching her, not really sure what to believe now.

'Can I come in?' Lainey called, knocking on the door.

'Yes,' Tierney called back.

'So you're up at last,' Lainey remarked as she went to open their curtains. 'It's almost midday, you know.' Turning to regard them, as though checking for hangovers, or worse, she said, 'It sounded as though there was quite a party going on at the pool last night. How many people did Max bring back with him?'

'Just Brett and Ricky,' Skye replied, tissuing off

her smudged mascara. 'I'm sorry, it was me making all the noise. They kept splashing and acting stupid, you know, the way boys do, and we forgot to keep it down. I hope we didn't wake you.'

Lainey's eyebrows rose, making it clear that they had. Then, making no further comment, she began picking up clothes as she said, 'Stacy took the boys over to Adriana's with her earlier, so I wondered if you two – and Max – might like to do something with me today.'

Grabbing back a bikini top before it disappeared in the wash, Tierney said, 'Like what? I thought you were going to try and find the woman who was Granny's friend today, Carlotta what's-her-name.'

'Calduzzi. That was the plan, but Marco just rang to say that he made some enquiries in the village this morning and although she lives in Cortona now, so not too far away, apparently she's on holiday in France till the beginning of next week.'

'So what about the priest in Tuoro? Weren't you hoping to talk to him?'

'Yes, but I don't expect he'll be able to tell us much, seeing as he wasn't even here at the time. Is that pile there to be washed, or hung up?'

Glancing at it, Tierney said, 'Hung up.'

'So,' Lainey said, heading for the door, 'how do you fancy having a look around Assissi, or Perugia?'

Glancing at Skye, Tierney groaned. 'Oh, Mum, it's too hot to go traipsing round churches. Dad always makes us do that and it's so boring.'

Lainey's eyes seemed to dim slightly as she said, 'I admit it can be at times, but in Italy it's where most of the major art is displayed . . .'

'Great, so we can look at boring paintings in churches and in galleries,' Tierney broke in. 'Is Max around yet? He said he was going to take us to the designer outlet place over by the autostrada today. Why don't you come there with us? You can treat us to lunch and pay for our shopping?'

With one of the wry smiles Tierney loved so much, Lainey said, 'That's what really gets to me about you, you're all heart.'

Tierney laughed, but as Lainey started to leave she felt suddenly bad. 'If it means you're going to be on your own today, we'll come,' she offered, ignoring the way Skye's head came up.

Surprised and clearly touched, Lainey said, 'No, it's OK. You go on and do your thing. I'll pop down to the village and see if I can rouse up a few ghosts – or I might take Marco up on his offer to drive over to Montepulciano for a look around while he sees one of his suppliers.'

Tierney stared at her. She was going out with Marco again.

'OK?' Lainey asked teasingly.

Tierney shrugged. 'If that's what you want.'

Blowing her a playful kiss, Lainey continued on to the boys' room to sort out their washing, leaving Tierney to turn back to the mirror and carry on brushing out her hair. 'I know what you're thinking,' she said to Skye, whose silence was so charged she might just as well have been shouting.

'I'm thinking the same as you,' Skye responded, scrolling through her phone. 'This'll make two days in a row that she's been out with Marco.'

Tierney put down her brush and rummaged for a scrunchie to tie up her hair.

'Jesus, you can be such hard work at times,' Skye told her. 'You really need to lighten up, do you know that?'

Feeling a stupid rush of tears stinging her eyes, Tierney kept her head down as she tied up her hair.

'Have you heard from *him* today?' Skye asked, still playing with her phone.

Tierney's heart contracted. 'What do you think?' she snapped. 'He's texting all the time.'

'So what did he say?'

'The same as always, that he really wants to see me when I get back.'

'Well, all this is telling me,' Skye declared, springing up from the bed, 'that you must have been pretty amazing, the way he's going on.'

As she disappeared off to the bathroom, Tierney shuddered with misery, more shame creeping over her. It wasn't always obvious it was her in the photos he kept sending, but in some it was and she wasn't sure whether it was seeing her own face that made her feel so sick, and scared, or the fact that he seemed to be using them as some sort of threat.

Don't tell anyone what happened, or I'll send these to your parents.

Of course, he never actually said that, it was the way she was reading it, but what if she was right?

She had to find a way of making him stop, but she just couldn't think of one.

'So, we hear from Zav that his dad is the famous Tom Hollingsworth,' Marco was saying as he spread a rug on the grass ready to lay out the picnic he and Lainey had brought with them.

Given how relaxed – and impressed – he sounded, Lainey felt certain that was all Zav had told him. She wished Marco hadn't mentioned Tom though, because now he had it was almost as if Tom was there, trying to spoil this time for her with a reminder of how much she missed him.

'I have probably read all his books,' Marco continued as he went to fetch the hamper from the car. 'In Italian, mostly, but a few I have read in English.'

Realising he must be wondering why Tom wasn't here with his family, Lainey tried to think what to tell him. Not the truth, obviously, she didn't know him well enough for that, and anyway it would embarrass him horribly if she suddenly started offloading how her husband had been deceiving her for years, and she, fool that she was, had only just found out. 'Do you have a favourite?' she asked, falling back on her usual response for these occasions.

He frowned as he thought. 'I suppose I was most drawn to the one set in Hungary,' he said. 'He must know Budapest very well, the way he writes about it. Did you go there with him?'

Having to shake her head, while wondering if Kirsten had, perhaps Julia too, Lainey said, 'No, he usually likes to do his research trips alone.' She almost added, *It's where he is now, researching for a new book.*

If only it were true.

Seeming to sense that she didn't want to discuss her husband any further, Marco set about uncorking a bottle of chilled white wine, which he'd produced from a small fridge in the boot of his car. The homemade antipasti she was unpacking looked scrumptious – she just hoped she could summon an appetite to eat it.

They were in the shade of a leafy maple, high on a Tuscan hillside to the west of Montepulciano, where the views, stretching for seemingly endless miles, were of valleys crowded with vines that climbed and sprawled over the banks of the opposite hillside as though trying to reach the golden town at the top. It was a remote and tranquil spot, its beauty almost timeless.

'Why do I get the feeling you've done this before?' she teased, as he poured the wine into two small stemmed glasses he'd taken from a cool bag. Their frosted coating was melting fast in the heat, causing translucent droplets to drip over his fingers and on to the rug.

He had beautiful hands, she noticed, very masculine, yet elegant.

His smile was gently amused as he passed her a glass. 'This is a very fine Pecorino,' he told her, passing the question by. 'Have you had this wine before?'

Surprised, she said, 'I thought Pecorino was a cheese.'

'*Si*, it is a very good cheese, but also it is a wine from the Pecino region of Le Marche, which is east of Umbria. You taste, but first you smell and tell me what fragrance you detect.'

A little self-consciously, since she wasn't practised at this, she carefully swished the wine around the glass and closed her eyes as she inhaled the shy release of a bouquet. 'It's a little spicy?' she said, glancing to him for guidance.

He nodded and gestured for her to continue.

Taking a sip, she allowed the flavours a few moments to settle over her tongue, before saying, 'I think liquorice, maybe . . . Is it jasmine?'

'You are very good at this,' he told her, smiling. 'Are you picking up the apple as well?'

313

She wasn't sure about that, but nodded all the same. 'It's delicious,' she declared, truthfully, and felt her heart falter as she thought of how much Tom enjoyed discovering new wines.

She had to stop making everything about him.

If only she knew how.

As they ate and drank Marco talked about the region and the winemakers he was due to visit later, making her laugh with his descriptions and mimicry of their idiosyncrasies and passions. He went on to tell her, because she asked, that he spoke English so well because he'd studied it at the University of Rome, and when she led him to the subject of his musical tastes she felt pleased when he declared a preference for opera. He'd inherited it from his parents, he told her, who'd died in a car crash just over ten years ago.

He asked about Alessandra and Peter, and seemed sad when she told him about Peter's dementia. His other grandmother had suffered the same way, he told her, and in the end it had been a blessing when she'd finally let go.

Feeling a lump tightening her throat at the thought of her father doing the same, Lainey swallowed more wine to try and help the moment pass. She was ringing every morning and evening to check how he was, and Aunt Daffs always put him on the phone. Sometimes he had nothing to say, didn't even seem to understand that he was supposed to speak, but last night he'd thought she was a child again, hiding somewhere in the house waiting for him to come and find her.

'Coming, ready or not,' he'd announced.

'He was the best father in the world,' she told Marco. 'We were very close – we still are, but obviously it's different now.' She held out her glass as Marco offered more wine. 'It's why,' she said, after taking a sip, 'I don't need to have a connection with my real father. I simply wanted to see if I could find out who he was, and if I might still have family here. Now, of course, I'm beginning to understand why my mother never wanted me to know.'

'We still haven't got to the truth of everything yet,' he reminded her. 'I admit it was easy to let Signor Donata's story lead us to the conclusions you are believing now, but we have yet to speak to Carlotta Calduzzi. She might have a very different story to tell.'

Grateful for the straw to cling to, she took it and used it to push the ugliness of her suspicions to the back of her mind. Perhaps she should let them stay there; after all, what good would it do to know any more about her roots? Whoever her real father was, wherever her grandparents might be, it wasn't going to change what was happening with Tom, and though she was trying to use this search as a way of not thinking about him, the truth was, nothing mattered more. In fact, she longed to cut the holiday short now and go home, but what difference would it make if she did? Kirsten was still going to be his main concern, and while a part of her understood that, another part was finding it impossible to accept.

'Excuse me, I should answer this,' Marco said, checking his mobile as it rang. 'It is one of my afternoon appointments. Maybe he wants to change the time. *Pronto*,' he said, taking the call.

As he got up to walk back to the car, Lainey watched him go and felt an admiration for him rising above her troubles. He hadn't mentioned his wife at all today, so she had no idea how he might be feeling inside, but she knew that if he was experiencing similar emotions to her, she'd want to help him in any way she could. However, it wasn't in her power to cure heartbreak any more than it was in his, though spending time with him was proving a balm of sorts.

She could only hope it was the same for him.

Lying back on the rug, she closed her eyes against the sunlight dappling through the maple and listened to the chafing rhythm of cicadas. If she could only get Tom out of her mind she knew she'd be enjoying every moment of being here, but the instant she stopped talking about other things, or even thinking them, she could feel the ache in her heart growing heavier, stronger, deeper . . .

Taking a breath, she let it out slowly and made herself focus on Marco again, and how his life was all about food, wine, people. It was embedded in the natural world and enriched by reality, while her life and Tom's seemed more like some sort of fiction.

Sitting up swiftly, as though to escape the thought, she poured more wine into her glass and drank it. It was warm, acidic and burned her throat, but as moments ticked by and Marco continued to talk on the phone she felt herself relaxing again. If she simply listened to him, allowed herself to enjoy the melodic sound of his words, immersed herself in the here and now, perhaps the ghosts of her past, and present, would stop finding a way in.

She must have dozed off, because the next time she opened her eyes Marco was sitting beside her sending emails or texts on his phone. She felt embarrassed about sleeping, but didn't alert him to the fact she was awake just yet. Instead, she lay watching him through the dark lenses of her glasses, feeling grateful to him all over again just for being there. It wasn't until Skye's words staged an unwelcome appearance at the front of her mind, about finding another man to make Tom jealous, that she sat up. It was true, Marco was very attractive, but no one could ever replace Tom, either in her heart or in her bed.

'Max, that's just mean,' Tierney cried angrily. 'You can't do it. I won't let you.'

Max regarded her with some amusement. 'And you're going to stop me, how?' he asked, seeming genuinely interested.

Tierney only wished she knew. 'I'll think of something,' she told him hotly.

'Then you'd better make it fast, because I'm about to text Lainey to make sure it's OK.'

Glancing up to check that Skye wasn't on her way back to the café yet, Tierney said, 'Does Christie know anything about Skye?'

Max threw out his hands. 'What's to know?' he demanded, as if there really wasn't anything.

Tierney daggered him a look.

'We have an understanding, you know that,' he conceded. 'Friends with benefits. No strings.'

'OK, then *you* tell her that Christie's coming, because I'm not doing it.'

Sitting back to rest an arm on the chair beside him, he said, 'I know what's bugging you . . . OK, you're trying to stick up for your friend, but really you're all strung out about Dad, aren't you?'

Wishing it was only that, though actually it was probably the worst of it, she countered, 'Aren't you?'

He shrugged. 'I've been here before, remember?'

'Yeah, when you were like five. It's got to feel a bit different now.'

'Maybe, maybe not, but I'm worried about you. Skye's a good girl, in her way, but she's the way she is because her dad left, and I don't want you turning out the same . . .'

'No way is that going to happen,' she cried, 'and anyway, who says Dad's going to leave? He just has to be there while this woman's sick . . .'

'If she's sick, and we only have his word for it.'

'He wouldn't lie about something like that.'

'Wouldn't he?'

'Stop it, Max.'

'I'm just saying, that's all. I don't want him to go either, but if it's what he wants . . .'

'It won't be.'

'OK, have it your way. I'm just trying to let you know I'm here for you.'

Feeling herself on the brink of tears, Tierney said, 'Have you spoken to him since we got here?'

'Nope. Have you?'

She stared down at her phone as she shook her head. 'Zav has, and Mum.'

'Lucky them.' Though he sounded as if he didn't care, Tierney felt sure he did.

'Do you reckon we ought to ring him?' she asked.

'No way! Well, you can if you want to, but personally I've got nothing to say to him, so why would I?'

Since she wasn't sure what she'd say either, Tierney decided to return to the subject they'd started with. 'You've got to realise there are going to be serious problems if Christie comes here next week. Skye's not going to like it, and if she starts causing trouble . . . Well, I don't know what she'll do, but it'll ruin everyone's holiday, that's for sure, including yours.'

Whatever Max was about to say didn't materialise, since his phone rang and by the time he'd finished the call Tierney was on the edge of panic as she stared at another text from Guy.

Have to see you. Tell me where you are and we'll find a place to meet.

'What's up?' Max asked, noticing how pale she'd gone.

'Nothing,' she said, feeling herself starting to shake. 'I just . . . It doesn't matter . . .'

'Oh, right. Brett's just told you he's heading back to England on Sunday. You got a bit sweet on him, didn't you?'

'Not really,' she mumbled, wishing she could show Max the text and ask him what to do. Feeling suddenly nauseous at the very idea of him ever finding out what she'd done, she got up from her chair and fled to the loo.

By the time she came back Skye was at the table, surrounded by designer bags and yakking on to Max about the great bargains she'd found at Armani. Whether he was particularly interested or not he was putting on a good show, until his mobile rang and after checking who it was he clicked on. 'Hey, Lainey. How's things?'

Tierney tensed. *Please don't let him say anything about Christie now with Skye right there.*

'Yeah? That's cool,' he was saying. 'Why not? Sounds good. Yeah, they're here, I'll ask them. We're being invited to Adriana's for dinner tonight,' he relayed. 'Do we want to go?'

Tierney looked at Skye.

'Yeah, we're up for it if you are,' Skye told him.

'Did you get that?' Max asked Lainey. 'Count us in,' and after assuring her they'd be back at the villa within the hour, he rang off.

'So, did she go out with Marco today, or down to the village?' Skye asked as her coffee arrived.

Apparently perplexed by the question, Max replied, 'No idea, I didn't ask.'

Skye glanced at Tierney. 'We reckon,' she said, 'that something could be going on between them.'

'What do you mean, *we*?' Tierney protested. 'It's you who said that, and I just wish you'd shut up about it.'

'OK, OK, cool it,' Skye responded, holding up her hands.

Watching them closely, Max said, 'Do you mean you think Lainey and Marco are getting it on?' He seemed both surprised and curious.

'It's not what I think,' Tierney assured him.

'Only because you don't want to,' Skye informed her. 'And I don't blame you, I didn't want to think my mum was seeing someone else when my dad left us. I kept telling myself they'd get back together, but no one ever does once they've broken up.'

'That's such bullshit,' Tierney said hotly.

'OK, tell me someone who has.'

Tierney took a breath, but she couldn't think of anyone. She looked to Max for help, but remembering that their dad hadn't gone back to his mum, she felt a sudden, ridiculous urge to cry.

'Plenty of people do,' Max said, coming to her rescue, 'but whether it'll happen for Lainey and Dad . . . If you ask me, she'd be better off with someone like Marco.'

'How can you say that,' Tierney almost shouted, 'when you don't even know him?'

'Well, he seems a nice enough bloke, and we know what a bastard Dad is, so I know who I'd pick if I were Lainey.'

'Well, you're not her, and to start saying things like that about her and about Dad just goes to show how ignorant and immature you are.'

'Wow!' He laughed, backing up. 'I'm definitely hitting some wrong notes with my little sister today. Ease up, T. None of it's a big deal. If Lainey wants to have a little play around while she's on holiday, you can hardly say she doesn't deserve it, given what Dad's been up to.'

It was on the tip of Tierney's tongue to tell them both to shut the fuck up about sex all the time, but afraid she'd sound like a weirdo or some stuffed-up virgin who knew nothing about anything, she decided to ignore them.

Luckily the subject changed then, and after finishing their coffees they wandered back out to the car, where Tierney's few purchases were already stored in the boot. Normally she'd have bought more, but she just hadn't been in the mood today, and now this text had turned up she couldn't imagine being in the mood for anything ever again.

'What am I going to do?' she asked Skye, when they were finally back at the villa and in the privacy of their room.

Not appearing overly concerned, Skye said, 'Just ignore it, same as usual.'

'But if I don't tell him where we are, he can easily find out from Nadia.'

Skye paused for a moment, then shook her head. 'There's no way he'll just turn up here,' she decided. 'How would he explain it to your mum?'

'I don't know, unless he brings Nadia with him.

She's joined us on holiday loads of times in the past.'

Seeing there really might be a problem brewing, Skye said, 'Look, if you're definitely not interested . . .'

'Are you kidding? How can you even say that?'

'. . . then tell him to drop dead, or fuck off. That should do it.'

Only wishing it would, Tierney gazed down at her mobile, feeling so worried and wretched she could hardly make herself think. In the end, she decided she had to tell Skye about the photos, otherwise she would never understand why the situation was so serious.

By the time she'd finished her admission she had Skye's full attention.

'OMG,' Skye murmured, 'the sneaky bastard.'

'He hasn't threatened to show anyone, or anything,' Tierney quickly assured her, 'but the way he keeps sending them to me . . .'

'Let me see,' Skye interrupted, holding out a hand for the phone.

'No way! Anyway, I've erased them, and somehow I've got to make him do the same.'

Skye didn't deny it. 'The trouble is,' she said, 'he's obviously really getting off on them, so . . .'

'I don't need to hear that,' Tierney cried. 'I just want you to tell me what to do.'

After giving the matter some careful consideration, Skye said, 'How about you turn the tables on him? If you threaten to tell your dad . . .'

'Are you out of your mind?'

'I don't mean actually tell him, but if you say you're going to . . .'

'He'll know there's no way I'd do that.'

Skye thought again. 'Tell you what, if he does turn up here I'll deal with him. I'm probably more his type anyway, given all the stuff he's into . . .'

'Skye, this isn't a joke. If I don't do what he wants he might turn nasty.'

'I'm trying to help you here,' Skye insisted crossly.

'And you think shagging him is going to do that?' Turning away in frustration, Tierney pressed the phone to her head and tried not to cry.

'Listen,' Skye said, coming to give her a hug, 'think about this sensibly. There's no way in the world he's ever going to show those pictures around. It would be the end of him if he did, because everyone would want to know how he got them.'

'He could say someone sent them to him.'

Skye was shaking her head. 'Then they'll want to know who it was, and when they find out there's no one they'll realise it was him who took them. OK, it won't look good for you, but it'll look a whole lot worse for him.'

Seeing how that could be true, Tierney wiped away her tears as some of her tension ebbed.

'Don't worry,' Skye said gently, 'we can handle this. It'll all be fine, I promise.'

Chapter Seventeen

'I think you'd better take a look at this,' Stacy said, carrying her laptop from her bedroom into the kitchen where Lainey, still in her nightie, was wrestling with the coffee machine.

Lainey looked up and immediately wished she hadn't moved her head so quickly. Having stayed late at dinner with Adriana and Lorenzo last night, she really wasn't feeling her best this morning. 'What is it?' she asked, stifling a yawn. 'God, how much did we have to drink last night? No, don't answer that. How come you're up so early?'

'It's gone ten o'clock,' Stacy pointed out, though she too was still in her nightie. 'I thought I'd work from home this morning, i.e. bed, and when I went online to check my emails Diana had sent me a link to this.'

Feeling the onset of unease crawling through her hangover, Lainey took the computer and went to sit down. The small headline on page nine of the tabloid leapt out at her, turning her hot and cold. *Trouble at Hollingsworth Hall?* (This was how some of the tabloids referred to Bannerleigh Cross.)

With a horrible tightening in her chest she scanned the short paragraph, as though only skimming the words would somehow make their detail less real.

However, there was no escaping their ugly intrusion into her life, so, taking the coffee Stacy was handing her, she returned to the beginning and read more carefully.

When news reached us that Tom Hollingsworth had recently moved out of the family home we couldn't have been more surprised. This was a marriage that had always seemed rock solid from the outside, however, sources tell us that Lainey, Hollingsworth's wife of 16 years and mother of two of his children, is devastated by the break-up and has gone away for a while to try and come to terms with it. Nadia Roundtree, Hollingsworth's literary agent, said yesterday, 'I am not aware of any kind of rift in Tom's marriage. It's not unheard of for Lainey to take the children away while Tom is finishing a book. I don't think you should read anything into it.'

So we won't, for now.

Feeling sick and angry, Lainey looked up as Stacy came to sit with her. 'Where the hell did they get this?' she snapped. 'And anyway, it's wrong. He hasn't moved out . . . Or not that I know of.' Her heart was pounding with dread. What if he'd waited for her to leave before coming to collect his things?

'How could he have done that without your Aunt Daffs knowing?' Stacy protested when Lainey voiced her fear. 'Think about it sensibly. If he's been there packing you can be absolutely certain she'd have told you.'

Of course she would have, and besides, Tom would never be so underhand. He wasn't a coward . . .

She'd never thought he was a liar and a cheat before, either.

'You know the gossip columnist's maxim,' Stacy

was reminding her, 'never let the truth stand in the way of a good story.'

Lainey shot to her feet, hot tears scalding her eyes. Why was this happening? Why couldn't she escape it, even here? Yesterday had been so wonderful, picnicking with Marco, exploring Montepulciano, dining with his family last night. Now, this morning, it was as though the world was mocking her, forcing her to remember what a mess her life really was and how very much she was hurting. 'He hasn't even rung,' she said angrily.

'He might not have seen it yet,' Stacy pointed out.

Lainey waved a dismissive hand, as though trying to detach herself. 'It doesn't matter,' she declared. 'Let's try to forget it. I ought to go and check on the girls, make sure Skye isn't still mad at me after last night.'

Sighing, Stacy said, 'What the heck was the girl thinking? I could hardly believe my eyes when I saw her come out of the pool house. None of us could.'

Shuddering simply to recall the shocking vision of Skye stalking towards them in a swimsuit cut so low at the front it might have exposed her pubic hair if she had any, and almost totally revealing her boobs, Lainey wasn't sure whether she wanted to groan or give in to her hangover and throw up. Almost as bad was the scene that had followed, when she'd leapt from her chair and pushed the girl back into the pool house.

'What on earth do you think you're doing?' she'd hissed. 'You're making a complete exhibition of yourself. Now either take it off and put on a proper swimsuit, or get dressed, but you're . . .'

'You can't tell me what to wear,' Skye had protested angrily.

'I can while you're in my care, so do as you're told or get in the car and we'll all go home.'

Skye glared at her mutinously.

'Is that what you want,' Lainey challenged, 'to ruin a lovely evening for everyone? Because that's what's going to happen if you don't make yourself decent *right now.*'

Whatever Skye had muttered in response Lainey hadn't caught, though she was sure it was something about her being jealous and out of touch. Well, Skye could tell herself that if she wanted to – what concerned Lainey far more was the kind of influence the girl could be having on Tierney.

Lovely, something else to worry about along with everything else.

How much worse is it going to get?

Don't even go there with the suspicion of Tierney being involved with a married man, it can't be real, I simply won't allow it. Nevertheless she had to find a way of broaching it with Tierney again, just to be certain.

'Lainey, are you in here?' Max said groggily as he came in through the door. He was another who'd had more than a skinful last night, though thank goodness he hadn't become aggressive or obnoxious. He'd simply hit more than his usual number of bum notes on the guitar, and managed to knock a glass of wine all over himself.

Would the Stefanis ever want to entertain them again?

'I'm here,' Lainey said, as Max peered through his sunglasses, trying to find her.

Spotting her in a shaft of sunlight he said, 'Ah,

right. Daffs just rang. She's trying to get hold of you, she said, but you're not picking up.'

Lainey's heart contracted. *Please God Aunt Daffs wasn't about to confirm what it was saying in the paper.*

Remembering that she'd turned her phone off on the way to the Stefanis last night (to try to stop herself hoping for a call from Tom), she went to dig it out of her bag. If he had tried contacting her this morning he wouldn't have been able to get through, which was small comfort when he could easily have done what Aunt Daffs had and rung one of the children.

Sensing Max's eyes on her as she waited for her phone to fire up, she attempted to give him a smile. Why was he looking so much like his father this morning? Why was his mere presence making her heart beat faster and harder?

'Are you OK?' he asked.

She was about to say she was fine, when she found she couldn't, and turning to the laptop, she pushed it towards him. 'You might want to read that,' she said, and leaving him to it she went out on to the terrace to call Daffs.

'Sorry,' she said as soon as she heard her aunt's voice. 'I had my phone turned off. Is everything all right?'

Sounding as breezy as ever, Daffs replied, 'Yes, sweetheart, everything's fine with us, I was just a bit concerned about you when I couldn't get through.'

'We're all OK, don't worry. How's Dad this morning?'

'The same as usual, just about to go for a walk with Sherman, as soon as he's finished his breakfast.'

She ran on almost seamlessly, 'So how's the search going for your mother's family? Any luck yet?'

'Some,' Lainey admitted, 'but there's still a way to go. Have you . . .?' She tensed as Max suddenly shouted, 'Fucking bastards!'

'Oh dear,' Daffs murmured. 'Was that Max?'

'I'm afraid so. I probably ought to go and talk to him, but before I do, have you – have you seen anything of Tom since we left?'

'No, dear, he hasn't been here. I expect he's engrossed in his book, down there at his friend's place in Cornwall.'

'I'm sure you're right.' Lainey smiled, wanting to hug her aunt for confirming that Tom hadn't packed up and left behind her back.

After ringing off, she stayed where she was, gazing out over the valley, so peaceful and perfect, trying to stop her emotions getting the better of her. It seemed so wrong to be here without him, so unsettling and strange, especially when it was a place for romance, laughter, love . . . Not for trying to deal with betrayal, and all the heartache and lies that came with it.

Checking her phone as it rang, her heart jolted when she saw it was him. She allowed it to ring several times before finally clicking on.

'At last,' he exclaimed accusingly. 'Where have you been? Did you get my messages?'

So he had rung. It should have made her feel better, but somehow it didn't. 'Not yet,' she replied, 'but I've seen an online version of today's paper if that's why you're calling.'

'I tried ringing last night,' he ranted on. 'Where were you, for God's sake?'

'With friends.' The words felt oddly like a door

closing. This was the first time since they'd been together that she'd had friends he didn't know.

'I thought something had happened when you didn't pick up,' he told her. 'I've been worried out of my mind.'

'Then why didn't you call one of the children?'

'I was about to if you hadn't answered now.' Taking a moment to get himself in better check, he said, 'So you've seen the piece . . .'

'I just told you I did. How did they find out?'

'I've no idea. Please tell me it wasn't from you.'

She gasped. Incensed, she cried, 'How dare you even think it, never mind say it?' and before he could utter another word she cut the line dead. 'Jesus Christ,' she seethed, as tears rushed to her eyes.

'Was that him?' Max growled from the doorway.

Lainey nodded, keeping her head down.

Coming to slip an arm round her shoulders, he said, 'Forget the bastard. He's a waste of fucking space.'

Too upset to wish he wouldn't swear, Lainey had to turn away. His male scent was so much like his father's.

'What are you going to do?' he asked.

She could only shrug.

'The others are up and about,' Stacy cautioned, coming out to join them. 'I was wondering if you wanted Tierney and Zav to see the piece?'

Lainey's eyes moved to Max. 'I suppose Tierney should,' she said uncertainly.

He nodded. 'I don't think Zav needs to, yet.'

Agreeing with that, she accepted the tissues Stacy was offering and dried her eyes. 'I should go and shower,' she said. 'What are we meant to be doing today, can anyone remind me?'

Glancing at his watch, Max said, 'Brett and Ricky should be here in about an hour. Some mates of theirs are in Siena today. They've invited me and the girls to tag along, but we don't have to go . . .'

'No, carry on with your plans,' Lainey insisted. 'I'll take the boys to Assisi.'

Looking awkward, Stacy said, 'I think you arranged for them to go sailing with the Stefani children today.'

Recalling the conversation through the fog of last night, Lainey agreed, 'You're right, I did. Was I supposed to be going too?'

'I'm not sure. I didn't hear that bit. Do you want me to ring and find out?'

Lainey gave it some thought and nodded. 'Yes, if you wouldn't mind, and if I am meant to be going can you say I've got a headache – which won't surprise them – so would it be all right if the boys came without me?'

'That means you'll be here on your own,' Stacy objected. 'I'm meeting Lorenzo today to talk olive oil, but I could always cancel . . .'

'No, no, don't do that,' Lainey came in quickly. 'I'll be fine, honestly,' and deciding to leave her phone on the table she took herself off to her bathroom.

As soon as the door was closed she began sobbing. She'd been trying so hard to hold on, to be strong for the children and for herself, but hearing him so angry on the phone, knowing he must be worried for Kirsten far more than for her, was tipping her over the edge. And how could he have thought she'd contact the paper herself?

It was so awful, so devastating, everything she treasured falling apart like this, that she just couldn't bear it. Nothing mattered without him, not who she was, why she was here, or even what her future might be.

Unable to catch her breath, she leaned over the sink and turned on the taps. She didn't want anyone to hear what a state she was in. She needed to get herself under control, force herself into the shower and back out there to face the world. The mere thought of it was making her cry even harder. She couldn't cope with this; she was going to pieces. She wanted her father so badly she hardly knew what to do. It didn't matter that he wasn't himself any longer, he was still the only person in the world who could put an arm around her and make her feel as though she was special, and right now she needed that more than she ever had before.

'Do you reckon I should go and apologise to your mum?' Skye was asking as Tierney came back to their room.

'No, she's really upset at the moment,' Tierney told her, feeling close to tears herself after standing at her mum's bedroom door and hearing how hard she was crying. She'd stayed there for ages, wondering if she should go in, but for some reason she hadn't felt able to. 'There's stuff in the paper today about her and Dad breaking up,' she said, staring at nothing as she sat down on the edge of the bed.

'Oh no, that really sucks,' Skye responded sympathetically. 'At least my mum never had to deal with anything like that. I guess it's what happens when you've got a famous dad.'

Tierney didn't reply. She was barely even listening. If Brett and Ricky hadn't already turned up she'd have gone downstairs to chat to Max, but she couldn't say anything in front of them. Actually, she wouldn't have minded going in to have a little cuddle with Zav, but he hadn't seen the piece on Stacy's laptop yet, so if she did he'd think she was weird.

So she was stuck here with Skye.

Though she felt horribly guilty about wishing Skye would go home, she couldn't help thinking it would be better if she did. For one thing she, Tierney, wouldn't have to worry about what might happen when Christie turned up next week, presuming she was going to. And for another, Maudie might be able to fly out and take Skye's place. Both her parents really liked Maudie – not that her dad counted any more, and as far as she was concerned he never would now.

However, she still had to sort out what to do about Guy, because if he did turn up here she was depending on Skye to help get rid of him.

'Did you hear what I said?' Skye asked, turning to find out if Tierney was listening.

'What?'

'I asked what they're saying in the paper about your rents.'

Tierney's mouth turned dry as her nails dug into her palms. At least they hadn't mentioned the other woman and Julia, but they would once they found out and then the whole world would know that her parents were breaking up because her dad had gone off with another woman.

'Was it bad?' Skye prompted.

Tierney tried to shrug, but it wasn't easy when she was so close to breaking down. Picking up her brush she began pulling it through her hair.

'Suit yourself,' Skye muttered when she realised she wasn't going to get an answer.

They were supposed to be driving over to Siena in a minute, but Tierney didn't want to leave her mum on her own, not while she was this upset.

'Listen to me,' Skye urged, in response to Tierney's reason for staying. 'She's shut herself away so she can do her thing in private where none of you can see her. I'm telling you, you have to give her some space. It's what she needs right now, not to stress about how you're feeling about things.'

Wishing she could get Maudie's opinion on that, Tierney wandered to the window to stare out at the view. Her instincts seemed to be telling her to put her mum first, while the fear of seeing just how upset she was kept holding her back. However, she wasn't going to allow herself to be pathetic. She needed to be strong for her mum, and even if there wasn't anything she could do to make things better, at least her mum would know that someone cared.

She'd just drawn breath to tell Skye that her mind was made up, she was staying, when a car arrived at the top of the slope. She knew instantly whose it was, so it was no surprise when Marco got out. As he crossed the lawn she could feel her heart pounding. They didn't need him here now; he was just going to complicate things, confuse and upset her mother even further.

When he reached the terrace he was only feet from her window, but she didn't let him know she was there. She simply listened to him talking to Stacy, telling her he'd brought a new pool boy with him because the regular one had broken his arm. Then he asked if Lainey was around, and Stacy told him she wasn't feeling well. He said something that

Tierney didn't quite catch, then finally he turned around and started back to his car.

Tierney was about to breathe a sigh of relief when she heard her mother calling out, asking him to stay.

'She'll be all right now,' Skye murmured, as Marco returned to the terrace.

Tierney tensed. She hadn't realised Skye was watching, and suddenly she wanted to slap her, or push her out of the way, or tell her to get the next flight home and never come back. Instead, she picked up her phone, stuffed it in her bag and went downstairs to join Max and the others.

'Thank you,' Lainey said, as Marco handed her a coffee he'd poured from a flask. With a smile she added, 'You know, I could get used to picnicking with you.'

Smiling too, he sat down beside her and rested his elbows on his knees to gaze out over his own Sangiovese vines that, from this perspective at the top of his estate, seemed to flow right down to the shores of the lake. 'I used to come here,' he said, 'when I was feeling as you are now.'

As her heart caught on the words, she sipped her coffee and let her eyes travel from the shining clusters of grapes in their tangles of leaves, across to the acres of olive trees and on to the red tiled roofs of his farmhouse at the heart of it all. Just beyond the farmhouse was the *colombaia* – dovecote – belonging to Lorenzo and Adriana's barn conversion, and in the dusty yard in front of the wine caves she could see Adriana leading a small clutch of visitors off on a tour.

Marco had brought her here after her eyes had

welled with tears as she'd tried to answer a simple question back on the terrace.

'Good morning, how are you?' he'd said, and to her embarrassment the lump that formed in her throat had left her unable to speak. In the end, in a strangled voice, she'd said to Stacy, 'Please show him,' and while he'd read the piece she'd gone back to the bathroom to pull herself together.

When she'd returned, she'd seen straight away how concerned he was. 'I want you to come with me,' he'd said, and taking her hand, he'd led her to his car. They'd driven first to the farmhouse, where he'd filled a flask with coffee, then he'd brought her here.

'If you would rather be alone,' he said now, batting a fly from his face, 'I will come back for you later.'

She didn't have to consider it for long. 'I like you being here,' she told him, meaning it. There was something calming about his presence, supportive yet not intrusive, perhaps because he was little more than a stranger. With someone she knew well she'd feel compelled to talk, even to make sure they weren't worrying about her.

Then, realising this must be bringing back painful memories for him, she said, 'You must be busy. If you'd rather go . . .'

His eyes remained on the leafy lanes of vines as he replied, 'I have no pressing engagements this morning.'

'But don't you – don't you mind being here? I mean, if it's where you used to come . . .' She wasn't sure how to phrase the rest of the question, so she simply let it fade.

He glanced at her briefly. 'Things are different

now,' he told her. 'The hurt – most of the hurt – has gone away.'

Because she needed to know, she said, 'Did it take long?'

Snapping off a blade of grass, he said, 'It would have taken longer if my wife hadn't decided that she'd made the wrong choice.'

Lainey felt a stab of something that might have been jealousy, or perhaps it was a hope that the same would happen for her.

'I expect Zav told you what Benito told him,' he went on, 'that Anna left to be with another man?'

Lainey glanced at his profile. 'I'm sorry,' she said softly. 'It must have been very hard.'

His jaw was taut now, his eyes less focused. 'She went more than a year ago,' he said, flicking away the blade of grass. 'I had been suspicious for a while, then one day she said she could not bear to go on pretending. She loved him, she said, she had to be with him, so she was leaving.'

Since she knew exactly how he must have felt in that moment, Lainey made to put a hand on his arm, but pulled back at the last. She didn't want him to think she was offering the kind of comfort that would end up embarrassing them both. 'Where is she now?' she asked.

'In London. She is not with him any more, she tells me. I'm not sure what happened between them, why it didn't work. She says, after being with him, she realised she'd made a terrible mistake, but it is hard to know what to believe.'

Understanding how difficult it must be for him now, she dared to ask, 'Do you still love her?'

He barely hesitated. 'Yes, I love her very much,

but I am afraid that it will not be enough to repair what has happened. There is no trust now, and without trust it is hard to see any happiness for our future.'

The poignancy of his words burned into Lainey's heart. The trust had gone for her and Tom too, and no matter what happened in the future, she couldn't imagine anything ever bringing it back.

'I feel it is important for Benito,' he continued, 'that I try with his mother. Of course, because I love her, I want that very much, so I guess it is for both of these reasons that I am now trying in my heart to forgive her. If I can do this, perhaps a time will come when I can begin to trust her again.'

Both afraid of finding herself in the same position, and terrified she might not, Lainey began examining her own heart to see if she might be capable of the same sort of forgiveness. Considering how desperate she felt right now, anything seemed possible, but she knew how dramatically her emotions could change from one hour to the next.

'I'm sorry, I didn't bring you here to talk about my problems,' he apologised. 'Please let's change the subject.'

Lainey smiled. 'As long as it's not to my problems.'

He twinkled, but instead of agreeing he said, 'I don't want to pry, but it might help you to talk.'

Though she couldn't feel sure of that, she knew she was incapable of thinking about anything else right now, so, in a halting, self-conscious way she began telling him about her marriage, and how she'd always feared that she loved Tom more than he loved her. Though there were moments when Marco turned to look at her, his eyes seeming as intense as the heat, he didn't interrupt once, simply absorbed her words as though nothing else in the world could matter more.

In the end he reached for her hand and held it so tenderly that she had to fight down yet more emotion. She wondered how his wife could have betrayed him, when he was the kind of man most women only ever dreamt of. She wondered how Tom could have betrayed her, and for so long.

'Do you realise,' she said, after a while, 'we might have been lifelong friends by now if I'd grown up in Tuoro.'

'Yes, I have had this thought too.'

Shaking her head in wonder, she said, 'It's incredible to think I'm as Italian, by birth, as you are. I keep trying to feel Italian, and sometimes I do get a sense of something, but I couldn't really tell you what it is. Probably a love of the wine.'

He laughed, and though he let go of her hand then, it was a long time before the feel of it went away.

'So where is she?' Tierney cried, all kinds of confusions tearing at her heart. 'She never goes out all day without telling us where she is.'

'She's with Marco,' Stacy reminded her. 'They left here . . .'

'I know when they left,' Tierney cut in rudely, 'I was here, remember, but it's nearly seven o'clock now, so where's he taken her, and why hasn't she rung me?'

Stacy said, 'I take it you've tried ringing her?'

'Of course, and she's not answering.' Her expression turned suddenly wild. 'Oh my God, something's happened to her. What if she's had an accident? They drive like maniacs here . . .' She turned to Max in a panic.

'Cool it,' he advised, offering her a beer. 'She needed to chill after that crap in the paper, so that's what she's doing.'

'But she's in a highly vulnerable state right now. We should never have let her go off with him.'

'Tierney, sweetie,' Stacy came in gently, 'you've met Marco, you know how lovely he is . . .'

'It could all be a front,' Tierney raged. 'Some people are like that, they use their looks and everything to make you feel safe, then they turn out to be weirdos or psychos or . . .'

'Stop, just stop,' Stacy said more firmly. 'I don't know why you're telling yourself these things when she's only been gone a few hours.'

'Nine!' Tierney shouted. 'She's been gone for nine hours and she's not answering her phone. Tell me that's not strange. Have you got Marco's number?'

'No, but I have Adriana's.'

'Can I have it please?'

With a sigh, Stacy said, 'If I give it to you . . .'

'Just give it to me,' Tierney growled.

'T, you're way out of order,' Max informed her.

'You want them to break up too,' Tierney yelled at him. 'Everyone does, except me and Mum, because she still loves him, and I know he loves her too, and I hate it that he's not here, and nor is she now, and I hate you all for shouting at me . . .'

'Hey, hey, hey,' Stacy soothed, pulling her into an embrace as she started to sob. 'Everything's going to be fine, sweetheart, I promise.'

'No, it isn't, not now Dad's with that other woman. Oh God, I don't want him to leave us, Stace . . .'

'Ssh, ssh,' Stacy murmured, smoothing her hair.

'How can he be so mean?'

Coming through the door, Lainey said, 'What on earth is going on here?'

'Mum!' Tierney gasped, and rushed to hug her. 'I've been really worried about you. Where were you? I thought you'd had an accident.'

Holding her close while regarding Stacy and Max curiously, Lainey said, 'Well as you can see, I'm all in one piece, so no need for all this drama.'

Tierney pulled back to look at her. 'Why didn't you answer your phone? I kept ringing and ringing . . .'

'I'm sorry, sweetheart. I turned it off while Marco and I went to talk to the priest in the village, and I only remembered to put it on again as I got back here.'

'Where's Marco now?' Max asked, glancing towards the door.

'He dropped me at the gates,' and clutching Tierney's teary face in her hands she planted a kiss on her forehead. 'You're a daft old thing, getting yourself so worked up over nothing.'

'It's not nothing,' Tierney protested.

Lainey's eyebrows rose. 'No, I guess it isn't,' she agreed, 'and I think you and I need to have a talk. Where's Skye?'

'Down at the pool with Brett and Ricky. They're going back to England on Sunday.' She almost added she wished they'd take Skye with them.

'And you're going on Saturday?' Lainey said to Stacy, feeling a flutter of dread at the parting.

Looking decidedly fed up about it, Stacy said, 'I have to, I'm afraid. I'm seeing Diana and the others on Sunday, ahead of a big meeting on

Monday. But you don't have to worry about driving me to the airport, because Lorenzo's offered. Apparently he has to be in Florence on Saturday night, and he's insisting that Pisa's not too far out of his way.'

'That's kind of him,' Lainey remarked, going to take a beer from the fridge, 'and actually it could work out quite well, because Marco heard from Carlotta Calduzzi earlier. It seems her family, here in Tuoro, got in touch with her after his call to say why he wants to talk to her, and so she's decided to come back early.'

Stacy's eyes widened in surprise. 'She's cutting her holiday short in order to see you?'

Lainey shrugged. 'I'm not sure it's the only reason, but she's definitely agreed to meet me. Now, aren't you going to ask me what the priest had to say?'

Dutifully repeating the question, Stacy went to perch on the edge of the table, tossing Skye a towel as she came dripping through the door.

'Sorry, I forgot to take one with me,' Skye mumbled, and keeping her head down she scuttled on through to the bathroom.

Lainey looked curiously at Tierney, as though seeking an explanation for Skye's unusual reticence, but Tierney's eyes were on Max.

Breezing past the moment, Max prompted, 'Priest.'

Taking her cue, Lainey slipped an arm round Tierney again as she said, 'He turned out to be a very sweet man, and the church in the village is . . . Well, I'll come on to the church, but unsurprisingly, I guess, Father Benedict had never heard of Melvina and Aldo Clementi.'

'What about Alessandra?' Stacy asked.

Lainey shook her head. 'However, he had heard of the Valente family and the villa is still there, about halfway between here and Cortona.'

'So is that where you've been?' Tierney asked, her face still pinched. 'To have a look at it?'

Lainey nodded. 'Only from the outside. It's a home for dementia sufferers now, but you can see it was really quite grand in its day.'

For some reason they all fell silent, until Max said, 'The church? You were going to come on to it?'

'Oh, that's right. It's really peculiar, but I had an amazingly strong sense of déjà vu while I was in there. It seemed to come out of the walls at me. I wondered if I might have been baptised there, but even if I was, being less than a month old at the time I couldn't possibly have any memory of it. Anyway, I guess it's fair to say that my Italian family has a history there, because I'm sure it'll be where Melvina and Aldo got married, possibly my great-grandparents too. Granny would almost certainly have been baptised there, probably had her confirmation there too, and the confessional would have heard details of all their transgressions. If that small box could only speak . . .' Though she waggled her eyebrows playfully, inside she was reliving the sense of unease she'd experienced during those few short minutes in the church. 'Even if it could, we know it'd never yield up its secrets,' she continued, 'but I'm telling you, I had a really odd sort of feeling when I was there.'

'I expect it was God giving you your calling,' Max told her. 'Maybe he wants you to be a nun.'

Rolling her eyes, Lainey let go of Tierney and took out her phone. Time, she told herself, to put the strangeness of the afternoon behind her and get back to reality. 'Where are the boys?' she asked, checking her texts.

'Zav rang about an hour ago,' Stacy told her. 'They're having dinner at the Stefanis and Adriana or Lorenzo will pop them back after.'

Lainey nodded, and made herself smile as she looked up. No messages from Tom. 'So, what are we going to do about food?' she asked brightly. 'Will Brett and Ricky be staying?'

'I'll go check,' Max responded, and picking up his guitar he ambled off across the terrace, strumming a lazy tune as he went.

'OK,' Lainey declared in a businesslike fashion, 'I guess we should . . . What is it?' she demanded, noticing the expression on Tierney's face.

Tierney barely looked up from her phone as she started for her bedroom. 'Nothing,' she mumbled.

'Is it from Dad?' Lainey couldn't help calling after her.

As the door closed behind her, Lainey turned to Stacy and felt suddenly sorry she'd come back after such an easy day with Marco.

'She seems pretty wound up about things at the moment,' Stacy confided, 'so I think your proposed talk with her would be a good idea.'

Pushing her hands through her hair, Lainey nodded distractedly. Then, because it was the only sensible thing to do, she set about preparing dinner.

Tierney was waiting as Skye came in from the bathroom, wrapped in fresh towels. 'Look at this,' she urged shakily, but as she tried to thrust her mobile at Skye, Skye brushed on past.

Tierney regarded her uncertainly. 'What is it?' she asked.

'What do you think?' Skye snarled, rounding on her. 'Exactly when were you planning to tell me about Max's *girlfriend* coming over? And don't pretend you didn't know, because he told me you did.'

Not sure what to say, Tierney glanced at her text again.

'Just what kind of friend are you?' Skye raged. 'You know I'm his girlfriend, so who the hell is this muppet? How long's he been seeing her, that's what I want to know.'

Tierney felt helpless. 'A few months, I suppose, and you always said you were just friends with benefits, or shag buddies . . .'

'Yeah, but that doesn't mean he should be inviting someone else to stay while I'm here, and I'm not standing for it. You've got to tell him to uninvite her, OK? If you don't, he'll be finding out about you and Guy.'

Tierney paled. 'You can't do that,' she cried. 'He'll go mental. He'll tell Mum or Dad . . .'

'So make him uninvite her.'

Tierney was desperate. 'I don't know how to. I mean, I already tried, but he won't listen to me.'

'You'll have to make him.'

'Skye, please don't be like this. I need your help. I've had this text, look.'

Flaring her nostrils, Skye snatched the phone. As she read the message her eyes grew wide.

Guess where I am.

'Fuck,' she murmured.

'What am I going to do?' Tierney begged. 'If he's here . . . Do you reckon that's what he's saying?'

Skye tossed the phone back on the bed. 'It might

not be,' she said, without much conviction. 'Text back and say, "Give up."'

Tierney quickly tapped it in and pressed send.

'Wherever he is,' Skye told her, 'no way are you getting any backup from me until you make Max uninvite that bitch.'

Chapter Eighteen

It was Saturday morning now, and though Lainey realised it was probably hating seeing Stacy go that was making her so edgy, she still couldn't shake a feeling of growing anxiety.

She hadn't spoken to Tom since their angry words about the tabloid article, nor, thank God, had anyone from the press tried to contact her. However, she'd learned from her aunt that he'd turned up unexpectedly yesterday evening, and as far as Lainey knew he was still there. Thinking of him at home, in his study, moving about the kitchen, probably sleeping in their bed, had made her want to go rushing back to be with him.

Please God don't let him be packing.

'Has he said how long he's intending to stay?' she'd asked her aunt first thing.

'No,' Daffs had replied, 'but I expect he'll tell us when he comes down. I must say we're enjoying having him here; he ate with us last night, and put your father to bed, after letting us win a game of Scrabble.'

As moved by that as she was worried by how hard she was going to find it to manage her father alone, Lainey said, 'I don't expect he mentioned it, but we've had a bit of a row.'

'Oh dear, I'm sorry to hear that,' Daffs responded. 'I'm sure you'll make it up soon enough. It would be good if you could, because I must say, he's looking quite strained.'

The churning in Lainey's heart was increasing painfully. He'd brought this on himself, so how could she feel sorry for his suffering, particularly when she had her own and Tierney's to consider?

These past two days Tierney had been unusually quiet, barely eating, and not even joining the others when they'd gone off on their jaunts. She'd even slept in with Lainey last night while Max and Skye went discoing, and as far as Lainey knew she was planning on coming to see Carlotta Calduzzi with her later today.

'I promise, I'm fine,' Tierney told her again, 'and *no*, I'm not involved with a bloody married man. I don't even know why you're saying that. I'm not involved with anyone.'

'So why are you seeming so . . . low?'

'Why do you think? It's you and Dad. I don't want you to break up. Mum, *please* don't break up with him.'

Swallowing hard on her emotions, Lainey said, 'It's not what I want, you have to know that, but if it's what he wants . . .'

'It isn't. He still loves you, I know it. It's just because this woman's ill. Once she's better he'll come back to us. You wait and see.'

Lainey could only wish she herself felt so certain, but she didn't. Quite the reverse, in fact, even though she supposed there was a chance it had already happened. After all, he was at Bannerleigh Cross now, so maybe Kirsten's treatment was over?

Maybe she should ring to find out. She would if

everything didn't feel so fragile between them, so capable of shattering beyond any chance of repair if even one wrong word was spoken.

'I've thought about taking Skye to one side,' Lainey confided to Stacy as they waited for Lorenzo to arrive, 'and I will later, if Tierney doesn't seem any better.'

'Is she still going with you and Marco to see Carlotta Calduzzi?' Stacy asked, checking she had her passport and boarding pass.

'If she is she'll have to get her skates on, because Marco's due here at ten and it's already twenty to.'

Glancing up at the sound of a car arriving, Stacy said, 'That must be Lorenzo,' and turning to Lainey she wrapped her in her arms. 'I'm so sorry to be leaving you now,' she said. 'I feel such a useless friend, bailing when you need me the most.'

'I'm fine,' Lainey assured her, despite feeling far from it. 'It's great that you have this job, and you're going to be brilliant at it.'

This was something she was probably going to have to find for herself in the not too distant future, a job that didn't involve Tom. The thought of it was crushing, for it was impossible to imagine there being such a void in her life when organising his world, running their home, and bringing up their children had given her such purpose and fulfilment. 'But you surely want something for yourself,' friends had commented over the years, but what was her family if it wasn't hers? She had no desire to push paperwork around the legal system, or give herself a breakdown trying to make shareholders even richer than they already were. Much less did she want to hand her children over to someone else to bring up so she could pursue an ambition she didn't really have, just to satisfy the feminists out there who seemed to feel it was vital for women to 'have a career'. She was a wife and a mother and felt no need to apologise for it, or to try and escape it, since for her – and she wasn't ashamed of this, indeed she'd always been proud of it – there was no more important job in the world.

How on earth was she going to rethink that and find another way, when up to now her family-centred existence had always felt so honest and right?

'I'll be at the end of the phone, day or night,' Stacy reminded her, as they walked towards Lorenzo's car.

'Thanks,' Lainey whispered.

Since Max and Skye had taken Zav and Alfie to the village for breakfast, there was only Tierney left for Stacy to say goodbye to, but when Stacy reached the bathroom door the shower was running and music blaring. Nevertheless she called out to let Tierney know she was on her way.

After a moment the volume went down and Tierney called back, 'Bye, Stace, have a good flight.'

'Thanks,' Stacy replied, 'and you enjoy the rest of your holiday.'

'I will.'

Going back to the terrace, where Lorenzo was loading her bags into the car, Stacy linked Lainey's arm as she said, 'Maybe you could work it so that Skye goes home early, since they're so clearly not getting along.'

Sighing, Lainey said, 'Easier said than done without hurting the poor girl's feelings. Anyway, I think what Tierney really needs is to speak to her father. I'd do more to encourage it if I weren't afraid of what he might say, and how it might end up making things worse.'

'Is he still trying to call her?'

'I think so, which'll be making her feel terrible, because she won't like hurting him. I'll have to sit down and talk to her again. We need to sort through this somehow.'

'Marco is on his way,' Lorenzo announced, coming to join them. 'He was dropping the children for their horse-riding lessons, so may be a few minutes late.'

'That's fine,' Lainey assured him. Thank goodness she had something to do today, or she might just find herself packing up and joining Stacy on the next flight home.

Home. Where Tom was.

Unless he'd already left again.

Embracing Stacy and fighting back the tears that seemed determined to spill, she said, 'Call when you land to let me know you've arrived safely.'

'Of course,' Stacy promised. 'And good luck with Carlotta. I'll be longing to hear all about it.'

Suppressing a shiver of nerves, Lainey stood back to watch her get into the car.

Moments later they were gone, and Lainey was trying not to feel the loneliness of being here without her best friend. Not that they'd spent much time together over the past week, but just knowing Stacy was around and there to talk to if she needed to offload had made the darkest moments a little easier to bear.

Suddenly the need to speak to Tom was so overwhelming that she couldn't stop herself dialling his mobile. After the third ring her aunt picked up, which was odd, but a relief too since it must mean he hadn't left yet.

'He's taken Peter for a walk,' Daffs told her. 'I only realised his phone was still here when you rang. Of course I wouldn't have answered if I hadn't seen it was you.'

'Has he told you yet when he's leaving?' Lainey forced herself to ask.

'No, but he took a few things out to the car earlier, so I suppose it's sometime today. Would you like me to give him a message?'

Unable to speak, Lainey urged the despair to pass, but it wouldn't.

'Are you still there, dear?' Daffs asked worriedly.

'Yes, yes, I'm here,' Lainey managed with a sob. 'I – um . . . No, no message. He'll see that I've rung and if he wants to call back, he will.'

Picturing him with her father as she rang off, she covered her face with her hands and tried so hard not to cry that it wasn't until Tierney came to wrap her in her arms that she realised the battle was already lost.

'Oh, Mum, don't, please,' Tierney wept, 'I know you're going to miss Stacy, but it'll be all right, I promise. We'll make it all right, me and you, OK?'

'Yes, of course we will,' Lainey replied, loving her for trying to be so grown up. She squeezed her tight, loving her even more for being Tom's daughter, a link to him that could never be broken. 'Are you ready?' she finally made herself ask. 'Marco'll be here any minute.'

'Actually,' Tierney said, as they started towards the terrace, 'I thought I'd stay here and wait for the others to come back.'

Surprised, Lainey said, 'Are you sure? They

shouldn't be long, but if they decide to go on somewhere . . .'

'I'll text and get them to come and pick me up.'

Deciding that a reunion with Skye could only be a good thing at the moment, Lainey let the matter rest. It would be easier not to have Tierney around while she and Marco were talking to Carlotta Calduzzi, if only because Tierney would be sure to keep interrupting. Besides, if Carlotta was going to confirm her worst fears, that she, and therefore her children, were the progeny of incest, Lainey would rather have some time to put it into her own words before breaking it to them.

As soon as the gates had closed behind Marco's car, Tierney took out her phone to send a text. Her fingers were shaking, she was close to sobbing, but she didn't have any choice. She had to do this or nothing in her life would ever be all right again.

The interior of Carlotta Calduzzi's apartment turned out to be as grand as the building that housed it, set high in the hilltop town of Cortona on a narrow, cobbled street, which meandered off towards the Sanctuary of Santa Margherita. The salon's spectacular view over the town's cluttered red rooftops and dazzling sweep of the valley below was framed, like a painting, in a highly ornate window with a table and chairs in front of it, and the inevitable crucifix above. In a way, the room was a little like a church, with its stained-glass panels in the doors leading to the hallway and kitchen, and fading tapestries hanging from the yellowing walls.

Signora Calduzzi herself, though no beauty in the obvious sense, was as elegant as any woman her age could wish to be, with small, precise features, neatly combed fair hair and a bearing that perfectly suited her expensively cut dress. Though her eyes were still moist after the rush of emotion she'd experienced on opening the door to find herself confronted by a *fantasma dal passato* (ghost from the past, Marco had provided), they were shining with fondness now and a touch of sadness too.

'She is so very young to die,' she murmured in heavily accented English, drawing the sign of the cross in front of her again, while repeating what she'd said when Lainey had broken the news of her mother's death. '*Dio fa che la usa anima riposa in pace.*'

Knowing this meant God rest her soul, Lainey smiled her thanks and sat down at the table, in the chair Signora Calduzzi was offering.

'*Grazie,*' *la signora* said to Marco as he held out a chair for her. 'Will you have a drink?' she asked, seeming almost fearful that they might refuse.

'I'd love one, thank you,' Lainey assured her, having no idea what the lemon-coloured liquid was in the crystal jug between them. However, she was eager to try it, if only to be polite. 'Shall I pour?'

'*Si, si, le mie mani tremano 'in questi giorni,*' she replied, gesturing for Lainey to continue.

'She's saying that her hands shake a little these days,' Marco explained, and seeing Lainey grimace as she lifted the heavy jug, he took it from her and did the honours himself.

Though the drink was sugary it was refreshingly cold, and as soon as Lainey realised Signora Calduzzi was awaiting a verdict, she declared, '*Delizioso.*'

Seeming almost childlike in her delight, *la signora* chuckled happily and took a sip herself. She spoke rapidly then to Marco, and for several minutes

Lainey simply listened, picking up on the odd word here and there, but unable to make any real sense of what was being said.

'She is telling me that you have a very strong resemblance to your mother around your eyes and the shape of your face,' Marco explained. 'Your colouring too, and she is wondering if your spirit is as mischievous.'

Breaking into a smile, Lainey turned to *la signora*, saying, 'Hopefully only on her better days.'

Marco translated and *la signora* clapped her hands in amusement. She then continued in Italian, telling Lainey through Marco how close she and Alessandra had been as girls, and how very much she'd missed her friend after she'd left for England. Apparently she'd written to Alessandra many times in the early years, but Alessandra had only replied once, to tell her that she would never come back. After that, all Carlotta's letters had gone unanswered, until eventually she'd stopped writing. But she'd never stopped praying for Alessandra to change her mind and return home, she said, or simply to send word.

'And now,' she sighed, a little tearfully, 'she is with the Blessed Virgin. I am always afraid for this, that I am never seeing her again. *Era malate da tanto*?'

'Was she ill for long?' Marco translated.

Already warming to this woman, simply for seeming to care so much about her mother, Lainey said, 'She had cancer.' She glanced at Marco, but *la signora* said, '*Si, si*, I understand. This is very sad, but you were with her?'

'Yes,' Lainey replied. 'My sisters were too, and my father.'

'You have sisters?' She seemed surprised and pleased.

355

'Two, Sarah and Esther. They're my half-sisters, and Peter is my adoptive father.'

Carlotta nodded gravely.

'Peter's a wonderful man,' Lainey told her. 'My mother was very happy with him, and I couldn't wish for a better father.'

Carlotta smiled. 'I hear long time ago from Maria, your great-grandmother, that our beloved Alessandra marries a nice Englishman. It is very good for my heart when I hear this.'

'You knew Maria?' Lainey asked.

'*Si, si*, I know all family of Alessandra. We are children together in Tuoro and on the island where live my grandparents – and Maria.'

Reaching into her bag, Lainey said, 'I have a letter here, or part of one, that I found amongst my mother's belongings. I was wondering if it might have been from Maria?'

Having put on her glasses, Carlotta took the single page, and while reading she touched her fingers to her lips as though to stop any emotion escaping. '*Si*,' she said softly, 'I believe this is from Maria. She is very sad when Alessandra leave. It break her heart. You understand, she was like a mother for Alessandra. She care for her very much.'

Lainey swallowed. 'Why do you think my mother told Maria she'd named me after her mother, Melvina?'

Carlotta's eyes darkened as she lowered them. 'Did Alessandra never tell you what happen between her and her mother?' she asked.

Lainey shook her head. 'I know something did, but she'd never talk about it. It's why I'm here, to try to find out why she left her family when she was still so young.' She hesitated a moment. 'I was also hoping,' she went on cautiously, 'that you might be able to tell me who my real father is.'

At that, Carlotta rose to her feet and began pacing the room. She seemed so agitated as she spoke to Marco in Italian that Lainey almost wished she hadn't broached the subject. She looked at Marco, who discreetly raised a hand, indicating she should allow *la signora* to finish whatever she was saying.

As she waited Lainey realised, with an awful churning inside, that there couldn't be much doubt now that her ugliest suspicions were being confirmed. It was the only truth she could imagine that would cause such a reaction, and as the shame of it burned into her heart she felt so wretched, and so afraid for her children, that she hardly knew how she could go forward from here.

In the end, as Carlotta seemed to calm down, Marco attempted a translation.

'Basically, she is saying,' he began, 'that as your mother never told you about your father then she feels that she cannot either. It is a truth that is far better to die with those who have kept it a secret all these years.'

Lainey turned to Carlotta, understanding why she wouldn't want to put the shame into words, but she couldn't simply let it go. 'It was Luigi Valente, wasn't it? He was both my father and grandfather?'

Carlotta frowned in confusion and looked to Marco. After he'd translated she turned back to Lainey, shaking her head. 'No, no, child,' she exclaimed vehemently, 'Luigi Valente is not your father. Maybe your grandfather, but I think even your grandmother, Melvina, does not know this for certain. Aldo, he always believe Alessandra is his, and Melvina, this is what she tell the world, that Alessandra is the daughter of Aldo. After what happen to her son . . . Do you know this, that Melvina had a son who die very young?'

Lainey nodded and waited while Marco related what they'd been told by Signor Donata.

'*Si, si,* I think this is true about the wife of Valente,' Carlotta responded. 'She was not a good woman. Of course, I am not born at this time, but my mother, she tell me when I am older about the curse on the son of Melvina. I know it is hard to believe in such things, but I am sure it was right for Melvina to tell everyone Aldo is the father of Alessandra. This way they keep her safe.'

Coming to sit at the table again, she took one of Lainey's hands and held it in both of hers. For a long time she simply gazed at Lainey's fingers, seeming absorbed by the neutrally painted nails, the creases around her knuckles, the platinum band of her wedding ring. 'I understand you want to know who is your father,' she said in the end, 'but, *mia bambina*, it is not an easy story to tell, and I think it is,' she glanced at Marco, '*piu difficile per te sentire.*'

'More difficult for you to hear,' Marco translated.

Lainey nodded, and attempted a smile of reassurance. Whatever the truth, she'd come this far, so she wasn't going to allow herself to turn back.

Carlotta's eyes drifted for a moment, and when she spoke it was hard to read her expression. However, the bitterness of her tone was enough to convey her feelings. 'It was Melvina, your grandmother, who cause the trouble,' she stated bluntly. She looked at Lainey. 'My mother always she say no one understand how gentle soul like Maria can have daughter like Melvina.' She took a breath and shook her head. 'You speak already of Valente,' she continued, 'so you know that he and Melvina . . .'

When she stopped Lainey realised she didn't want to put Melvina's carnal sins into words, so she nodded and said, 'Yes, we know.'

'But he is not your father,' Carlotta assured her. 'I cannot be sure if he is your grandfather, I can only tell you what my mother tell me, that when Melvina is on the island after the death of her son, Valente does not go there during this time. Only Aldo is there and when they return to Tuoro she is pregnant with Alessandra. Perhaps Valente and Melvina find a way to see each other when she is on the island, I do not know, but Aldo always say that Alessandra is his. Whether he believe it only he knows, but the world pity him, because they know that Melvina is crazy for Valente. She have no care for her child, or her immortal soul, she care only for this man.'

Looking down at Lainey's hand again, she folded her own more closely around it.

'The trouble, it begin,' she said, 'when your mother, Alessandra, is sixteen and Valente see her for first time since she is grown. Like her mother, she is very beautiful, very how you say, *sviluppata*?'

'Developed,' Marco told her.

'*Si*, she is much developed for her age, and of course she is young and Melvina is now not so young. I do not know how Melvina find out that Valente want her daughter, maybe he tell her himself, or maybe she understand this from seeing him with Alessandra. Alessandra, she is how you say, playful with the boys. Not in a way to cause trouble, you understand, but she flirt a little and she like to have the attention. And the boys . . . they give her the attention. Always when we do *il passeggio*, she is the one they choose and it depend on her mood if she will walk with them. Sometimes she will, sometimes she will not. Some people say, after it all happen, that she bring it on herself with the way she is, but this is not true. It is her mother who make it happen. It is her mother who is so *gelosa* that she is the one who will suffer for all eternity for what she do to her daughter.'

Realising her throat had gone dry, Lainey picked up her drink and took a sip. She couldn't even begin to guess what Carlotta was about to tell her, nor did she want to try. It was in the past now, so whatever it was, it couldn't hurt her – please God.

'Alessandra, she swear to me,' Carlotta continued, 'that she never do bad things with Valente. He want her, he beg her, but she is good Catholic like her grandmother, Maria. And Valente, he is old man. *Never* she want him. She tell her mother this, but Melvina is crazy with the jealous. She does not believe her. She send her to the island to be with her grandmother, so Valente does not see her, but Alessandra she come back to Tuoro, and Valente, one day he come to the apartment when only Alessandra is there. Melvina find them laughing together and Alessandra, because she is angry with her mother, she flirt with Valente in a way to make Melvina think something happen with them.'

Carlotta's hand was shaking noticeably as she took a sip of her drink and dabbed her mouth with a tissue. She was no longer meeting Lainey's eyes; instead she was staring blindly, painfully into the past.

'Melvina she do nothing until Valente is gone,'

she continued, 'then she take Alessandra by the hair and she drag her into Piazza Marconi where is their apartment, calling her terrible names. My mother and me, we hear the screams, and we run out to see what happens. Melvina is in terrible rage. She drag Alessandra to the church and push her into *il confessionale*. Padre Angelo he come and Melvina tell Alessandra to confess her sin. Alessandra swear she has no sin but Melvina does not believe her. The padre, he try to make Melvina calm, but Melvina cannot control her rage. She tell Alessandra she is no longer her daughter, she cannot come home. Alessandra beg her to listen, but when they get to the apartment Melvina slam the door in her face and say she never want to see her again.

'Alessandra is very scared. She run back through the village and down to the lake. She want to get to her grandmother, but it is dark now and there are no boats. She say she never hear anyone coming behind her, she only know when she is forced to the ground and the terrible things begin to happen to her.'

As Carlotta stopped to take a breath, Lainey could feel herself recoiling from the horror of her words. *Her mother was raped. This was how she was conceived.*

'After it is over,' Carlotta continued, 'the attackers, there are two of them, they leave her where she is and it is my uncle who find her the next day. He bring her to us and she tell me she is sure one of them is the priest, because he wear a long black gown, but she did not see his face. She knows she cannot say this to anyone, because they will never believe her. So she keep it to herself, and ask me to do the same. Then, few weeks later, while she is with Maria on the island, she learn she is pregnant and she is so unhappy she want to die.' Carlotta's lips were trembling now, her face pale as tears filled her eyes. 'You understand, Elenora, she did not know you then . . .'

'Of course I understand,' Lainey assured her. What mother would want a child who'd been fathered in such a way? In fact, if Alessandra hadn't been Catholic Lainey was sure she'd never have been born.

'I do not know if God in His mercy will ever forgive Melvina for how she turn her back on Alessandra, both before and after the attack. She is afraid, of course, that Valente is the father, and this she cannot bear. So she send Alessandra back to the island and tell her she must never leave.'

Lainey's pity for her mother was overwhelming. She could fully understand now why Alessandra had never wanted to see Melvina again. She even understood why she'd wanted Melvina to think she'd named her daughter after her. It would not have been what Melvina wanted to hear: it would have been like a punishment, an attempt to add to her shame.

'I am sorry, Elenora, for what I am telling you,' Carlotta said, tightening her hold on Lainey's hand. 'Whether God will forgive those who do this to your mother, only He know. Maybe the men they confess and receive absolution, but Melvina . . .' She shook her head hopelessly.

Swallowing the bile in her throat, Lainey asked, 'So what happened after she went back to the island?'

Carlotta sighed. 'It is very difficult time for everyone, because Alessandra, she will no longer go to the church and this upset Maria very much.

It upset Aldo too. He think, like Melvina, that Valente is the father of the child, and he want, when the baby come, that Alessandra give it to the nuns. But when the time come Alessandra will not do it. At first I think she keep you to punish her mother, she say this is true, but then, when it is clear how much this is hurting Maria, she still will not give you up. In the end Maria write to her cousin in England to ask if you can go to her. So after *il battesimo* Alessandra agree to this. She take you with her to London and we . . . we never see her again.'

Feeling almost as emotional as Carlotta at the thought of her mother, so young and alone, making the journey to a life she could barely even imagine, in a country whose language she couldn't speak, Lainey had to let a moment pass. 'And Melvina?' she said hoarsely. 'We were told that she left the village.'

Carlotta nodded. 'Yes, in the end she go too. She have to, it is not possible for her to stay because when Valente find out what Melvina do to her own daughter because of him, he is disgusted. He will not see her any more, and for Melvina this is terrible. So Aldo take her away. They go south to Calabria where there is distant family of Aldo. I think they also live for a while in Sicilia, but it is many, many years before they return to Umbria.'

Lainey blinked. 'They came back?'

Carlotta nodded. '*Si, si,* they are here now, not so far from Tuoro.'

Lainey's heart turned over. 'Are you saying . . .' She was hardly grasping this. 'Are you saying my grandparents are still alive?'

Carlotta's expression seemed to close. 'It is how you say, *un'ironia*?' she asked Marco.

'An irony,' he replied.

'*Si*, it is *una strana ironia* that Melvina now live in the villa of Valente. My mother say this is always the dream of Melvina and we see that it now come true, but today the villa is only for the old people who have *la demenza*.'

'Dementia?' Lainey asked, glancing at Marco.

He nodded.

What an irony indeed, and still trying to take it in, Lainey said, 'So who has dementia? Both of them . . .?'

'No, it is only Melvina who lose her mind. Aldo, he have small apartment in new part of the villa that is next door, and he go every day to see Melvina in the place where are the people who must have special care.'

Lainey looked at Marco again, not sure what she wanted to say.

He spoke quietly to Carlotta in Italian, and after she'd replied, he said, 'I asked if it is possible to visit them, and *la signora* say that it is. She thinks it is not likely that Melvina will understand who you are, but she is sure that Aldo will.'

Lainey was still finding it hard to make herself think. After hearing all that she had, she couldn't be sure what she wanted to do about anything now. What she did know, however, was that right at this moment she'd give almost anything to be with Peter.

During the drive back to Tuoro Lainey sat quietly, almost numbly, gazing out of the window, still trying to absorb what she'd been told. Her mind was in a turmoil of indecision. She'd already turned down Marco's offer to detour to the old Valente villa, not because she was ruling out seeing her grandparents, but because she simply didn't feel ready for it yet. She needed some time to think, to try to come to terms with the way they had turned their backs on Alessandra – and on her.

Her eyes closed as her mother's terror on that night seemed to come alive for her. The fear, degradation, helplessness and sense of betrayal she must have felt was beyond anything Lainey could imagine. She understood completely now why Alessandra had never been able to tell her about it; why she'd found it so hard to have a normal relationship with her. It must have been all but impossible for her mother to look at her and not remember how she'd been conceived. Lainey wondered if she'd ever detected signs of the priest in the shape of her daughter's eyes, her mannerisms, or sound of her laughter.

She asked herself, would she, in her mother's place, keep a baby who'd come to her that way? Since she wasn't a Catholic, and was living in a different time, it wouldn't be the same sort of issue for her, but for Alessandra it must have been truly devastating when she'd learned she was pregnant. So why hadn't she let her baby go to the nuns? It could surely only have been as Carlotta had said, to punish Melvina, and though Lainey didn't blame her mother for wanting to exact her revenge, fearing that was all she'd meant to Alessandra was making her feel wretched. Yet she was sure her mother had come to love her over time, even if she hadn't at the start. She must make herself hold on to that now, and turn away from the dreadful self-pity that was struggling to swamp her.

'We are close to the turning for the old Valente

villa,' Marco told her, 'if you would like to change your mind . . .'

She shook her head. 'No. Thank you.' It wasn't only that she needed more time, it was the fact that it didn't seem right to go there with Marco. He'd been so kind, so supportive throughout everything, but the person she really wanted to see was Tom. Her heart twisted as she realised she was going to have to get used to him not being there for her any more. Nevertheless, if she rang to tell him what she'd learned today she felt sure he'd listen, even though it was unlikely to affect him now. She was not his main concern.

'Would you like me to come in?' Marco offered, as they pulled up outside the Villa Constantia. The doors and shutters were all closed, telling her no one was at home.

'Thanks, but I'll be fine,' she assured him.

He didn't appear convinced. 'I'm truly sorry for what you've learned today,' he said softly.

Her smile was flat. *Her father was a rapist who might also have been a priest.* 'I'll call you later,' she promised.

After he'd gone she went to stand on the terrace and gazed down at the village, scattered on its own small hilltop overlooking the lake. She thought of the secrets buried in its heart, and of how nothing, no amount of regret, forgiveness or penance, could ever right the wrongs inflicted on her mother. Her eyes travelled on to the silvery blur of the horizon, where the mountains seemed part of another world. A tear rolled on to her cheek as she remembered how Alessandra had called out for her grandmother at the end. She wondered if, on some level, Maria had heard her.

In her heart she was calling out for her mother now. She wanted to see her so much, to tell her she understood and how sorry she was for all that had happened to her. She waited as though expecting a whisper on the breeze, or a sign in the shimmering air, but the world was quiet and still.

She had never, she realised, felt so utterly alone. Her mother was gone for ever, and nothing could bring her back, Peter was slipping away, and Tom was leaving too. How was she going to make herself go forward from here?

Hearing the gates opening and a car coming through, she dabbed at her tears and went to unlock the door. She didn't want the children to see how anguished she was, it would only upset them, and it was going to be hard enough telling them what she'd learned today. She could already imagine Tierney's shock, Zav's confusion, Max's disgust. It wouldn't surprise her if Tierney ended up wanting to visit Aldo with her, should she decide to go, and maybe she'd let her. She mustn't shut her out the way Alessandra had shut her out; no good could ever come of that.

A few minutes later Zav and Alfie were wandering across the lawn to the terrace, while Skye stood at the car, talking to Max.

'Where's Tierney?' Lainey called out.

Max and Skye looked up. 'I thought she went with you,' Max replied.

Lainey's heart caught on a beat of unease. 'No. She decided not to come in the end. She said she was going to give you a call.'

Max shrugged and started towards the villa. 'She must be inside,' he said, 'or down at the pool.'

Lainey went through to check while Zav ran down to the pool.

'She's not here, Mum,' Zav called as he started back.

Lainey looked at Skye, who merely repeated what Max had said: 'I thought she went with you.'

'She must have gone for a walk,' Max decided, pulling out his mobile.

Lainey was searching frantically for a note.

Skye was already busy texting, and remembering she hadn't checked her messages since leaving Carlotta's, Lainey began scrolling through them. At last she found a text from Tierney, sent a couple of hours ago.

I'm all right, Mum. Please don't worry about me.

As confusion jarred with alarm, Lainey showed her phone to Max. 'What does that mean?' she demanded. 'Where is she?'

At a loss, Max turned to Skye, who shook her head. 'No idea,' she answered, convincingly.

Lainey was dialling Tierney's number. Finding herself going straight to voicemail, she said, 'Darling, where are you? I'm very worried, please call me the minute you get this.'

Chapter Nineteen

It was Sunday morning now, and Lainey was beside herself with worry. Tierney hadn't come home all night, nor had she rung to say where she was. At least she'd texted, but only to repeat *Promise I'm OK. Please don't worry.*

But how could Lainey not worry when she had absolutely no idea where Tierney was, or who she might be with? Max seemed genuinely to have no clue, and Skye was insisting she didn't know what was going on either. Lainey wasn't sure she believed her, but short of threatening her with something drastic if she didn't speak up, she had no way of getting any information out of her. However, if Tierney wasn't back by the end of the day, Skye was going to find herself in very deep trouble.

'I keep thinking about this married-man business,' Lainey said to Stacy on the phone, 'but she swore it wasn't true. Of course she would, she'd hardly admit it, would she?'

'Has she taken any clothes?' Stacy asked.

'Yes, a few things are missing.'

'Have you told Tom?'

'Not yet, but I'll have to if she isn't back by tonight. I've even considered going to the police, but she's sixteen, for God's sake, and she's in touch, sort of,

369

so I don't suppose they'll be interested. Oh God, I dread to think of what she's got herself into – and of what Tom's going to say if I have to tell him I don't know where she is.'

'Let's hope it doesn't come to that. I'm sure she'll show up at some point today.'

'After spending the night somewhere with someone she doesn't want me to know anything about? This isn't good, Stace. There's definitely something wrong, and if anything happens to her, it'll be all my fault for being so damned wrapped up in myself.'

Downstairs in Max's apartment Skye was saying, 'All you've got to do is stop your girlfriend coming here and I'll tell you where your sister is.'

Max was in a filthy enough mood already; this was making it a whole lot worse. 'Don't fucking threaten me,' he growled. 'Just tell me where the hell she is.'

'No way . . .' She sprang back as he started towards her, but he was too fast and grabbed her wrist. 'If anything happens to her,' he snarled, 'I'll hold you personally responsible. Now where the fuck is she?'

Accepting she wasn't going to win this, Skye said, 'Actually, I don't know where she is . . .'

'What the fuck . . .'

'. . . but I think I know *who* she's with.'

He waited.

She glanced at him nervously, certain Tierney wouldn't want her to tell him, unless that mental case, Mr Grey, had turned up here and forced Tierney to go with him . . .

'Skye,' Max warned.

'All right, but actually, I don't know his name,' she confessed. 'I mean, it's Guy something-or-other. You know him though, because he's married to your dad's agent.'

Max looked as though he'd been struck. He surely to God hadn't heard that right. 'Tell me that's not true,' he demanded in a dangerously low voice.

She only looked at him.

'Jesus Holy Christ,' he thundered. 'That bell end's old enough to be her father . . . Shit, if Dad ever finds out about this . . . We can't tell Lainey. We can't tell anyone. Where's he taken her?'

Skye shrugged. 'I've got no idea. She didn't even tell me she was going to see him . . .'

'She's bound to have . . .'

'I swear she didn't. All I know is that he sent her a text saying, Guess where I am.'

'And?'

'We assumed it meant he was here.'

Opening up his mobile, he scrolled fast through the numbers. He didn't much care what kind of trouble he was about to cause now, all that mattered was blowing that jerk right off the planet so he could never lay a hand on Tierney again. 'Hey, it's Max Hollingsworth,' he told Nadia as she answered. 'Sorry to bother you, but I don't have a number for Guy and I kind of need to talk to him.'

'I'm afraid he's not here,' Nadia replied, sounding all bunged up. 'He's at the office . . .'

'On a Sunday?'

'We've got a lot on at the moment.'

'OK, great, I'll call him there. Thanks,' and ringing off he found the office number and connected. A girl picked up on the third ring.

371

'Is Guy there?' Max demanded. 'It's kind of urgent.'

'Uh, I'm not sure,' came the reply. 'Can I ask who's calling?'

'Max Hollingsworth, Tom's son. I'll hold.'

As he waited, his eyes went to Skye's, but seeing her unease he quickly looked away.

'Is he there?' Skye whispered anxiously.

'That's what I'm trying to find out.'

'I'm sorry,' the girl said, coming back on the line, 'I thought he was here, but it seems he's stepped out for a while. Shall I ask him to call . . .'

'Have you actually seen him today?' Tom interrupted.

Sounding baffled, the girl said, 'Not personally, but . . .'

'OK, when did you last see him?'

'I guess it must have been Friday, just before I left for the day. Can I ask . . .'

'No you can't. Sorry, I just need to get hold of him. Do you have his mobile number?'

'Yes, but I'm not supposed . . .'

'I'm Tom Hollingsworth's son,' he reminded her, 'you can give it to me.'

Minutes later he was connecting to Guy Whittaker's mobile. It rang half a dozen times before Guy's voice came down the line, saying, 'If this is a telemarket . . .'

'It's Max Hollingsworth,' Max cut in. 'Where's my sister?'

There was a beat of silence, before Whittaker said, 'Why on earth would I know where your sister is?'

Max glanced menacingly at Skye. If she was making this up . . . 'Because you've been texting her, stalking her more like . . .'

'You need to get a grip, Max,' Guy broke in, 'because I've got no idea . . .'

'You're full of shit, Whittaker. I've got her friend right here and she's told me everything.'

'And you believe her?'

'As a matter of fact I do. So I'm asking you again, where the fuck is my sister? Is she with you now? Put her on.'

'I can't do that . . .'

'Just do it!'

'I told you, she's not here.'

'Where's here? Are you in Italy?'

'What the . . .'

'Did you send her a text telling her to guess where you were?'

'What? *No!*'

'He did,' Skye cried. 'I saw it, and I know it was from him, because I saw all the others he sent too.'

'Did you hear that?' Max demanded.

'I did, but she's getting it all wrong . . .'

'He's a weirdo,' Skye shouted even louder. 'He's into all sorts of . . .'

'Max, give me a break,' Guy interrupted angrily. 'You know what girls that age are like, they get an idea in their head and your sister . . .'

'Is a child,' Max seethed.

'She's sixteen,' Skye reminded him.

'Next to him, that makes her a child,' Max retorted, 'and if I ever find out you laid as much as one finger on her . . .' he threatened Guy.

'He shagged her,' Skye broke in wildly. 'He was her first . . .'

'That is not true,' Guy shouted back.

Max's head was spinning.

'Yes, it is true,' Skye insisted. 'You did stuff to

her like in the book and you keep wanting to do it again, but she's not interested, so now you won't leave her alone.'

'I'm not listening to any more of this,' Guy snapped. 'I don't know where your sister is; I'm sorry if she and her friend have been spinning you a load of lies, but it's not my problem,' and the line went dead.

Max glared at Skye.

'I swear I didn't tell her to get involved with him,' she gasped, 'and I didn't . . .'

'Shut up, I'm trying to think.'

'Charming,' she muttered.

After a moment he slapped a hand to his head, and calling up Tierney's number he pressed to connect. Once again he was pushed through to voicemail, but not before he'd heard the double ringtone. 'She's in England,' he declared. 'She's gone to that fucking lowlife . . .' He was already digging through his holdall, turning out his passport and wallet.

'What are you doing?' Skye cried.

Ignoring her, he ran upstairs to Lainey. 'I know where she is,' he told her, 'or I kind of do. I'll find her. Just don't tell Dad yet, OK? Let me get to her first,' and before Lainey could utter a word he was dashing to his car, turning it around and speeding off down the drive.

Tierney hadn't cried at all yet, but she'd come very close more times than she could count. Yesterday, Sunday, had been the worst, when she'd caught a train to Pisa with Brett and Ricky. They hadn't been thrilled about letting her share their tent, which they'd pitched at a campsite close to the airport, but at least they'd helped her get on the same flight as them first thing this morning. This meant she'd ended up at Gatwick, so she'd travelled into London with them where they'd left her to go on up north.

She was on another train now, her mobile clutched tightly in one hand, her bag nestled in her lap as she stared out of the window. It was raining, which seemed weird after all the sun in Italy. She wondered what her mum was doing now, and felt her heart tightening as more tears stung her eyes. She hated making her worry like this, which was why she kept texting to say she was all right. Skye had sent loads of messages too, but Tierney hadn't answered any of them. She was so mad with Skye. She'd only gone and told Max about Guy, so now Max was sending texts saying he was on his way and would *sort the bastard out.*

Oh God, what was he going to do?

Getting to her feet as the train rolled into the station, she pushed her way along the aisle and out on to the platform. She'd have to take a taxi from here, but that was OK, she had enough money. Her heart skipped a beat as she wondered if he'd be waiting outside. She'd texted to say she was coming, but she couldn't remember now if she'd told him which train she was on.

Choking back a sob as she merged with the crowd exiting the station, she looked around but could see no sign of him. Was he in his car, waiting to spot her?

She stood still, thinking it might make it easier for him to see her, but she was only bumped and pushed aside, knocked with umbrellas and splashed by feet hitting the puddles around her. The crowd cleared and he still wasn't there.

Joining the taxi queue she checked her mobile, as a new text dropped in.

Where are you? What the hell have you been telling your brother?

Her heart churned with fear; her fingers were trembling so hard she could barely tap in a reply. In the end, she stopped trying.

Twenty minutes later, the taxi was preparing to stop. She was so tense she couldn't even feel her nails biting into her palms. What was she going to do if he wasn't there? How was she going to make everything all right if he didn't want to listen?

She felt sick with dread. It was all going wrong. She shouldn't have come, but how could she not have? She'd needed to do something, but now she was here she wished she was still with her mum.

She saw his car, and a huge sob escaped her.

Then she saw him, coming out of the door, and leaping from the taxi she ran straight into his arms.

'Dad, Dad,' she choked, clinging to him with all her might. 'Oh, Dad, you're here.'

'Of course I'm here,' he said tenderly. 'Didn't you get my messages?'

She didn't know. She didn't think so, but maybe she'd been in too much of a state to realise what she was reading. It didn't matter – all that did was that he was at home, where he belonged, and now, together, they were going to make everything all right between him and Mum. She couldn't tell him about Guy, though. That was a problem she had to try to ignore, for now.

Keeping her with him, he went to pay the driver, and after taking her bag from the back seat he led her into the kitchen. There was no sign of Auntie

Daffs or Grandpa. Maybe they'd gone to Age Concern, or church, seeing as it was a Sunday.

After putting her bag down Tom wrapped her in his arms again. 'So what's all this about?' he asked softly.

'Please don't go,' she sobbed wretchedly. 'Please stay with us. Mum still loves you . . . so do we . . . nothing will ever be right without you.'

'Hey, hey,' he soothed. 'Take a breath now.'

'You're not listening to me . . .'

'Of course I am.'

'You don't understand, Mum's . . . Oh my God, you're going back to her,' she cried, spotting his bags on the floor. 'Dad, don't, please, please . . . We really love you and I think you love us. OK, I know you've got Julia to think about, and her mum's not well, but it's not fair if they take you away. It just isn't, when you're our dad too . . .'

Cupping her face in his hands, he said, 'She isn't taking me away from you. No one could ever do that.'

'So why are you . . .?'

'Will you please let me get a word in?'

She gave a jerky sort of nod as she hiccuped another sob.

He was regarding her closely. 'Before we go any further,' he said, 'does Mum know you're here?'

Realising it wouldn't do any good to lie, she shook her head. 'I've sent her lots of texts saying I'm all right, but I know she's really worried. I just didn't want to tell her, in case she tried to stop me.'

He gave her a look of fond despair. 'We need to call and let her know you're safe,' he declared. 'Then, my darling, we're going to sit down and have a good long chat about everything that's been happening . . .' He broke off as she suddenly began sobbing again, harder than ever. She was shaking so violently that he could barely hold her still. 'Tierney, what is it?' he urged worriedly. 'There's more, isn't there? Tell me what it is.'

'I can't,' she gasped. 'I mean, there's nothing.'

'I think there is.'

She turned away, using her fingers to try and blot her tears. 'Let's ring Mum,' she gulped, and reaching for the phone she handed it to him.

As he dialled his eyes kept coming back to her, searching for whatever she was hiding.

'Please be nice to her,' she said hoarsely, as she heard the ringtone.

'Aren't you going to speak to her?' he asked.

The shake of her head could have been a nod. Her mobile rang, and seeing it was Max she felt herself shrivelling inside as she tried to decide whether or not to answer. She couldn't with her dad there, but she had to know what was going on, so taking the phone into the hall, she clicked on.

'T? Are you there?'

'Yeah, I'm here,' she whispered. 'Where are you?'

'On my way to get you. Didn't you pick up my messages?'

'Yes, but I'm OK, honestly. You don't have to come.'

'I do, if that slimy bastard's . . .'

'I'm at home, Max, with Dad.'

There was a moment's stunned silence. 'With Dad?'

'Yes, I can put him on if you like.'

'No thanks. What are you doing there? Skye said . . .'

'I know what she said, but I had to see Dad, that's why I came.'

'So why the fuck didn't you tell anyone?'

'Because you'd have tried to stop me.'

'Jesus Christ, T. I've just got off a plane . . .'

'You didn't have to come.'

'I did if you're seeing that arsehole.'

'I'm not, I promise.' She started to cry.

'What's he done to you, T? I need to know if any of what Skye told me is true.'

She tried to say it wasn't, but couldn't make herself speak.

'It is, isn't it?' he growled.

'Don't,' she sobbed. 'I didn't mean . . . It's not . . .'

'He's going to fucking pay for this,' he snarled, and before she could utter a protest the line went dead.

Remembering the door code to Nadia's South Kensington offices, Max punched it in and was about to race up the stairs to strangle Guy Whittaker when his mobile rang. Seeing it was Tierney, he quickly clicked on.

'What now?' he demanded brusquely.

'What are you going to do?' she asked shakily.

'What a fucking question! I'm going to make sure that stinking lowlife never comes near you again, that's what I'm going to do.'

'Max, listen, I don't want anyone to know.'

'No kidding?'

'If Dad ever finds out . . .'

'I'm on it, all right. Now, if you'll let me . . .'

'He's got photos, Max. I mean, of me.'

Max stopped in his tracks. 'Tell me I'm not understanding this correctly,' he warned.

No reply.

'Jesus Christ, Tierney, what were you thinking?' he cried, spinning round and thumping the wall. 'How could you let *anyone*, least of all that jerk . . .'

'Don't shout at me. I messed up, all right? But you've messed up too, loads of times . . .'

'Not like this. OK, maybe worse than this. Actually, maybe not.' He was trying to think. 'How the fuck am I supposed to get the photos back?'

'I don't know, but you have to.'

'Dead right I do.'

'Max?'

'What?'

'You won't look at them, will you?'

If he weren't so mad he might have laughed at that. 'Right, so when I get them deleted or whatever, I'm going to have to take his word for it that they're of you, because I can't look at them. Tierney, get real.'

'But, Max, they're, like, you know . . .'

'Yeah, I'm getting the picture, literally.'

'Don't say that!'

'What is it with you? Don't you get you're a paedo's dream?'

'I'm sixteen . . .'

'Just. Did you do anything with him before your birthday? If you did, that bastard's going to jail.'

'Shut *up*. I don't want anyone to know, and anyway, we didn't do anything before.'

'That's the only bit of good news you've given me today – apart from being with Dad. Where is he now?'

'On the phone to Mum.'

Leaving that for another time, he said, 'Anything else you need to get off your chest?'

Miserably, she replied, 'No, that's it, but Max?'

'What?'

'If you do get them, you won't look at them for long, will you?'

Rolling his eyes, he said, 'Frankly it's weirding me out just thinking about them . . .'

'Oh my God, got to go, Dad's coming.'

As the line went dead Max pocketed his phone and took the stairs three at a time. At reception he came up against a locked door, but he knew that code too and rapidly let himself in.

Since it was lunchtime the place was deserted, but he wasn't leaving until he'd checked Whittaker's office, just in case.

'Max?' Nadia said, coming out of her office. 'What are you doing here? Is everything all right?'

Max was about to respond when he caught a glimpse of Whittaker quickly closing his door. 'Hey you!' he raged, going after him. 'I want a fucking word with you.'

'Max!' Nadia cried in shock.

Ignoring her, Max shoved open the door to find Whittaker standing behind his desk, arms raised in the air.

'Max, I told you on the phone . . .'

'I want the pictures,' Max snarled.

Blanching, Whittaker said, 'I don't know what you're talking about.'

'I think you do.'

Behind him, Nadia asked in amazement, 'Max, for heaven's sake, what's going on?'

'Ask him,' Max growled, pointing at Whittaker. 'Let him tell you what he's been doing to my sister.'

Nadia's face turned grey as she looked at her husband.

'He's making a mistake,' Guy insisted.

'The photos,' Max demanded.

'What photos?' Nadia cried. 'Guy, *what* is he talking about?'

'He's crazy,' Guy snorted, backing away as Max rounded the desk.

'Is that right?' Max snarled, and his fist slammed hard into Whittaker's jaw.

Nadia gasped, and shouted, 'No!' as Whittaker's punch knocked Max back into the desk, sending a pile of manuscripts to the floor.

Grabbing Max as he leapt up ready to fight on, Nadia yelled, 'That's enough! Pull yourselves together.'

Max and Whittaker eyed one another balefully.

'This isn't sorting anything out,' Nadia said sharply. 'Now please tell me what the hell this is about.'

Using a sleeve to wipe the blood from his nose, Max said, 'Are you going to tell her, or shall I?'

'For God's sake,' Whittaker muttered, rubbing his jaw, 'there's nothing to tell. She came on to me, right . . .'

Max made to lunge for him again, but Nadia hauled him back. 'You mentioned your sister,' she said shakily.

'I did,' Max confirmed, still sneering at Whittaker, 'and it turns out that bastard has been corrupting her.'

'He's off his head,' Guy shouted.

'He's got photos,' Max insisted. 'The arsehole took pictures of her . . .'

'Guy, tell me this isn't true,' Nadia warned, her voice threaded with shock. 'Tell me you've never laid a hand on Tom Hollingsworth's daughter.'

'You just heard him say she came on to him,' Max butted in, 'but that's not how it was. He made out like he was that jerk from the book everyone's reading. He got her to do stuff . . .'

'What the hell's she been telling you?' Whittaker practically shrieked. 'No way did I get her to do anything she didn't want to. She was up for it every step of the way. She'd have done anything . . .'

'Guy! For Christ's sake,' Nadia cried, her face slack with horror. 'Tierney Hollingsworth's a child . . .'

'She was sixteen before I even touched her, and if she's saying anything different . . .'

'She isn't,' Max cut in savagely, 'which is lucky for you, because I swear to God, if she'd been underage . . .'

'If she had, I'd be reporting him to the police myself,' Nadia cut in fiercely. To Guy she said, 'What about the photos? Did you seriously take . . .'

'He's going to lie,' Max snarled as Whittaker started to protest. 'We need to see his phone, *and* his computer.'

'Over my dead body.'

Nadia was already pulling the laptop towards her.

'You can't be serious,' Whittaker shouted.

Her eyes were glittering with intent as she opened the files.

He glanced at the door, but sensing he might make a dash Max went to block it.

'Oh my God,' Nadia murmured, as she arrived at the pictures of Tierney, or at least of a naked young girl bound and gagged, each shot taken from a different, highly explicit angle. Feeling faintly sick, she asked, 'Is this her? It is, isn't it?'

'You tell me,' Whittaker retorted smartly.

Turning to Max, she said, 'She won't want you to see this.'

'Dead right she doesn't,' he replied. 'Can you tell it's her?'

Nadia shook her head. 'Not really, but the fact this is happening . . .' Her eyes returned to Whittaker. 'I don't know what I'm finding harder,' she told him, 'that you did this to a friend's daughter, or that you've knowingly put my entire business in jeopardy.'

Whittaker's expression was sour as he said, 'You're making way too much of it . . .'

'Don't say any more,' she snapped. 'We're going to delete every last shot you have . . .'

'We need to know if he's sent them to anyone,' Max reminded her.

'Have you?' she said to Whittaker.

'Give me a break,' he sneered.

'Do you know how to check?' she asked Max.

He shook his head.

'I sent them to her, OK?' Whittaker told them. 'She wanted to see them, she got off on them . . .'

'No more,' Nadia cried, as Max looked like he might go for him again. 'I'll deal with this now, Max, but before you leave, I need to ask, does your father know anything about it?'

Max shook his head. 'Not from me, and Tierney's terrified of him finding out, which is lucky for you, Whittaker, you lowlife piece of scum, because if he did know you'd be more than fucking toast, you'd be six feet under the fucking ground.'

As the door closed behind him Nadia regarded her husband in disgust. 'It's lucky for you,' she informed him, 'actually it's lucky for me, that after

384

my first husband's betrayal nothing can ever affect me like that again. Which doesn't mean this hasn't hurt me, because it has, but at least I know I'll get over it. Now I want you to clear out your desk and then go to the house and pack up your things there. Please be gone by the end of the day.'

'Nadia, for God's sake . . .'

'I don't want to hear anything you have to say. Take your own clients if you want to, but make no mistake: you are no longer a part of this agency, or of my life,' and not entirely sure what she was going to do next, or indeed if this might end up hitting her a lot harder than it was right now, she left the room.

Lainey was in Tuoro, walking towards the church. Almost twenty-four hours had passed since Tom had called to let her know Tierney was safe. The relief had been overwhelming, as had the surprise, particularly as it had then raised the question of where the heck had Max gone dashing off to, if he'd known Tierney was going to her father? Actually, she knew Max was in England because he'd told her when she'd rung him, but where in England, and who he was with, she had no idea. All he'd said was, 'Everything's taken care of, T's with Dad, and I'll be back sometime in the next couple of days with Christie.'

There was obviously more to the story than either Max or Tierney were telling her, and Skye's elusive manner since then had as good as confirmed they were hiding something. In fact, Skye had spent most of her time since Tierney's disappearance at a neighbouring villa, where another English family with teenagers were staying. On the odd occasion she popped back for more clothes, or whatever else she needed, she always seemed to be in such a hurry there was no time to talk.

Had the rest of the conversation with Tom yesterday not been so unsettling, Lainey might have been giving more time to the mystery surrounding Tierney. As it was, her mind was in such turmoil that she barely even knew how to think, never mind what to do with the thoughts when they came. Her reaction to what Tom had said had been so hostile that he had been forced in the end to hang up on her.

'Kirsten wants to meet you,' he'd told her. Just like that. As though it was something she might welcome, or perhaps he thought Kirsten was doing her some sort of favour.

'Well, how very sweet of her,' she'd retorted acidly. 'Shall we join the ladies-who-lunch club, or did she have something a little less formal in mind?'

'Lainey,' he'd admonished, an edge creeping into his voice. 'She's trying to reach out to you . . .'

At that, outrage had robbed her breath. 'I don't need her reaching out to me, thank you very much,' she'd seethed. 'In fact, if she thinks for one minute that I want to sit there listening to her bleating on about how much she loves you, and how wonderful you've been during this time, and how she can't give you up now, she is out of her mind. Just tell her from me, she's welcome to you, because personally I'm not into lying, cheating bastards who deceive their families . . .'

That was when he'd hung up on her, and though she knew she should call him back, perhaps even apologise, she simply couldn't bring herself to. Not yet, anyway. And even when she did, what on earth was she supposed to say? OK, she was sorry Kirsten was sick (though she had to admit, perhaps not as sorry as she ought to be), and she was truly sorry for how scared Julia must be, but that didn't make it any easier for her to deal with how it was affecting her and her family. If anything it was making everything worse, because how was she supposed to fight for Tom when even she understood that Kirsten and Julia had to come first?

Walking into the shadowy interior of Santa Maria Madelena, she felt the cool air brushing her skin like a balm. There was no one around; the place was so quiet and still that her heart, her mind, seemed impossibly loud and fast. Sliding into an empty pew, she sat forward to rest her head on her hands. She wasn't entirely sure why she'd come, what comfort she'd thought it might offer, but after Zav and Alfie had finished their breakfast at the café a while ago and taken off to explore more of the village, she'd felt herself being swamped by a terrible loneliness. She couldn't seem to shake the pitiful sense of never really being wanted, not by her mother, her real father, and now her husband. The only one who'd ever truly cared was Peter, and thinking of him had brought such large, scalding tears to her eyes that she'd been forced to leave the café before anyone noticed.

She'd walked, almost unwittingly, to the Piazza Marconi, where she'd gazed up at the cluttered balconies, netted with washing, and spruced by flowers. She'd wondered which of the apartments had belonged to Melvina, and for a fleeting, horrible moment she'd seemed to hear her mother sobbing to be let in. There was only a cat on the piazza, watching her from a shady doorway. She'd gone towards it, but it had sprung up and disappeared inside. Was this the door, she'd wondered, that Melvina had refused to open the night her daughter had been raped?

Having no answers for her questions she'd turned to follow the Via Matteotti to the church, very probably walking the same route Melvina had dragged Alessandra on that terrible night.

This, she was thinking now as she turned to the confessional, was where Melvina had tried to force her own daughter to ask forgiveness for a sin she hadn't committed.

In such silence it was hard to imagine the commotion there must have been, the priest's shock, Alessandra's hysteria, Melvina's madness, for she surely had been mad to do what she had. And yet something of it seemed to echo beyond the stillness. She looked around at the Futurist paintings, the stained-glass windows, a handful of candles flickering next to the altar. In front of the pulpit a portrait of an impossibly handsome young Christ made her think of Max. She wondered if he was already on his way back, and if he might bring Tierney with him. She hoped Tierney would come, because she was feeling a need for her now that was as deep and powerful as the need she felt for her mother.

Going to the confessional she placed a hand on the ornate, dark wood, as though the touch might quietly unlock its secrets. She wondered if it really had been the priest of that time who'd raped her mother, along with another man. Marco had since learned that the priest had left the village only weeks after the crime. When news had reached him of Alessandra's pregnancy, perhaps? Had he ever asked God to forgive his unforgivable sin? Were a few Hail Marys all it had taken to wipe away the stain of such unspeakable shame? Had either of those men ever truly suffered for what they'd done? How much thought did they give it now, if either was still alive?

Though it might be possible to trace the priest and even force a paternity test, Lainey had absolutely no desire to know anything about him, or his accomplice, not even their names. All she wanted was to feel a connection to her mother, to somehow let her know that she understood why it had been so hard for her to look at Lainey and not remember.

Hearing Zav and Alfie outside, she dabbed her eyes with her fingers and turned towards the open doors. Whatever was waiting for her in the future, it could never be as bad as what had awaited Alessandra when Melvina had locked the door on her that night. If her mother could survive that, then surely to God she could survive what was facing her.

Stepping outside, she waved to Zav and Alfie and turned on her phone. No calls while she'd been inside, but there was a text from Max.

Be there tomorrow.

Swallowing her disappointment that he wasn't coming today, she pressed in Tierney's number to find out where she was and what she was planning to do. If she'd decided to stay at home, would Tom stay with her? Going through to Tierney's voicemail she said, 'Call me when you get this, because if you're not coming back to Italy I'll have to arrange to send Skye home.'

'Can we go back and get in the pool now?' Zav asked, making a deliberate crash into her and turning it into a hug.

Smoothing his hair, Lainey said, 'Of course. We'll just pick up something for lunch . . .'

'From Speedy Benny,' Alfie cried, making Zav laugh, and with their arms jutting like aeroplane wings they set off back through the village.

Deciding not to retrace her mother's and Melvina's steps again, she cut across the piazza beside the church, and answered her mobile as it rang. 'Hi, Marco,' she said, feeling pleased to hear from him, 'how are things in Rome?'

'Hectic,' he replied, 'but I always enjoy being here. I was wondering how you are today. Adriana says she called in to the villa earlier, but you weren't there.'

'I'm in the village,' she told him. 'Should I ring Adriana? Is it something urgent, do you know?'

'She didn't say, but I think she wants to make sure you are not too much on your own after what we learn about your mother on Saturday.'

Touched, but feeling awkward about becoming a liability, Lainey said, 'She mustn't worry, honestly. I'll be fine.'

'But she likes to worry, and besides, we have decided that you are a part of our family now, so it is our job to worry.'

Almost coming undone by his kindness, Lainey said, 'Then I feel very honoured, thank you. I'll give her a call as soon as I've finished speaking to you. Have you decided yet when you're coming back?'

'Actually, it was going to be tomorrow, but when I spoke with my wife this morning we agreed to talk, so she is going to fly here tonight. Perhaps, when I return to Tuoro on Wednesday, she will come with me. If she does, I would like you to meet her.'

Thrown by the echo of Tom's words, and feeling ludicrously choked by the fact that her own marriage wasn't even close to being mended, was in fact heading in the other direction, she said, 'That would be lovely. I'll look forward to it.'

After ringing off she quickly called Adriana to assure her she was fine, then picked up the few groceries she needed before ushering the boys back to the car. The heat was almost unbearable by now; sweat was rolling down her back and her hair was sticking to her neck. The thought of jumping into the pool, fully clothed, as soon as she returned had an irresistible appeal, until she found herself remembering the times she and Tom had done just that on holiday.

Feeling a terrible heaviness in her heart, she began the drive up the hill, only half listening as Zav and Alfie chattered on in the back.

'Mum!' Zav suddenly shouted.

'What?' she cried, instinctively braking.

'Where are we going? You missed the turning.'

Realising she had, she mumbled an apology and turned the car round.

Several minutes later she was in the kitchen unloading the shopping, while Zav and Alfie, stripped to their shorts, dashed down to the pool. It was as well she had them to take care of, she was thinking, because left alone she'd be an even worse mess than she already was – though seeing how ridiculously hard she was crying right now, that was hard to imagine. Tears were splashing all over her hands and the fruit, while painful sobs were racking her body.

'Mum,' she whispered raggedly, 'I need you to tell me what to do.'

'Who are you talking to?' Zav asked, appearing in the doorway.

Quickly trying to pull herself together, Lainey said, 'No one. I was just . . . It doesn't . . .'

'You're crying,' Zav accused, his mouth starting to wobble. 'Please don't cry, Mum,' and rushing at her he plastered his wet body to hers.

'It's OK, I'm fine,' she assured him, reaching past him for her ringing phone. Seeing it was Tierney, she almost sobbed again. It was as though her mother was sending her children as a reminder that she wasn't alone.

'Hello, sweetheart,' she said into the phone.

'Hey, Mum,' Tierney came back brightly. 'Can you open the gates please?'

Lainey blinked, certain she was dreaming. 'Why, are you here?' she asked cautiously.

'Duh, yes, so can you open up, please?'

'I thought Max said . . .' Realising Tierney had gone, she clicked off her end and pressed a kiss to Zav's forehead. 'Your sister's here,' she told him. *Thank you, Mum,* she whispered in her heart, *thank you, thank you, thank you for bringing her back.* She knew it was nonsense, but it was how she felt.

After releasing the gates, she and Zav went on to the terrace to watch the taxi arriving. Had Tierney come all the way from Pisa in it? She must have, and was no doubt assuming her mother would pay when she got here. Lainey would, happily, because no price was too high for having her daughter back.

She was on the point of going inside for her purse when Zav suddenly shouted, 'Dad!' and as he took off across the lawn Lainey watched in a daze as Tom opened his arms to catch him.

Was he really here? *Please don't let this be a dream.*

His eyes came to hers, and she felt herself starting to sway.

Why had he come? What was this about?

She had no idea, nor any breath to ask. She could only watch as he came towards her, his eyes never leaving hers, until finally he was taking her hand and pulling her into his arms.

Chapter Twenty

'Are you OK now?' Tom asked gently.

Lainey tried to nod, but though the tears had finally stopped, she still seemed to be sobbing.

'Here you are, Mum,' Tierney said, bringing her a glass of wine. 'Would you like one, Dad?'

'Thank you,' he replied. His arm was still round Lainey, but as she lifted her head from his shoulder he let her go.

She wished he wouldn't, she wanted to go on standing with him for ever, but she still had no idea why he'd come, and now she was past the first throes of shock she was starting to realise that his kindness was very probably an attempt to soften the blows to come. 'I'm sorry,' she said, drying her eyes, 'I don't know what came over me. I just . . . I'm fine now . . .'

'No you're not,' Tierney cut in.

Lainey blinked in surprise.

'Where's Max?' Zav asked, bringing out the plate of cold meats Lainey had prepared before going to pieces.

'Put it there,' Tierney instructed, pointing to the bowl of tomatoes she'd brought out herself. 'Max isn't coming back till tomorrow, which reminds me, where's Skye?'

Lainey shook her head. 'I haven't seen her today, but I imagine she's down at the other villa.'

'Which other villa?'

'Zav will tell you,' Lainey replied, anxiously watching Tom as he walked to the edge of the terrace to take in the view. She didn't know what to say to him, still couldn't quite believe he was here. It felt so right, and yet so horribly unnerving.

Turning around, he looked at her, and as their eyes held it was as though the children, the villa, the lake, were fading away. It was just the two of them, their history, and the love she felt tangled in the pain of losing him.

'Don't cry again, Mum,' Zav pleaded, as a latent sob escaped her.

'I'm not,' she promised, though she was very close. Her eyes were still on Tom's; it was as though his intensity, his strength were physical forces holding her up. What was he thinking? Why didn't he say something?

'OK, that's lunch for you two,' Tierney announced, setting a salty focaccia on the table, along with the opened bottle of white wine in a frozen sleeve. 'We're having ours down by the pool.'

Tearing her eyes from Tom's, Lainey watched Tierney loading Zav with a picnic basket before picking up a bottle of Coke and three plastic glasses. She was being so efficient, so forthright, that Lainey realised she must have planned all this before getting here.

'We're going to leave you to talk now,' Tierney informed them as she ushered Zav towards the lawn, 'and Dad?'

Tom's eyebrows rose.

'Tell her everything, OK? And when I say

everything, I mean *everything*. Now come on, Zav, I know you're starving.'

'How do you know?'

'When are you ever not?'

As they traipsed across the grass Lainey felt herself being submerged by so much feeling that she wanted desperately to hug them. They were hers and Tom's, and if Tom wasn't equally over-whelmed right now, then he was no longer the man she'd married.

Seeing that he did indeed look moved, she smiled shakily and glanced at the table where their impromptu lunch was waiting. She had no appetite, but if he'd taken the early morning flight he would surely be hungry.

'I came, because . . . well, because we can't go on like this,' he told her, in a tone that was both wearied and sad.

Her eyes closed as all the hopes she hadn't dared to formulate began to fade. 'No, we can't,' she agreed, 'but I don't want to meet her. I can't get involved in what's happening to her when I feel the way I do about you. I'm sorry, I just can't.' There was no anger or bitterness in her voice, only resolve.

Coming to her, he tilted her face up and gazed searchingly into her eyes. 'There's a lot to explain,' he said, 'because the way you're understanding things isn't real.'

Her eyes came challengingly to his. 'So are you saying you don't have a sixteen-year-old daughter with a woman . . .'

'No, I'm not saying that, because Julia does exist, but what you need to know, and what I should have made much clearer when I first told you, is that I was completely unaware of the fact that Kirsten and I had a daughter together until Kirsten got in touch, *two months ago*, to tell me.'

Lainey felt suddenly light-headed. *Two months ago?* He hadn't known until then that *he* was the father the press had longed to identify?

'Stop doubting me,' he growled, as though reading her mind. 'For once in your life try to accept what I'm telling you . . .'

'But you had to have known,' she protested. 'The whole world knew Kirsten Bonner was pregnant, and if you'd been sleeping with her . . .'

'I wasn't the only one.' Tom sighed. 'You surely remember how rife the speculation was? I don't want to speak ill of her in that way, but she had a lot of admirers, for want of another word, and yes, I was one of them. In fact, we were pretty close, at least I thought we were, but then I met you . . .'

'Didn't you at least try to find out if you were the father?' Lainey broke in.

'As a matter of fact, I did, and she said I wasn't . . .'

'And then you never saw her again?'

'Until two months ago, when she got in touch to ask for my help.'

She looked at him steadily. She wanted to believe that, she really did, but it was hard. 'So why are you only telling me this now?' she challenged. 'Why have you allowed me to think that you've been having an affair all our married life if it isn't true?'

He regarded her helplessly. 'To be honest, I didn't realise at first that you were thinking that way. I thought I'd told you that I'd only just found out myself, and that you were just refusing to believe me.'

'You didn't tell me.'

'I realise that now, and I'm sorry. More sorry than I can ever say. My only excuse is that I was so thrown by it all, so mixed up about what I should do, how to be a father to a child I didn't even know at such a difficult time in her life . . .' He sighed heavily. 'I accept I've handled everything badly. Worse than that, I've hurt you in ways I'll probably never forgive myself for.'

Not quite sure what she wanted to say to that, she picked up her glass and took a sip of wine. If he was being truthful, and God knew she wanted to believe him, then there had been no affair, and if there had been no affair . . .

'If Kirsten was sleeping around back then,' she said, 'and even told you you weren't the father, then why would you believe her now?'

'Because I insisted on having tests, which take a while, and when the results came back . . . Well, they proved that Julia is mine.'

Lainey was regarding him incredulously. 'So you were going through all that without me even knowing,' she accused. 'I'm your wife, you should have told me . . .'

'God knows I wanted to, but if Julia hadn't turned out to be mine . . .' The fight suddenly went out of him. 'I guess I still couldn't have turned my back on Kirsten,' he admitted, 'not when the only family she has is a sister in Scotland who has three children of her own, and a distant cousin somewhere who she's never in touch with. But if Julia hadn't been mine it would have cast a different light on things. We, you and I, could have helped them together. Or that's what I told myself. As it was, she did turn out to be mine, and once I was convinced of that, Kirsten made me promise to be there for Julia while she went through the chemo. Of course I agreed, how could I not, but though I tried I could never seem to find the right time to tell you. I know how cowardly that must sound, and I admit it was, but I hardly knew where my head was during that time. I was still trying to get over the shock of it all, and at the same time I was having a nightmare with the latest script . . . Anyway, in the end Kirsten sent you a text . . .' He pressed his fingers to his eyes, showing how tired he was. 'She'd got tired of waiting, so she wanted to push me into action.' He took a breath. 'I don't know if it's the drugs she's on,' he continued, 'or if she really has changed from the woman I used to know, but the anger in her, or that was in her before the treatment started . . . This is her second time round with cancer, and she's terrified she isn't going to make it. I guess it's fear that's making her so hard to reason with, and say or do things that don't make much sense. It's not quite so bad now, but after she'd sent the text she made me swear I wouldn't tell you she had cancer. I tried to make her understand that I couldn't possibly hide it from you, but she said if I didn't she'd tell you I'd known all along about Julia, and that I'd been cheating on you for years.' There was a sad irony in his eyes as he said, 'It seems you didn't need any help with believing that . . .'

Lainey swallowed drily as guilt surfaced in her heart. 'Why didn't she want me to know she has cancer?' she asked.

'Because she doesn't want anyone to know. She has it fixed in her head that the press will descend on her and start trying to find out again who Julia's father is, and I guess she's not wrong about that, because they probably would. It wouldn't be a good time for it all to start coming out now.'

'But she surely doesn't think I'd tip them off?'

He shook his head. 'Frankly, I don't know what she tells herself from one minute to the next, I only know that I couldn't hold it back from you, so I told you and . . . Well, we know how it went, but I blame myself entirely for not handling things better.'

Though he certainly could have done so, Lainey was feeling more for the turmoil he'd been struggling with alone than for the mistakes he'd made. 'If her cancer is a secondary,' she said, 'why didn't she contact you the first time around?'

'I don't know, she just didn't, but frankly, right now, today, she isn't really the issue, is she? We have to think about us, and the way we've started to come undone over this when I think, I hope, it's the last thing either of us wants.'

Loving the sound of those words, she whispered, 'Of course it is.'

'What's hard for me,' he told her, 'is how ready you were to believe that I'd cheated on you. As far as I'm aware I've never done anything to make you doubt me, and yet as soon as this happened . . . OK, I should have been clearer about it, but your lack of trust, your readiness to believe the worst of me . . .'

'I'm sorry,' she broke in. 'I realise now how awful that must have been for you, and that I was only thinking about myself. I should have listened . . .'

'I'm not trying to make you blame yourself. I'm just trying to find a way for us to deal with this.'

Wretchedness showed in her eyes as she tried to think of the right thing to say – or a way to undo how suspicious and paranoid she'd been.

'I know you've always believed,' he continued, 'that I left Emma and Max because of who your father was, rather than because of how I felt about you, but the reason I left, Lainey, was to be with *you*. I've told you that so many times over the years, but you never seem to hear it. It's like you don't want to hear it, or you can't accept that anyone actually cares for you, when you're at the very centre of our world. We'd none of us – me, the children, your father, Max, even Stacy – be who we are without you. You're the most vital part of our lives, you give us so much, so generously and support-ively. I only wish you'd do the same for yourself.'

Her eyes moved away as she tried to absorb his words. It wasn't that she hadn't heard them before, God knew he'd tried many times to tackle her lack of self-worth, but this time she was hearing it, and the reality of how much damage she'd done to herself, and to him, was finally starting to hit home.

'Obviously, I know your problems stem from your relationship with your mother,' he went on. 'The way she was with you at times was enough to make God Himself feel insecure, but I had no idea it had driven you to a point where you could believe me capable of deceiving you on such an epic scale.'

Lainey tried to marshal her thoughts into some form of defence, but failed.

'I have no secrets,' Tom emphasised. 'I've never kept anything from you, until now, and believe me, I don't intend making the same mistake again.'

Tears shone in her eyes as she looked at him.

'These past weeks have been hell,' he told her. 'I've missed you and needed you so much . . .'

'I'm here now,' she whispered. 'And if Kirsten's ready to meet me . . .'

Putting a hand to her face, he said, 'Are you sure?'

'Of course. She needs us. Are you the only one caring for her? Didn't you just say she has a sister?'

'She has a nurse living at the house, and Rosa, her sister, comes as often as she can. Mostly, though, Rosa has Julia to stay with her.'

Feeling deeply for the child, Lainey asked, 'How is Julia coping?'

He turned his head to one side, as he said, 'That's probably the hardest part of it all . . . She isn't . . . Well, she isn't like other girls her age.'

'In what way?'

'You'll see when you meet her.'

'I guess what's important is how she's responding to you.'

He almost smiled, as he continued to gaze into the distance. 'Yes, well,' he replied, seeming slightly disconnected from his words. 'She's a sweet girl . . .'

'Oh, Tom,' she murmured, putting her arms around him. 'I've been such an idiot.'

'No, I have,' he insisted, wrapping her tightly to him. 'What I've put us through . . . I haven't even been here for you while you've tried to find out about your family. I know how much it means to you . . .'

'Actually, less now than I expected,' she came in gently, 'and whichever way we look at it, Kirsten's and Julia's need was always greater.'

Cupping her face between his hands, he gazed so lovingly into her eyes that she could only wonder how she'd ever allowed herself to doubt him. Not that she imagined her insecurities were at an end, but in that moment there was simply no room for them.

It was a long time before he released her from his kiss, and when he did it was only to look into her eyes again.

'Go on, say it,' she whispered.

He smiled, but as he started to speak they heard a scuffle nearby and looked round to find Tierney doing an about-turn. 'Don't mind me,' she called out. 'I'm not here.'

With no small irony, Tom said, 'Well, at least she didn't say *gross*.'

'Doesn't mean she didn't think it.'

'She definitely will if we disappear for a while.'

'Do we care?'

'Not really.'

Laughing, Lainey leaned against him as they started inside. 'Can I take it you've already put her straight about Kirsten and Julia?' she asked.

'You can.'

'Which is why she told you to tell me everything. I assume you did.'

'I did.'

'So what exactly did she think you'd miss out?'

'Actually, it was the bit I was about to say when she put in an appearance.'

Lainey's eyebrows rose questioningly.

'That I love you,' he murmured.

Feeling the words coasting magically through her, she said, 'So you admitted to her that you have trouble saying it?'

'I'm afraid so, and I've regretted it ever since, because I've been having lessons all the way here.'

Laughing at the thought of it, Lainey went to take another bottle of wine from the fridge before leading him on through to the bedroom. Of course, there was much more talking to be done, but for now this was far more important.

Though they emerged from the bedroom to take the children to the village for dinner later, and again for breakfast the following morning, they spent the best part of the next twenty-four hours behind closed doors, enjoying their reunion. Apart from treating the time like a second honeymoon, they talked a lot too, and ended up deciding that for Julia's sake, they should return to England sooner rather than later.

'What, you mean like tomorrow?' Tierney asked, when they told her.

'No, at the weekend, if we can get flights,' Tom answered, reaching for his coffee. 'Are you OK with that?'

Tierney shrugged. 'I guess so. I mean, I don't suppose you'd let me stay here without you. Although Max is on his way back . . .'

'Don't even think it,' Lainey interrupted. 'Anyway, I'm getting the impression things aren't great with you and Skye, so this might be a good way out. Where is she, by the way? Did she come back last night?'

Looking distinctly sniffy, Tierney said, 'She texted to say she was staying with Zoe, her new best friend, and frankly I hope she stays there, especially if Max is bringing Christie with him.'

Tom's eyebrows rose as he and Lainey exchanged glances.

Realising her mistake, Tierney jumped in quickly. 'Forget I said that. It just came out the wrong way.'

'Is there something going on between Max and Skye?' Lainey asked bluntly.

'No, not really,' Tierney replied, beginning to clear the table. 'I mean, she's got a sort of thing about him, but I expect she's found someone else by now.'

Lainey was still frowning.

'I hope Max hasn't been leading her on,' Tom ventured. 'He can be a bit full of himself . . .'

'It wasn't him, it was her,' Tierney cut in defensively.

Tom regarded her with interest.

Lainey said, 'Actually, I find that easy to believe, and so would you if you'd seen the way the girl has carried on since we've been here.'

'Yeah, so don't start blaming Max, the way you always do,' Tierney warned her father. 'He's been really brilliant lately, hasn't he, Mum?'

Lainey blinked. 'Well, yes, if you can call not seeing much of him brilliant. And now we're on the subject, perhaps you can tell us where the heck he is.'

Tierney rapidly scooped up a pile of plates and carried them inside. 'You'll have to ask him,' she tossed over her shoulder, 'he never tells me anything.'

Lainey looked at Tom. 'Did you see him before you left to come here?'

Tom shook his head, and checked his mobile as it rang. 'I'd better take this,' he said, his eyes coming to hers.

'Is it Kirsten?' she asked.

He nodded, and as he answered the call his tone was so tender that Lainey couldn't help the flare of jealousy that caught her. 'Yes, I can talk,' he said, reaching for Lainey's hand as though sensing what she was feeling. 'Mm, pretty hot.' As he listened he was gazing absently at the view, seeming to see Kirsten's world rather than the one he was in. Eventually, he said, 'We can do it whichever way you prefer . . . OK, you think about it. I'll be back at the weekend . . . Yes, Lainey's fine about meeting you. Of course Julia too. Is she still at Rosa's? I see, well, you don't have to commit to anything now. We'll speak again later.'

After he'd rung off he sat quietly for a moment, clearly immersed in thought as he toyed with his phone.

'Are you thinking we should go home before the weekend?' Lainey asked.

He shook his head. 'No. She has the nurse there. She's going to let us know when she feels up to meeting you.'

'Will we go to her home?'

Tom glanced at Tierney as she came back on to the terrace. 'That would probably be the best,' he replied.

'So what's Julia like?' Tierney asked. 'Do you have any photos?'

Tom was eyeing her carefully. 'I don't, but I guess I should have,' he told her.

Though Tierney was doing her best to hide it, Lainey knew she was jealous.

'Is she pretty?' Tierney wanted to know.

He cocked an eyebrow. 'I think she is, yes, but I'm not getting into who's the prettiest, you or her.

All I'm going to say is you're very different, and I hope very much that you're going to get along.'

Tierney wasn't looking thrilled. 'So is she like, into the same kind of stuff as me?'

Seeming to find that amusing, Tom said, 'As I've no idea what you're into, my darling, I can't even begin to answer that.'

'I mean, like the same sort of music, and fashion, and stuff.'

'Tell you what,' he said, bracing himself as Zav came bounding across the lawn towards him, 'why don't we let her answer for herself,' and catching Zav over his shoulder he wrestled him to the ground.

'I thought you were coming down to the pool,' Zav complained. 'We've got the boat all blown up ready. It's hilaire trying to get into it.' His eyes sparked with mischief as he looked up at Lainey. 'I reckon we should get Mum to try.'

'What's so funny about watching me make a fool of myself?' Lainey protested. 'Get Dad to do it.'

'That would be even funnier,' Tierney decided. 'Come on, let's do it.'

'Hang on, hang on,' Tom protested, as they tried to drag him off. 'I'm still waiting to find out if we're going to see your great-grandparents today.'

'If you go,' Tierney said, tossing back her hair, 'I want to come too so I can tell that evil old bag, Melvina, exactly what I think of her.'

'She probably won't understand you,' Lainey replied.

'And besides, you're not coming,' Tom informed her.

'You are so dictatorial,' Tierney protested. 'What if Mum wants me to come?'

'I don't,' Lainey assured her.

'So who's going to stay and look after us?' Zav wanted to know.

'Tierney's sixteen now,' Tom reminded him. 'She can be in charge.'

'No way!' he cried. 'I'm not being bossed around by her.'

'Actually,' Lainey said, 'I don't think it's a good idea just to drop in on Aldo before we leave at the weekend. I should give him some time to consider whether or not he wants to meet me, and if he does, I can't just rush off again. It wouldn't seem right.' She was looking at Tom.

'It has to be your decision,' he told her, 'but I agree, I think you should allow more than a few days to do it. We can always come back at a later date, when we can spend more time getting to know him.'

'If he's still alive,' Tierney piped up. 'And if it's what he wants.'

Lainey's reply was drowned by the sound of a horn blasting through the peaceful afternoon. 'That can only be Max,' she commented drily.

'Yay!' Zav cheered, and leaping up he tore across the lawn to meet his brother.

'That's what I love about Zav,' Tom commented, 'he's just like Peter, always pleased to see everyone. I reckon he'd even be the same with burglars.'

Lainey smiled. 'Aren't you pleased to see Max?' she asked Tierney, noticing how edgy she suddenly seemed.

Tierney shrugged. 'Course. Did I say I wasn't?'

Lainey's eyes moved to Tom.

'There's no point looking at me,' he told her, 'I gave up trying to understand my children a long time ago.'

'What about Julia?' Tierney challenged. 'Do you understand her?'

'Probably not,' he conceded, 'but she's definitely not as complicated as you.'

At that, Tierney's eyes widened. 'Was that a compliment or an insult?' she asked her mother.

Laughing, Lainey said, 'I'll let you decide,' and getting to her feet she was on her way to welcome Christie when she caught sight of Max's swollen right eye. 'Wow,' she murmured as he sailed past her into the kitchen, with Zav throwing punches behind him.

'What happened to you?' Tom demanded.

'You should see the other guy,' Max retorted, tugging open the fridge.

Lainey and Tom looked at each other.

'Excuse me,' Tierney mumbled, pushing Max back inside as he made to come out again.

'Hi, I hope it's OK for me to be here,' Christie said, her wide blue eyes seeming uncertain as she let everyone know she was there.

'Yes, yes, of course,' Lainey assured her, remembering her manners. 'Come and sit down. How was the journey? Would you like a drink?'

'I'm on it,' Max called out, and sliding past Tierney he carried two beers to the table and handed one to Christie as he began downing the other.

Lainey was still intrigued by the bruise around his eye.

'An explanation,' Tom prompted.

'Max!' Tierney shouted.

Max shrugged helplessly. 'Be right back,' he told his father.

Tom turned to Christie.

'Apparently someone tried to mug him while

he was in London and he fought back,' she told them.

Not at all sure she believed that, Lainey said, 'Did he go to the police?'

'I don't think so. I didn't ask.'

Lainey looked at Tom. 'Tierney's involved in this somewhere,' she informed him.

His eyebrows rose. 'Really?' he responded, though his tone was far more relaxed than she might have expected. 'We seem to have another visitor,' he announced.

Lainey looked round, and her heart sank to see Skye coming across the lawn in a tight bikini top and low-slung shorts. 'At last,' she said, 'we've been wondering where you were.'

'I texted Tierney,' Skye replied, her flinty eyes fixed on Christie.

Trying to ignore the tension, Lainey went on, 'We've decided to fly home at the weekend, so we should call your parents to let them know.'

'Hello, Skye,' Tom said cheerily.

Her eyes darted briefly to his.

'I'm Christie,' Christie said, holding out a hand to shake.

'Yeah, right.' Skye ignored the hand. 'Don't bother calling my parents,' she told Lainey, 'I won't be going back with you. Zoe's family have invited me to stay with them, so I'm only here to pick up my stuff.'

Trying not to be irritated by the curtness, Lainey said, 'I'll have to clear it with your parents first, so if you could let me have their number . . .'

Skye was still glaring at Christie, her weight shifted on to one leg, a hand on her hip, while Christie looked back in bemusement.

Certain Skye was about to cause a scene, Lainey tried to think what to do and almost jumped when Tom reached for her hand.

'Zav,' he said, pulling Lainey to her feet, 'run in and get Max, will you? Then meet us down at the pool. Mum and I are going to try out the boat.'

Startled, Lainey allowed herself to be led away. 'Don't you want to get to the bottom of what's going on?' she whispered.

'Not really,' he replied. 'They're all grown-ups, or they like to think they are, so why don't we let them sort it out for themselves?'

In Tierney's room Max was saying, 'What the fuck did you want me to do, let the douche bag get away with screwing my sister?'

Tierney's eyes were bright with horror. 'Of course not, but the fact that Nadia was there . . . Oh my God . . . What am I going to do if she tells Dad?'

'She's not going to tell Dad, moron. She won't want him to know any more than you do.'

This was true. She had to remember that. 'But what if he tells someone?'

'If he does, we just deny it, but no way is he going to do that. He doesn't even have the photos any more, so he can't prove it.'

Tierney's cheeks paled. 'Tell me you didn't look at them, please say you didn't.'

'I didn't. Nadia took care of it, and she texted after to say they were all deleted.'

'Oh my God, she must hate me now.'

Max shrugged. 'I doubt it, but who knows. Anyway, a thanks would have been nice, but . . .'

'Thank you, thank you,' she cried, throwing her

arms around him. 'You're the best brother in the world, and I'm sorry you got a black eye. Did he do that?'

'Yeah, but I can promise you he's looking a lot worse. Hey, Zav, what's up, little man?'

'Dad said I had to come and get you,' Zav told him.

Max was about to respond when Skye shoved Zav out of the way to get into the room. 'Hey, don't take your shit out on him,' he growled.

'You are such a fucking loser,' Skye hissed at him. 'You all are,' she added, glaring at Tierney. 'No way am I staying around here while you've got that slapper out there . . .'

'She's not a slapper,' Max informed her, 'and no one's forcing you to stay. If you need a ride to the station I'll be happy to help out.'

'Max!' Tierney cried, as Skye turned white. 'That was just mean. Why did you have to say that?'

He seemed confused. 'I thought I was being friendly,' he replied. 'I mean, how else is she going to get there?'

'Just go,' Tierney told him.

'And I've informed your *girlfriend* that you've been screwing me all this time,' Skye snarled after him, 'so happy holiday, you fucking bell end.'

'Cool,' Max muttered as he swaggered out of the room.

'Don't,' Skye snapped, as Tierney tried to comfort her. 'Just leave me alone, OK?'

'But you're really upset, and . . .'

'I said, leave me alone. You've got everything you want now, your brother's sorted out the psycho, your dad's back with your mum, you've even got a new best friend out there on the terrace, plus a sister waiting in the wings, so what do you need me for? I'm just in the way . . .'

'That's not true.'

'Yes it is, so do me a favour and get out of my face.'

Not knowing what else to do, Tierney stood watching Skye as she began stuffing her clothes and make-up into her bags. 'I don't want to fall out with you,' she said lamely. 'Can't we just . . .'

'No! We can't do anything. You're just an immature, snivelling, spoiled little brat. I don't know why I ever bothered with you. I suppose I felt sorry for you. Actually, I still do, because your family is seriously fucked up and so are you.'

Ashen-faced, Tierney retorted, 'It's your family that has the problem, not mine, and for your information, if Christie asks me if it's true about you and Max I'm going to tell her it was all in your head,' and still feeling terrible for Skye she stalked out of the room.

Down at the pool Lainey was sprawled out on a lounger, aching with laughter at Tom's attempts to get into the boat. He'd made it now, just, but was lying on his front, not daring to turn over in case he ended up with another dunking.

'Come on, Dad, you can do it,' Zav cried, jumping up and down at the shallow end.

'Just go really slow,' Alfie advised, pushing a ball under the water and letting it shoot up in a fountain.

'No, I'm nice and comfy like this,' Tom assured them, clinging to the sides with one leg still in the pool.

Lainey practically howled she laughed so hard.

'Whoa, Dad, need some help there?' Max offered, appearing with Christie.

'Not from you, thanks,' Tom muttered.

Passing Lainey her phone, Max said, 'It kept ringing.'

Taking it, she said to Christie, 'Why don't you get changed into a swimsuit?'

'We're about to go and move her stuff into the apartment,' Max replied, 'so you won't be seeing us for a while.'

'Too much information,' Tom grunted.

Max regarded him thoughtfully, until noticing the boat was drifting close to the edge of the pool, he went to give it a hefty shove back to the middle.

'You'll pay for that!' Tom warned.

Max grinned, and tossing Alfie's ball back to him he slipped an arm round Christie to walk her up to the car.

'Adriana's inviting us for a barbecue tonight,' Lainey told Tom as she read her texts.

'Sounds great,' he replied, his voice skimming along the bottom of the boat.

'Apparently Marco's wife is going to be there.'

'Dad, do you want your phone? It's been ringing,' Tierney said, coming to sit on the edge of the pool.

Tom almost reached out a hand. 'Oh no, I'm not falling for that,' he told her.

'Honest.' She laughed. 'You've got three missed calls.'

Before he could answer Skye screamed from the top of the steps, 'You're all a bunch of fucking losers. I can't wait to get out of here.'

Lainey sat up; Tom lifted his head and the next instant he was under the boat.

As everyone exploded into laughter Lainey realised Skye would think they were laughing at her, but by the time she had rushed to the top of the steps Skye was already getting into a car at the gates.

'I feel really bad for her,' Tierney said, coming to stand with her mother.

'So do I,' Lainey sighed, giving her a hug. 'I'll go and check on her later to make sure she's told at least one of her parents where she is.'

'She hardly ever sees her dad, so she won't have told him.'

Understanding this was almost certainly at the root of Skye's constant need for male attention, Lainey tightened her hold on Tierney.

'She was really close to him once,' Tierney said. 'Like I've always been with Dad.'

'And nothing will ever change that,' Lainey assured her.

Tierney didn't answer.

Turning to her, Lainey put her hands on her shoulders. 'You're thinking about Julia, aren't you?' she said.

Tierney nodded. 'Aren't you worried about it too?' she asked.

Lainey held her close as she tried to find the right words. 'I'm not saying it won't take some getting used to,' she said, 'but we'll have to keep remembering how difficult things are for her, with her mother being ill.'

Tierney nodded glumly. 'I know, and I feel sorry for her about that, honestly, but what if she turns out to be a bitch?'

'I'm sure she won't. Dad says she's very sweet . . .'

'He would, wouldn't he?'

Keeping an arm round her shoulders as they started back to the pool, Lainey suggested, 'Why don't we make a pact, you and me, that no matter what, we'll always be there for each other.'

Instantly accepting this, Tierney said, 'I'll definitely be there for you, Mum, and if there's ever anything you want to talk about you know you can always come to me.'

'Thank you,' Lainey replied with a smile. 'Same goes for you.' She waited, but since nothing was forthcoming she said, 'I'm not going to insist on knowing what's been going on lately, but if you do ever feel the need to discuss . . .'

'Don't worry, I won't. I mean, nothing's been going on, and anyway, everything's all right now, because Dad's here. What I'm saying is . . .'

'It's OK,' Lainey interrupted, 'I was your age once, so I understand there are always going to be things you really don't want your mother to know . . .'

'Just like Granny didn't want you to know things about her.'

'Precisely, and we can't blame Granny for wanting to keep her secrets to herself, can we?'

'Definitely not. So do you think it might have made a difference when you were growing up if she'd told you the truth?'

Since this was a question Lainey had asked herself several times these last few days, she was able to say, 'I'd certainly have understood things better, and I probably wouldn't have gone through such intense periods of self-doubt, or of resenting her the way I sometimes did. Now, back to you: just promise me you're not in debt, or involved in drugs, or pregnant.'

'I swear I'm none of those things,' Tierney responded with feeling.

'And I was definitely wrong about the married man?'

'Definitely.'

'Good. Then we'll leave it there.' She was watching Tom, now sitting on the edge of the pool and clearly waiting for her to join him.

Chapter Twenty-One

For Lainey, the very best part of being back at Bannerleigh Cross was seeing her father's face light up as she walked through the door. It moved her straight to tears as he wrapped her in his arms, seeming almost like his old self for those few precious moments.

'How was the show?' he asked. 'Were they good?'

'Excellent,' she assured him, having no idea what or who he was talking about. 'You'd have loved it.'

'I'm sure I would.' He beamed. 'Did your mother enjoy it too? Where is she?'

Hugging his arm, she led him back to his chair. 'She'll be here soon. She stayed on for some shopping, but the children are with me.'

'Sarah and Esther? I don't ever see them now.'

'Actually, they popped in yesterday,' Daffs corrected, her kind, fleshy face creased with affection as she shared her brother's pleasure at having his eldest daughter home.

'They did?' Lainey said, surprised. Her sisters almost never came.

Daffs continued to smile as she shook her head. 'I find it distresses him less if he doesn't feel neglected,' she murmured.

Having no argument with that, Lainey said, 'So how have you been, Dad? It looks as though Aunt Daffs' cooking has agreed with you.' In truth, he appeared to have lost weight, and her aunt confirmed it when she asked.

'He doesn't seem to have much of an appetite,' Daffs confided, as Tierney and Zav hauled their bags in through the door.

'Grandpa!' they shouted in unison, and as Peter looked up in confusion Tierney flew into his lap, while Zav collapsed over Sherman.

'It'll probably come back now you're home,' Daffs added.

'How has he seemed otherwise?' Lainey asked, glancing past her aunt to where Tom was outside, still unpacking the car, while talking to someone on the phone.

'Well, actually, I was a bit worried yesterday,' Daffs confided. 'He wasn't himself at all. He couldn't hold his cup, or get his food to his mouth. We wondered if he'd had one of those mini-strokes again, you know, like he had a few months ago, but by the time the doctor came he seemed much better.'

Concerned, Lainey turned to look at him, but he was smiling so happily at the fuss being made of him by his grandchildren that apart from the weight loss, she could see nothing to be alarmed about for now.

'Did Tom come back with you?' Daffs asked, going to put the kettle on.

'Yes, he'll be in shortly,' Lainey replied, suspecting he was talking to Kirsten, and trying not to resent the fact that she'd barely allowed him to get off the plane before she'd started ringing again. Over the past few days it had felt almost as though she was in Italy with them, she'd called so often. Whether they were sightseeing in Perugia, barbecuing with the Stefanis, or struggling to watch the Palio in Siena, she was constantly on the phone, and though Lainey was trying to be understanding it wasn't always easy.

'I don't want to pry,' Daffs said quietly, 'but is everything OK between you two now?'

Brightening, Lainey said, 'Yes, it's fine. I'll explain it all later, but we're more or less back to normal. Where's Uncle Jack?'

'Oh, he's taken Marty to the garden centre to pick up some plants for the old people's home. They were here playing cards this morning. Your father actually managed a snap!'

Looking suitably impressed, Lainey began unloading the olive oil and pasta she'd brought back for her aunt, looking up curiously as Tom came in with more bags. 'Is she OK?' she asked.

'Actually, it was Max,' he responded as he dutifully embraced Daffs. 'He wants you to text instructions on how to make a tagliata, and if I can get his Internet reconnected by the time he comes home he'll be my friend for life.'

Lainey couldn't help but laugh at the drollery in Tom's expression.

'So Max stayed on, did he?' Daffs asked.

'For another week,' Tom confirmed, starting to carry the heavier bags into the hall. 'Come on, you two,' he called out to Tierney and Zav, 'let Grandpa breathe and help get this lot upstairs.'

'Can Maudie come over?' Tierney asked, as she sauntered past her mother to scoop up the smallest of her bags.

'If you like,' Lainey responded, looking curiously at Tom as he beckoned her to follow him into his study.

Once the door was securely closed, he caught her in his arms and pulled her against him.

'Wow!' She smiled, feeling how aroused he was.

'All the way back on the plane,' he murmured, 'I kept looking at you and thinking how damned lucky I am to have you.'

She nodded agreement. 'Yeah, I suppose I can't argue with that,' she teased, 'but do you think now is the right time to do something about it?'

He had to shake his head. 'I guess not, but you look so damned sexy in those shorts and with a tan that I don't know if I can wait till I get back.'

She frowned and pulled away. 'Back from where?' she asked.

The expression on his face was answer enough.

'Oh, Tom, we've only just got here . . .'

'I know, I know, but I promised I'd be there for when Julia gets home.'

'Exactly when did you make that promise?' she enquired frostily.

'Last night. I didn't say anything sooner, because I didn't want to spoil what little time we had left and I knew you probably wouldn't be happy.'

Sighing, she said, 'You're right, I'm not, but if Julia's expecting you I suppose you can't let her down. I just want you to remember that we need you here too, and if I'm going to support you through this, which I am, I think we need to start setting a few ground rules.'

'Anything,' he declared rashly.

She smiled. 'I'll work on them while you're gone, but most importantly, both you and Kirsten need to understand that no matter how sick she is, not everything can be about her and Julia.'

'I'll remember that,' he promised, sliding a hand into her hair, 'and with any luck the worst of it's already over now her treatment's complete. Anyway, I ought to get the heavy stuff upstairs before I go, and I haven't even said hello to your father yet.'

'Aunt Daffs thinks he might have had another of those mini-strokes,' she told him.

Turning back, he said, 'When?'

'Yesterday, but he seems fine now. He's obviously glad to have us all around him again.'

'Are you going to tell him what you found out in Italy?'

She shrugged. 'What's the point? He won't understand it, and even if he did, how's it going to help him now?'

Pulling her back into his arms, he said, 'I haven't forgotten how hard all that must have been for you.'

'I'm sure I'll survive.'

'Of course you will, but knowing what your mother went through . . .'

'The good thing is she ended up meeting Dad, and we can't ever doubt how happy she was with him.'

'As happy as you are with me?'

Her eyes narrowed teasingly, but before she could answer there was a loud thump on the door behind them.

'Mum! Are you in there?' Tierney called out. 'Alfie's dad's on the line wanting to say thanks for everything, and you told me to remind you to ring Skye's mum.'

'Coming,' Lainey called back. Tom's eyes were still on hers, and as he smiled she could feel herself starting to melt. 'I love you, Tom Hollingsworth,' she whispered, and after kissing him lingeringly, she went off to deal with the phone.

'So where is he now?' Stacy was asking the following day, having come over for coffee.

'Still over there with Kirsten,' Lainey replied, popping a chicken into the Aga. 'You're staying for lunch, I hope?'

'I'd love to. How many will we be? I'll set the table.'

Counting on her fingers, Lainey said, 'Actually, only five, unless someone turns up out of the blue. You, me, Tierney, Maudie and Dad. Zav's over at Alfie's, and Aunt Daffs and Uncle Jack set off early this morning. Poor Aunt Daffs, she was really shaken up when I told her what I'd found out in Italy. She was certain Dad never knew, or if he did he never told her. I guess it's not a secret you really want to share with anyone, is it? I almost wish I didn't know it myself.'

'But you had to have answers,' Stacy reminded her gently. 'It's been driving you nuts for years.'

'Maybe it's a lesson in being careful of what you wish for,' Lainey commented wryly. 'Anyway, there's no unknowing it now, so I'll just have to live with the fact that my real father was a rapist, my grandmother was a she-devil, and my mother could never look at me without remembering how she'd come to have me. In other words, my Italian roots have sadness and shame all over them, and what little family I still have there might very well not want to be reminded of how badly they treated their daughter. However, on the upside, I'm probably the luckiest person alive to have been adopted by Peter, because I defy anyone to have a more wonderful father.'

Stacy smiled fondly as she looked over to where Peter was sitting quietly in his chair, gazing at a newspaper he could no longer read. 'So when are you expecting *your* children's father back?' she asked, going to fish out the cutlery.

'I'm still waiting to hear,' Lainey replied, checking the oven's temperature. 'He texted last night to let me know he'd arrived, and to say that apparently Julia isn't coming back until Tuesday or Wednesday now.'

Stacy's eyebrows rose expressively.

'I know what you're thinking, and I've no idea if Kirsten knew that before she asked him to go, or she found out later. I'm trying to give her the benefit of the doubt.'

Stacy's expression mirrored Lainey's irony. 'So when are you meeting her?'

'I don't know yet,' Lainey replied, and scooping up the phone, she said, 'Hi, Max, how's it going over there? Yes, we're all OK this end. Missing you like crazy, of course.' She laughed at his response, and after giving him directions to the supermarket nearest to the villa, she rang off. 'OK, enough about me,' she declared, as Stacy seemed about to return to the subject of Kirsten and Tom. 'I want to hear how things are going with the launch. Have you set a date for it yet?'

'Actually, we've hit a few problems,' Stacy confessed, 'all to do with finance, of course, but the guys are on it so we're definitely not giving up yet.'

Lainey regarded her sympathetically.

'It was to be expected,' Stacy insisted. 'These things never go without a hitch, you know that. It'll be fine, I'm sure. It's just in this current climate everyone's playing safe.'

Lainey looked at her father as the paper slid from his hands. 'He has so many contacts,' she said, going to prop his head against a cushion. 'I'm sure he'd know who to call if only he could remember. I wonder if Marty could go through his address book with me . . .'

'You've got enough to be dealing with,' Stacy told her, 'but don't worry, if things get really bad I might come back to you on that. And there goes the phone again.'

'Tom,' Lainey said, reading the caller ID. 'Hi, darling, how're things?'

'. . . if you can . . . then I'll give you . . .'

'Sorry, you're breaking up.'

'. . . hear me now?'

'Only just.'

'. . . to say that if . . . Kirsten feels . . .'

'It's no good, Tom. Can you go somewhere with a better reception, or maybe try sending a text?' Before she'd even finished the line had gone dead.

Putting the phone down, she said, 'There's surely got to be a landline over there, so why doesn't he use that?'

'Some people have cut them off since mobiles,' Stacy reminded her. 'Except that doesn't make much sense in Kirsten's case, if she can't get reception. Unless she has a different server, of course.'

With raised eyebrows Lainey picked up the phone again. 'Hi, Nadia, this is a nice surprise. How are you?'

'Yes, I'm fine,' Nadia replied hoarsely. 'Sorry, I've got a bit of a cold, nothing serious. I wasn't sure if you were back yet . . .'

'We arrived yesterday, but Tom's not here I'm afraid, if that's who you're looking for. You can always try him on his mobile, though I'm not sure you'll get through on that either.'

'It's OK, it's not urgent. Just have him call when he gets home.'

'Of course. You do sound rough, I hope you're taking something?'

'It'll pass, I'm sure. These things always do. Actually, before I let you go, I should probably tell you that Guy and I have decided to go our separate ways.'

Shaken, Lainey said, 'Oh no, I'm really sorry to hear that. Are you OK? Do you want to come over?'

'I'm fine. Well, I'm probably not, if the truth were told, but I know it's the right decision. On a different subject, did Max come back with you, by any chance?'

Wondering at the question, Lainey replied, 'No, he stayed on with his girlfriend, but I'm not sure how long they're going to last trying to fend for themselves.'

With a weak laugh, Nadia said, 'Is he . . .? Do you know . . .? Sorry, I'm a bit scatty at the moment. I should ring off, but if you could get Tom to call that would be lovely.'

After putting the phone down Lainey turned to Stacy, her expression drawn into a frown. 'She didn't sound good,' she said, glancing round at the sound of Tierney and Maudie coming down the stairs. 'Apparently she and Guy have broken up.'

'Oh no, that's really tough,' Stacy commented,

'especially when she's already been through it once. Not that I ever thought he was right for her, but it's not what I think that counts. Did he meet someone else?'

'Who?' Tierney asked, sailing into the kitchen and helping herself to an apple.

'Guy Whittaker,' Lainey answered. 'Apparently he and Nadia are no longer together.'

Tierney's face paled. 'Oh my God,' she mumbled.

Putting an arm around her, Lainey said, 'I know break-ups are painful, but they're a part of life, and Dad and I . . .'

'I know. It's not that.'

'Then what is it?'

'Nothing. I'm cool. Come on, Mauds, let's go.'

As they reached the door, Lainey said, 'Lunch in an hour. Don't be late.'

'We won't,' Tierney replied, without turning back.

Watching them crossing the garden to the footpath, Lainey said, 'I hate the fact that she hides things from me, but I guess I have to get used to it.'

'I'm afraid you do, now she's the age she is.'

Sighing, Lainey reached for her mobile as it bleeped with a text. 'I always thought we'd be able to talk about anything, no matter what age she was,' she remarked, 'but I guess that was a bit delusional.' After reading Tom's message she passed Stacy the phone for her to read it too.

Kirsten is asking if you'd be willing to come here tomorrow?

Stacy's eyes went to Lainey's.

'You don't know how much I wish I could say no,' Lainey told her, 'just so we're not doing

427

everything her way, but that would be petty, wouldn't it?'

'You've got a busy life,' Stacy pointed out.

'True, but I guess I'd rather get it over with, so for the moment I'm prepared to let her call the shots. It might all be different after I've met her. We'll see.'

Chapter Twenty-Two

In spite of Tom's careful directions, Lainey wasn't surprised when Kirsten's rural retreat turned out to be almost impossible to find. For some reason it seemed likely that Kirsten would be at the back end of beyond, though quite why she'd chosen to live so remotely, and for so long, Lainey guessed only Kirsten knew.

During the drive through Herefordshire she'd struggled with so many conflicting emotions that she knew her perspective was in danger of slipping. Everything was seeming disturbingly surreal, as though this charade – and that was what it felt like, a charade – was happening apart from her, because she surely couldn't really be about to visit her husband in the home of another woman. A woman with whom he had a child, and God only knew what kind of relationship now.

One step at a time, Lainey, she cautioned herself. *Remember, you're supposed to be keeping an open mind, and you trust Tom, you really do.*

By the time she finally turned off the leafy lane she'd already driven up and down twice on to a bumpy track leading to a sprawl of ramshackle outbuildings with a slightly shabby but quaintly thatched cottage at their heart, it was already past midday. She was half an hour late. She looked more closely at the cottage. Not exactly the kind of dwelling she'd imagined for the glamorous Kirsten Bonner, but then what did she know of her today?

Spotting Tom's car next to an old Range Rover she felt herself being drawn into a knot of apprehension, which only tightened when he came out of the cottage to meet her. He, and his car, gave the appearance of being very much at home here.

'I was starting to get worried,' he told her as he opened her door. 'Did you get lost?'

'A little,' she admitted, picking up her bag and wondering if Kirsten was watching from behind a curtain.

'Thanks for coming,' he said, wrapping her in his arms. 'Is Peter OK? Who's with him?'

'Marigold,' she replied, referring to one of the agency nurses she called on in times of need.

'That's good. He always seems to relate well to her. So, are you hungry? There's some soup for lunch. I could say I'd made it myself, but I know you wouldn't believe it.'

Hating the way he was playing host, making her feel as though she was no more than a casual visitor, rather than his *wife*, come to meet his *ex-mistress and please God it really was still ex*, she said, 'I'm fine, thanks. You seem very comfortable here.'

At that his eyes narrowed, but he apparently decided not to voice whatever he'd drawn breath for, and simply watched her survey the cluttered yard with its scavenging ducks and chickens, towering hay bales, and rusting bits of old farm machinery. Behind a row of rundown stables a couple of horses stood in a field, while the countryside beyond stretched out to the horizon in a lazy patchwork of shimmering greens. It was certainly peaceful around here, she was thinking, and secluded, though she guessed the new estate she'd passed just now was probably only a short walk away.

'You should go in,' he told her.

She turned to him in surprise. 'What about you?'

'Kirsten thought it would be best if you two talked alone, at least at first, so I'm going to exercise Julia's horses.'

Lainey's heart jarred. She'd forgotten he could ride, since the last time she'd seen him on horseback was during a holiday in the Camargue, before Zav was born. Apparently these days it was a pastime, perhaps even a passion, he shared with his elder daughter. She couldn't help wondering how Tierney would feel about it, but quickly pushed the thought away. That was something she'd have to deal with later.

'Is there anyone else inside?' she asked.

He shook his head.

Lainey glanced at the cottage. 'Actually, I'm not sure I want to speak to her alone.'

'It'll be fine,' he assured her. 'You're always great with people, and she's looking forward to meeting you.'

If that were true, she could only wish she felt the same. 'Aren't you at least going to show me in, and make the introductions?' she said rather desperately.

'You don't need me to do that. All you have to do is go along the hall into the kitchen. She's waiting for you there.'

'So she's not in bed?'

'No, but she hasn't regained full strength yet, so please try to bear that in mind.'

Not liking how protective he was sounding, she turned back to the car.

'What are you doing?' he protested. 'Lainey, for God's sake, you can't come all this way only to . . .'

'My phone,' she explained, retrieving it from the charger.

Sounding less tense, he said, 'I'm afraid you won't get any reception.'

'I'd still like to have it with me. How long will you be gone?'

'Half an hour, I guess. Look, I know this isn't easy for you, it isn't for her either, but I promise, you'll like her. There's nothing not to like, and by the time you leave you'll be saying the same.'

It was on the tip of her tongue to ask if he'd be leaving with her, but she decided to save it until she knew whether Julia was coming back tomorrow or Wednesday.

After watching him trudge off to the stables, she made her way to the cottage and in through the open front door. The entry hall was narrow and shadowy, with a vivid, childlike mural of farmyard scenes covering one wall and a wooden staircase running up the other. The place smelt both musty and fresh, as though lemons had been squeezed over old clothes. With so little light it was hard to tell how clean it was, but the sense of age and need for refurbishment was plain in the scuffed panels of the floorboards and scratched paintwork on the doors.

She couldn't quite gauge how she was feeling now, apart from apprehensive, and out of place, as she followed the hall into a misty pool of light that, when her eyes adjusted, turned out to be illuminating a spacious kitchen. With its heavy oak beams, large battered table and flagstone floor it was certainly a homely space, though there didn't appear to be much in the way of modern units, or even appliances. Plenty of dried herbs and copper pots hanging from the ceiling, though, and the fridge was covered in drawings, photos and magnets. She noticed a saucepan on the range, presumably containing the soup, and two bowls next to it with a ladle resting on the top.

'Do come in.'

She spun round, but could see no one in the dimly lit enclave where a vast inglenook fireplace was surrounded by several armchairs. Beneath the window to one side was a desk, and she noticed Tom's laptop straight away. It appeared as at home here as he did.

Catching a movement, she waited and watched as a woman in jeans and a pale blue kaftan stepped into the light. Her breath became shallow as she realised she was looking at Kirsten Bonner, seeming almost ethereal in the misty bands of sunlight that engulfed her. As she passed out of the rays Lainey could see her blotched and swollen face, a travesty of what it had once been, and a wave of pity surged through her. Kirsten had been so beautiful, so slender and fair. Now she was bloated, covered in sores, and beneath the turquoise silk scarf wrapped around her head she was presumably without hair.

'You manage to mask your shock better than most,' Kirsten told her, her voice not much more than a rasping whisper.

Lainey had no time to respond.

'I told Tom you were lost, not involved in an accident, but he seemed intent on worrying. Would you care for a drink of something? He went to the

433

supermarket this morning, so there's lemonade and juice in the fridge. You can have tea if you prefer, but I'm afraid you'll have to make it yourself.'

'I don't need anything, thank you,' Lainey replied. 'But maybe I could get something for you?'

Ignoring the offer, Kirsten pulled out a chair and sat at the table, gesturing for Lainey to do the same.

Once they were opposite each other, Lainey found herself under almost intimidating scrutiny. The piercing grey eyes, that appeared so much more alive than the sallow skin of Kirsten's face, swept over her with a frankness that was close to offensive. It wasn't possible to tell what the woman was thinking, but Lainey wasn't feeling any of the welcome Tom had led her to believe she'd receive.

'I wonder,' Kirsten began, 'if you have any idea how often I've imagined this day.'

Since this was far from the opening Lainey had expected, she felt her mouth turn dry as she tried to think what to say.

'You don't have a clue,' Kirsten declared. 'You've never given me a single thought over the years, and why would you when you had what you wanted? For me never a day has passed that I haven't resented every single bone in your body, to the point I often wished you dead.'

Lainey could hardly believe what she was hearing. Since Tom hadn't prepared her for anything like this, she wasn't remotely ready to deal with it.

'That's an irony, isn't it?' Kirsten continued. 'Me wishing you dead, and now I'm the one who's most likely going to ship out early. No, don't look at me like that, I've got cancer; cancer kills people and this is the second time it's come for me. I suppose it's what I get for thinking so many evil thoughts about someone who probably doesn't even know what an evil thought is.'

Finding her voice, Lainey said, 'I don't understand why you're . . .'

'No, of course you don't understand. How could you, when even now you still have no idea what you took from me back then? No one knew. I never told a soul, apart from my sister – and *Tom*.' As her eyes glittered the challenge, Lainey felt the shock ripple through her.

'Are you saying that Tom's always known you have a child together?' she asked hoarsely.

Kirsten smiled, and the beauty of it was almost an insult to her inflamed, puffy face. 'You're really afraid of the answer to that, aren't you?' she said.

Lainey couldn't deny it.

'Ever since finding out about Julia you've been wondering if Tom and I have been together for as long as you've been with him, only in secret of course. You've tormented yourself with the fear of it; you've imagined him leading a double life, being as happy with *our daughter* as he is with you and yours, possibly even happier. It's been tearing you apart, making you want to lash out in ways you've probably never thought yourself capable of. In fact, I'm sure you've wished me dead a thousand times. Maybe I should blame *you* for the way I am.'

As Lainey stared at her, she was wondering if Tom had any idea just how bitter this woman was. Surely he'd never have let her walk into this if he had.

'God, I've envied you,' Kirsten told her bluntly. 'I still do, because nothing's ever been difficult for you, has it? Having Peter Winlock as a father, your glamorous mother . . . They made sure their little angel never wanted for anything. You were spoiled rotten from the day you were born, never had to work for anything, or wonder how you fitted into the world . . .'

'You don't know anything about me,' Lainey broke in defensively.

Seeming not to have heard, Kirsten said, 'Incidentally, I was impressed when I read about the way you cared for your mother at the end. It wasn't what I'd have expected of someone who's much more used to taking than giving.' Her eyes bored into Lainey's, seeming to demand a response.

'If that's what you want to think of me, then go right ahead,' Lainey told her, her mother's fire sparking in her eyes.

'It's hard to think otherwise when as far as I can tell you've had it *all* for as long as I've known you, or at least known of your existence. The ideal wealthy family, a wonderful husband, two perfect children, your looks, your health, more friends than you know how to keep up with. In case it interests you, I had to work hard for *my* success, short as it was. I didn't have parents who could throw open doors for me, push me through and make all the right introductions. In my world there was no one there when things didn't go so well, apart from my gran who was deaf, and my sister, Rosa. Our parents died when I was thirteen, but I guess I at least have the satisfaction of knowing that I made something of myself through my own efforts, even if it didn't last for as long as I'd have liked.'

Lainey was trying to assimilate this new image of a younger Kirsten, who she'd always assumed had come from a similar background to her own.

'Of course, it would have lasted if Tom hadn't

met you and got you pregnant,' Kirsten pressed on. 'We'd have been together then, the way we should have, bringing up our child, perhaps having more, while continuing with our careers. That's what would have happened if you'd been anyone other than Peter Winlock's daughter. But unfortunately that's who you are, and because Daddy's girl always gets everything she wants, there was never any doubt that she was going to get Tom Hollingsworth too. So he divorced his wife, married you, and spent the next sixteen years pretending to love you . . .'

'I don't have to listen to any more of this,' Lainey told her, getting to her feet.

'Sit down,' Kirsten barked.

Staying where she was, Lainey said, 'I realise now why you didn't want Tom here while we talked. He wouldn't let you get away with what you're saying, because none of it's true and if you knew anything about me . . .'

'I know you'd like it not to be true,' Kirsten smiled, 'but the problem is you don't believe he loves you either, do you? No, don't bother to deny it . . .'

'Why are you doing this?' Lainey broke in angrily. 'What on earth do you think you're going to gain from so much . . . resentment and malice?'

'I don't suppose I'll gain anything, apart from a brief sense of satisfaction. I say brief, by the way, not because I could be on the final leg of my journey, but because payback is rarely as sweet as we expect it to be. For instance, I can't say I'm experiencing much in the way of gratification right now, though I thought, before you came here, that I would.' She threw out a hand, as if to show she could accept she was wrong. 'Do tell me,' she pressed on, 'how it feels to realise you've been despised for years? I know it won't change anything, we can't have the time over, but it must be a whole new experience for you, who's always been so adored and . . .'

'As I said,' Lainey cut in sharply, 'you know nothing about me, and now I'm going to find Tom, because if we're to continue this I think he needs to be here.'

'Hiding behind him?'

Lainey's face tightened.

'Why don't you have the courage to let me finish?' Kirsten demanded.

'To finish what? Making me feel that I'm the cause of all your misery? Whatever happened between you and Tom *sixteen years ago*, what you expected of it, what he promised, even, is never going to change the fact that he married me. If he'd wanted you no one would have stood in his way . . .'

'Apart from your father.'

'No, not my father, because indulgent as he was, he'd never have wanted Tom to marry me if he'd thought he was in love with somebody else. And contrary to what most people seemed to think, he wouldn't have blocked Tom's career either, because my father simply isn't like that. So tell me, do you think Tom was in love with you back then? Perhaps you think he still is.'

'I don't think, I *know* . . . that he isn't, and probably never was. But what I do know is that for years I've believed he knew about Julia and deliberately shut her out of his life. And the reason he did that was because *you* and your father made him.'

'I repeat, my father and I never forced him into anything. We didn't even know that Tom had had a relationship with you, much less that your child might be his. As for Tom, he swore to me that when

438

he asked you if the baby was his you told him it wasn't.'

Kirsten's chin came up as she took her time to consider that. 'When I was pregnant I told him what he wanted to hear,' she said in the end. 'He was terrified I was going to spoil things between you two, and believe me, I was tempted to. The problem was, I could tell that even if I were able to prove the child I was carrying was his, it wouldn't make a difference. He didn't want me, he wanted you and all you and your father could offer.'

'But if you didn't tell him the baby was his, how could you have spent so many years believing he'd turned his back on you?'

Kirsten treated her to an approving look. 'Because after Julia was born I wrote him a letter telling him I'd lied, that she was his,' she confessed, 'and he never replied. He says now that he didn't receive the letter, and I suppose, after this time of seeing him with Julia, that I'm coming to believe him. He really doesn't seem like the kind of man who'd turn his back on his own child. Unless, of course, he was forced to.' Her tone rang with the challenge.

Lainey's jaw tightened. 'Do you seriously think anyone can force Tom into doing something against his will?' she cried. 'If you do, then you really don't know him.'

'I don't think it now,' Kirsten admitted, 'but I did, for a very long time.'

Long minutes ticked by, during which neither of them spoke. Lainey watched Kirsten's eyes as they drifted to a place only she could see. After a while she felt sure she could sense the fight draining from Kirsten, as though the effort of maintaining a position she'd already lost had become too much.

Eventually she looked at Lainey and sighed shakily. 'To be honest, there's so much I wish I'd done differently,' she murmured. 'Things I wish I hadn't said, or believed, except we're not supposed to admit to regrets, are we?'

Hearing the sadness in her voice, Lainey sat down again as she said, 'I'm getting the impression that you've caused yourself more pain than you have anyone else.'

Kirsten didn't argue. 'I hope that's true, but I can't deny that I wanted to hurt you today. You see, I'm still jealous of you, perhaps even more than ever, because not only did you get Tom and go on to live as his wife for the last sixteen years, you've got your health, your family, your friends, and I . . . Well,' she threw out an arm, 'shall we say I've made some bad choices and I'm not sure now whether life, or perhaps I should say death, is going to allow me enough time to make up for them.'

Moved by how desperate she must be feeling, Lainey asked, 'Is it really that advanced?'

Kirsten merely shrugged. 'They're saying it's still too early to tell, but with something like this, you have to be prepared for the worst.' Another silence fell as she gazed down at her hands and let her thoughts go to places she apparently didn't want to reveal. After a while she looked at Lainey again. 'I really didn't want to like you,' she said frankly, 'and the last thing I wanted was your pity, but I don't think things are going my way on either count.'

Responding to the first hint of a connection, Lainey said gently, 'Why don't you tell me about Julia?'

Kirsten seemed surprised. 'Tom hasn't already done that?' she asked.

'Not really. I know how old she is, of course, and I guess she likes horses.'

Using a crooked finger to block a tear, Kirsten said, 'He's never mentioned that she . . . well, that she isn't like most other girls her age?'

Lainey regarded her curiously.

'She has Down's,' Kirsten told her.

Lainey became very still. Why on earth would Tom have omitted to tell her something so vital, something that would have made such a difference both to her and to Tierney? Surely he wasn't ashamed? That wouldn't have been like him at all. 'I understand now why you feel so protective of her,' she said.

'And why I didn't try to push her on him sooner?'

'I don't think you're pushing now. I think you're doing absolutely the right thing in bringing them together. Not only for her sake, but for yours. You need to know that should the worst happen, and obviously we're hoping it won't, she's going to be as loved and cared for as she is now.'

More tears shone in Kirsten's eyes. 'I don't understand why you're being nice to me after the way I've treated you today. I guess you just feel sorry for me.'

'Of course I do,' Lainey responded, 'but not in a patronising way, only as one woman to another, one mother to another. And I don't blame you for being afraid, because in your shoes anyone would be.'

Kirsten only looked at her.

'It can't have been easy,' Lainey continued, 'bringing up a special needs child alone, especially when you thought Tom had abandoned you.'

'Actually, she's not too bad,' Kirsten assured her.

441

'Well, I guess she's typical of someone with her condition.'

Lainey smiled, already feeling enormous affection for the child. 'Tell me, why didn't you get in touch with Tom again after you sent the letter telling him about Julia?' she asked. 'It must have crossed your mind that he didn't get it.'

Kirsten put her head back, as though to sink her tears. 'Believe me, I thought about it and I came close several times,' she replied, 'but I knew I wouldn't have been able to stand it if he didn't want to see her. Your little girl had been born by then, and she was perfect . . . You all looked so happy . . . I saw the pictures in the press, you and Tom with Tierney and Max and both your parents. You seemed so complete as a family. He had the wife and children he wanted, the career, the in-laws. It didn't feel as though there was any room for us.'

Understanding how different a public image could be from reality, Lainey said, 'We'd always have made room for you, I promise.'

'But how was I to know that? I thought you simply didn't care about anyone but yourselves.'

'That's not who we are, any of us.'

'I didn't know that then. Frankly, I'm not even sure of it now.'

Lainey's eyes narrowed. 'Yes you are,' she countered. 'Since you told Tom about Julia you've tested him over and over, and I don't think he's let you down at all. Now you're testing me, trying to turn me against you, but it's not going to happen.'

Kirsten's missing eyebrows arched, but she said nothing.

Time ticked by until Lainey asked, 'Why are you set on making this harder for yourself?'

Seeming to find that intriguing, Kirsten said, 'Is that what I'm doing?' She thought about it, and conceded, 'Yes, I suppose I am. I guess I just wasn't prepared to find myself . . . liking you, though Tom said I would.'

Lainey smiled. 'If there's to be a relationship between your daughter and her father, then perhaps a friendship between us is a good place to start?'

Kirsten's mouth trembled. 'I won't argue with that,' she managed, 'but I should tell you that Julia's already very attached to her father.'

'That's good.'

'She's a child who needs a lot of love.'

'Don't they all?'

Kirsten nodded. 'Of course.' Sweat was starting to bead on her upper lip; the sores on her cheeks looked livid. 'You'll meet her,' she said. 'She's back tomorrow. Tom will bring her to you. Promise me you'll be kind to her.'

'Of course I promise that. Please don't think it could be any other way.' She frowned as Kirsten touched a hand to her head. 'Is there anything I can do?' she asked. 'You're not looking well.'

'I just need to lie down for a while. Why don't you go to find Tom? Tell him . . . Well, you know what to tell him, you don't need any advice from me for that.'

When Lainey got outside there was only one horse in the field, so guessing Tom must still be riding she sent a text to let him know she was waiting, and opened up her messages. The third was from Marigold, saying she'd called the doctor to Peter following a 'little episode'. Immediately she tried Marigold's number, but the service was so poor the connection kept failing, so after making a quick search of the downstairs of the cottage and finding no landline she quickly forwarded the text to Tom and jumped into her car. Though the past half-hour was still crowding her mind, and there remained much more to discuss, she was far more concerned about her father now than anything else. Tom would be there for Kirsten after she'd rested, and when he read the text from Marigold he'd understand why she, Lainey, hadn't stayed.

She'd been driving for around ten minutes before her mobile began ringing with voicemails, so quickly pulling over to the side of the road she pressed to connect. To her relief there was a message from Marigold letting her know that the doctor had left now and Peter seemed fine.

'Just a bit of a dizzy spell,' Marigold added, 'but he turned a funny colour, so I thought it best to be on the safe side.'

Glad that she'd taken that decision, Lainey clicked on to the next message, which turned out to be from Tierney, left only a few minutes ago.

'Hey, Mum, hope it's going OK. Just wanted to let you know that Heather from the village has been in touch asking if we're up for the Christmas panto this year. Obviously that means she's hoping Dad's going to stump up some cash to help pay for it, but it's all going to a good cause, she reminded me, and she's offered us parts if we want them. You were so awesome as Cruella de Vil last year that you've totally got to do something again. I think they're doing a kind of *Harry Potter* thing this year – actually Dad ought to play Dumbledore, don't you think? I'll tell him that. Anyway, call me back when you get this. I want to know . . . Oh my God! Maudie, quick. Oh God, what am I going to do? Don't let her see me . . .' After that there were a lot of muffled sounds and footsteps before Tierney said, 'Oh shit, I'm still connected to my *mother*,' and the line finally went dead.

Not sure whether to be concerned or amused, Lainey tried to call back, but finding herself going straight through to messages she simply told Tierney she was on her way home and rang off. A moment later a text arrived from Tom.

Call as soon as you can to let me know about Peter. I'll come back if you need me to, otherwise will stay with Kirsten till Julia comes home. PS Did you and K get along?

Easily able to picture his concern, she sent a text back saying *P fine, apparently. K not what I expected, but we can talk when I see you. Let me know when you're bringing Julia and if you think Tierney and Zav should be there.*

'Oh my God, she's still down there,' Tierney whispered in a panic as she tiptoed back into her room. 'What am I going to do?'

Loyally worried, Maudie said, 'We'll just have to stay up here till she goes.'

Still pale from the shock of seeing Nadia pull up outside, Tierney nodded and went to join Maudie on the bed. 'She has to be here because of me,' she stated for the umpteenth time. 'She must be so mad. I mean, her marriage has broken up . . . Oh my God, it's all my fault . . .' Tears were welling in her eyes as her lips trembled with dread. 'I never really thought about her when it was all, you know, happening . . . It was like she didn't exist or something, but I can hardly tell her that, can I?'

'You don't have to tell her anything,' Maudie reminded her.

Taking comfort from that, Tierney reached for a tissue and blew her nose. 'At least the doctor said Grandpa's all right,' she sniffed. 'He's had funny turns before and . . .' She froze in dread as a knock came on the door.

'Tierney, are you in there?' Nadia asked.

Tierney's eyes bulged with horror as she looked at Maudie.

'Marigold said you were in,' Nadia told her. 'I'd like to talk to you. It won't take long.'

'What am I going to do?' Tierney said faintly.

'You'll have to let her in,' Maudie whispered helplessly.

'I can't.' Her heart practically flatlined as the handle of her door went down and a moment later Nadia was staring at them sitting on the bed like trapped rabbits.

'Please don't look like that,' Nadia said gently, 'I'm not going to . . .' Breaking off, she asked Maudie, 'Would you mind giving us a moment?'

Maudie turned her traumatised eyes to Tierney.

Tierney wanted to beg her to stay, but Maudie was already getting to her feet, doing as she was told.

When the door closed behind her Nadia came to sit on the stool beside the bed. Tierney couldn't help noticing how upset and kind of drawn she looked.

'I want you to know,' Nadia began, 'that I'm really sorry about what happened. He, that is, Guy, shouldn't have done what he did. He should have known better.'

Tierney could only look at her; she had no idea what to say.

446

'He won't ever bother you again,' Nadia promised. 'Me neither, come to that.' The irony was so pathetic, so sad that Tierney felt worse than ever.

In the end, she said, 'It was kind of my fault as well. I mean, I, well, you know . . .'

Reaching for her hand, Nadia gave it a squeeze. 'You mustn't blame yourself. You're too young to have a real understanding yet of how men work. All you were doing was responding to all the new hormones you've got firing off in there, and he took advantage of that.'

'But I kind of, you know . . .'

'Yes, I expect I do know, but what's important is that you put it behind you. But before you can do that you need to decide if you want your parents to know . . .'

'No, no, I really don't,' Tierney jumped in, bursting with panic. 'Please don't tell them. Oh, Nadia, please . . . Dad'll be so furious and I'll never be able to face him . . .'

'It's OK, it's OK, I'll do whatever you want me to do. I just didn't want you to think that I'm keeping it from them for my own sake.'

'But you should,' Tierney hastily told her, 'because if Dad was ever to find out he might not keep you as his agent.' She frowned as another thought occurred to her. 'Actually, now Guy's not with you any more I suppose you don't have to worry about that.'

'Don't concern yourself about me. You're the one who matters here, and what's been done to you. I don't know if you feel in need of any sort of counselling . . .'

'Oh no, I'm fine. Honest. My head is totally straight.'

'OK, but if you do ever feel confused, or as if you could use some help, I want you to promise to come to me.'

'I will, honest, I swear. I mean, I don't expect I will feel any of that stuff, but if I do I'll come straight to you.'

Nadia smiled, but as she started to get up Tierney said, 'I know you're saying it's not my fault, but it was, in a way, and I wish it had never happened, mostly because of what it's done to your marriage.'

Nadia regarded her with teary eyes. 'It would have happened anyway, sooner or later,' she assured her. 'He was too young for me, and to be honest, I always knew that the only reason he married me was to get his foot in the door of the agency.'

Appalled, Tierney said, 'That really sucks.'

Nadia didn't disagree. 'And I suppose he was my last grasp at youth,' she confessed. 'So time to start acting my age.' She twinkled in a way that made Tierney smile.

'You're still really lovely,' Tierney told her earnestly.

Nadia almost laughed.

As she started to leave, Tierney scrabbled in a drawer for her Chloe bangle and put it on. 'I so totally love this,' she declared. 'It's my favourite bangle ever.'

Coming to drop a kiss on her head, Nadia said, 'I was hoping it might be,' and cupping Tierney's face between her hands she gazed down at her fondly. 'I know you'll take this as a compliment,' she told her, 'but it's not really meant as one. You look much older than your age, and though you might think that's good, I'm afraid it makes you far more vulnerable than you realise. Luckily nothing too terrible happened this time.'

Tierney continued to regard her.

'I hope that doesn't sound as though I'm trying to put you off men,' Nadia continued, 'I just want you to be aware of how unpredictable they can be when it comes to sex. So next time, and there will be a next time, please make sure you're safely in a relationship before you start down that road, preferably with someone closer to your own age.'

'I will,' Tierney whispered, meaning it. Then suddenly not wanting Nadia to go, she said, 'Shall I make you some tea? Mum should be on her way back by now, and I know she'll want to see you.'

It was another hour before Lainey came in the door to find Nadia, Maudie and Tierney sprawled out on the sofas with Peter, watching one of his favourite black and white movies. The fact that Peter had tears rolling down his cheeks seemed to have gone unnoticed, but when Lainey went to sit with him his face lit up again.

'Sandra,' he whispered, smoothing her hair. 'I've been waiting for you.'

Chapter Twenty-Three

'They're here!' Zav shouted up the stairs.

Having primed him to let them know the instant Tom's car entered the drive, Lainey hurried out of the bathroom, almost colliding with Tierney, who was in front of the mirror looking doubtful about her fourth outfit of the morning.

'What about this?' she said anxiously. 'I really love these jeans, but they're not designer . . .'

'Don't be ridiculous,' Lainey scolded, moving her aside so she could get past. 'She's hardly going to care about something like that.'

Tierney pulled a face. 'No, I don't suppose she will. Oh, Mum, what am I going to say to her? I've never met anyone with Down's before.'

'Just be friendly and make her feel welcome,' Lainey instructed. 'Now let's go down. I don't want her coming into an empty house.'

'Where's Grandpa?' Zav asked, coming along the landing to find them.

Lainey's eyes widened with alarm. 'He should be in his chair,' she cried. 'Please don't tell me he's gone walkabout.'

'I don't know, I only looked in his room,' Zav responded, going to bounce on the bed. 'Why are you getting so worked up?'

Ignoring the question, Lainey raced down the stairs to find her father where she'd left him half an hour ago, in his chair, after a long and particularly difficult start to the day.

Heaving a sigh of relief she cast a critical look around, trying to imagine how the place might present itself to Julia. Did it appear welcoming, or imposing? Ostentatious when compared to the ramshackle cottage Kirsten had apparently inherited from her gran? Cold, too big, overcrowded? No one was here today, apart from immediate family, and the place was never normally this uncluttered. Even Sherman's bed and bowl had been tidied into a corner. The Italian biscuits she'd made to one of Adriana's recipes were still cooling on the Aga, and the aroma of fresh coffee was mingling with the natural smells of their home (which she could no longer detect). She just hoped they weren't off-putting in any way.

'They're outside now,' Zav announced from the door, and tugging it open he charged off to meet his new half-sister, apparently totally unfazed, or perhaps unaware, of the enormity of it all.

'He's weird,' Tierney decided, straining to see past him to catch her first glimpse of Julia as the passenger door of Tom's car opened.

Lainey was right behind her, trying to push her outside.

'Oh my God, she's *fat*,' Tierney whispered in shock.

'Shut up,' Lainey hissed under her breath, and quickly stepping past Tierney out of the door, she watched the heavy-set blonde girl turn around to look at her.

The smile that lit up Julia's sunny moon face was

so radiantly happy that Lainey could feel it glowing straight into her heart.

'Oh my God, Mum,' Tierney murmured.

Lainey moved forward, but Tierney was the first to get to Julia, and the way she wrapped her new half-sister in her arms brought hot tears to Lainey's eyes.

'Oh Julia, Julia,' Lainey sobbed, joining in the embrace. 'How lovely it is to meet you.'

'. . . to meet you,' Julia said, her awkward voice muffled by Tierney's shoulder.

'I'm Tierney,' Tierney said, still squeezing hard.

'I'm Zav,' her brother announced, watching with amusement.

'I'm Julia,' she told him, as Tierney let her go. Despite her distinctive Down's speech she was easy enough to understand, and the sun that shone out of her seemed more dazzling than ever. 'I'm very pleased to meet you,' she slurred. She looked adoringly at Tom and raised her shoulders in glee.

Pressing a hand to her mouth to stop herself sobbing, Lainey watched him smooth Julia's wispy blonde hair and wondered if she'd ever loved him more.

'We've got biscuits,' Tierney was saying while keeping a proprietorial arm around her new half-sister as she steered her towards the house, 'and juice and squash and everything. My favourite's apple, what's yours?'

'Apple,' Julia repeated, though whether to be friends, or because it was true wasn't possible for Lainey to know.

'Grandpa's inside,' Zav informed her. 'He'll be your grandpa too. You'll really love him, even though he's not like he used to be. Do you like dogs?'

'Yes, I like dogs. And horses.'

'Mum said you've got two horses. What are their names?'

As they moved away Lainey turned around to find Tom opening the rear passenger door. Only then did she realise that Kirsten had been watching from the back seat.

Waiting until Kirsten was out of the car, looking tired, yet somehow indefatigable, Lainey said, 'Why on earth didn't you tell me you were coming?'

'I only realised as they were leaving,' Kirsten answered honestly, 'that I wanted to see for myself how . . . well, how . . .' Her mouth was trembling; a tear dropped from her lashless eyes. 'Your children . . . They've taken my breath away.'

'They often do that to me,' Tom told her wryly. Though his eyes were on Lainey, Lainey's attention was wholly on Kirsten as she watched the children disappearing into the house.

'I won't be able to stay for long,' Kirsten said, as Tom ushered her in behind them.

'It's lovely that you're here,' Lainey told her, going ahead to rearrange the pillows on the most comfy sofa, 'but we'd have come to you. It would have been so much easier for you.'

'Maybe, but I'm stronger than I might look, and to be frank, I wanted to see where you live.' As emotion fractured her voice, Lainey sat down with her and held her hands. She was a different woman to the one she'd met yesterday, and she knew instinctively that she was now meeting the Kirsten who lived behind all the pain and fear.

'I wish I knew how to make things easier for you,' Lainey said softly.

453

Kirsten's gaze was fixed on Julia, who was on the floor with Zav fussing Sherman while Tierney explained to Peter that he had a new granddaughter. 'You already have,' Kirsten assured her. 'Seeing how warmly you greeted her . . .' She took a breath, and before she could continue Julia brought her face out of Sherman's fur to say, 'Mummy, it's a dog. His name's Sherman.'

'He belongs to Grandpa really,' Zav informed Kirsten, 'but he doesn't mind us playing with him, do you, Grandpa?'

Peter smiled as he patted Zav's head.

'Would you like some coffee, or tea?' Tierney offered Kirsten.

Kirsten managed a smile. 'Water is fine for me,' she replied. She watched Tierney go to the fridge. 'She's a lovely girl,' she commented, almost to herself. 'Very like her father.'

Understanding what must be going through her mind, and how difficult it must be, Lainey tightened the hold on her hands. Though there was nothing she could do to change the way Julia was, or to make up for the time she'd lost with her father and siblings, she was already determined that her new stepdaughter was going to be a huge part of their lives from now on.

'Julia, sweetheart, only one biscuit,' Kirsten chided as Julia grabbed a handful from the plate Tierney held out. 'You know what we've said about your weight.'

Obediently putting the extras back, Julia stuffed the remaining one in her mouth and grinned widely as Tierney did the same.

'It looks easy when she's being like this,' Kirsten said quietly, 'and on the whole she has a very sweet nature, but there are times when she can be very challenging.'

Not doubting it for a minute, Lainey concurred, 'Show me a child who isn't, but I understand her needs are different. I'll make sure I know what they are for when she comes to stay. You can tell me, and I'll get advice from specialists too, so please don't worry. We'll manage, I promise.'

Kirsten's eyes followed Tom as he went to pick up the biscuit Peter had dropped into his lap.

'Daddy,' Julia said, beaming up at him.

'Julia,' he said, smiling down at her.

'He's my dad too,' Zav told her.

Julia nodded, up and down, up and down.

Without saying where he was going, Tom turned away and left the room.

'I'm still not sure how well he's coming to terms with being the father of a Down's child,' Kirsten admitted. 'Men often think it's their fault.'

Realising that was something else she'd have to learn about, Lainey said, 'I'll go and talk to him. Will you be all right here for a moment?'

'Of course,' Kirsten assured her, and patting the seat next to her she said to Tierney, 'come and tell me all about you.'

Finding Tom in his study, Lainey closed the door behind her and looked across to where he was standing, staring out of the window.

'Why didn't you tell me about Julia?' she asked.

He didn't answer, and realising he was too choked with emotion to utter a word, she went to rest her head on his shoulder. 'She's a lovely girl,' she said softly.

He nodded.

'It can't have been easy for Kirsten, bringing her up alone.'

'A thought that almost never leaves me,' he responded hoarsely.

More minutes ticked by as they felt the burden of Kirsten's struggle, and the guilt of not having been around to help her. Finally Lainey braced herself to ask the question she knew she couldn't avoid any longer.

'Did you get the letter Kirsten sent all those years ago?'

When only silence followed she knew, with a horrible, wrenching dismay, that she had her answer. 'Oh God, Tom,' she murmured, pulling away. 'And when you cancelled seeing her . . .?'

'Before you start jumping to conclusions,' he broke in, 'I didn't open the letter, so I never knew Julia had Down's.'

'And if you had known?'

Pressing his fingers to his brows, he said, 'I keep asking myself that question, and honestly, I don't know what I'd have done. Obviously, I couldn't have turned my back on her . . . I'd never have done that, and yet now it's like that's exactly what I did do.'

'Without realising,' Lainey reminded him.

'It's no excuse. To think, all these years, when we've been so happy, so blessed with our children . . .'

'You surely can't think Kirsten's any less blessed. Julia's as special to her as Tierney and Zav are to me.'

'But Kirsten needed me there. She shouldn't have had to bring her up alone. I know you, you'd have embraced her as warmly back then as you have today. We could have made such a difference to their lives.'

'Of course, but it's not too late. We can be there for them now, and God knows Kirsten could do with our support while she's going through this, especially if, God forbid, she doesn't pull through. She'll need to know that Julia's going to be loved and cared for in a family that's genuinely hers.'

His eyes were gazing wondrously into hers. 'You are so generous,' he responded, 'but I don't think you realise what an enormous commitment it would be if we did take her on. No, hear me out,' he objected as she made to interrupt. 'You've already given me so much of your life . . . When I met you, you were so young, so fresh and full of possibilities. Yet you were willing to give up your studies, all the travelling you'd planned, the adventures every young person should have, the wonderful, exciting risk of just living, in order to be with me. And God help me, I let you because I couldn't bear the thought of being without you. You meant everything to me, you still do, always will, but I can never reconcile myself to all you've missed out on because I turned you into a wife and mother before you even had a chance to be yourself.'

Lainey could hardly believe what she was hearing. 'Are you crazy?' she cried. 'After all these years of knowing me, of living with me, have I ever seemed to you as though I felt I was *missing out*, or not being myself? I love being a wife and mother. It's who I am, what I do, how I think, even, and I'm not ashamed of it. I'm proud of it, because what I do here, taking care of our children, of you and all that comes with you, is, for me, the best career in the world.'

With love shining in his eyes, he said, 'But Tierney's going to be leaving home soon, and it's not so many years until Zav will too. What's going to happen then if we do have Julia with us? You'll be stuck here with a husband who's turning into an old man before your eyes, and a stepdaughter who's never going to be able to leave. She could be your responsibility long after I've gone, do you realise that? You'll have sacrificed your entire life for me and a child who's not even yours. I can't let you do it, Lainey. You deserve your life . . .'

'Tom, will you please listen to me,' she cut in forcefully.

'No. You've taken care of your mother, and your father . . .'

'You will listen,' she insisted. 'You're my family, all of you, and that's what matters to me. Maybe it's the Italian in me. OK, I wasn't set much of an example, but taking care of you all, Max and Julia included, loving you, being with you and doing what I can to make you happy is what makes me happy. So please don't keep going on with all this nonsense about sacrifices and what I deserve. I love you, Tom Hollingsworth, more than I know how to put into words, and sadly I can't rely on you to provide them because you can't seem to say it at all.'

Laughing past his frustration, he caught her to him and held her tight. 'I'll find the words,' he promised.

Tilting her head back to gaze up at him, she said, 'It's not really about words in the end, is it? It's about being together, getting through the bad times and enjoying the good, sharing everything of each other and knowing we'll always be there for each other.' She wrinkled her nose. 'That was a lot of words, wasn't it?'

Losing his kiss to another laugh, he suggested, 'Maybe you should be the writer in the family.'

'I have my job, thanks, and I happen to think I'm quite good at it.'

'You're certainly that,' he told her softly.

Their kiss was long and tender, and might not have ended there if they hadn't been forced to remember their visitors.

'I've been giving this some thought,' she said, linking his arm as they started for the door. 'OK, not for long, I admit, but I'm pretty sure about it already. I think Kirsten and Julia should come here to stay while Kirsten's recovering. That way she'll be able to see Julia settling into the family, and will be able to feel a part of it herself.'

Tom's eyes closed as he shook his head in quiet amazement. 'I don't know why I'm surprised, when I know you as well as I do,' he murmured, turning her to face him. 'In fact, I should have seen this coming.'

'Do you think Kirsten will go for it?'

'I've no idea, but I do know that this is why I find it so hard to tell you I love you, because where you're concerned the way I feel goes so far beyond those three words that they're not even beginning to express the strength of it.'

Chapter Twenty-Four

Though Kirsten was perfectly able to see the merits of Lainey's suggestion, she still didn't prove easy to persuade. As far as she was concerned, she couldn't possibly allow herself to become such a burden. However, for Julia's sake, she finally agreed to come for a few weeks, which ended up turning into a couple of months, then three, then four, as Julia seemed so settled and Lainey was so insistent that they really ought to hang on till after Christmas.

By then Kirsten's recovery was making some progress, and since Max was now in London, renting a studio flat from Nadia while he helped out at the agency by day and gigged around town by night, she and Julia had taken over the annexe.

Though Lainey and Tom were seeing little of Max at Bannerleigh Cross, hardly a day went by when he wasn't in touch with his father, or Lainey, usually because he needed something, while his Skyping with Tierney, Zav and Julia was solely because Julia seemed to love it so much.

'I suppose there's hope for him yet,' Tom was occasionally heard to sigh, after he'd watched Max serenading his half-sister with lyrics written specially for her. Her pleasure at being made to feel so special, coupled with the sheer joy of having brothers and a sister, was as heart-warming to behold as her delight in being an extra in the Christmas panto. Or as touching as watching her running out of school with drawings for everyone clutched in her hands, and marks that showed the very real worth of her inclusive education. Though she wasn't able to go to Tierney's school in Stroud, she'd fitted in straight away at The Farnaways, where Lainey and Tom had both recently become governors.

Julia also had a desk in Tom's study where she was allowed to do her homework if she was quiet, and her beloved horses were in stables the other side of the village. Since they'd been moved there the whole family had taken up riding, and because of how much they enjoyed it Tom and Lainey had set about building a stable block of their own.

Next to riding her horses, rehearsing for the panto, Skyping with Max, reading to her mother or father, and hanging out with Tierney and Maudie, Julia's greatest pleasure in life was taking Peter and Sherman for walks – either down to the duck pond, or over to the stables. Quite what Sherman thought of his new lead, since he'd almost never worn one, was impossible to tell. However, he never seemed to mind when she clipped it on, and there was definitely a wag in his tail whenever the three of them – four when Zav or Tom joined them – set off down the drive. For his part Peter rarely failed to smile when he saw her, much as he did with his other grandchildren, though it was doubtful he really knew who she was. The only names he'd spoken in a while now were Lainey's and Sandra's, and it was evident he had them confused.

November came, and Tom's new book was published. As usual it went straight to number one, both sides of the Atlantic, and because this was the first time Kirsten and Julia had been around to celebrate with them they'd thrown an especially big party. However, a week after publication other matters once again overshadowed Tom's fictional world.

Now, as Lainey surveyed the neatly kept gardens of the crematorium where more mourners than either she or Tom had imagined were starting to gather, she was remarking the colours of the trees and how bare some were, while others still seemed slow to shed. The sun was bright, glistening in puddles and flashing off windscreens like laughter. The sadness of the occasion seemed to be passing nature by.

There were many faces she recognised, some only by sight or from TV, others whom she knew fairly well, mainly through Tom. She felt touched by their need to pay their final respects, saying so softly as she shook their hands. Everyone was welcome at the reception following the service.

There was a marquee in the field where caterers were even now setting up for the event, while the gardener and his assistant were clearing pathways through the piles of fallen leaves.

As time ticked on more people arrived, dressed in black and carrying memories they were already starting to share. She wondered what Tom would make of so many luminaries when he saw them. No doubt he'd know who they all were. She could see the hearse turning into the crematorium now, with a black Mercedes behind that she knew was carrying Tom, Max, Tierney, Zav and Julia. Lainey had come on ahead with Stacy and Kirsten's sister Rosa. Rosa's husband was here too, as was Nancy, many teachers

462

from Julia's school, and most of the village including the owners of the stables. Her sisters, Sarah and Esther, had turned up a few minutes ago with their husbands; even her own self-appointed Italian family had flown over to lend their support: Marco and his wife, Adriana and Lorenzo.

As the hearse came to a stop beside the low red-brick building, Lainey looked at the coffin, covered in flowers, and tried not to think of the body inside. It wasn't a person any more, only the remains after the spirit had soared. She wasn't going to break down, she really wasn't, but she was close, and seeing Tom and the children getting out of the second car she felt a tear splash messily on to her cheek. Their grief was so evident it was impossible for her not to feel it too.

Tom's eyes found hers, and for a fleeting moment it was as though all sounds stopped and no one else existed.

Feeling Stacy's arm go through hers, Lainey pressed it to her side and watched Tom joining his brother, Grant, and four more dark-suited men to hoist the coffin on to their shoulders. The children were surrounding her now, struggling with their emotions, needing to be close.

'Are you ready?' Stacy whispered as the pall-bearers began edging forward.

Lainey nodded, and holding Julia's hand she started to follow, but stopped as she saw Sherman, loyally walking behind the coffin.

'It's all right, Mum,' Tierney sobbed as Lainey buckled. 'It'll be all right.'

Max's and Stacy's arms were around her, holding her up.

'I'm fine,' she tried to say, but the words wouldn't

463

come. *Daddy, Daddy, Daddy*, she wanted to scream, but of course she couldn't.

He was gone. Her wonderful, gentle, devoted father had left to be with her mother. It was where he belonged, she knew that, but how was she going to bear being without him?

The service passed in a blur as she sat with her head on Tom's shoulder, her hand resting in his. Her eyes only left the coffin when Tom got up to speak, at length, about Peter, his friend, mentor, father-in-law and inspiration. He stirred up long-forgotten memories for many of those present, making them laugh and cry and laugh again. He spoke about Lainey and how special she had been to her father, while tactfully, if not truthfully, including her sisters. He said something about how much the best father in the world was going to be missed, and she wanted to tell him that he was that person, but realised it would have to wait until they were alone.

Two of publishing's top executives spoke about Peter too, saying how valuable and inspirational he had been to the industry, and emphasising the importance of his legacy. Even Father Michael from her mother's church stepped up to say a few words, followed by Bannerleigh's local vicar. Then Max, with his guitar, sang a song he'd composed specially. Lainey could only imagine how many tears were falling; she could tell by how stiffly Tom was holding himself that he was finding this the hardest part of the service so far.

When it was finally all over and time to leave, Sherman was once again Lainey's undoing, since he couldn't be moved. He simply stood by the coffin, waiting for Peter to need him. In the end Tom had to carry him outside, and when the dear dog turned his tragic brown eyes up to Lainey, she could only hug him and sob into his fur.

'We'll take care of you,' she promised brokenly, 'just like you took care of him.'

By the time they returned to the house the sun had yielded to a bruising sky and a fine mist of drizzle. Kirsten, who'd received the devastating news, only yesterday, that the cancer had spread to her lungs, was, perversely, looking stronger than she had for some time as she waited in the marquee, having overseen the arrangements in Lainey's absence.

Seeing her, Lainey walked into her arms and held her tight. They'd become good friends these past few months, and knowing that she was going to lose her soon, too, was proving especially difficult today. 'Thanks for doing all this,' she whispered, drawing back to look at her. 'Are you OK?'

'High as a kite.' Kirsten tried to twinkle through her tired eyes. 'How did the service go?'

Lainey grimaced. 'Probably best not to ask, and definitely don't mention Sherman.'

'Did he go too?'

'Yes. Poor thing, if he could have jumped into the coffin, he would have. He's going to miss him so much. We all are, except of course he hasn't been the dad I knew for quite some time.'

Kirsten looked up as Tierney and Julia came into the tent, followed by Tom, Zav and Sherman.

'I didn't feel right about leaving the dog on his own,' Tom admitted, 'so he's come to join us.'

Loving him for thinking of it, Lainey stooped to give Sherman another hearty hug, while Julia went to link hands with her mother.

'We said goodbye to Grandpa,' she told her. 'It was very sad.'

'I'm sure,' Kirsten responded, stroking her face, and thinking, Lainey imagined, of the day, not too far distant, when Julia would be saying goodbye to her.

'Daddy carried the coffin,' Julia announced.

Kirsten smiled at Tom. 'That's because he's big and strong,' she said teasingly.

'That'll be me,' Tom agreed, looking round at the sound of voices as everyone starting arriving.

'Are you sure you're up for this?' Lainey asked Kirsten.

'I've put myself on a table close to the exit,' Kirsten assured her, 'so I can slip away at any time.'

Knowing that a part of Kirsten was actually looking forward to this potentially last opportunity to see some people from her own past, Lainey squeezed her hand and went to join Tom, who was greeting Nadia.

Though it took a while for everyone to assemble, the atmosphere was becoming almost light-hearted as long-time friends caught up with one another, and extended family joined in playing host. It was exactly, Lainey was thinking, as she watched the children mingle with trays and drinks, how her father would have wanted it to be. No more tears, only laughter as old stories were retold and new ones took their place. She could almost see him standing in the middle of it all, the catalyst between past and future, loving the fact that busy lives had been put on hold for a day, allowing everyone he cared about to remember why they cared about each other.

'Mum, I've got something to tell you,' Tierney announced in a whisper.

'Do I want to hear it now?' Lainey asked, also in a whisper.

'Yes. Definitely. I've decided that when I go to uni I want to study to become the kind of doctor, or nurse, that takes care of people like Julia.'

Lainey's eyes widened with surprise, but as she turned to make sure Tierney wasn't teasing her Tierney slipped back into the crowd.

Just wait till she told Tom this astonishing – and perhaps unreliable – piece of news.

Spotting Stacy sitting with Kirsten, she knew without asking what they were discussing: the article Stacy was going to run in her new magazine, to be written jointly by Kirsten and Lainey, that would reveal Tom as the father of Kirsten's child.

Deciding she might like to join them, she started on her way but was waylaid by Marco and Adriana.

'Your father was clearly very well loved,' Marco commented as he gave her a hug. 'It pleases me a lot to see this after what you learned about your family in Italy.'

'But you have us now,' Adriana reminded her. 'You are welcome always in our home, please to know that.'

'Thank you.' Lainey smiled, keeping hold of Marco's hand as she felt a renewed gratitude for how much easier he had made that terrible time. His own marriage was working out fine now, apparently, though she could tell by the haunted look at the back of his eyes that the trust still hadn't fully returned.

'Have you decided what you want to do about Aldo?' Adriana asked, replacing her glass on a passing tray.

Since Melvina had died, a month ago, Lainey had

felt a stronger desire to meet her grandfather than she had before, provided he wanted to meet her, of course. 'We're hoping to go and see him in the new year,' she replied, leaning against Tom as he came to slip an arm around her. 'You never know,' she said, 'he might be happy to find himself with a family again, even if it is ours.'

'I think he will,' Adriana assured her. 'From everything Carlotta tells us he is a lonely man, and perhaps in need of knowing that Alessandra's life became a good one – and that her daughter has grown up safely.'

Not until they were able to steal a moment alone did Lainey say to Tom, 'Am I safe?'

He gave it some thought. 'Only because all these people are around,' he decided.

She gurgled on a laugh, and linked his arm as they headed towards Kirsten and Stacy. 'Well, at least we know one thing for certain,' she said, looking around her.

'We do? What's that?'

'That whether you love me or not you're doing your level best to keep me tied to you, the kitchen sink and your very many children.'

Turning her to him, he asked, 'Are you sure you don't mind?'

'About being pregnant? Why would I mind, when I've always said being a wife and mother is what I do best?'

'No.' Tom shook his head. 'What you do best is shame me for not being able to tell you how much I love you.'

'Ah, but you're pretty good at showing me.'

With a waggle of his eyebrows, he said, 'I like to think so. In fact, I could tell you too, if you like.'

Intrigued, she said, 'Go on then.'

'OK. I love you, Lainey Hollingsworth.'

She frowned. 'Is that it?'

'I told you it wouldn't be enough.'

Funnily enough, it didn't seem to be.

'I could shout it so everyone can hear,' he offered.

At that, her eyes sparked with mischief. 'Go on then,' she challenged, knowing full well that he'd expected her to back away from the very idea.

To her surprise he took a breath, but before he could get the first word out she clapped a hand over his mouth. 'It's OK, I believe you,' she muttered, smiling at those nearby.

He gave her a quizzical look. 'Are you sure, because I don't have a problem with everyone knowing it.'

'I'm hoping we can assume they already do. Anyway, I prefer it when you show me.'

'Aha.' His eyes narrowed with interest. 'I can do that, except maybe not right now.'

Loving the way this was going, she said, 'OK. Then what are you doing later?'

'You know, I wasn't sure before,' he smiled, tilting her mouth to his, 'but I am now.'

'And?'

'I'm going to start a new book, all about how much I love my very beautiful wife.'

Acknowledgements

An enormous thank you to my lovely friend Carlo Cocuzzi who helped so patiently and tirelessly with the Italian translations. Any mistakes (and hopefully there are none) will be completely down to me. I'd also like to thank my good friend Ruth Kelham for introducing me to Stroud.

Last, but by no means least, I'd like to thank my wonderful stepsons Michael and Luke for providing so much inspiration and entertainment while we were in Italy researching the book.

Getting to know

Susan Lewis

Read on for an insight into *The Truth About You*,
all about Susan and her links to the charity
Breast Cancer Care

For those with a love of Italy I hope that your stay in Umbria, via this book, has been an enjoyable one, even if a little turbulent at times. I imagine we've all been through challenging family holidays when it's hoped that getting away from it all will prove the antidote to stress, until you find it's all come with you. In Lainey's case, of course, she walked right into the middle of more.

It was through her that I have tried to reach the hearts of people who, for whatever reasons, don't feel as secure in themselves, or their relationships as they'd like to. I believe a very big part of what makes us strong is knowing we are loved, and when the doubt sets in is when things start to go wrong.

It always fascinates me how courageous people can appear, how strong and capable, when inside they are falling apart. It makes me look at people differently, always wondering what their story really is. We all have secrets of some sort, and sometimes they can make us feel very alone. It's my aim, with most of my books, including this one, to reach out to those who might be feeling that way in the hope that it helps to diminish, at least for a while, the sense of isolation.

I must mention in this letter that after many years of feeling alone 2013 was the year in which I acquired not only a wonderful husband, but two wonderful stepsons. They were with me during the time spent in Italy, and though the story here is not based on them (or not entirely anyway!), I have to admit they provided some splendid inspiration.

I hope you have enjoyed the book. It's always a great treat to hear from readers as so many of you have such fantastically uplifting things to say, so please don't hesitate to be in touch. You can reach me through the contact link on my website: www.susanlewis.com or on the Official Susan Lewis Facebook page: www.facebook/susanlewisbooks

Susan

I was born in 1956 to a happy, normal family living in a brand new council house on the outskirts of Bristol. My mother, at the age of twenty, and one of thirteen children, persuaded my father to spend his bonus on a ring rather than a motorbike and they never looked back. She was an ambitious woman determined to see her children on the right path: I was signed up for ballet, elocution and piano lessons and my little brother was to succeed in all he set his mind to.

Tragically, at the age of thirty-three, my mother lost the battle against cancer and died. I was nine, my brother was five.

My father was left with two children to bring up on his own. Sending me to boarding school was thought to be 'for the best' but I disagreed. No one listened to my pleas for freedom, so after a while I took it upon myself to get expelled. By the time I was thirteen, I was back in our little council house with my father and brother. The teenage years passed and before I knew it I was eighteen . . . an adult.

I got a job at HTV in Bristol for a few years before moving to London at the age of twenty-two to work for Thames. I moved up the ranks, from secretary in news and current affairs, to a production assistant in light entertainment and drama. My mother's ambition and a love of drama gave me the courage to knock on the Controller's door to ask what it takes to be a success. I received the reply of 'Oh, go away and write something'. So I did!

Three years into my writing career I left TV and moved to France. At first it was bliss. I was living the dream and even found myself involved in a love affair with one of the FBI's most wanted! Reality soon dawned, however, and I realised that a full time life in France was very different to a two week holiday frolicking around on the sunny Riviera.

So I made the move to California with my beloved dogs Casanova and Floozie. With the rich and famous as my neighbours I was enthralled and inspired by Tinsel Town. The reality, however, was an obstacle course of cowboy agents, big-talking producers and wannabe directors. Hollywood was not waiting for me, but it was a great place to have fun! Romances flourished and faded, dreams were crushed but others came true.

After seven happy years of taking the best of Hollywood and avoiding the rest, I decided it was time for a change. My dogs and I spent a short while in Wiltshire before then settling once again in France. Perched high above the Riviera with glorious views of the sea. It was wonderful to be back amongst old friends, and to make so many new ones.

Casanova and Floozie both passed away during our first few years there, but Coco and Lulabelle are doing a valiant job of taking over their places – and my life!

Everything changed again three months after my fiftieth birthday when I met James. For a couple of years we had a very romantic and enjoyable time of flying back and forth to see one another at the weekends, but at the end of 2010 I finally sold my house on the Riviera and moved to a delightful old barn in Gloucestershire with Coco and Lulabelle. My writing is flourishing and over thirty books down the line I couldn't be happier. James continued to live in Bristol, with his boys, Michael and Luke – a great musician and a champion footballer! – for a while until we decided to get married last year!

It's been exhilarating and educational having two teenage boys in my life! Needless to say they know everything, which is very useful (saves me looking things up) and they're incredibly inspiring in ways they probably have no idea about.

Should you be interested to know a little more about my early life, why not try *Just One More Day*, a memoir about me and my mother? The story then continues in *One Day at a Time*, a memoir about me and my father and how we coped with my mother's loss.

1. What made you want to become a writer?

It's something I instinctively felt would happen one day, though I didn't do much about it until I began working in TV drama. Editing scripts, pulling together storylines, dreaming up characters and their backgrounds was something I enjoyed so much that when an agent suggested I turn one of my projects into a book I decided to give it a go. That book was never published, but the bug had bitten and the rest, I guess, is history.

2. Describe your routine for writing and where you like to write, including whether you have any little quirks or funny habits when you are writing.

I have a study at home that overlooks a beautiful spread of lower Cotswold countryside where I aim to be by ten each morning, through until six or seven in the evening. For a long time I wrote seven days a week taking a break only when I was so exhausted I couldn't do any more. Now, I pace myself a little better by doing only five or six days, but even that is pretty gruelling. I don't have any quirks particularly, but I do have a very bad but thoroughly enjoyable habit of drinking a glass or two of wine when I read back over what I've written during the day.

3. What themes are you interested in when you're writing?

I'm always interested in the strange or terrible things fate inflicts on innocent people and how courageously (or not) they strive to overcome it.

4. Where do you get your inspiration from?

The most obvious source of inspiration is life itself. Added to that there are certain authors I find very inspirational in the way they write, such as Lionel Shriver; Jodi Picoult; Anita Shreve; Susan

Howatch and Irène Némirovsky whose book, *Suite Française*, played a very big part in my own book, *A French Affair*.

5. How do you manage to get inside the heads of your characters in order to portray them truthfully?

It's all done through imagination, I guess – I can't think that there would be any other way.

6. Do you base your characters on real people? And if not, where does the inspiration come from?

Very occasionally they're based on people I meet, but as a real character is so highly complex it would only ever be one or two aspects of them. I guess you could say that personality traits are perhaps more inspiring than actual characters.

7. What's the most extreme thing you've ever done to research your book?

I once allowed myself to be locked up in a Filipino jail when researching *Last Resort* – that was pretty scary, and it didn't smell too good either!

8. What aspect of writing do you enjoy most?

I enjoy it all, especially when exciting and pivotal things happen that I hadn't seen coming!

9. What's the best thing about being an author?

For me it would definitely be doing the second draft when all the really hard work is done, and the smoothing out is underway. After that comes a lovely freeing time when I hold onto the book before giving it to my editor – this is a period when there is no pressure at all, or anxiety about whether or not she is going to like it. That begins the moment I send it from my computer to hers.

10. What advice would you give aspiring writers?

Probably that you have to be serious about writing to make it work, not simply think 'I'm going to write a bestseller' or 'I'd write a book if I only had time.' It takes a huge amount of dedication and belief in yourself; if you have that then I think the best advice I could give is pay great attention to your characters and who they are, and don't forget to listen to them. It's uncanny how often they'll help out when you find yourself stuck.

11. What is your favourite book of all time and why?

There are many books I could list here, but I'm going to settle for *Suite Française*, because it's the only book I've ever finished reading and then gone straight back to the beginning to read it again.

12. If you could be a character in a book, or live in the world of a book who or where would you be?

I wouldn't mind being one of Georgette Heyer's heroines back in Georgian times, but as they didn't have much in the way of anaesthetic then, perhaps I'd rather be Claudine in my own book, *Darkest Longings*.

Susan Lewis

and

breast cancer care

I lost my mother to breast cancer when she was thirty-three years old and I was nine. This was back at a time when women, even doctors, spoke in hushed tones about the dreaded Big C. Nothing was discussed, no counselling offered; there was even a kind of shame attached to having fallen victim to this terrible disease.

Luckily, all that has changed. Today someone is always there to offer advice and support to those who need it, or simply to lend an ear if all that's required is to talk. Many of these people are doctors, nurses, or members of the healthcare professions; but just as many are women who selflessly give up their time to be there for those in need. Stephanie Harrison of Breast Cancer Care is one of these very special people, and it is because of her that I have become associated with this extremely worthwhile organisation.

Read on to learn more about Steph in her own words . . .

In June 2008, I was sitting in my doctor's office hearing the words 'Stephanie, you have breast cancer'. As those words reached my ears I felt like I'd been kicked in the stomach, and for a moment or two I sat in a daze of numbness and shock. I then heard, 'Is there any history of breast cancer in your family?' to which I replied 'No, but trust me to start a new trend'. Everyone in the room laughed, and I decided from that moment on I would try to fight this disease with humour.

At my diagnosis I received all the information I would need about treatment, lifestyle and aftercare, which was provided by Breast Cancer Care. At that time I had no idea just how important this organisation and its staff would become in my life. Subsequently they gave me so much help and support throughout my fight with cancer. I consider myself very fortunate that I was offered their support because now I realise it really is second to none. What I didn't realise at the time is that not everyone is aware of the support they offer. Therefore I decided to help raise awareness for this amazing charity by choosing Breast Cancer Care for my own fundraising activities.

It seems odd to say that my life has got better since being diagnosed with breast cancer, but in a lot of ways it has. It has focused my mind and made me realise life is short – that old cliché 'life is not a dress rehearsal' is so true. Seeing that this disease has no respect for age, colour or creed was a real eye-opener for me and it made me realise I had to do something to help others who would hear this devastating news. So I set out on my path as a fundraiser for BCC. During this time I have been overwhelmed by the love and support of so many people and their willingness to help me, as well as by the support of those at Breast Cancer Care. I have met so many amazing people, many of whom have become good friends and some of them have changed my life in more ways than they will ever know. One of those people is Susan Lewis.

In the spring of 2011 I was given a copy of the first part of Susan's autobiography *Just One More Day* and it changed my life. I wasn't sure reading a book about someone dying from breast cancer as I approached my third annual mammogram would be a fun thing to do, but how wrong could I be. From the very first few lines I was hooked and I spent the next two days laughing and crying as I experienced all the ups and downs of Susan's family's lives; a family being torn apart by illness and secrets. Three things struck me immediately. One was how well written it was. Then I wondered how Susan wrote so effectively from the point of view of a child. I was also overwhelmed by Susan's honesty. By the end of the book I was so moved that I had to speak to Susan and tell her how it affected me. The mother/daughter scenario she described got me thinking about my own mum and just how important this book is and on so many levels. I have since read many of Susan's novels, and the wonderful *One Day at a Time*, the second part to Susan's autobiography. Every book is not only a joy to read but also a learning experience about life. The first time I met Susan I realised I was in the presence of a kind, caring and truly genuine human being and working with her is one of the greatest joys of my life. I am proud to call her my friend and know that we will do wonderful things to help Breast Cancer Care help those who suffer from this life-altering disease.

Being told you have a life-threatening illness totally puts your life into perspective and makes you realise just what is important. It is also one of the scariest things any of us will ever have to face but with the love and support of others we can hopefully make the lives of those diagnosed in the future a little easier. It is a joy and an honour to represent Breast Cancer Care and the wonderful work they do.

There are more than half a million people in the UK today who have been treated for breast cancer and every year another 50,000 or so – including around 300 men – hear the devastating news that they have the disease. They'll probably feel frightened and confused – and their family and friends might need help too.

Breast Cancer Care is just a phone call or mouse click away for anyone affected by breast cancer. Their free helpline and information-packed website offer a friendly ear and expert guidance to anyone dealing with the turmoil of this life-threatening illness. Across the UK, they also provide skilled emotional and practical support through a range of confidential, face-to-face services, helping people every step of the way.

Their unique strength lies in the way they combine their understanding of people's experience of breast cancer with the clinical expertise of their team of specialist nurses. They care because they've been there, and they know how to help.

Breast Cancer Care helpline:
0808 800 6000

Breast Cancer Care website:
www.breastcancercare.org.uk

Read my story...

To find out more about my family's experience with breast cancer then you can read *Just One More Day* and *One Day At A Time* – two memoirs that will hopefully make you laugh as well as cry! For some they may prove entertaining trips down memory lane; for others they will hopefully show how fortunate we are to be living in the times that we are.

Available at your local bookshop or online

Look out for Susan's new novel,
Never Say Goodbye, out in hardcover
27 February 2014

How would you cope with the threat of losing someone you
love?

Josie Clarke is a loving wife and mother. She and her
husband Jeff don't have much and it's often difficult to make
ends meet. But Josie will do anything to protect her family
and keep them safe.

Bel Monkton is a successful property developer, living in a
beautiful house by the sea. She seems to have everything
going for her, but she's lonely. And she's let the shadows
from her past cloud her future.

Josie's life couldn't be more different to Bel's. But three years
ago, tragedy tore Bel's life in two. Now it's happening to
Josie.

And faced with uncertainty and heartbreak, they come to
treasure their growing friendship.

CENTURY

Join

Susan
Lewis

online

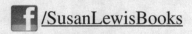

Sign up for her newsletter
at www.susanlewis.com

Get in touch via the
Official Susan Lewis Facebook Page:

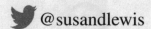 /SusanLewisBooks

Or follow Susan on Twitter:

@susandlewis